HELL
OR
HIGH
WINTER

HELL OR HIGH WINTER

A NOVEL BY

ANDREW RUBIN

RARE BIRD
LOS ANGELES, CALIF.

THIS IS A GENUINE RARE BIRD BOOK

Rare Bird Books
6044 North Figueroa Street
Los Angeles, California 90042
rarebirdbooks.com

For more information, address:
Rare Bird Books Subsidiary Rights Department
6044 North Figueroa Street
Los Angeles, California 90042

Set in Minion
Printed in the United States

10 9 8 7 6 5 4 3 2 1

Library of Congress Cataloging-in-Publication Data available upon request

For my family.
To my dad. Thank you teaching me how to dream.
Your memory will always be the greatest blessing.

CHAPTER ONE

SNOW FLURRIES SETTLED ON the saintly alabaster faces that watched over Saint Peter's Square. At the foot of the world's largest cathedral, a Swiss Guard emerged from his small booth, boots sliding on slush covered cobblestones. He rubbed his hands against the chill. It could get cold in Rome, but rarely did it snow, and if this guard of the Holy City were more theologically open-minded, he might have bent to the ground and whispered a condolence or a brief *"just hang in there"* to the ancient Greek goddess Persephone, whose annual three-month imprisonment in the Underworld had caused this ungodly polar vortex.

The Swiss Guard stomped the snow off his boots, and turning back to his booth, he noticed, above the empty Saint Peters Square, the Vatican residence glowing like a Christmas tree. *Strange for three in the morning.* There were plenty of secrets in the Vatican. Secrets within secrets, they jokingly told him when he started this coveted, plushy assignment. The old man must be an insomniac. Or something was weighing on his conscience.

But then again, *that* wasn't any secret.

***

Inside the papal apartments, the midnight oil burned—or it would have, if they still used oil. Really, the midnight halogen lamps were buzzing. The Vatican refused to switch to any of those wussy incandescent hippie bulbs. They had only recently acknowledged the Jews didn't kill Jesus. Wasn't that enough for one millennium?

So, beneath the soft orange glow of the halogen lamps in the stately drawing room outside the pope's personal quarters, a flock of cardinals blinked sleep from their eyes as they huddled in fractured groups, whispering and passing furtive glances. They had gathered here as fast as they could be roused, waiting with the conspiratorial excitement of summer camp boys planning a jailbreak from their bunks.

A toilet flushed. They pivoted and bowed as a privy door opened and a frail Pope Benedict—eighteenth, nineteenth, whatever—emerged. He adjusted his robes and wiped his hands on a Vatican cloth, which he passed off to a waiting tweeny-bop valet, who accepted the dirty towel with reverence.

The red sea parted. Concerned faces offered the Holy Father reassuring smiles before the heads shook and sighed behind his back. The pope shuffled through their channel like a geriatric ghost until the thin-faced and mafia-connected Cardinal Angelini blocked his path.

"Your Holiness," Angelini said.

The pope smiled inwardly. He knew Angelini really meant, *Die, you old bastard, I want your job.* In truth, Benedict was quite spry, exercised often—albeit slowly—and had regular bowel movements—"exorcising the demons," as he jokingly called them.

Hey, even the pope's human.

Pope Benedict could have won an Oscar for his old cripple performance. It was his way of playing the Vatican game. They thought he was senile and deaf and therefore spoke loudly in front of him and said things they would normally have waited to say in private. He didn't care. Besides, if he really stepped up to the role, they'd probably have him killed. It hadn't happened in a while, but there was precedent.

Then again, his cardinals were right about one thing: Benedict was hearing voices. To be fair, they weren't in his head, and they weren't voices as in plural, but a voice. And to further clarify, this was not *The Voice.* That really would be insane. However, this voice was waiting for him on the other side of his bedroom door and belonged to none other than the Archangel Gabriel.

He shared that fact with one of his more trusted cardinals, the oh-so-Irish Cardinal Farley—a man of large faith and large appetite—and of course the cardinal told all the other cardinals. Now everyone thought the old man had finally gone off the rails. Maybe it hadn't dawned on them that their pope was experiencing a bona fide divine revelation, like those descried in the oldest and most sacred texts of the faith they purportedly preached. Was it so rare? Had they become so rote in their holy work that they were now immune to that cornerstone of faith—the miracle?

Gabriel woke the pope tonight, just as he had so suddenly one week ago, and faithfully repeated every night since. It struck Pope Benedict as odd that Gabriel would decide to show up around midnight and continue his private salons until dawn. He considered asking Gabriel why they needed to have these conversations in the dead of night—and why it was so important to discuss the state of Italian football—but as a mere mortal he quickly reconsidered questioning a figure of Holy Authority. The Lord works in mysterious ways, right?

Yet it was always around three in the morning, upon returning from his clockwork visit to the lavatory, when he was at his most fatigued, that the debate would take a turn for the serious and mystical. The witching hour. In a thunderous voice, Gabriel would preach about the corruption of the Church, the infiltration of evil into the blessed bureaucracy, and a coming apocalypse. Some of the pontifications—those related to corruption—made sense to the pope. Most of them did not. Overall, it had the desired effect of scaring the crap out of him, which would most likely have happened in front of the Archangel if his internal clock hadn't already taken care of that plumbing minutes before.

The message was simple: something radical had to be done to save the Church.

Since Gabriel's arrival, the pope's days were filled with a dreaded anticipation for the nightly discussion to come—a distraction his cardinals misread as a rapid mental decline. The fatigue had become so acute that Benedict's handlers canceled a high-profile trip to Latin America and a low-profile appearance at the bar mitzvah of Mordechai Kopciovsky, the son of the chief rabbi of Rome. The pope had never cared for choreographed PR stunts, but now, in the face of the Archangel's impending revelation, they were downright irrelevant.

Tonight, he knew, he would have his answer to save his Church and the one billion Catholics who worshipped the one true God.

"Your Holiness…" Cardinal Angelini repeated.

Right. Him. Benedict was jogged from his thoughts in time to notice Angelini raise an alarmed eyebrow at the rest of the cardinals before flashing a patronizing frown meant to pass for respect.

"Please. Let me hear your confession. I fear these voices are devil's work."

"Just one voice. Just one." Benedict patted the man's hand. He stepped around his subordinate, entered his private chambers, and shut the door, the lock clicking definitively.

Cardinal Angelini instantly pressed an ear against the wood to listen. The other cardinals crowded beside him for a spot. Several feeble bodies were roughly displaced by Cardinal Farley, who ignored the grumbles as he wedged himself in, his cheek spreading against the wood like pancake batter on a griddle.

"Is he talkin' to himself again?"

"SHHHHHH!" they hissed back.

* * *

The pope's private bedroom was elegant in its simplicity, but there was an emptiness that struck Benedict as soon as he entered. Not so much empty as in lonely empty—it was empty as in someone-else-was-in-here empty.

A cold sweat stained his virgin-white robe. His tongue stuck to the roof of his mouth; his cataract eyes scanned the faint outline of gilded chairs, a large king bed, pillows and duvet embroidered with those double golden keys that he hoped would one day get him into heaven. His heart accelerated, near to its weak limit. Perhaps he'd get those keys tonight.

A voice slithered in the dark. "Pope Benedict, do the red snakes continue to whisper their lies?"

Benedict swiveled. The voice came from everywhere and nowhere at once.

"The red snakes make you question my existence. Do you need me to reveal myself to you?"

"Is it truly you?"

"Yes."

Benedict gasped and spun to the Archangel Gabriel seated in a large chaise lounge, an arm draped lazily over the cushions as his fingers strummed the seat. He possessed a casual sophistication—the oozy charm of an A-list celebrity on the late-night couch. He had dark olive skin, power coursing through his noble frame, and, of course, the smile of an angel. His gaze, which had witnessed ages pass, now burrowed into Benedict.

Benedict dropped meekly into the opposing chair.

Gabriel asked, "What troubles you?"

"This...game." The pope glanced up from his lap to the angel. "My cardinals are incessant in their criticism. They say you are not an Angel of the Lord. They deny your prophecy."

Gabriel leaned forward. "Were they supposed to believe you? The true test of any faith is ridicule and doubt. It is the mud and dirt the snake calls home, from where it slithers into your conviction and strikes you with its poison."

Benedict lifted with a resurgent confidence. His younger days debating theology stirred within him—or perhaps it was just the reminder that he was the pope. He led a billion Catholics, after all. Could he not speak to the Archangel as an equal?

"But why can they not see you as I see you? Or speak to you? Why am I the only one to hear this dire warning? Every night you come to my city and—"

"My city?" Gabriel smiled. "You lease, not own."

Benedict cocked his head. Was that sass? Did an archangel just sass him? Chastened, he sealed his lips—like a good pope.

"It is as it has always been throughout time. We do not casually present ourselves to anyone who kneels and prays, to anyone who professes devotion. Otherwise, there would be chaos. There are few who are truly open to receive. It is a very delicate and weighted decision. Sometimes it takes a millennium. Who among the humans do we offer this gift of experiential faith? It must be someone ready to accept it, process it, bring it to the masses."

"But why me?"

"Because you're the pope, for God's sake!" Gabriel snapped.

The Archangel issued a long exhale, pinched his brow, and shifted in the sofa to regain his composure.

Weren't angels supposed to have infinite patience and compassion?

Though Benedict realized he had upset the angel, he nevertheless dug in. "You say we are at a crossroads, a time of pluralism, but how can the Church be under attack from other gods when there is only one true God? Is it not antithetical to all that we have been led to believe? I can't reconcile it. Neither can my cardinals, my most trusted confidants. I can't blame them. It's as preposterous as if you said Hell did not exist. Or Heaven! Who could believe the story you weave every night? You beat it into my head like a drum. Then you talk about the difference between American football and rugby, and debate me about the virtues of birth control, and rant about how much you loathe email. Not just loathe…how you have a wrath for email! No wonder no one will listen to me. It's all madness." He took a deep breath. "Their doubts about what you say—about you—are so…well…rational."

Rational. Dirty word.

"And you, Benedict? Formerly Hanz Klein Schlepper of Quedlinburg. Do you doubt me?"

Gabriel rose from the sofa, enveloping the room with his grandeur. Two great wings unfurled off his back as if to proclaim: You want proof? Here is your goddamn proof!

Benedict cowered, and tears ran freely down his quivering cheeks. Ashamed, he cast his gaze to the floor. He had doubted Gabriel. Not just Gabriel, he realized then. He had doubted everything. He covered his face.

Gabriel crossed the room, light as the feathers fluttering above his shoulders.

Benedict studied the purple carpet between his fingers as two brightly colored Converse high-top sneakers stepped into his sight. Not sandals? Weren't those shoes for rappers and American tourists?

"You have seen my wings," Gabriel rumbled.

"Yes. I have seen your wings, Gabriel." Benedict's wrinkled hands fell from his face, revealing the deep shame of a pope who stood at the apex of his faith and yet felt nothing under his feet. "If what you say is true, how can I save the Church? You must give me absolution."

Benedict fell to his knees, hands pressed in a triangle. If he was going to believe—and by God, he was going to believe—then he was all in.

"Tell me what I must do."

Gabriel smiled.

***

The pope's antechamber quieted with anticipation as Benedict stepped out among his worried flock. Angelini and Farley quickly darted into the pope's bedroom. If, perchance, the pope wasn't crazy, they meant to catch the unauthorized visitor—celestial or human—before she (or he) could sneak out through some secret passageway. Their eagerness reminded Benedict of the nuns at his parochial school checking the boys' beds for the residue of sin. He always thought the nuns seemed disappointed to come back without a single bedsheet. The same was true of Angelini and Farley, who'd found only an empty bedroom, no evidence of an intruder.

A sense of theological clarity filled Benedict—a clarity he had not felt since he was a promising young deacon in Germany, long before he accepted this burdened office. Benedict met their worry with this saintly stoicism. His hand suspended for silence, the Holy Father took a long, sanctifying breath. The cardinals waited.

"Effective immediately, I resign Saint Peter's Throne," Benedict announced—words that had not been uttered in over six hundred years. A shockwave blasted through the room, and one by one the cardinals began to process the bombshell, their shock turning to an uproar. Benedict continued, his hand still requesting a silence that would never be restored. "I relinquish the papacy to your vote. May God cast mercy upon this Church."

It was done. He dropped his hand to his side. And for the first time in recent memory, not a single eye was fixed upon him.

Scarlet robes churned as the cardinals began to plot their succession. Pope Benedict—or the Benedict formerly known as pope—searched the turbulent sea. Gabriel wore a matching red robe, easily blending into the crowd as he slipped away. So engrossed were the cardinals, they didn't even notice the stranger, who hiked up his ill-fitting costume, caught Benedict's dumbstruck stare, and offered a final wink before disappearing into the confusion.

Benedict whirled back to his relinquished flock and frantically waved for their attention, but he had stepped beyond the velvet rope, was no longer the center of their universe. And once you're out, you're out.

What have I done?!

The pope emeritus wanted his throne back.

***

Glory be to me, Gabriel thought, grinning like a schoolyard punk as he strutted down the Vatican's grand hall meant for kings, queens, and presidents. Spotlights illuminated the stained-glass windows, painting the corridor with refracted passages from the Bible. His silk cassock swished luxuriously on the Roman marble floor depicting the stars and planets and inlaid with the Keys of Heaven. Tonight had gone exactly as planned. The clock had started. Now the real work would begin.

Yet, as Gabriel stepped through the fractured light, his angelic features began to flicker and bend like an old television caught between channels. Passing through the rainbow, his dark hair turned gold, his skin lightened—a lenticular shifting perspective. By the time he reached the end of the hallway, that impish grin had transferred onto an altogether different face.

Hermes shed his skin as smoothly as a snake. He was the god of tricksters, after all, and the art of disguise was among his many gifts. Stealing the appearance of the actual Archangel Gabriel was just showing off. Hermes could have disguised himself as anyone—or even appeared as his plain old self. The pope had never seen an angel before, let alone the Archangel, so what difference would it make?

Makes a difference to me. Hermes prided himself on the details of his tricks, their elaborate, multi-faceted dimensions. It was overkill, yeah, but there was a certain *je ne sais quoi* to it. Transforming himself into the guise of a dull mortal? Child's play. A parlor trick most gods employed to get laid. Stealing the guise of another deity required a level of mastery found only among the greats. The fact that he had used this highly developed skill for such a selfish end was irrelevant—or so Hermes assured himself.

Already, Hermes could feel his moment of triumph slipping away. A Voice deep inside (capital "V")—sometimes friend, mostly foe—casually uttered the truths he preferred to bury in the basement of his psyche. The Voice had found an old standard: *Are you, Hermes, just wasting time?*

That light step was growing heavy.

Hermes had met Psyche once, briefly, during her sojourn to the Underworld. She was cute but hopelessly lovesick to please Aphrodite, who by then had jumped ship for the Romans and rebranded herself Venus. Personally, he was underwhelmed. Hermes never understood how humans developed such an extensive (and painful) belief system from Psyche's little romantic adventure. Hermes had tried psychoanalysis once, hearing it involved a couch and thinking it had something to do with Psyche—but it was just an hour lying in uncomfortable silence while an old man breathed through his mouth. Whatever fetish that was, Hermes wasn't interested.

Am I really just killing time?

Hermes fired back a question of his own: *Why not?* What some called narcissism took a serious level of devotion. Narcissism—another Greek invention. *We really nailed civilization.* The tricks made him feel vibrant and indestructible. Like base jumping. Or revenge after a contentious breakup.

Ahead, the sun crested the Eternal City, tinting the snow-dusted piazza a perfect shade of pink. Snow. He hated snow. It always made him miss Persephone.

Hermes shrugged off his cardinal's robe to drape over a homeless man shivering beneath one of the massive columns harvested from the ruins of a former temple dedicated to one of his fellow gods. The cold did have one positive effect: it refocused him on what he had achieved—what he had set in motion. Hermes was determined to enjoy what came next.

***

Several months before his round of nightly visits to the Vatican, Hermes took a sweltering summer vacation on the eastern coast of India, in the state of Odisha. Hermes loved India. He loved the smells, the crowds of people, and the fact that even after he ate their spiciest curries, he still couldn't get the runs—a feat he imagined should be added to his list of attributes when kids studied him in middle school classrooms. His letter requesting this inclusion had so far been ignored by the Texas State Board of Education.

The Hindis seemed to have a boundless appreciation for the gods and were adding new ones all the time, which Hermes appreciated. They worshipped in an innocent way, feeding, clothing, and bathing their gods as if playing house. There was no uniformity among the temples either, each offering a different interpretation of the same god. Their traditions and belief systems were as colorful as their garb, and Hermes admired them for their flexibility and envied the fluidity that kept their faith alive across millennia without the erosion that afflicted so many of his immortal peers. Plus, when they got married, the groom rode a horse down the aisle. How cool is that?

Hermes wasn't in India for the curry—though he tasted plenty. He had already been to China, Babylon (he still liked to use the old name), and Mexico, where after a brief and unsuccessful visit he was chased out of town by two spry Mayans: Xbalanque and Hunahpu, the hero twins with a history of roughing up gods who got out of line and who were apparently still miffed over his accidental involvement in several Latin American coups back in the twentieth century. Hermes swore he was only there for the drugs—the Amazon boasting a wide variety of hallucinogens—and he thought they'd be over it. No matter, he'd try again in a hundred years.

It was easy to brush off the rejection because Hermes had a lot of friends—if you could call them that, which you probably couldn't. They were gods, minor and major deities, and monsters that Hermes cultivated during his time as the Messenger of the Gods, when he had access to all the realms beyond Earth—all the heavens and hells of all the world religions. A singular position. Then worship declined and the Greeks lost their prominence. Hermes' services were required less and less—and eventually not at all. He would take an occasional interfaith mediation job, but then along came the Internet and, well, fuck email. No god hated it more than Hermes.

He spent the summer globetrotting, dropping in on his fellow tricksters and thieving gods to cut them in on a potentially lucrative score. They all respected him for his ingenious heists that took years to plan and certain, precise execution. The gods lined up to take part—or so he told himself, the last few decades yielding fewer *yeses* than gentle *nos*. Several of his tricks had gone spectacularly wrong. Who would have thought convincing an ifrit to set itself on fire in the middle of a Tunisian square would set off an Arab Spring? Eshu, Hermes' bestie—Trickster of Africa's Yoruba people—asked Hermes if he'd heard of something the humans now used called a Facebook and a TikTok. No, he had not, thank you very much. Hermes didn't understand much of this modern world, and he prided himself on his stubbornness not to find out. If it existed on the Internet, Hermes vowed he wouldn't touch it.

He spent the day waiting for Krishna outside the Jagannatha Temple in a city called Puri, watching the throngs of pilgrims crowd the dusty pink square beneath the jagged pyramids to cheer on the famous Ratha-Yatra chariot races held in honor of their Supreme God and its avatars. Almost no one in the crowd pulled out a cell phone to compulsively snap pictures or take meaningless videos. They were more in touch with the ancient traditions, and it relaxed him to be among the grit and physical gears of life and away from the sterility of the Western cities.

Under the pink temple, large chariots were constructed—towering, rickety structures topped with triangular canopies all pattern and color. Each carried an image of a god venerated at the temple. The word *juggernaut*, derived from Lord Jagannatha, came from this racing event and these formidable chariots. The chariots, so massive, would often barrel out of control and run over the spectators. Hermes liked that part. He didn't like himself for liking it, but it was still funny.

Hermes was on his sixth Kingfisher beer at a dirty sidewalk café when the festival began to wind down and families dispersed down dusty streets. A parade of chili lights lit up the temple, rival folk bands on opposite street corners competed for most obnoxious melody; India was a country designed to overwhelm the senses.

Without warning, a Dalit in a sweat-stained wife-beater and frayed khaki shorts dropped into the chair across the postage-stamp table and helped himself to Hermes' beer. The beggar had a thin mustache and a sour smell.

"Hey!" Hermes protested. "I don't have change. Shoo."

"Is that how Hermes treats his hosts?" the beggar asked.

Hermes leaned back and crossed his arms. "Krishna? Is that you?"

"Indeed. The one and only."

"Eighth, actually."

The Supreme Deity had disguised his trademark blue skin and royal attire—puffy yellow pants and a bedazzled cape—opting to take this untouchable's form to join the night's festivities. Unlike other deities, Krishna enjoyed taking part in the ceremonies that honored him, though he preferred the humans never know of his presence.

Having finished the beer that was not his, Krishna flagged down a waiter, lit a cigarette, and waved for Hermes to start talking. There could be only one reason the Greek god would drop in on his festival: a job.

Six beers later, Hermes had finished detailing his master plan, and now Krishna silently hemmed and hawed, like he always did, his blue skin turning a deeper shade of navy as the night darkened. He compulsively twirled the jewels draped over his chest through his fingers.

"Clever, yes," Krishna finally said, dipping a toe into the conversation.

"Of course it's clever," Hermes trumpeted. "They're always clever. So…you're in?"

Hermes flagged the staff for more beer. More beer was what was needed. Unfortunately, it would take a truckload before they even felt a buzz. A waiter quickly deposited a frosty bottle at the table, which to any human looked as if it were occupied by a sweaty European tourist fascinated by an Indian beggar.

"It's just that I'm so busy these days…"

Busy. That dreaded word.

Hermes flicked the condensation off his bottle. "This isn't a yearlong proposition. It isn't even a month. One night. One night is all I'm asking for, because that's the only chance we'll get."

"I have sixteen thousand wives and only two hands." Krishna popped a few papadums into his mouth and munched. "Do you know how long it takes to pinch thirty-two thousand nipples?"

Hermes rolled his eyes. "You've always been a big baby."

"I'm impressed, don't get me wrong. You'll be the first."

"We'll be the first."

Krishna pushed the bowl of crackers away, then settled back with his arms folded over his belly to watch crowds of men trolling for a late-night coda to add to the day's celebration.

Hermes could see the temptation. Feel it. "Don't make me pinch your nipples."

Krishna grinned. Hermes smiled back.

Next stop, Africa.

CHAPTER TWO

HE HADN'T SAID NO, but he hadn't said yes, either. Among his many attributes, Eshu was the god of crossroads, and he never eliminated possibilities. He came tonight to leave his options open, to consider all the angles. The West African god wore an elegant black suit accented by a red tie—appropriately dapper for Rome. An avid people-watcher and scholar of human behavior, he deliberately parked himself along the string of news trucks ringing Saint Peter's Square, where the broadcast lights enhanced the carnival atmosphere of this otherwise solemn gathering. A cold rain pelted the writhing sea of ponchos and umbrellas under which an assortment of clergy, nuns, devout Catholics, and tourists awaited the main attraction. Leaning against a barricade beneath a gentlemanly parasol, Eshu smoked his kuba pipe, amused by the throngs uniformly staring up at a tiny tin chimney strapped to the roof of the Sistine Chapel.

Eshu's followers prayed to him for protection whenever they traveled, for he held the power of both fortune and misfortune and was the personification of the Road of Life and its intersections. Therefore, he represented both the beginning and the end and could be feared as much for his power over death as he could be celebrated for his ability to create life. Since his domain included the road, the other sub-Saharan gods relied upon him to act as their communicator, translator, and ambassador. It flattered him to hold such importance despite his humble position. Never underestimate a small seed, for it could grow into a mighty baobab.

These weren't the attributes that brought him here tonight. Hermes had sought Eshu in the jungles of Africa because, above all else, he was the West African god of tricksters and mayhem—with a capital "T" and capital "M"—and there existed a small fraternity of gods who appreciated a little mayhem and the lessons it could impart. Eshu loved duality. And for him, the art of a trick was the takeaway. He delighted in sending mortals into the maze of the mind or a carefully laid trap to witness them return enlightened. If his follower did not return at all—or went mad in the process—then the trick could also be called a success, for its logic dictated that only those who learned the hard way had learned something at all.

Despite his godly presence, the Catholics ignored Eshu. To Europe's xenophobes, Eshu represented another migrant infecting their streets: either a pimp, a terrorist, or a vendor of tchotchkes and designer knockoffs sold on street corners outside their monuments—a hawker of calendars bearing twelve unique photos of Pope Benedict in various awkward yet endearing snapshots, like the one of Benedict wearing a sombrero in Mexico. The calendar, printed in Bangladesh and packaged in China, cost the American company less than half a penny to produce, with a resale value of thirteen euros a pop—a biblical markup. And with the pope resigning, the crap calendars, along with all the other crap souvenirs in Rome, were now collectors' items. A miraculous flood of profit was washing upon every corner kiosk and gift shop. Despite the long-term turmoil for the Church, in the short run, it was a boon to the local economy.

Eshu wasn't selling anything. Not even those cheap, one-use umbrellas. A group of Americans gave him a wide berth as they instinctively clutched their bags and stuffed hands into pockets. Eshu was used to their suspicion. The Italians shot him daggers, as if he'd just decamped from a migrant boat, and the occasional nun would shine him a sympathetic glance and drop him a few euros. He nearly had enough change to buy a pack of cigarettes. The nicotine would be needed after tonight.

In front of Eshu, a Ryan Seacrest–wannabe with too-white teeth and a wave of chemically enhanced hair used his reflection in a camera lens to apply a subtle gloss of lipstick. The reporter had honed a thousand shades of amazement during his endless fluff assignments. Eshu guessed the baby-bro journalist had an Ivy League degree in political science, sang a cappella, and dreamed of anchoring the national news. Instead, he'd been stuck covering winter airline delays until the network plucked him from obscurity and dropped him into the middle of history. A plum assignment that promised career advancement—and he was eating it up.

Inside the open news van, monitors ran a live feed from New York, where a national anchor facilitated a three-way among so-called experts. Eshu admired modern news—so efficient at sowing chaos, misinformation, and fear among the masses. It was as close to a god as you could get.

Eshu exhaled. The tobacco vapor stretched through the air like a trained snake. It wrapped around the news camera, turning it on before slithering past a bored producer eating a bowl of *cacio e pepe* and into the news van, where it finally infiltrated the control board. The monitor shimmered with static, and the panel discussion switched to a live satellite feed of the reporter puckering up to the lens.

The producer's earbud suddenly screeched with frantic voices. The control room back in New York had lost control, with no way to cut to commercial or back to the news desk. Eshu had his smoky claw firmly in place. Mr. Pepe dropped his dinner, whirled to the monitor, and, with a mouth full of pasta, tried to both whisper and shout, "Derek! Derek, we're live!"

Derek, the once up-and-coming star of the network, froze mid-kiss, the red light staring back.

And just like that, Derek became a meme.

Eshu shook his head. *Go home,* he wanted to shout. *All of you go home!*

"LOOK!" a spectator shouted excitedly, and the world pivoted to the black smoke coiling from the Vatican chimney.

Derek found his footing. "Um…Looks like something's happening. We have the first vote!" Derek got into the groove. "Black smoke. No decision!"

Eshu checked his watch. *Way to call that one, Chief.*

"Now, as a reminder, the cardinals are burning ballots from the last vote. If the smoke was white, it would mean we have a new pope. Let's zoom in on that so everyone can get a closer look. Can you guys see the black smoke from the studio?"

Eshu snuffed out his kuba pipe with his thumb and tucked it into his breast pocket. He checked his field watch—time to go anyway. The crowd remained too distracted by the black smoke puffing out of a tin can to witness the real miracle as Eshu began to shimmer, the very molecules holding him together disintegrating, turning him opaque like a dirty pane of old glass, until he dissolved entirely into a cloud of smoke. A breeze picked up, and his smoky image thinned and vanished.

Eshu reassembled himself at the base of Castel Sant'Angelo, an imposing circular fortress that hugged the icy Tiber, capping the wide boulevard to Saint Peter's Basilica. The castle had once been the decadent home to popes, with a not-so-secret passageway built within the aqueduct that connected it to Vatican City. For a long time, it was a place of refuge when the city was in turmoil or invaders threatened. The Church later reconstituted its halls as a prison and house of torture—but before all that nonsense, it had been a Roman tomb, encased in the brilliant marbles harvested from his continent. That meant the blood of the old gods flowed through its veins.

Rome was a city reconstituted—"the old whore," as some called it—built layer upon layer, recycling the past to construct the present. Monasteries placed upon old churches upon pagan temples. It was dirty and tired and yet kept chugging along. History, forever vertical.

Inside the castle's ward, the entrance descended into a grand, vaulted foyer. Eons ago, epic slabs of colored marble and frescoes had adorned these walls. Eshu took a moment to acknowledge the passing of the torch from one religion to another and finally to the inanimate gods of commerce that rebranded this place into a tourist attraction. He grumbled at the little model that depicted that past and began to climb a narrow corkscrew passage. The wall sconces were empty, replaced by embedded track lighting that wove around the cordoned-off remains of ancient mosaics that once covered the floor. The castle resonated, grumbling at this ancient and exotic god infiltrating its darkened halls constructed for popes, dukes, and emperors. Or perhaps it was simply saying hello to a long-lost relative.

Eshu ignored the military apartments that had been converted into galleries displaying overflow Catholic iconography. He ignored the conveniently placed café and gift shop situated at the top of this ride, and he ignored the exhibits that preserved the pope's bedroom and Raphael's frescoes. Never in history had a single religious order mastered patting itself on the back like the Catholics—the epitome of self-aggrandizement. Eshu finally emerged atop the keep. The rain had abated, leaving low, wrung-out clouds. Rome unfolded with its twinkling hills, ruins aglow like beacons, warning the old gods to stay away from these craggy shoals.

Across the battlement, wearing his silly Converse high tops, waited Hermes. A massive sculpture preened above: the Archangel Michael returning his sword to its sheath. *With what Hermes has planned,* thought Eshu, *the Archangel might want to keep that sword at the ready.*

Hermes leaned over the balustrade, watching the ripple of camera flashes. The crowd below hummed, supercharged by the twin powers of prayer and social media. It truly was a circus. A big, noisy, madhouse circus. Exactly as Hermes intended.

"You made a mess," Eshu called.

"Or cleaned one up," Hermes said, and disconnected from the Vatican show.

"You had to get rid of a pope?"

"If I recall correctly, you said it had to be one grand distraction. Well…" Hermes gestured to the ballot smoke curling through spotlights. "The world's all looking up—we go down."

"I thought we were speaking hypothetically," Eshu grumbled.

"Lilith had what we needed. For a price." What price a Hebrew demoness required for such confidential Heavenly documents, Hermes left unsaid.

"What does Persephone think of this?" Eshu asked.

"It's winter. All this will be forgotten by spring."

A hymnal rose from the crowd.

"You've created uncertainty with one of the superpowers. The other religions are nervous. The Orishas think I'm prowling the Congo, not here with you."

"Where are the others?" Hermes asked, suddenly realizing it was just the two of them.

"There are no others. No one's touching this."

"Not even Krishna?"

"Not even me. You're on your own."

Hermes wilted. "That's disappointing."

Eshu stepped forward. "What are you trying to accomplish, Hermes?"

"Accomplish?" Hermes scoffed.

"You're risking the desecration of a sacred city. What are you trying to prove? Why do this?"

Why? Why do anything?

It wasn't as if he needed to steal from the Catholics, nor did he hold a particular grudge—no more than his disdain for any other religious authority. *Why?* The universe needed gods like Hermes to balance things out. Everyone was way too serious. Hermes existed to thumb his nose at dogma and tell the fanatics to chill the fuck out. What was wrong with a bit of fun, especially at someone else's expense?

"You're creating friction," Eshu said with the disapproving tone of a kindergarten teacher.

"There's always friction," Hermes said.

"And there are times of peace. Like now. You may have lost your worshippers a long time ago, but not the Yorùbá. We survived. Barely. I can't provoke the Christians. They nearly wiped us out once, and they might decide to finish the job this time."

"You still have plenty of followers in Nigeria."

"War is brewing. Muslims against Christians. Christians against Muslims. Christian against Christian. Muslim against Muslim. We won't be spared. And my people scattered across the globe, forced to convert generations ago—they smuggled us with them, hid their devotion. It did not go unnoticed. Only tolerated. If the Christians decide to notice, we will be expelled, ruined."

Hermes recognized this was a sore subject. Many smaller religions were only small because the majors had decimated them over several brutal centuries. The religious community had become critically homogenized. An increasing number of gods straddled the endangered species list before joining the painful club to which Hermes belonged. True, religions naturally rose and fell, just as human empires did (most often linked), yet at some point the whole business had become horribly lopsided. The new monotheistic religions were mostly to blame; they enjoyed the luxury of despotism. The ancient religions had too many cooks in the celestial kitchen. They were entirely unprepared for the organized onslaught of this new kid on the block. Hermes considered himself lucky that his religion had died a gradual, rather painless death, and not from the violent corporate takeover endured today. Those massacres had left a lot of lost and angry spirits roaming around.

A tenuous peace had finally been brokered only two centuries ago. Monotheism had consented to a ceasefire—to refrain from miracles, from influencing geopolitics, or even, as they did in ancient times, from literally joining the humans on the battlefield. But Monotheism had its fingers crossed behind its back. The monotheists knew they didn't have to get involved anymore. Their worshippers would do all the work for them. A deft sleight of hand. Keep the smaller religions focused on the Big Guy in Heaven while legions of human missionaries did all the damage on Earth. The minor religions should have known: the whole conversion play was written right there in their bibles.

Except for the Jews—those wacky elders in the monotheistic family tree who kept to themselves. The only conversion they cared about was when it related to one argument against another. Their unofficial motto being: *No, thank you very much.*

It was unfortunate the monotheists had such large appetites. In the game of gods, worship was currency, and for the new players it wasn't enough to have eighty or ninety percent market share—they wanted it all. In provoking the Catholics, Hermes was walking a tightrope over a volcano. The fear was real, and it burned white-hot in Eshu.

"Why fuck up our peace by tricking the pope to resign? And worse, masquerading as the Archangel Gabriel!"

"Since when has he been so sacrosanct?"

"Since year zero! When he first showed up. You've embarrassed them. There will be consequences."

"Eshu, Africa's god of mayhem, lobbies for restraint…in defense of a crucified god. A mortal born among animals in a barn. A carpenter," Hermes said, dripping with sarcasm. "Might as well have been a plumber. At least Hades is a blacksmith."

"Exactly. With a billion followers and counting. A child knows not to touch fire. You thrust your hand into it. I know my fate if I'm caught, but have you thought of yours? Your wings, for starters. They would tie you down and clip them. You would walk upon this Earth like just another human. Unable to cross between realms, unable to enjoy the privileges of a messenger. That is, if they do not do something more radical, like entomb you beneath a mountain. Or banish you to your Underworld. Or worse—force you to return to Olympus. That desolate, lonely retirement home in the sky. Do you think the Catholics, in retribution, in their boundless capacity for rage and retaliation, would subject you to some simple punishment?" His chest heaved, out of breath from the speech.

"This is the Middle Realm. We're all equals. They can't touch me here, and they know it. Besides, they would need Zeus to agree. Like that'll ever happen."

"Don't be so sure. You think the Dodecanese would object if the full might of the monotheists came knocking on Olympus?"

"They'd need to drag me off Earth. To do that, they'd have to catch me first. Fat chance."

"They let you alone. You leave them alone." Eshu stabbed his words.

"That's rich. After they dragged your people from Africa to the Caribbean, to South America, and robbed you of your shamans. After all the mistreatment of your people—the way they wipe their holy ass with your treaties, trample on your traditions?"

"I own my own grudges and live with them as I please."

"You're afraid," Hermes shot back.

Eshu shook his head. "We've never pulled a trick for retribution. If we go down that road, we'll become just like the humans."

"This is getting far too philosophical. We're about to break into the Vatican vault. Think about that. The *real* vault. And I know what you suspect they have locked away in there."

"I'm thinking about more than myself. I am still called by my people. Krishna must tend to his," Eshu answered.

"You have all eternity to tend to your flock. If you're so lucky."

"And you were once the god of luck."

Hermes clenched but wouldn't show the hurt. Not to this asshole.

"I abstain," Eshu declared.

"You'd better leave, then," Hermes said. "Wouldn't want what happens next on your permanent record."

***

Beneath Rome existed a secret network of tunnels. Unlike the catacombs carved from soft limestone by humans, these were chiseled out of serious bedrock by divine power. They spread for miles upon miles and served as a prison for the magical beings who once inhabited the lands of Europe. The horrific genocide started during the Inquisition. Any nymph, beast, or fairy that didn't flee or go into hiding was imprisoned in this maze of underground cells.

Hermes shuddered as his lonely footsteps echoed in the dark, the stench of sulfur thick in his nose, a faint trickle of running water somewhere within the walls. To find his way back, Hermes left a trail of chalk markings bewitched to light up upon his—and only his—return.

The map he purchased from Lilith proved remarkably accurate. Lilith was a demon of the night and once roamed these halls not as captive but captor. She relished getting her hands dirty, and perhaps her help was a form of absolution. Perhaps it was simply payback, since she claimed to have been promised a promotion to angel for her unsavory services. It had been a long night spent in her company, coaxing this map out of her deeply disturbed mind. He now understood why the Bible described her as a screech owl.

Cell after cell gaped back at him, each a gallery of some forgotten horror and woe. Signs of the madness and desperation these forgotten prisoners endured were carved into the walls by claws and magic, painted in blood and excrement. No mythology ever recorded the sad stories of those poor pagan spirits entombed here for centuries.

Hermes rounded a passageway, and the sound of water grew more pronounced. Lilith instructed, if lost, to simply follow the stream. The tunnel abruptly ended. He studied his map. This looked right. More than that, he could feel the presence of a portal. As a messenger god, Hermes regularly navigated the entry points between worlds and was a master at recognizing the subtle variations in planes.

"Damn," he said, admiring the handiwork of the smooth brick wall as it hummed with a divine presence.

Lilith's map offered no further instruction.

All very arcane, he mused, running his fingers along the grout. For those who knew the language, magic could be read like Braille. His fingers stopped on a brick about two-thirds up, near the middle. It was warm…alive. Intuition told him to knock, and the brick wiggled in response. He slowly removed it from its slot as if defusing a bomb. The tunnel shuddered.

On the right track, he studied the wall, minus the one brick. He thumbed the surrounding bricks, then settled on one directly above the vacant space. The brick shifted down with a satisfying click, a lock recognizing the first right move in a combination. Only this lock didn't just have three numbers, or nine, or fifteen. It would require perhaps hundreds of moves among a thousand bricks. It was a three-dimensional slide puzzle, and every move needed to be accurate—or else. According to Lilith, this little obstacle represented the only way between the underground torture chamber and the heart of the Vatican.

Another four choices faced him: move the same brick up, slide the left brick to the right, slide the right brick left, or drop the top brick down.

He chose the left brick.

Click. Right again.

Hermes grinned. He totally had this.

He maneuvered brick after brick—left, right, down, up. Moving faster, he descended into the puzzle, feeling his way. Hermes dealt with worse security back when religions one-upped each other in fantastical stagecraft. The Catholics could have designed a difficult challenge if they weren't so afraid to tap into the deep magic. *Give me a fire-breathing dragon or a maze with a giant half-bull, half-man ready to gouge your innards any day.* This puzzle amounted to workplace efficiency memos and data-point observational whatever. At some point the shifting gap magically widened, creating a new dimension to the game. The bricks could be turned sideways or at an angle.

Hermes cracked his knuckles.

A pattern emerged: a series of horizontal and angled bricks began to resemble two crossed keys—the pope's seal. It was his door, of course. So obvious. Finally, one brick was missing to create the last tooth of the skeleton key. Hermes spun around to the empty tunnel.

"You guys woulda loved this," he said to no one.

With all the fun vacuumed out of a high-five–able moment, Hermes placed the first brick back as the last brick to create a complete image of the two crossed keys. Take that, Dan Brown. The wall rippled, its bricks turned to water, and the whole wall collapsed like a tipped fish tank, revealing a narrow stone staircase spiraling up to a place no other religious deity had dared to trespass. Hermes took a triumphant step forward and sank into three inches of foul red mud that encased his precious sneakers. *Ruined!* he thought, then squished forward. *Everything's ruined. Screw 'em. He would do this alone, by God. Because he had to. Because there was no one else.*

* * *

The Vatican had two secret libraries, though officially there was only one. The official secret library was one of the oldest in the world. Coveted by conquerors, visited by scholars, and the source of endless conspiracy theories, it was famous for its nearly two million precious literary artifacts. The unofficial secret library was older, just as coveted, visited by no one, and the proof that those conspiracies were not just theories at all.

A Swiss Guard noisily patrolled, his pantaloons flaring like a circus tent. He had a thick bone structure, wide jaw, and heavy, elongated eyebrows as if his features had been carved by a blind stonemason. A face so ugly it could scare off evil spirits. No wonder they'd shoved the guy down here. His boots clomped across the stone, punctuated by the clunk of his poleaxe.

Clomp—Clomp—Clunk. Clomp—Clomp—Clunk.

The Swiss Guard paused a moment to sniff the air like a bear in the woods.

Smelling nothing out of the ordinary, he moved on.

Clomp—Clomp—Clunk. Clomp—Clomp—Clunk.

He reached the end of the aisle, pivoted into the central corridor, then pivoted again into the next aisle like a lawn mower seeking neat rows.

Clack—Clack—Clunk.

Once the sound of the patrol faded, a funny thing happened in the library: a hand thrust straight out of the floor, as if the marble had turned to water. The rest of Hermes emerged thereafter from the secret access to the Vatican's dungeons.

The super-secret secret archives were hidden below the normal-secret secret archives. Unlike the official secret library, which was showcased in a grand marble cathedral, the unofficial secret library was housed in a disappointingly dull, unadorned warehouse on the sub-sub-sub-basement level. There were no study desks, reading nooks, or microfilm machines. This was not a library meant to disseminate knowledge but rather to stifle it.

Its first outside visitor in a thousand years, a triumphant Hermes surveyed the chamber. Sacred texts of all shapes, sizes, and materials lined simple metal shelves under track fluorescent light. Among the collection was a first edition *Egyptian Book of the Dead*, scrolls thought to have been burned with the Great Library of Alexandria, Sumerian parchment edicts, and collectible box sets of magical spells bound in human flesh. There was also a tiny scrap of paper that offered a passkey into the Akashic Record. None of this interested Hermes in the slightest. Instead, he set off down the aisle, sneakers whispering on the marble.

A mile in, Hermes stood on a catwalk overlooking a sunken antiseptic white room and a single, massive red blast door the size of a shipping container positioned on rollers. The hair on the back of his neck prickled. Things just got complicated. Hermes assumed that he could simply waltz into the Holy of Holies. Lilith never said anything about this additional security—wouldn't have even known about these upgrades. A digital inset on the steel door foretold worse trouble.

Digital. That word. Hermes felt the outer edges of defeat crawling along his skin.

How could I have been so naïve!

Maybe all the critics were right. Maybe all of his trickstering and thievering merely represented an attempt to fill a sliver of his immortal time. It suddenly felt as if the weight of an ocean was pressing in on his ears and crushing his lungs. His palms became sweaty.

Is this a panic attack?

"Underneath Michelangelo, a secret city designed to survive Armageddon," said a familiar voice.

Startled, Hermes spun around as Eshu formed from a puff of smoke. The African god of mayhem removed his kuba pipe and snapped his fingers to ignite the tobacco and resume a steady locomotive puff.

Hermes gave his old friend's shoulder a squeeze, more relieved than he'd ever admit.

"Look at all this shit," Eshu said, waving dismissively. "All my worshippers need to summon me is a drum, fire, and a strong drink. And they'll sing till morning."

Hermes smirked. "What do you have against doomsday capsules?"

"A religion offering immortality hedges its bets..." Eshu rolled a glance his way. "Interesting."

Hermes shrugged. "I dunno, I kinda like a bit of infrastructure."

"Columns and marble. You demanded much of your people." Eshu exhaled his musky tobacco. "It really has been many years since you've been worshipped, my friend."

Was that pity?

Eshu removed an old pouch made of dried, wrinkly elephant skin and took a pinch of something that wasn't tobacco. He stuffed his pipe, inhaled deep, and then blew a great puff into the chamber. Magic smoke billowed, uncovering a series of crisscrossing red lasers.

"More toys," Eshu grumbled.

Hermes whistled, impressed. "I thought those were a fake TV thing."

Eshu sucked on his pipe. "I don't understand."

"If you break the light, it sets off an alarm, everyone shoots us," Hermes explained.

"So what are we to do, great trickster?"

"You wear revealing black tights—that's one of the rules, for some reason—then you drop from the ceiling on ropes and dance over the lights. One time these cat burglars...it might've been James Bond. No, sorry, it was Tom Cruise...no, wait, I'm pretty sure it was Bond. Yeah, Bond. He froze the room with liquid nitrogen, though I'm not sure that's a thing."

Eshu stared blankly. "You watch too much television."

"What made you change your mind?"

"I'm unpredictable," Eshu said.

"Admit it, you're here for the glory."

His eyes burned, matching the coal at the end of his pipe. "I'm here to reclaim what was stolen from my people."

What am I starting?

"Friction," Eshu replied, as if reading Hermes' mind.

Can he read minds? Fuck.

"And no, I can't read minds," Eshu said, further confusing Hermes. Then Eshu clattered down the stairs.

"Wait!" Hermes snatched the back of his blazer. "Goddamnit, stop! You'll trigger the alarm."

Eshu easily slipped out of Hermes' grasp and continued into the fancy red lasers. Hermes braced for alarms, but the beams simply passed right through him as if he were made of smoke. Tricky. Eshu reconstituted at the touchscreen panel, gave it an aggressive tug, and ripped the device out of the wall. The lasers vanished and the blast door unlocked with a satisfying pop.

"No need to be fancy," Eshu said, lifting the electronic guts like a severed head on the battlefield.

"I could kiss you."

Eshu spun the large wheel and the blast door slid along its lubricated tracks, revealing a tunnel burrowed into granite.

"We're gods—did they really think this would stop us?"

***

Entombed at the heart of the church, the Vatican vault hid fifteen hundred years' worth of global domination, treasure, and artifacts of tremendous importance from cultures the world over. Upon entering the cavernous warehouse, Hermes and Eshu were greeted by the Peacock Throne. Made of solid gold and encased in precious stones, the famed dais once adorned the Taj Mahal and represented the seat of power in India. Not seen in over three hundred years, most scholars thought it had been melted down by the Persians after they sacked the Mughal Empire.

Nope.

The Peacock Throne, the *pièce de résistance*, held the highest street value of all the items they would encounter, and yet Eshu strolled right past it without a glance. Hermes rolled his eyes. The god of mayhem really needed to take a chill pill.

Hermes ran his hands along the throne's gemstone-encrusted feathers. If only he'd brought a sled. "Too bad Krishna bailed. You think this'll fit in my apartment? Couple pillows, this would make a killer TV chair."

"You want the shiny shit, you're on your own," Eshu called out from deeper in the vault, triggering a chatterbox—a literal wooden snuffbox that incessantly dispensed small talk. A sadistic Russian sage had invented the torture device for the czar sometime in the eighteenth century. Its relentless prattling drowned out the rest of what Eshu had to say.

Curious as to the friction he'd unleashed, Hermes decided to spy on his friend. The chatterbox was babbling on about the differences in wheat varieties along the Volga when Hermes caught sight of Eshu. The African god passed an assortment of royal crowns, then abruptly paused at the crossroad of two aisles.

Hermes hid between two Celtic stone heads housing the spirits of druid priests that whispered furiously in his ears—apparently, they were in a centuries-old feud. Tuning them out, he watched Eshu deliberate. Two paths. One choice. This was his jam.

Eshu strummed the air with his fingers, as if playing an imaginary instrument, and decided on the right path. Hermes followed trepidatiously, keeping to the shadows, which wasn't hard with the overhead lights pulsing feebly against the forces of magic. He continued to stalk Eshu for what felt like an age.

This is wrong, he thought. A pit opened in his stomach the size of a fig—but not as substantial as, say, a melon—so it couldn't be that wrong.

Eshu finally stopped beneath a handwritten sign in Latin that read *"Sacred Stones and Rocks,"* and Hermes tucked himself beyond a golden statue of Horus.

Beyond the geological eccentricities was a series of display cases containing row upon row of sacred tribal staffs stolen from Africa, each one secured in place by a silver ring. The collection was organized by region, tribe, and the god whose powers they channeled. Eshu's eyes swept over his people's magic. Made of dark woods and light woods, some unadorned, and some intricately carved with bright patterns, or depictions of African beasts and grotesque human faces grinning, pouting, and sneering. Depending on their geographic and cultural origin, the staffs could be decorated with a mix of shells, animal skulls, human bones, hair, or beads. They signified centuries of ceremonies conducted over roaring bonfires in remote jungles and open savannahs. Though the tribes lived among vast deposits of gemstones and precious minerals, there were no ostentatious displays of gold, silver, diamonds, or sapphires. Their shamans knew of a stronger way to access the spirit realm. The staffs, wrought from the earth, represented old magic—elemental and powerful.

Hermes feared for the dark thoughts surging through his friend. Eshu had been the one to warn of retribution, yet now he seemed ensnared in its orbit. The rage was understandable. Justified. The mere existence of this collection was an insult. These important tribal relics had been rendered lifeless, on display for no one. Museums around the world paraded his culture for the price of a ticket, as if his religion were some long-extinct curiosity. Eshu clearly ached to liberate his heritage—museum by museum—end the shame and insult, but to seek justice would be to break the fragile treaty with the Christians. An invisible force pulled him down the row until he came upon that which he and his people had been unjustly denied.

"They take simply because they can take…" Eshu muttered.

The display glass vibrated, cracked, and then exploded.

Hermes permitted himself a grin. He knew Eshu wouldn't be able to resist the chance.

The sacred dance staff of the Yoruba flew into Eshu's hand. Liberated at long last! Carved from bronze, the three-foot icon crouched on a small drum; its narrow face and wide features captured a mischievous expression that bore a remarkable likeness to Eshu. It was topped with a phallic, conical headdress like one of Santa's elves, and its little wooden hands gripped a phallic staff between its little legs like it was going to churn butter. Phalluses were kind of a thing with the old religions. A necklace of cowrie shells and a black cloak with a red, yellow, and green triangle pattern adorned the shoulders.

The actual staff, a polished lenke branch, was lost many centuries ago, but that didn't matter. The power remained preserved in the icon. In Eshu's world, the cosmos consisted of two overlapping realms: the *Orun*, which held the spirit; and the *Aye*, which consisted of the physical. Because Eshu essentially operated the tollbooth on the supernatural highway and was the appointed guardian of its travelers, he also maintained the responsibility of protecting the sacred rituals allowing his people to pass between the realms. Hot tears swelled in his eyes as his hands balled into tight fists around the icon. He brought them down with a roar.

Fuck, Hermes thought, and then immediately followed that with: *Fuck it.*

While Eshu was distracted with his fancy dance stick, Hermes slipped back to the other side of the vault, stepping on the fig-sized pit in his stomach and squishing it flat.

On the way back, he liberated a few items of his own, including an Indonesian tribal mask that summoned demons from other realms, and a tiny knockoff Ark of the Covenant that he knew a wealthy Iraqi jinn had long coveted. He had considered absconding with one of the flying carpets but couldn't decide which he liked most. Then there was the collection of chalices that could heal the sick. He swiped one and poured a generous shot of ouzo from the bottle he kept handy in his backpack. The licorice spirit always calmed his nerves.

That's when he heard footsteps.

Hermes rose on his tiptoes to peer over the artifacts. "Yo, Eshu?"

Eshu approached from the main aisle. "What?"

"How'd it go in phalluses and accessories?"

"Tell me again how your people used to vape volcanic gas and divine the future."

"Ouch."

The Greeks used to build temples on gas vents, get high, and claim an oracle was speaking inside their heads—a good parlor trick.

Eshu stepped into the light with his icon. "This is my people's magic."

"Who doesn't like a magical stiffy?" Hermes smiled. "You finished shopping?"

"Yes."

"I have a lot of people on my Christmas list this year. Here, load up!" Hermes tossed an empty duffel that soared past Eshu and straight through the face of a mirror that cast no reflection.

"The rest is not mine to take," Eshu said.

"It's already stolen, so technically we're not stealing."

"Let the others come. It's not my job to right every wrong, just the ones done to me and mine."

The Eshu that filled the shadows could send armies trembling: wild, gleaming white eyes set within an onyx face, a wave of hair sprouting from the top of his head like the horn of an ibex, gold disks dangling from his ears and woven into the fearsome lines of his face. An abrupt about-face—the old African trickster returned, the same god Hermes would chill with on a Friday night.

But the disquiet remained. An axis had shifted from fun to not. To Hermes, this holy grail of heists (incidentally, now stashed in his bag was the actual Holy Grail) represented street cred, party favors, and get-out-of-jail-free cards. To Eshu, the only thing hoarded in this vault was pain. Lots and lots of pain. Perhaps Hermes really had opened Pandora's *pithos*, releasing all the old grudges that should have been left undisturbed. Hermes had named the girl, after all, and cunningly delivered her to wed Epimetheus, Prometheus's brother.

Really, he should have known better.

Despite all the high-tech security that normally kept cat burglars like them out of this vault, the Vatican's real deterrent had always been their superpower status. Who would want to start a war that was unwinnable? Yet the bigger the size, the bigger the target. After centuries of indignity, the displaced gods had nothing left to lose. Cue insurgency. Hermes, who never took responsibility for anything, shuddered to think of the consequences. He realized he was a one-celled organism asking a complex being *how's the weather*. And it wasn't about the weather. He realized then that he longed for Eshu's pain. His existence amounted to nothing. Who did Hermes have to fight for? No one. What people did Hermes serve? None.

The heavy sacks of treasure suddenly felt awful light.

***

Back in the library, Mr. Cro-Magnon and his excessively large cheekbones took exactly one hour and twenty-two minutes to complete a patrol that encompassed aisles eighty-one through eighty-three, section XXIV, which meant that exactly one hour and twenty-three minutes after Hermes slipped inside the vault, the clack, clack, clunk abruptly stopped. Registering an infinitesimal scent somewhere between Axe Body Spray and olive oil, Cro-Magnon sniffed the shelves, nostrils pausing at the base of his pole, where a queer diamond pattern was rendered in mud on an otherwise pristine stone floor: the unmistakable imprint of a Converse sneaker. A second pair of prints—another, then another—trailed off in the direction of the vault.

***

"Hold on a second," Hermes said just before reaching the exit to the archives. "I'm forgetting something."

Eshu tapped his foot impatiently, clutching his icon like a teddy bear won at a carnival. "What now?"

"Lilith!" Hermes sprinted back into the artifacts, abandoning the puzzled Eshu.

Lilith had made one demand in exchange for the entrance code to the Vatican archives. It was a strange request, but small enough to be nearly inconsequential, especially when compared to the buffet of magical tchotchkes. He plunged deeper into the vault, parsing through stranger items: a wall of pinned butterflies fluttering against a wall of silk; jars of colored smoke that followed him as he passed. *Just open the lid! Let us free!* they seemed to scream.

Then he found it. He never would have believed it existed.

The collection of feathers filled many cabinets, framed in little glass compartments presented on velvet cushions. They ranged from flamboyant tropical feathers to gray-and-white plumes plucked from your garden-variety pigeon, tiny hummingbird wings to long peacock quills and jet-black raven pens. The sheer variety was overwhelming, but Lilith had been extraordinarily specific. Her chosen plumage came from an extraordinarily long Yucatán bird once called a Baach, a shade of blue so startlingly bright it seemed to possess an inner light. A placard on its door listed "H. X. CK." Maybe that meant the bird was extinct.

Hermes snapped the padlock and reemerged with the ridiculous feather tucked behind his ear.

"I don't want to know. Don't tell me," Eshu said, brow pinched in frustration.

Hermes offered Eshu one of the three duffel bags as they entered the tunnel back to the library. "You want to carry one of these?"

"No. I'm good."

"You're good? That's good."

Eshu gave him a side-eye. "It would make me culpable."

"Little late for that."

Eshu sighed and thrust out an arm.

"Thanks." Hermes smiled as he handed off the third duffel.

They exited the vault, dragging an awkward silence. Hermes' shoulders protested under the weight of his loot. He slid the vault shut with a resounding thud. Eshu tapped him on the elbow. The kuba pipe dangled from his lips, idol cradled under one arm, eyes firmly fixed on the catwalks, where nearly two dozen heavily armed Swiss Guards waited.

Hermes whistled. "Glocks, assault rifles, and striped pantaloons…"

"Oh my," Eshu finished.

"We're just a pair of grave robbers. No big deal." Hermes slipped the Baach feather from behind his ear and into his jacket, which caused the Swiss Guards to shoulder their firearms. *Suicide by Holy See.*

"You got anything left in your bag of tricks?" Hermes mumbled.

Eshu took a deep breath, which lifted the kuba, then blew—*puff!* Smoke exploded from the pipe into the chamber, surging over the catwalks like a tidal wave.

Gunfire erupted in the concrete box like a firework show going off all at once. Goodbye, eardrums. Muzzle flashes rippled along the catwalks. Temporarily deaf and blind, Hermes and Eshu groped for the stairs and climbed behind the line of fire, tumbling into the quieter and smoke-free library, where Mr. Cro-Magnon happened to be standing guard in case the intruders escaped—which they just did. The threesome froze. Cro-Magnon's gaze seesawed from Eshu to Hermes, then down to his Converse sneakers caked in mud. A second after the snarl came the poleaxe.

The steel whistled. Hermes ducked, and the sharp blade buried into a wall of precious, gold-plated volumes. Eshu, nimble as wind, stepped inside the swing and snapped the Swiss Guard into a crumpled squeezebox. Hermes grimaced. This was not part of his master plan.

"Shouldn't he be dead?" Eshu nodded to Cro-Magnon as the body twitched and molted. A scaly arm burst through his uniform, meaty claws slashing the air as they searched for flesh. Then came a snarling, drooling face, gray and scabby, the texture of warts.

Eshu stepped away, disgusted. "That's not human. What is it?"

Hermes sidestepped another claw. "A gargoyle."

"Gargoyles?!" Eshu shouted furiously.

"I guess humans were too much to hope for."

Cro-Magnon dragged itself closer, leaving a trail of drool.

"You knew?!"

"No, not exactly—" Hermes kicked aside a paw. "I mean, it was possible."

Eshu glared, and Hermes held up a hand.

The vault had gone silent. The smoke dissipated.

Then the chamber filled with mighty roars. Mr. Cro-Magnon had a lot of gargoyle friends.

Despite being gods, Hermes and Eshu ran like devils into the archives, splitting into parallel aisles, keeping apace between book spines and through the periscopes of scrolls. The horned gargoyles pursued them like a stampede of angry rhinos. Saliva frothed between their nubby teeth, and long lizard-like tongues licked the air. Their runty wings flapped uselessly while their beefy arms swung side to side, constantly bumping into one another. When a gargoyle got a little too excited, it lifted inches off the ground. Gargoyles, though persistent, were a clumsy and dull breed.

Hermes reached the end of his aisle, took a hard turn, and nearly collided with Eshu.

"Your secret entrance?" Eshu indicated the muddy Converse footprints. "Bush league."

Hermes had never felt so foolish.

They followed his inadvertent trail back to the portal, only to find the floor had returned to solid stone. Hermes frantically pried at the seams of what had been the passage.

"Open it already!" Eshu snarled as the thunderous sound of gargoyles bore down. Only the very existence of his religion was on the line.

"I don't know how it works in reverse!" Hermes finally admitted.

"Fool!" Eshu shouted and tried to bash through the marble with his idol, but it didn't even make a scratch. The ground trembled; books toppled off the shelves. Then the mass of gargoyles exploded into their aisle.

Hermes yanked Eshu off the floor. "Executive decision: we're taking the full tour."

The two gods zigged and zagged between aisles until they located a Fibonacci staircase and tore their way up the corkscrew, assuming up was better than down. Behind them, the gargoyles squeezed into the narrow passage, the gray, stinking mass of them like a backed-up toilet erupting.

The dizzying sprint abruptly ended. Momentum carried Hermes and Eshu through brick and plaster and a quaint tapestry depicting the martyrdom of Saint George, before they landed in the traditional Vatican library.

Hermes rose and shook off the debris. "Meet me at the rail station." Eshu spun around. "There's a rail station?"

But his partner was already gone.

***

Gargoyles can really huff it on those chubby legs, but I can fly like lightning. Hermes pumped himself up as he entered the Vatican's private offices, stained glass and cornices giving way to safety glass and drywall—a sharp downgrade from gilded to institutional. A night janitor with a dried fusilli mustache buffed the floor. His jaw dropped as the Greek god charged past.

"Run!" Hermes shouted at the janitor.

A second after his warning, the gargoyle avalanche exploded through the office doors. The janitor leapt behind a column as the gargoyles flattened his buffer and continued after Hermes.

Hermes banked onto a patch of freshly polished travertine, high tops squeaking. Behind them, gargoyles skidded out in a tangle of arms and limbs, face-planting on the slip-n-slide. A handy tourist map with a smiley-face sticker outside the Vatican cafeteria (*overpriced, bring your own water*) marked his position. Hermes located the Sistine Chapel and tapped it on the map.

Perfect.

Hermes vaulted down the stairs, a soaring vestibule flanked by colonnades of swirling purple and white marble. He took a quick selfie before sprinting to a pair of giant oak doors sealed by a silver chain. An iron padlock with the pope's insignia supposedly meant security. *Cute.* Hermes drummed his fingers on the padlock, and the iron shattered.

Hermes slipped into a thick, reverential silence. Beneath Michelangelo's subversive opus, the College of Cardinals milled—weaving alliances, choosing sides, selling votes. *Cardinal Byrne for Class President!* Long tables extended from a dais, where the vote counting occurred. Hermes located the little potbelly stove connected to the pipe that led to the ceiling and emitted the famous smoke. He magically morphed into a matching red-and-white-robed replica of Cardinal Angelini. Head down, careful his bags of loot didn't attract attention, Hermes blended into the conclave. *Don't bump into the real Cardinal Angelini,* he thought, uttering a few Hail Marys and hoping Eshu was faring better.

***

Eshu was not.

He escaped the Vatican Museum into a dusty piazza, Hermes' loot jangling on his back like a cow calling the wolves to dinner. Two paths confounded him: take the dark alley to this-god-doesn't-know-where or the well-lit cobblestones to the Sistine Chapel? The god of crossroads stuck at a crossroad. *Damn Hermes.* A manhole burst open, releasing an infestation of gargoyles, forcing him toward the famous medieval shoebox—rather unimposing up close.

Two Swiss gargoyles cut him off. One swung a poleaxe, but Eshu quickly split into three Eshus. The steel sliced smoke before thumping into his comrade's chest. The real Eshu snapped the other gargoyle's neck with a bottle-cap twist. Another dozen gargoyles advanced from the piazza. His back was literally against a wall.

***

Inside the Sistine Chapel, Hermes edged toward the potbelly stove. A baseball glove of a hand grabbed his arm. "What in God's name are you doing with those sacks?" Cardinal Foley nodded at the duffels.

It took Hermes a moment to remember he was still disguised as Cardinal Angelini.

Keep it simple.

"More ballots," Hermes responded.

"I thought you were securing Cardinal Imbutu's block?"

Hermes reached for a cover story but was coming up short. Luckily (*god of luck, remember*), the chapel doors burst open.

In the presence of the cardinals, the angry gargoyles instantly shifted back to human form faster than the old men could put on their glasses.

"How dare you violate procedure!" Cardinals parted for the real Angelini. "Get out! Lock the room!"

Ignoring Angelini's protests, the Swiss gargoyles, cloaked as humans, pushed into the room. *Unprecedented!* Stunned cardinals grumbled and shot indignant stares that went ignored.

"The conclave has been breached!" Angelini continued shouting.

No one listened.

Foley spun between Angelini and the doppelgänger, stuttering like he was having a stroke. *Two Angelinis! The work of the devil?* Hermes morphed back to his Greek self and Foley signed the cross to keep from fainting.

"Good luck integrating this." Hermes gave him a pat and hurried off to the stove.

The sound of breaking glass sent heads swiveling up to the rafters. Eshu elbowed out a stained-glass window and flopped onto the gallery wrapping the chapel.

The room gasped.

Eshu spotted Hermes on the chapel floor. In the commotion between the Swiss Guards and the appearance of a cat burglar on the roof, no one had noticed the errant god. Hermes flung open the ballot stove. *Fumata nera* billowed into the chapel.

Eshu gripped the rail, eyes screaming *Don't do it!* Hermes shrugged—*Sorry, can't help myself*—and raised two closed fists, as if to make Eshu guess which one held disaster. He opened the right fist. Empty. Then the left—*Grenade!* Hermes smiled, tossed it into the stove, and spun around to plug his ears.

BOOM!

The grill blasted off its hinges and took out a painted cherub. Cardinals flattened, leaving Hermes in full view of the Swiss Guard. *Oops.*

Before the guards could react, muffled cheers rose from Saint Peter's Square, and the befuddled cardinals peeled off the floor.

Gallery windows shattered as the gargoyles in pursuit of Eshu stormed the chapel. Shards rained down onto fleeing cardinals shielding their heads. Hermes joined the chaos, eluding the frustrated Swiss Guards, who were seizing random robes. Eshu gave Hermes the middle finger and climbed a narrow ladder that led to the roof.

Hermes and the cardinals surged onto the central balcony of St. Peter's Basilica to thunderous cheers from the faithful gathered in the square. One by one the cardinals pointed to the famous chimney now spewing rainbow smoke.

Could it be? The first openly gay pope?!

After months of planning, this was the moment Hermes should have relished. *Should have.* Instead, he leaned over the balustrade, scanning the empty rooftops.

Where was Eshu?

Hermes spotted him vaulting from the Sistine Chapel onto the Papal Residence. A troupe of gargoyles leapt after him, unseen by the crowd still fixated on the rainbow smoke. Out of roof, Eshu dropped onto the pope's private balcony. Gargoyles followed, chubby tumbling boulders. Pikes raised, they cornered Eshu against the balustrade.

Hermes spun to the piazza.

"Habemus papam!" he bellowed unnaturally loud into Saint Peter's Square. The effect was instantaneous. *The world gasped.* A new pope!

The gargoyles kneeled in reverence, giving them the appearance of, well…gargoyles. *The king is dead. Long live the king!* Spotlights pinned the African god as cameras swiveled to the pope's balcony. Around the world, fourteen billion eyes blinked in confusion. *A black pope?*

Suck it, hegemony. A stunned Eshu gazed upon the crowd, now wild with enthusiasm, and made his first pronouncement as Holy Father.

"Oh, fuck."

Hermes chuckled. He'd pay for this one later, but it was so worth it.

He gave Eshu the thumbs-up just as everything electronic suddenly crashed. Phones. Cameras. Lights. *Dead. Total blackout.*

Interesting, Hermes thought as he folded into the shadows.

***

Eshu waited in the parking lot, trembling as he relit his pipe, radiating animosity at Hermes over the flame. Hermes had managed another in-flight wardrobe change and was now disguised as an innocent seminary student newly arriving with his two duffel bags at the Vatican's private rail station.

"I'm not impressed," Eshu grumbled.

"The blackout? Wasn't that you?"

"No. You screwed me, Hermes. Worse, you screwed my people."

Eshu would've given Hermes a larger piece of his mind, but a distinctly large shadow glided overhead. A hole in the clouds was ringed by fire, the night sky visible through the porthole.

The Archangel Gabriel landed with the conviction of a kamikaze, shattering the streetlamps. Tall, dark, and handsome, he was a true Angel of the Lord. Hermes congratulated himself. He'd really gotten the whole physiognomy right, captured the spirit of Gabriel down to the olive skin and model looks. Unlike Gabriel's stained-glass counterparts, typically depicted in a gold-plated centurion costume or simple white toga, the Archangel before them wore a sharp suit with a silver tie and $10,000 camel-skin loafers complete with diamond-studded clasps. *Tithes were good at the top.* The only detail Hermes missed was the ivory horn murse.

"Thieves," Gabriel said with all the menace of a loaded gun cocked and aimed.

"Liberators," Hermes corrected. "You're upset. He's angry," Hermes nodded at Eshu. "I'm sober. Why don't we find a decent bar, have a little tête-à-tête, get it all out in the open, do some historical accounting?"

Gabriel's stare could freeze vodka, which did not bode well for any alcohol diplomacy.

Hermes stepped forward, palms raised. "Hear me out. I give you back the Holy Grail—yours, obviously. But. But…I want the flying carpet."

Gabriel slipped the lamb's horn from the holster and brought it to his lips.

"Crap," Hermes muttered as Gabriel blasted a roaring B-flat at the sky.

The shofar thundered, ripping the ozone with a thunderous note that signaled a flock of angels in trim Armani suits to perforate the clouds—literally waiting in the wings. The angels nose-dived, their outstretched swords shimmering in the moonlight. Hermes felt the bull's-eye on his forehead.

"Yes…" Gabriel said. "You should run."

Hermes and Eshu took the advice and bolted into the Vatican rail station.

The terminal windows exploded as Gabriel and his angels smashed through the stained glass. His large brown-and-black wings created a shock wave with each thrust. They were eagles, and Hermes and Eshu were a pair of mice trying to cross an open prairie.

"Get into the metro," Hermes yelled and leapt onto the tracks.

Eshu slid off the platform. Gravel crunched.

Darkness pooled. No light at the end of this tunnel.

They heard the crush of angel wings flapping in the tube behind them. While they ran, Eshu unzipped one of the duffels bouncing on Hermes' back.

"Hey, that's mine!" Hermes protested.

Eshu scooped out a handful of treasure and pitched the priceless artifacts over his shoulder. Golden chalices and bejeweled totems took out a few of the angels, but there were still too many.

A screech of metal tore through the tunnel.

"Train!" Eshu shouted. Only there was no sign of one barreling down the tracks.

"It's the Rome metro." Hermes removed a pistol from under his frock.

"A gun?! You brought a gun…to a holy city?!"

"Absolutely." Hermes blasted the hinges off a service door to a parallel tunnel. On the

other side, the train hurtled past inches from their noses. Hermes hooked the last car and flung Eshu aboard moments before Gabriel shoved through the same entrance and took off after them like a rocket. He didn't like losing. Never had.

The track curved. White light reached over the train. *Salvation!* The angels landed just out of view of the station, wings melting into their bodies as the metro braked alongside a crowded Termini B platform under a vaulted red-and-white ceiling.

Hermes slipped into the disguise of an elderly *nonna* and tugged a grocery cart into the swirl of commuters.

Eshu dissolved and quickly hitched a ride with a chain-smoking Sicilian construction worker.

Angels climbed onto the platform and shoved into those exiting and boarding the train. Hermes glanced back from the stairwell and—despite *nonna's* cataracts—caught sight of Gabriel standing on a bench, scanning the crowd. Gabriel clearly wanted to smite something. Smite anything. Specifically, smite Hermes. He burned with a fierce and ugly hatred that stewed from a dark, un-Christian place. Thwarted, he punched the tile wall. And in that moment, Gabriel resembled nothing of an angel.

***

The Coliseum looked like a pair of old dentures. Cats prowled beneath a purple sky. Hermes and Eshu didn't stop running until they reached this graveyard of the ancient world, taking refuge in the nosebleed section, where the poor once sat, where weeds grew now. Weeds had conquered the emperor's box and the slaves' pit, too. It was all weeds. Eshu puffed smoke rings over the arena. Hermes waited for his friend to explode, but no outburst came. The silence was worse.

Hermes dropped the treasure and stretched his aching back. The stadium floor had been partially reconstructed, teasing visions of lions devouring slaves and gladiators in combat to the death. The humans secretly missed the old blood sports, waged without appropriately padded helmets. Humans were animals, despite all the ways they separated themselves from that truth. Suppressing the urges only led to the random, more destructive habits. *A bit like me*, Hermes thought, as he turned to a tuxedo cat nuzzling against his leg. He scratched its chin and listened to it purr gratefully. A convert.

Taking in the ruined world of his people, Hermes wanted to apologize to Eshu. But Eshu's silence intimidated him. He turned to the African god, outlined against the morning from atop a parapet, idol clutched to his chest. Eshu carried the responsibility of his people—all those prayers of want, need, and desire flowed through his god blood. Without followers, Hermes was untethered to that divine juice. He had nearly forgotten the feeling of human worship, when mortals visited his shrines bearing sacrifices and gifts, praying for him to intercede in their short, insignificant lives. The absence of their worship was like the floor missing from his existence. Despite being an animal, man was a most significant animal.

Was Eshu thinking about his people? Would the gods of Africa once again go to war?

Eshu's nations had suffered much in this modern, interconnected world. No balance, and none to be found. Everything was out of control and controlled by so few. Hermes often wondered if he could still be a god to the humans today. He wanted to say something to Eshu but couldn't bring himself to speak. He didn't have the right. And Hermes suddenly realized why: he was ashamed.

The tuxedo cat lost interest in Hermes and bounded away. Eshu's gaze followed as it slipped beneath a loose stone. He emptied his pipe of spent tobacco and pocketed it.

"What's next?" Hermes asked.

"What's next?" Eshu threw the duffel bag he'd been forced to carry at Hermes. "Next, I disappear."

Hermes pushed the bag back. "That's your share."

The duffel dropped between them, the metal loot clanging.

Eshu eyed it with derision. "I came for the staff."

"You're welcome," Hermes said bitterly.

"You want me to thank you, even begrudgingly, but I won't," Eshu said. "I return home a fugitive. The fault is mine. You merely provided the temptation. I lacked the self-control. Don't attempt to find me again; you're no longer welcome in our jungles."

"Miss out on Ebola? Pity."

"I gather the places you are welcome have become quite limited," Eshu said.

"There's always Canada." Hermes shrugged. He hadn't pissed anyone off in Canada—at least not so far as he knew.

"This wasn't mayhem and mischief. It was chaos and madness. And there will be a price to pay. You would be stupid not to feel frightened. Perhaps this won't end violently, but I can't read the future. I can only guide my people to the crossroads. They must choose the path."

"Use that for your people then. Help them," Hermes said, pointing to the third bag of loot.

Eshu turned away without so much as a glance at the treasure.

"It was never about money," Hermes called after him.

Eshu stopped to glance over his shoulder. "Which makes it harder for you. And now Gabriel's seen you, and you know how he is."

Eshu strolled to the edge of the Coliseum, stopping at the dais where a statue of a Roman emperor once gazed upon the gathering crowds.

"Good luck."

The god diminished into smoke, picked up by a breeze, and was lost to dawn.

Hermes stayed to watch the sun turn shapes into ruins.

CHAPTER THREE

Time had not been kind to the Underworld. A barren pomegranate orchard graced the long driveway of a half-complete imitation of Versailles, hewn from the great stone cliffs that made up Hades's palace. Empty scaffolding, partially collapsed, clung to the baroque walls. All signs pointed to a long-abandoned remodel.

During the height of his reign, Hades had ruled with an iron fist and spared no expense to make his kingdom desirable and opulent for his queen. He'd indulged Persephone's every insincere, halfhearted redecorating whim, harvested for her the finest works of art from the mortals, and, in a somewhat more insensitive gesture, expanded the very same pomegranate orchard that was the reason for her eternal imprisonment.

Hades liked pomegranates.

Around the eighteenth century, he'd tried his last grand hurrah and unveiled plans for a new palace. *We're living in squalor,* he exclaimed one evening upon bursting into her private quarters. It was decided that he would build her a palace to rival the most impressive in Europe, and she agreed. Kinda. More like shrugged her shoulders as she hunched over a book at her vanity. She had learned to read through his interruptions, and that night—it was always night in Hell—she was engrossed in a remarkable, newly published little novella, *Candide.* Thursday in Elysium was book club night. She was expected to hold her own against history's most notorious philosophers, and yet she hadn't finished the week's assignment, so she said yes, mostly just to get him to leave.

Hades ran giddily from the room, the *whap, whap, whap* of his bare feet slapping the marble receding down the hall. It was at that moment Persephone felt the first pang of guilt. Hades was sick. From then on, she increasingly found herself playing servant to his delusions.

Guilt, what a bitch.

Her guilt grew steadily over the centuries as Hades began, inexplicably, trying to please her, pining for her affections while no longer recollecting his original sin. It was Hades who'd engineered her imprisonment in this hellhole, and his violent temper continued; he wounded her at every chance and cried foul when she defended herself. The perp had reinvented himself as the victim.

Notorious for his temper, Hades could still be a cruel son of a bitch, but his outbursts came like squalls—infrequent, expending their wild punches, then forgotten shortly thereafter. Even physically he had changed, having slowly eroded into a withered old man. All his muscles from his years fighting the Titans and constructing his kingdom out of rock and dirt had simply picked up and left. His eyes were now more socket than sapphire, and his face drooped and struggled to shape expressions.

The week after his remodel pronouncement, Hades unleashed a team of contractors on the palace. They smashed the ancient façade and chiseled away at the mountain. Only, Hades had failed to notice the receding pool of free labor. There were too few slaves, and most were too feeble to complete the task. He continued to bellow orders with gusto, firing them off at random, and often at cross-purposes. The Mad King would tell one team of engineers to tear down a wall he'd told another to build. Other demands were downright confusing, including asking the masons to make him a ham sandwich or flirting with the craftsmen as if they were mistresses. And the further the fitful remodel progressed, the more unhinged he became. He issued new decrees daily, usually at whoever crossed his path. No soul dared defy a god, and each order was faithfully transcribed—no matter how nonsensical—then issued far and wide. Fridays were now Dress-Down Friday, and brunch was officially banned throughout the realm. Factories were required to increase pollution by five hundred percent over the next ten centuries.

The kingdom collectively scratched its head. His advisors warned that the decrees would soon be met with indifference, some with outright defiance.

Two hundred years later, and no one answered anymore. The sprawling complex once occupied by an army of servants, sycophants, petitioning souls, and demons now maintained only the few rooms that served a practical purpose for Hades and Persephone. The rest of the palace was devoid of the living and the dead. The king and queen of the Underworld had downsized mightily.

A positive change: the palace now boasted a wide variety of modern comforts smuggled down from Earth by a few entrepreneurial cacodemons—like toasters and TVs.

Only the black market thrived in the Underworld these days. Way back in the Greek heyday, mortals didn't produce anything a god would want. Who needed a clay pot? Not Hades. Not Persephone. But an iPhone? Not even Zeus could match the all-knowing power of Google.

Time moved slower in the Underworld. Three months crawled at the pace of an Earth year. When not rereading books, tending to her indoor garden, or watching CNN—yes, the boredom was that bad—Persephone spent her time mastering the art of avoiding Hades. Unfortunately, there would never be a palace large enough to house them both. Hades was unyieldingly needy and terrified of being alone. For a god as tough as Hades, he certainly was clingy.

She heard the familiar *whap, whap, whap* lapping the corridor outside her large, French colonial kitchen (the only good thing to come out of the remodel, and which she had personally overseen).

"Tonight," she heard him declare through the door, "we're going out!"

Go out? Go out where? There was no destination to "go out" to unless they felt inclined to wander the decrepit streets of Acheron, his sweaty, oily hand clutched over hers.

The *whap, whap, whap* receded. Another false approach.

Persephone ignored his poisonous flybys, perfectly content to hibernate. She had devoted the last twelve hours to mental centering exercises, then focused on the minute details for tonight's plans, which mostly involved her staying in. On her side of the palace. Alone.

The first of her tomatoes had ripened, and although they tasted a bit metallic, they reminded her of home. She would harvest them, make a ratatouille, put on a record—something classic, like Ella Fitzgerald—open a bottle of wine (Hades maintained impeccable taste in wine, to his credit), and just veg. By obsessing—ordering and reordering her activities, meticulously planning the evening, assembling a playlist, record by record—she found she could both kill time and carve out a respite. Let her mind wander, and Hades would send her into an emotional tailspin. It was a small, sad, claustrophobic existence. But she was determined to make at least this one part of it bearable.

Persephone was well into the ratatouille recipe when the *whap, whap, whap* returned. This time, Hades made good on his promise, bursting into her kitchen to blow her meticulously mapped evening all to Hell.

She twisted to her husband, knife in hand, pulp dripping off the blade, tomatoes bleeding out onto a butcher's block behind her.

His jaw dropped at her less-than-queenly appearance. The goddess wore a rustic lavender apron, yoga pants threadbare at the knees, and a faded *Eras Tour* sweater, sleeves rolled up. Yet the kitchen hearth blazed, haloing her auburn hair tied up in a messy ponytail. A black kettle sent up clouds of steam.

It was a bucolic picture lifted straight from a Julia Child fantasy, and from the glint in his eyes (and under his robe), it was clear he found it downright sexy. He was the luckiest god in…hell, anywhere. Persephone never lost that kidnappable quality. No wonder the muses continued to sing of her all-natural, irresistible, ageless, sensual beauty. The heir of Demeter, goddess of fertility, every curve of her body radiated gentleness and power—

"By God, those ham-hock hips were made for birthing," he said. Hades really knew how to deliver those pickup lines.

The sash on his robe slipped and…

Dear God. Her eyes quickly averted north, from his stained tighty-whities to his mischievous smile, which alerted her to the hand he held behind his back.

Ruggedly handsome was how Hades liked to describe himself. The blacksmith of the gods would profess—and generously so—that all his godly testosterone paired well with Persephone's virtuous femininity. In begrudging moments, she could admit he had certain attractive quali-ties—to certain kinds of women, that is.

But now? Now he looked like shit.

Worse, as he stood here attempting to ask her out on a date, he had no clue how slovenly he appeared. He still had a stallion mane of rock-star curly hair that flared over his shoulders, but his knotted, matted beard held a few week-old chicken nuggets and could reasonably contain the chicken coop that housed the chickens that became said nuggets.

Hades took in the kitchen. "My queen doesn't cook. Let the servants do that."

"Servants? What servants?" Persephone threw out her hands.

He looked around and had a revelation. "Microwave. Would you like one?"

Persephone laughed—then saw he was being sincere. She sagged into the counter. "I'm fine."

"We haven't been out in ages," Hades declared. "I've come to take you somewhere special. Where would you like to go? We can go anywhere."

"Tokyo," she mocked. "Or how about Niagara Falls? Paris?"

His lips tightened, nostrils flared, and with a grunt, sent a puff of flour across the counter.

Persephone lost her appetite to play along and returned to chopping. There would be consequences, but she was determined to disengage.

She felt him linger, his gaze boring into her back like a corkscrew opening a bottle of wine.

"Why don't you wear nice things anymore?" he asked.

Persephone had once employed hundreds of slaves to sew her elaborate gowns and dresses, which were envied throughout the realms. But what good were dresses when you had no reason to wear them? When nothing you wore changed how you felt on the inside?

"I wear what's comfortable," she replied, still chopping.

Hades moved closer. "Here." He thrust a bouquet at her. Six freshly picked detestable narcissus blossoms—putrid white petals with their revolting orange trumpets.

Persephone froze. The insensitive, senile bastard. The same flower he used to abduct her.

She set down her knife, lest she "accidentally" jam it into his neck.

"Take. Them. Away." She mashed the words through her clenched jaw.

"They're for you," he said with the confusion of a puppy who did bad but knows not why.

"Keep them."

"Damnit!" He suddenly upended the whole heavy counter. For an old god, he could still do damage. She recoiled from his tantrum, and he smacked her across the face with the petals. "I don't have to be generous. I own you!"

Persephone stood there, stunned.

For a moment, Hades realized he had gone too far.

Persephone turned and fled the kitchen.

Hades limped after. "Where are you going?" he called out. "You won't ruin this evening! I won't allow it!"

Her dinner was already ruined. That was the only tragedy of the evening. She didn't look back. "The only place I'm going is to my side of the palace. You stay on yours."

"WAIT!" he croaked with desperation.

Persephone swept down a long hallway lined with gilded mirrors separated by columns and floral patterns carved into the ceiling—an attempt to mirror the Hall of Mirrors.

"Once I cross that line, you don't follow anymore." There was a literal white line painted across the floor halfway down the hallway, leftover from a last-century feud. She could hear Hades panting behind her and quickened her pace. "I stay on my shitty side. You stay on your squalid side."

"Is that what this is about?" He hobbled faster to catch up, as if the line held actual power.

"You're embarrassed?"

She shook her head. "You're right, my love, this place is a dump. We'll have it torn down. Rebuilt. Redecorated. Grander than any castle or palace or church." He scrunched his face at that last word. Persephone shook her head again.

"We'll put the other religions to shame!" Hades bellowed.

She finally crossed her white line and whirled back, face pinched into a venomous scowl potent enough to freeze him in place. Fortunately, that place was on the other side of the infamous line.

"Another remodel? That's your big solution? Put the other religions to shame? Like they even know we exist! Look around—the only thing you've managed to screw up worse than the last remodel is your own kingdom. That is to say, if you've managed it at all."

He shook the ragged bouquet. "If the humans still worshipped—"

"You wouldn't need a pill to get it up. Same old story."

"You exaggerate."

Her anger flared. "You deny me every comfort, any company. If I claim a servant—just one—you banish the poor soul for your daughters to torture."

"Every servant I send you, you bed," he shot back. "And who knows how many more humans up there!" He jabbed the bouquet at the ceiling.

Her hands clamped her hips. "What I do on Earth is my business."

"Where's the sweet girl I found all those thousands of years ago?"

"You didn't find. You stole. And for the record, I fucking hate that flower."

He studied the mangled bouquet, finally did the math. Right. But apologies were not something the lord of the dead dispensed. Besides, he'd spent the better part of his afternoon picking these flowers from the meadows of Asphodel.

"They were from my heart. I love you."

She stared at him, frigid as the winter she left in her wake.

"You don't know what love is."

***

Hades didn't know where he was going. After Persephone strode into her side of the palace, he stood immobilized, letting the hurt wash over him. It always hurt, her rejection. He knew he had done wrong all those years ago. She was his brother's daughter. (At the time, not so reprehensible on the incest scale.) It wasn't his fault. The only thing that had changed was morality. It wasn't fair to apply present standards to past crimes. And really, was loving someone too much a crime? He only stole Persephone because he coveted her.

Hades had a big heart. It beat irregularly, and he wore it on his sleeve. All the Greek gods were notorious hotheads, philanderers, and sinners. Hades had simply lost the popularity contest. He felt unfairly judged—a victim of double standards, overzealous criticism, and extra scrutiny. Hades always got the short end, drawing the worst lot of his three brothers. The almighty, infallible Zeus (*pfft!*) claimed the heavens; pretty boy Poseidon was granted dominion over the sea; and meanwhile gimpy Hades was saddled with ruling over your dead grandparents. Even his birth was ill-fated—his leg mangled in his mother's womb as Zeus and Poseidon wrestled over the title of firstborn. No one would see his side of the story.

His mind ran laps of morbid self-pity. He wandered into rooms he hadn't visited in years, wings he'd forgotten even existed. The other gods enjoyed sunshine and laughter at the cool kids' table while he sat alone and despised in the dark. He wondered how smiles could come so easily to them, while joy, friendship, and love had no meaning for him. His brothers basked in an adoration they took for granted. Hades would trade anything—anything—for a moment of respect. To be loved the way he loved her. To hold her in his arms without her struggling against him. Of all the indignities Hades suffered—loneliness, the loss of mortal worship, the scorn of his fellow gods—nothing cut deeper than Persephone's indifference. He was willing to settle for friendship but afraid if offered, she would accept, forcing him to spend the rest of eternity in the friend zone.

Only when three tongues licked the coconut lotion off his hand did Hades realize he was lost. His three-headed hellhound stared up at him with her six puppy eyes and whined with concern. Cerberus could sense his mercurial moods, crawling into his lap when everyone else fled.

"Not now." He was in no mood.

The stallion-sized dog padded after him as he searched for his bedroom. Yet another night of reality dating shows awaited. Cerberus—his constant companion and primary instrument of torture—he had nursed her since she was a pup into the cutest cold-blooded killer and best friend a god could want.

He gave each gray muzzle a pat. Both dog and master walked with a limp. Sometimes, one of her heads would catch on a doorway, and she would scream until Hades freed her. Then there were the accidents—brown mountains and yellow rivers. It became hard for the slaves to keep up with the mess. The stench proved so overwhelming his demon warriors would faint while standing guard outside his bedroom. Hades never noticed.

The last time he unleashed Cerberus to punish a soul, she merely licked the man's face instead of mauling him. It took Hades shouting "Bite!" while flapping the frightened soul's arm to get Cerberus to rip him to shreds. Still, Hades could not bring himself to put her down. She had fight in her yet. Besides, it felt good to have someone who cared about him by his side.

He paused in a gold-tiled room with twelve bidets arranged in an inward-facing circle. A vague memory surfaced—some plan for this room—but that wasn't important. He was nowhere near where he was going.

Where was I going?

He slapped his thigh to signal Cerberus, and she padded after him as he tried to figure out just where in Hell he actually was.

It worried him, these lapses of memory. Names and faces had become as elusive as Artemis and her virtue. No one dared acknowledge his embarrassing mishaps or the less frequent episodes when his mind descended into an entirely different reality. His slaves would nervously play along—the task essential for their own survival—yet not exactly a recipe for stable leadership. Sometimes, when Hades returned to reality, he would continue the delusion simply to save face. Yet inside he was scared. Deeply, deeply scared.

After observing this decline for some time, the slaves began to take advantage and flee their bondage. Rooms began to collect dust. Stables were left unmucked. Extravagant feasts became microwaved meals. By the time Hades noticed, it was too late. He raged at his demons to catch the runaways, but even his most trusted soldiers had abandoned him. Then Hades was alone, and his quirks, memory lapses, and physical malfunctions were no longer embarrassing.

If a drunken god pissed himself when no slave was around to clean it, did it even really happen?

It took Hades several hours to find a room he recognized: the bowling alley, where he used to spend years obsessively practicing for tournaments. Hades had once been in a league with Aeschylus against the other great poets; their team's name was *The Tragics*. He sighed with relief, knowing he could find the rest of the way from here.

Indeed, he pushed open the great doors to a magnificent banquet room that once hosted the most decadent feasts of any realm. In his prime, Hades had made the Underworld the premier destination to satisfy one's sordid desires. The parties were legendary. Now it held court to dignitaries of dust and clutter.

He surveyed his sad collection of jewel-encrusted weapons, designer clothes and shoes, kitchenware, treadmills, and various exercise equipment with faded bows still attached—all his failed romantic gestures. His eyes landed on the skeleton of a unicorn and the marks on the wall where it tried to chew its way out. He probably should have set that gift free.

Hades suffered from stage-five hoarding disorder. Each gift signified his unyielding efforts to win over Persephone. Throw away one basket of shriveled fruit or one box of moldy chocolate, and he might as well throw away love itself. Half of him fantasized Persephone would one day find his collection and become overwhelmed by his devotion. The other half dreaded the same.

Hopeless, he thought, as he tossed the mangled bouquet atop all the other bouquets, dried and petrified from age.

***

A stack of books collapsed as Persephone slammed her bedroom door shut—an avalanche of worn-out spines and overread pages. Books were piled everywhere. She stormed the room, toppling each successive stack, a pent-up goddess who wanted to rattle her cage. Every year was the same, but without the distractions she could once rely upon, the Underworld had gone from prison to torture chamber.

She stopped, heaving in the dust.

Great, now I have a mess to clean too.

If she were truly being honest with herself, she needed a fucking Kindle.

Persephone fled her cozy bedroom, designed to resemble a French country cottage, retreating into an attached indoor garden, laid out in neat rows beneath grow lamps. The plants usually calmed her—the smell of soil, the soft fuzz of a new leaf, the tiny flower that promised fruit.

She turned to a window, expecting soaring mountains, an endless meadow, blue sky with towering clouds. Instead, she found a familiar wall of rock.

How could a goddess live like this? Like some wretched mortal in a cramped apartment with a view of an elevator shaft.

Her fingers dug into the wood of the windowsill, and she wanted to cry.

The sound of a television drifted in from her salon. She didn't remember turning it on. An overmodulated voice spoke excitedly:

"...nearly a thousand years since a pope resigned!"

Curiosity drew her from the window, past her rows of plants, and to the television, stuck on some twenty-four-hour game show that passed for news. A sense of dread rose within her as the reporter broadcast live from a packed and rainy Saint Peter's Square. Behind him stood a gathering of the poncho-wearing faithful with their cell phone cameras at the ready.

"The cardinals are now sealing themselves inside for the Conclave, an historic scene. Only hours ago, we witnessed the pope take off in his helicopter, leaving behind so many unanswered questions. Chief among them: Why? Why would Pope Benedict resign?"

Persephone gasped. No—she shook her head in denial. Popes resigned all the time. No big deal. Perfectly normal.

The reporter said it happened once…a thousand years ago.

She approached her blurry TV. The overly groomed reporter comported himself like a reality show host in a war zone. "Two popes! Unprecedented! Will they talk to each other? What if they disagree? What does that mean for the doctrine of *Ex Cathedra*?"

She ran her hands tightly through her hair until they found the back of her neck and squeezed. Suddenly, she felt sick.

"Damnit, Hermes, what have you done?" she asked the television.

The reporter tossed it back to the news desk.

CHAPTER FOUR

THE SUN GREETED ROME with striped pink clouds layered like swatches of fabric. The polished stone path leading to the Palatine Hill and the Roman Forum was slick from the rain. Hermes passed beneath the Arch of Titus with its depiction of the sack of Jerusalem and had the ancient city all to himself. In only a few short hours, a tide of tourists would wash over the temples once venerated to Jupiter, Vesta, and the other Greek gods who shamelessly sacrificed their identities on the altar of popularity.

Atop a hill overlooking the Italian capital, a maze of shattered brick walls marked what was once the Flavian Palace—ruins lording over ruins. He stopped atop the cliff where emperors once strolled a brilliant veranda. Below, a bulldozer traced circles through the empty, trash-littered Circus Maximus, no longer home to the chariot racers spurring on their horses to glory and death. Hermes sat in the cold, wet grass beneath a barren cherry tree. Its branches stretched across his vision. Slowly, the sun caressed the backside of the Palatine Hill, gently waking the city. A warm breeze kissed his cheek, interrupting winter's chill and shaking the branches around him. A faint pulse rippled beneath his other cheek, the beating heart of a slumbering Earth. All at once, and quite unexpectedly, the cherry tree exploded with pink and white blossoms like kernels of popcorn in a pan of hot oil.

And the brother of Persephone was suddenly happy. Spring had sprung.

***

Spring. Persephone had long since reached the apex of anticipation and slid down the other side into something akin to hibernation. For nearly a week she lay in bed, fingers clasped over her breast, staring past the peels of paint hanging from her ceiling. Her chest rose and fell like a metronome. Inhale. Exhale. Inhale. Exhale. She closed her eyes.

Inhale.

Her fingers twitched. The air hummed. Her skin tickled with an electric charge. Exhale.Her eyes opened to a warm stillness. Winter's grip had relented. It was time.

***

Persephone crossed the blood-stained marble, a prisoner meeting the parole board of one. She reached the lower steps and stopped. Hades waited for her on a simple bench atop the dais, as he did every year upon her release. His petulant silence stretched for an eternity. This was their ritual, the one bit of consistency in their marriage, and she hated its intimacy. It was her best and worst moment, her most vulnerable and most strong position. For God's sake, would he just say something? She wanted to scream, to shake him, slap him, force out his rage to justify hers.

She was angry at so many things that it was hard for her to pull them apart in her heart. But right now, she was particularly angry at his sadness, and that he thought he could hide that sadness from her. A god should never be pitied. It was unkind.

Most of all, Persephone was angry at her anger. Because its shadow was compassion. She raged against her empathy. Because how could the goddess of rebirth and renewal deny him? She was the original hypokritēs, the greatest pretender in all the universe.

She did not love Hades; there was no pretense there. She would never love him. Nor could she forgive his crimes. And yet, after so many centuries, he was all she knew.

She climbed the steps, placed a hand on his cheek, and softly kissed his forehead.

Hades remained a block of stone, unmoved despite the warmth of her lips and the sweet scent of jasmine, honeysuckle, and mint lingering in the air.

"Go," he commanded.

She pulled away, and he closed his eyes, listening as her footsteps receded down the long hall.

"I DON'T NEED YOU!" she heard him scream.

***

Dead pomegranate trees protested her departure, their thorns clawing at her dress. Eyes watched from within the bony thickets. There was always someone watching in Hell. She pressed on, into a forest of stalactites and stalagmites. Torches lit the narrow path, extinguishing as she passed, the Underworld turning its back on her. The black tidal wave swallowed all light, sound, and will. The Underworld had long ceased to scare Persephone with its petty games and theatrics. The last barrier to freedom was a smooth stone door polished into a mirror and rising to unfathomable heights. The rest of the Underworld was ringed by a fortress of razor shale, impassable even to the most powerful Titans, who endlessly plotted in the deepest, darkest depths.

Persephone married palms with her reflection. A great crack resounded as the tectonic plates ruptured. A fissure climbed from her fingers, a pair of stone lips opening just wide enough. Wide enough. A fresh breeze flirted with her hair, calling her home. She breathed in deeply, renewed, and began to climb. The chamber instantly sealed shut behind her. There was only up.

Twenty-four hours later, her thighs burned, her lungs screamed, and her tongue tasted of dirt. She regretted the lack of discipline surrounding her winter workout regime. *Didn't Hades buy me a StairMaster once?* He had, and she now remembered refusing it, calling the gesture insensitive. *Foolish me.* She vowed, as she heaved ever upward, to find out what happened to that strange, perfectly appropriate machine next winter. Perhaps she would turn the throne room into Hell's first Pilates studio.

Persephone grunted. There she went again: halfway to Earth, yet her mind was still trapped in Hell. No matter what she did, she couldn't untangle herself from him and that infernal prison.

Focus on the stairs, Persephone, focus.

The stairs took two months to climb, each step an affirmation. Round and round. On day twenty-three, the spirits of spring began to stir. She registered the slightest rise in temperature, the faintest hint of daylight. Round and round. The roots stirred. The Earth awakened. Round and round.

At long last: the sun.

***

Dense cumulus clouds parted above a mountain peak, setting its cap of winter ice to sparkling. The stairway from Hell opened into a narrow cave. Light danced through a waterfall shielding the entrance. The roar of the snowmelt sounded like the most joyous laughter. Persephone stepped through the icy shower, washing off the dirt and despair before wading into a clear baptismal lake and an overwhelming smell of pine. Bluebells and poppies crowned the shore. The Earth was so, so verdant. Her heart swelled. The rest of the Northern Hemisphere would take time to thaw, but here, spring had arrived in full bloom. She dipped backward, rinsing away the last of Hell, and finally turned to the forest. There weren't any woodland creatures poking through the trees. This wasn't a fucking Disney cartoon, and Persephone didn't expect any grand welcoming committee.

Who needs one when you have Hermes?

She expectantly scanned the shore. Where was Hermes? Hermes, who had nothing to do all winter but wait for her return? Persephone waited and waited, welcomed home only by a broken promise.

His promise.

She sighed and waded ashore.

***

Life on the run didn't suit a god like Hermes. The past two weeks had served as proof. Following Eshu's departure, Hermes took a train from Rome to the port of Ancona, where he slipped onto a ferry across the Adriatic to a picturesque little village on the coast of Croatia. Hermes could fly—sort of. More like hover at top speed, courtesy of the four embarrassingly tiny wings that fluttered off his ankles. For the sake of anonymity, those wings were tucked inside his sneakers. The day he lost his job as messenger, the gods had clipped his wings, a barbaric and mortifying ceremony of demotion. Slumming it like a human was about as embarrassing as it got for a god. With the dishonorable discharge, Hermes was forbidden to travel between realms or deliver messages, even after no one was left to care. Eventually, the feathers grew back, but he kept them covered to avoid any temptation to use them.

Once in Croatia, Hermes took two buses squished among sweaty, unwashed humans and their annoying offspring, followed by a three-mile haul on the back of a mule-drawn cart with his jangly loot before he made it to a town with a train station. Normally, he'd take a steamer to Tunisia and hop on a cargo ship to Canada, but North Africa wanted none of him these days, nor could he set foot in Greece. He was too hot to travel to Athens or any of the islands he once called home. Gabriel would no doubt have the place swarming with angels, and the Greek Orthodox pantheon would be more than happy to help. The Orthodoxy hated Hermes and longed for an opportunity to rid their country of him and his memory once and for all.

Bunch of bearded pussies.

It pained Hermes to bypass his native shores, riding a second-class ticket to Odessa, exhausted and ready for a transatlantic voyage that would put some much-needed distance between him and the Europe-wide god-hunt. He bribed a boatswain named Yuri with a pewter Viking chalice that, if filled with a certain type of Nordic beer, would temporarily give the drinker the strength of ten men (not that the walking steroid needed the boost) and boarded a Ukrainian shipping vessel. To sweeten the deal and assure discretion, Hermes also gave Yuri a strip from the Shroud of Turin. The cloth was a fake. Hermes always kept a few schmattas around for the purpose of bribing humans who couldn't tell the difference between a magical item and a knockoff—and often didn't care. They'd believe anything. The cargo ship would make a quick stop in Lebanon to drop off an arms shipment for the conflict du jour before turning west toward good ol' New North America.

Yuri, who smuggled him aboard and now coveted the fake Shroud, was a boiled Ukrainian potato spotted with moles and red everywhere else from prolonged sun exposure. He visited Hermes in the cargo hold on their first day at sea. Splotchy, unidentifiable tattoos stained his muscles, courtesy of his stint in jail for selling stolen televisions. He preferred to wear the same ratty "Keep Calm and Chive On" T-shirt, green camo cargo pants, and over-exuberant smile that craved companionship. Without an invitation, he squatted on a crate across from Hermes, who was playing solitaire.

The one-sided conversation continued for hours. Without prompting, Yuri told Hermes all about his miserable time in the military, his wife and three daughters living in Queens, whom he hadn't seen in years; his girlfriend in Odessa, whom he was afraid didn't love him; his girlfriend in Kiev, whom he didn't love; and his tabby cat, who was supposedly too cute for words.

And yet he found the words anyway. Didn't this guy have a ship to steer?

Hermes dealt a new hand as Yuri finally fell silent. He was afraid to look up in case it prompted him to keep talking.

"You're a god, aren't you?" Yuri finally said, his thick accent giving birth to each vowel.

Hermes glanced up. "Kinda."

Yuri's grin swelled into a smile. He wagged a pudgy finger. Sometimes people had the "gift." Schizophrenics, as Westerners liked to call them. Yuri clearly wasn't a shaman, but maybe his mother was a seer, or he kept the spark that allowed grown-ups to believe in Santa Claus.

"Could I pray to you?" he asked, like he was asking to touch a mascot at Disneyland.

Hermes revealed another card, three of diamonds. No moves. "Wouldn't do you any good."

"Praying don't do me no good now. At least I can see you, talk to you. And you talk back."

"Yeah, I can talk back." Hermes placed a queen of hearts. "Fuck off."

Yuri's laugh sounded like a lawn mower that wouldn't start. "You are my kind of god!"

"I'm no one's god." His game hit a dead end and Hermes restacked the cards.

"No One's God," Yuri repeated. "Where you from, No One's God?"

"Greece."

"Ah. Which one are you? Apollo?"

Someone knew his mythology. Sorta.

"No, I'm not Apollo," Hermes huffed, and began shuffling the deck. "Apollo would never ride steerage."

"You're not Poseidon, or you wouldn't need me to cross sea."

"And on the eighth day, Man discovered logic."

Yuri wagged that finger again. "God of Sarcasm."

"Bingo." Hermes threw his feet up on a crate, kicked off his sneakers, and let his four wings unfurl. It felt good to stretch them. Yuri gasped in wonder. Hermes abandoned the cards and began his ritual cleaning of the sneakers. From the awestruck silence, he knew that Yuri had never seen a miracle—though Hermes didn't count dirty feet as a miracle, either.

Mortals these days were starved for the divine. All the new religions were so hands-off. Kneeling and pressing palms together doesn't do much more than create a short boost of dopamine, just enough to keep coming back for the next fix—same as gambling. And as with all routines, these eventually lose their meaning too. Prayer becomes the bathroom rug that's never been washed. Seeing Hermes pick lint from between his toes was enough to transport Yuri to another realm of consciousness. A blissful tear rolled down his cheek. "I know who you are. You're Hermès."

"Nope. Those are the purses. I'm Hermes," Hermes said, polishing the yellow and green suede back to mint-condition shine. "My one endorsement deal and I can't even afford to buy a fucking bag."

"Why does Hermès—Hermes—need a purse?"

"To be fair, they started out selling harnesses for horses and, well, it made sense at the time. Why am I explaining anything to you?"

Yuri wagged a pudgy finger. "Ahhh, god of messengers. Ferrier of souls," he recited from his primary school knowledge.

"A-plus. Gold star."

Yuri suddenly beamed. "Wait!" And he scurried off into the darkness of the hold.

Wait. As if there was anywhere else to go. There was some commotion, the opening of a shipping container and fumbling about. Then, as if by his own powers to perform a miracle, Yuri returned with a golden Birkin bag and held it out for Hermes.

Hermes was slightly ashamed how quickly he snatched the treasured artifact out of Yuri's hands, and that he had been honestly more excited by a purse than the Ark of the Covenant. To be fair, one had better resale value. Priorities.

Yuri sat back down. "Gift. Or should I say offering?"

Hermes turned the bag over, and the gleam and dreams of Sotheby's drained from his eyes. The stitching was all wrong and it didn't feel like alligator skin. "Are these fake?"

"No..." Yuri said. Then "Yes," Yuri said.

"It's a knockoff." The word sagged with disappointment.

"I have container full..." he confessed, and then sheepishly added, "If you prefer other style, color, you let Yuri know. First one free, then I can give you a good deal on second."

Hermes had a quarter of a mind to turn Yuri in and three-quarters of a mind to sell the knockoffs himself. Instead, he handed the bag back to Yuri. "Thanks, but no thanks."

At the end of the day, Hermes, like Nike, was duty bound to protect brand identity.

Yuri didn't seem to mind. "This is fate. I...I am also ferrier of souls."

Uh-huh. Fate. Nice word.

"This must be a sign from above," Yuri said to the steel ceiling.

"Little lower."

Yuri clapped, eager as a birthday boy at a magic show. "Perform a miracle!"

Hermes did the next best thing and procured a bottle of vodka from his backpack, chugging half before extending it to his newest fan. "Prayer answered."

Yuri accepted the bottle and suckled as if it were nectar.

Hermes gently reclaimed the offering. He was going to need a drink after this conversation ended.

"I will serve as your most faithful and loyal and devoted servant," Yuri hiccupped.

"First, that's redundant. Second, I don't work with mortals. You have a habit of dying."

Undeterred, Yuri sprang from the crate and puffed out his chest, placing one hand over his heart and the other in the air like he was swearing an oath. "From now on." Big gulping breath. "Hermes, messenger of gods, ferrier of souls, is my god. I worship you. I pray to you. Oh, Holy One."

"For Olympus' sake," Hermes groaned. "I give you vodka, show you my wings, and now you won't leave me the fuck alone."

"I am Saint Paul walking the road to Damascus," Yuri said, clutching his heart.

"Did you just convert yourself?" Hermes buried his head in his hands, a headache marching over the horizon.

"Come, my god, you must follow me."

"I thought you were following me? I'm so confused."

Yuri studied Hermes' makeshift camp and frowned. "You can't stay here."

"What am I supposed to do, swim?"

"No. No. Inspections." Yuri had never said anything about inspections. He waved Hermes down the hold and Hermes reluctantly packed his cards, trailing along to the stern, where his annoying host worked the padlock on a rusty shipping container with several faded Banana Republic logos. A distinct, rank odor filled the air, and Hermes suddenly realized what Yuri meant...

"Oh, hell no," Hermes began.

"Very nice, very comfortable. You see!"

Hermes would smite Yuri before he slept in a steel shoebox with a load of spoiled fruit.

"Is practical." His accent thickened when excited.

"As your god, I command you!" Hermes tried to sound mighty, but Yuri had a habit of hearing only what he wanted to hear. "You try to shove me in there, I'll sink this ship."

Yuri lifted a latch and the container door swung open with an obnoxiously loud screech. A fluorescent glow flooded the cargo hold accompanied by an overwhelming stench—a pungent mix of sweat, urine, tobacco, and ramen noodles. Hermes heard scurrying within the tin can, then whimpering. Inside, nearly thirty Chinese men, women, and children were living, crammed into the container. Mattresses lay on the floor. Pilfered UN food packages were piled in a corner, cooking over butane lighters.

"See, I too am ferrier of souls. Many, many souls. To America. To new life." Yuri beamed. "They're small people." He held his hand four feet off the ground to demonstrate their hypothetically small stature. "Small people." Then he gestured at a speechless Hermes like he was the host of a sweepstakes show and Hermes had won a prize. "You stay with them, all good."

"You're mistaken." Hermes was not amused. "Check my reservation."

Yuri did that lawn mower laugh again. "Yes. Not fitting for a god. You wanted king suite. I know. This, this only fit for peasants. But we make do, right?"

Wrong. The tired, huddled mass watched Hermes with an intense uncertainty. He was a stranger among strangers in this strange place, all of them sailing to a strange land, fear and hope like cross currents fighting his internal god compass. The smuggled humanity clung to one another. Their fate, entirely out of their own hands, left to the winds, to Yuri…to Hermes. The whispering intensified, voices yearning and pleading, except the miserable faces that stared out from the container remained as still as stone, lips sealed, a determination to make it across the Atlantic. Only then did Hermes recognize the sound. It had been ages and ages since he'd heard anyone pray.

Hermes turned to Yuri, the human smuggler. "You can't lock them in here."

Yuri cycled through a range of responses, at first dismissive, then hurt and affronted. Finally, realizing he was dealing with an angry god, he grew mortified, as if he too were abhorred by this crime against humanity. "Yes. Of course. They are people. All God's—your creation. But see, I make them comfortable. Give them food, water, piss bucket. Settle them in New York. All a-okay."

He barked some order in Chinese at the makeshift camp, and a boy no more than twelve disentangled from his mother's arms and scampered to the back. Reaching behind a curtain, he retrieved a large bucket, pinching his nose as he dragged it to the front. Yuri smiled, sealed the fecal bucket with a plastic lid, and handed the boy an off-brand chocolate bar and a clean bucket. "See! I take care of them. Most people put them on boat and then goodbye. Not me. I care for them. Like they're family."

The boy, green and sickly, looked at the chocolate bar as if it were the last thing in the world he wanted. Yuri tussled his hair, the jolly uncle. When the boy didn't leave, Yuri impatiently shoved the kid back inside. "Go!"

Yuri started shouting vowels, but the boy wouldn't budge, eyes wide as saucers.

Hermes had forgotten to put on his sneakers, and now his four pixie wings were erect, twitching from his anger at Yuri. The kid's extended family jumped to their feet, vigorously pointing, making excited exclamations that sounded like a tropical bird aviary. The kid had produced a smartphone and was snapping photos of his feet.

Great.

Yuri smacked the kid on the side of the head and spoke broken Chinese, punctuating his speech with wild gesticulating. By all accounts, Yuri looked like a raving lunatic, but they must have understood because the group suddenly dropped to their knees and began bowing with pyramid palms pressed to their foreheads. All the heads bobbing up and down made Hermes think of those drinking-bird novelty toys kooky secretaries used to decorate their desks. Wait a second...they were showing their most esteemed reverence, they were expressing their veneration, they were praying to Hermes!

Yuri stood back, proud. And just like that, in the hold of a Ukrainian cargo ship carrying knockoff jeans, illegal weapons, car parts, and a load of Chinese immigrants, Hermes acquired his first cult of worshippers in nearly two and a half thousand years.

***

The rest of the journey passed in an uncomfortable rotation of prayers and dreamy gazes. Hermes tried to keep his distance from his new worshippers, which was hard in a forty-by-twenty-foot box. Yuri and the families started lighting candles by his winged feet until the shrine took up half the shipping container and raised the temperature to suffocating levels, forcing Hermes to blow them all out and forbid further veneration. Then they brought him offerings of food, grain alcohol, and tobacco. Being prudent, Hermes only partook of the grain alcohol and got seriously drunk. On the grand cosmological scale, the Greek god wasn't sure how this all stacked up or how it might affect his status as a fugitive on the run from the Catholics. He learned that the boy in charge of the poop bucket was named Wu. He had spiky hair and the personality to match. Hermes would wake to find the boy poking him in the ribs. He spent days studying Hermes as he lost successive games of solitaire, until one morning Hermes found Wu in the middle of a Klondike after swiping his deck. Hermes swelled with pride. Not long after, Hermes taught Wu how to count cards and shanghaied a couple of the elders into a poker quorum.

Sleeping, eating, shitting, laughing among these families, something profound and permanent began to take root. Despite his best efforts to remain unattached, Hermes was beginning to feel responsible for these humans. He learned the rest of their names, their deepest desires, hopes, and fears. Their prayers, which first sounded like conversations faintly overheard through an apartment wall, grew louder and more distinct. Often, he found himself staring at Wu (*not in a creepy way*), imagining the kid's future in America. The reality awaiting them wasn't pretty. Most likely Wu would spend his childhood paying off his family's debt, working eighteen hours in the dirty basement of a dim sum restaurant in Chinatown. The families, bound in a heritage of respect and care for their elders, would jettison off relatives one at a time, assailed by assimilation, financial hardship, violence and crime, the stresses of starting a new life. And what was Hermes supposed to do? Being accountable for their

62

lives frightened him. Other gods simply let their mortal worshippers run amok, interceding only on the rare occasion when it suited their self-interest, but Hermes wasn't sure he could operate from the same level of divine detachment. He never thought of himself as a god who could rule from a remote mountaintop.

On a chilly March night, three weeks after acquiring his new band of apostles and with the Manhattan skyline in view, Hermes dove overboard into a polluted Newark Bay. He emerged from the primordial ooze at the New Jersey Turnpike looking like a swamp monster. Actual swamp monsters lived in the vast Garden State wetlands—no surprise there—but those vile, half-man, half-salamanders preferred to burrow deep below the sludge.

He showered at a truck stop in Jersey City before checking into a cheap hostel in Spanish Harlem. Two fitful days passed tossing and turning on a squeaky metal bunk bed, disturbed by visions of his abandoned worshippers being passed off to some shadowy mobster as Yuri pocketed his cash, until, unrested, Hermes stepped over the bags of garbage piling in the hallway, past the meth dealers, and into America.

Hermes had one important stop to make in the Big Apple. He took the 1 train to Christopher Street and walked the maze of cobblestone streets to a brightly painted lesbian bar aptly called the Cubbyhole. It was noon and the place was busy with an eclectic mix ready for a spread in the Sunday Times. A few hipster women chatted loudly, and a group of self-conscious NYU students sipped cheap whiskey, trying to seem one with Manhattan. A man in a business suit winked at Hermes and patted an empty stool. Hermes kept walking, the top of his head brushing dolls and toys that hung as decoration from the ceiling.

He slid into a booth at the back of the joint, beside a jukebox playing Tina Turner's greatest hits. Five empty tumblers sat overturned on the table, arranged in a pyramid, behind which two eyes peered over the milky glasses. The woman rested her chin in her palms, dark crimson lips smelling of strawberry lip gloss, elbows jutting out so that she formed a perfect triangle of displeasure. She wore several rings adorned with owls on her manicured fingers.

Hermes slid the alcoholic shrine down the table to better see Lilith. "What's a sweet Jewish girl like you doing in a place like this?"

"Did you expect to find me eating a fucking cupcake? Chatting with my girlfriends on Bleecker Street?" She dropped her arm with a slap on the table. "You kept me waiting." Her sultry voice reminded him of a subway platform on a steamy August night.

"It's called deferred gratification. Here's your feather." He withdrew the long blue Baach feather from his pocket—the one from the Vatican vault—and set it on the table between them.

She didn't smile so much as drill him with her eyes. "The Holy See is roiling. I hear Gabriel's turning over every rock from Rome to Jerusalem."

"Then he's looking in the wrong place."

"For now," she replied, sing-songy.

"You gonna rat?"

"On you? No. I wouldn't want to be working cross-purpose. My little part in this stays silent."

His eyes narrowed. Hermes wasn't aware of any bigger picture.

"But I thank you all the same, darling." She produced a pair of tweezers from her purse, carefully plucked the feather as if it were a diamond, and slipped it into a cellophane package before it disappeared into her handbag.

Should he have been using protection with that thing?

"You want to know what it's for?" she asked, desperate to dish some juicy goss.

"Not really."

"Oh. Shame. I wouldn't have told you anyway." She cocked her head to one side. "Maybe if you tortured it out of me."

"I'm sure there are a few girls in here that are game."

"You're such a drag. Even for the West Village." She turned her attention to the bar. "What are you having?"

"No time. I just came to give you yours."

"You're off to see *her*, aren't you? It's nearly spring. Where's she holidaying these days? She has such good taste."

"Off-grid," was all Hermes was willing to share with this snake.

She made a cooing sound, as if someone had set a tray of dessert in front of her. "I like secrets. I'll tell you mine if you tell me yours."

"No. Don't care enough." He freed himself from the booth.

She smiled up at him. "You should."

Hermes dropped a few twenties and headed for the exit, wondering if he should have asked Lilith what in God's name (and perhaps for which god) she wanted with that feather. It was the one payment she required for giving up the secret entrance to the Vatican's Holy of Holies, and he hadn't even bothered asking why. After all, she had her pick of the world's most powerful and sacred objects from the vault, and she chose that one. Seemed like a fair trade at the time. Hermes had even felt guilty, as if she were getting a raw deal and he were taking advantage. Now, as he stepped out into the chic Lower Manhattan neighborhood, he wondered if he'd gotten it all wrong. The whole exchange soared miles over his head, and even though they'd never slept together, Hermes got the distinct feeling he'd just been fucked.

***

Hermes trampled wildflowers as he approached a lone cabin framed beneath the Mission Mountains, surrounded by a rolling green valley. Persephone spent her monastic summers here, tending a garden, communing with all that grew, flew, slithered, hopped, walked on four legs, and crawled. The crawling sometimes included Hermes coming off a hard winter binger. He hopped a rushing stream, smelled the richness of the damp earth. A path appeared, and he took its meandering course into Persephone's garden. Vegetables and flowers rose from freshly tilled soil to meet apples and peaches dangling from burdened trees. He smiled. Her magic was alive and well. Thriving, actually. This truly was paradise.

She appeared on the porch, lips pursed, auburn hair flowing past her shoulders, hands on her hips, a flower-patterned apron tied around her waist. Baking flour dappled her cheeks.

He dropped his duffels like a soldier returning from war. "I was detained."

"Wouldn't have to do with the Vatican, would it?"

He shrugged.

"Of all the religions, you had to poke the lion in the eye."

"I like lions."

She sighed. Her hands fell from her hips.

"So, can I stay till fall?"

"As long as you can work a hoe."

Hermes beamed.

"In the garden."

"Anywhere she wants it."

Persephone smiled despite herself, wondering how he always did this to her. No matter how infuriating his transgression, she couldn't help but forgive him. God, she loved him.

Hermes launched up the steps and wrapped his arms around her. "Thanks, Sis."

No one understood him, cared for him, listened to him, and called him out on his bullshit like Persephone. It was a large and lonely universe for a god, but when Hermes and Persephone had each other, immortality didn't seem so unbearable.

Then she pulled away and got serious. "Are we safe?"

"Don't worry, I zigzagged." He gave her a quick peck on the cheek and darted inside her cabin. She heard the rattle of the refrigerator opening and his muffled voice call out from her icebox: "What's for dinner?"

CHAPTER FIVE

IT WAS AN ODD time of year for a winter fire, seeing as it was the beginning of summer, but Hermes insisted. It complemented the cabin. Everything in Persephone's secluded mountain refuge was locally sourced, certified organic, and made of raw materials, from the interlocking pine log walls to the woven wicker furniture and goose-feather pillows. Hermes lay atop a nest of Navajo blankets. Persephone liked to honor the Native religions wherever she put down roots and had her home here in northern Montana decorated with the ceremonial artwork of the Blackfoot tribe, gifts from the spirits who sheltered her and kept her presence a guarded secret.

Hermes fed logs into the fire and stoked the embers, his mind—turbulent of late—now content to watch the flames play. All his troubles, along with the stolen Vatican loot, were buried off Highway 89, beneath mile marker 320, where they would wait until the first frost. He tried not to spoil his time with Persephone by dwelling on that day three months hence. Then he would dig up the duffel bags and begin his lonely winter, roving and waiting, as he did every year, for spring.

Empty bottles rolled across the floor as Persephone dropped beside him and uncorked an ancient vintage with her teeth. Wine spilled down her chin and neck. She wiped it off with her fingers and licked the juice.

"We're cleaning house. Well, I am anyway."

She held out the bottle. He refused and spread on his back. She shrugged.

He watched her drain half the bottle in one go.

"Knock that off. I've been deprived," she said.

Hell had always been well stocked in the vino department. The rest be damned, Hades would never let the Underworld go dry.

"Don't tell me the cellars are empty."

"Deprived of conversation...of good company...of my sanity."

Hermes rolled his head to stare up at the rafters. "What did he give you this year?"

She joined him on her back. "Flowers. *The* flower."

"Ouch. What is that? Ten years in a row?"

"Twelve." Her smile withered. "He's getting worse."

"You're feeling sorry for him?"

"No," she replied too quickly, intensely studying her antler chandelier.

"You are."

"Am not."

"Careful," Hermes warned, "you may start feeling something else."

She managed a flimsy smile. "Please."

Hermes commandeered the bottle. Admission by omission. The first few nights of their reunion were typically spent uncorking the resentments and misgivings they had bottled over the winter. This was supposed to be their safe place.

She took the bottle back and swigged. "But—"

"But what?"

"I was cruel."

"Cruel. That's new. Isn't it his fault you're down there? Why we all have to suffer?"

"You don't have to remind me."

"Apparently I do. I don't like you defending him."

"So what if I'm defending him?" The conversation was having a sobering effect, wearing thin alcohol's cushion. She retreated from the thought, eyes misty. "I'm not defending him. I'm just tired."

He pulled her against him and rested his chin protectively atop her head as she snuggled.

"I don't know which is worse: his cruelty or his senility." It poured out of her now. "He's being taken advantage of—by his daughters, by everyone. I don't know what to do about it."

"Is the prisoner supposed to run the prison?"

She lifted away from him, smudging tears, a wounded look that Hermes didn't understand.

"Why do you care so much?" he said. "It's not like you wanted any of this to begin with—to be his queen, his wife. Let it play out how it will without getting so wrapped up in it."

She abruptly stood, trying to determine the shape of her anger. "We can't all be as carefree as you."

He rolled his eyes.

"I'm serious," she shot back.

"Don't turn this."

"And why not?"

"Because we're talking about you."

"No," she blurted, too inebriated for this delicate task. "This is the perfect opportunity…the perfect opportunity to address your bad behavior."

Here we go.

Hermes smiled, though the smile didn't move past his lips. The evening came into sudden focus, her hands on the wheel, intending to steer the conversation toward this uncomfortable talk. The carefree dinner, the top vintages uncorked—she had orchestrated it all to get him relaxed;

then she thought she could tiptoe into his subconscious and go for the insecurities. Instead, she had just smashed in the front window and stomped on the glass.

"My bad behavior?"

"The way we've all been feeling about you. Yes."

"We?"

"The consensus."

"Among whom?"

Persephone bit her lip, paced in front of the flames that swayed behind her like backup dancers, then turned to him. "The gods that still care about you."

Hermes scoffed. He chafed at being mothered.

She added, "Who are few and far between."

"Like I give a shit. Besides, this was supposed to be your intervention."

"What do I need an intervention for?! I'm not the one crossing every religion," she shouted. So much for their safe space. "Creating conflict between the religions! Especially the powerful ones!" She took a deep breath, reset. "There's only so much mending I can do."

"Then don't mend."

"You need to find something for yourself. Find your thing—not tricks."

His eyebrows hit the ceiling. "Tricks? That was art."

"Don't. You're trying to pass this off as some grand public performance. There wasn't any moral lesson learned. You didn't better humanity. Or elevate the gods. Don't *art* me."

"It's not my fault the humans sold off magic for Google and cell phones."

"You used to be the Messenger of the Gods. Who do you think you're fooling?"

He stood and faced her.

She stared him down.

"Careful now."

Persephone smirked. "Oh, now you want caution. Because we're a little too close to the truth?"

"You? You're going to lecture me?" Hermes clenched. His chest heaved. "This is why the gods can't stand you! Why Hecate won't talk to you anymore. Why you don't have any girlfriends." He used air quotes to emphasize "girlfriends." "You act poor when you're anything but. We're not all so blessed with purpose as you. No one rewrote your myth. No other god co-opted your responsibilities. No one else's mom chose to disappear into the void to gift their only daughter the job of making sure humanity doesn't starve. All high and mighty. You and your divine fucking trust fund."

Her mouth was parched from adrenaline. "That's not an excuse."

"That's every excuse. You have a reason to get up in the morning!" He remembered there was a bottle of wine in his hand and chucked it into the fire, dousing the flames. "Sometimes I envy mortals. At least they can die."

She stood opposite his furnace of anger and couldn't move.

"What is the Messenger of the Gods supposed to do when there are no more fucking messages?"

"And there it is, the truth we've been circling for centuries." Persephone refused to back down. "You waste your immortality on trick after trick that accomplishes nothing—at the expense of the Catholics, this time. You're the poster child for unintended consequences."

That stung good and deep. They fell silent. The room crackled with the sound of logs splitting from the heat as wine bled from the hearth. Hermes looked her right in the eyes, disturbingly detached, voice flat.

"On second thought, you should feel sorry for Hades. I do."

***

That first night of their reunion, they had stumbled upon the edge of something, pulled back, and silently agreed never to return. They brooded in silence for the rest of the night. Sleep never found them, and as they stared at the darkness around their pillows with heavy thoughts, they came separately to the same realization: the bonds between them were far more fragile than they had suspected.

The next morning, they regarded one another warily. Hermes stood in the kitchen, slurping his Lucky Charms. Persephone took her egg-white omelet at the table. They stared past one another as they ate. Conversation no longer flowed easily; now it felt as if they were only filling silence. The words, when they did flow, amounted to small talk and trivial necessities.

Over the warming days and weeks, they eased back into a semblance of their former routines. Yet the shadow of the argument followed them everywhere, a lurking presence, there to be called upon and resumed at any moment. They could hear it breathing loudly when they worked outside, pressing on the windows at night when they sat down to read. It was the summer of eggshells, the opposite of the rejuvenation they once found in each other's presence. That was the worst of it all, though neither would admit they felt so uneasy.

They were done with revelations.

Polluted with the haze of distant wildfires, the sky took on a scorched hue in the early September heat. The bare mountaintops looked like a row of spearheads mounted on the gold-brushed grassland. Persephone scavenged her rows of stalks, harvesting the last of the summer corn, rustling in search of each sporadic ear to fill the basket under her arm. It was a windless day, and the work was tiresome. She turned back toward the cabin, visible over the sentinel reeds, and wiped her brow. Shielding her eyes, she spotted Hermes on the shaded porch, feet up, chair rocking back, cowboy cool.

"So much for helping," she mumbled while glaring up at him on his comfortable perch.

Hermes lowered his straw hat over his eyes.

"Heaven forbid the god of boredom pick up a fucking shovel," she raised her voice.

"Hell forbid the goddess of nags chill out for five minutes," he retorted.

She dropped the basket. "Love to. But dinner isn't going to pick itself."

Oh, game on. Hermes had just begun to respond when a cool wind suddenly gusted down from the north to swipe the hat off his head. The brim caught on the porch railing. But the breeze continued, bending the stalks of corn, slipping over Persephone's sweaty neck, sending a shiver down her spine, rustling her orchard, and finally escaping into a grove of aspens.

Seized with a sudden dread, Hermes gripped the porch rail, knuckles white, face ashen. Persephone spun to the forest, searching the wind's southern wake through the tired summer leaves. She instantly spotted the autumn petal, golden yellow. It caught the breeze like a full sail and struggled to hold onto its branch.

The breeze died down and the leaf, still clinging, shimmered with relief. Persephone turned to Hermes, eyes filled with a thousand apologies, all the regret of a wasted summer. Then, without a sound, the leaf slipped free, as if pushed from a ledge, and spiraled to the forest floor.

It landed with the thud of a boulder.

Persephone closed her eyes in a ritual of defeat.

Summer had bent the knee to fall. It was time.

***

That evening they sat on the porch swing, wrapped tightly in each other's arms, watching the sun douse the prairie purple, orange, and pink. He massaged the nape of her neck, felt her pulse flutter through her summer dress. Tomorrow Persephone would be gone, and Hermes would be alone.

He looked up to the first stars emerging above them. "Do you think there are other galaxies?" he asked. "Other cosmos? The humans say there are maybe a billion solar systems. Perhaps there are other gods and goddesses we don't know about."

"It's possible," she said, a tinge of sadness. Hermes felt her shrug.

"With other little creatures like the humans to worship them?"

She smiled. "And alien scientists to doubt those gods."

His eyes narrowed in rumination. The earth tipped and the horizon swallowed the sun.

"Do you think we exist because the mortals exist?"

"It would be rather one-sided if they didn't have some part to play in creation."

"I wouldn't go that far. Do you actually think the humans helped create Earth and the sky and the heavens?"

"They have power too. They just don't realize it. They're too distracted. And I'm not talking about power in the way they drive us nuts when they're not praying and leaving us presents. There's a more intangible connection. As a collective species, they have an enormous flow of—"

"Energy?" he mocked.

"Now you're being a jerk." She pretended to be insulted. "Forget how pseudo-spiritualists use the word. They've really fucked that one up for the rest of us. They don't own the word energy."

"Burning incense and candles in their beach houses while they commune with spirits. And their shamans who bill by the hour. Sounds like someone's been hanging out with too many SUV-driving, weekend hippies. Don't deny it."

"Ha. Ha. Ha." She pinched his side.

"Ow!" He squirmed, grinning. "Run away, run away! The goddess Persephone and her reign of horror knows no bounds!"

She pinched him again. Harder.

"Ow. Ow. Ow. Not fair."

"You're teasing me. But you know what I'm talking about. Good and evil. Heaven and hell. Male and female. Yin and yang. Give and take. Push and pull. Forces as old and fundamental as it gets."

"Gods and humans," he finished.

Fireflies sparked beyond the porch. They listened to the crickets.

Persephone sighed. "It would be so lonely without the humans, wouldn't it? Even if they stopped worshiping altogether."

He suddenly thought about Wu and Yuri, and the other families now somewhere in New York. And when he thought about them, he could feel them worshipping in his name.

Holy shit!

Hermes felt them. *Their energy.*

Somewhere on the planet, they were worshipping him. The connection was faint, clumsy. Tapping into the divine highway, Hermes could sense his new followers were lost and alone. But also together. And there was strength in that, a congregation of souls—the first strands.

Strands of what?

Community.

The word lodged itself in his skull. He fought an urge to tell Persephone of his new human followers because it would only lead to questions, questions that would inevitably bring them to the argument about his irresponsibility that they had so far managed to leave undisturbed. He didn't want to turn the boat around. Not now. Not when their hours were numbered, and she would soon descend, and the world would turn so bitter cold. He coveted her warmth, for as long as he could have it.

"How come we're not omniscient?" he said, almost angrily.

Persephone chuckled, but stopped when she realized Hermes was being serious. "I don't know. The humans, though—they seem to be closing in on it themselves, and all on their own."

"Do not say its name."

"You have to get over your beef with the internet."

"This isn't about the internet or email," Hermes insisted. "How'd the humans get to thinking that we had all the answers? What idiot god gave them the idea that we're all-knowing?"

"Why are you so hot and bothered about it?" Persephone asked.

"What good is being divine if we're as confused and frustrated as they are? Shouldn't we be the question and the answer? Both? At the same time?"

"That's a fun paradox," she said and then whispered to herself, "It would be nice to have all the answers."

She turned to him. "Where is this coming from?"

Before he could answer, they heard a distant engine, tires kicking up dirt and gravel. Headlights peered over her garden and blinded them, sterilizing the conversation. A pale blue and white 1973 Ford pickup crested the hill, bouncing along the dirt road. It parked, and an elderly man in his sixties climbed out. He was twig-thin yet broad-shouldered, with the brown complexion of a Florida retiree left in the sun too long. His salt-and-pepper hair was cropped along the sides, and he had a wide, flat nose like a sledgehammer, which complemented his high forehead. He wore a T-shirt and jeans and a friendly smile as he approached the cabin.

"Old Jim," Persephone called out with a weak smile. General circumstances this evening made being friendly an effort.

"Hiyya, Persephone, Hermes." He nodded at each as he leaned on the garden fence below.

"Hiyya, Old Jim," Hermes repeated, welcoming the interruption.

"How are the Niitsitapii?" Persephone asked.

Niitsitapii meant "the Real People," the traditional name for the Blackfoot Nation. Jim Old Bear LaBoueff was medicine man for the local Blackfoot tribe. He was also Persephone's neighbor, arbiter between the Spirit Realm and the human world, and just a darn nice guy. His voice was smooth and warm as bedtime tea with a tinge of the high-plains lilt that was a relative of the North Dakota "you betchas."

"We want to invite you two over. Martha had the boys set up the sweat lodge, which we know you like especially," he said, looking at Hermes.

Hermes grinned. "You drive a hard bargain."

"Best way to rid the body of toxins," Old Jim said. "Get a bonfire going. Figured we can do a journey before it gets too late. Potato salad."

"Potato salad? Did I hear that right?" Hermes exaggerated his enthusiasm.

Persephone elbowed him.

"You betcha," Old Jim said with pride.

Hermes slapped his thigh. "Sold!" Potato salad or not, Hermes swore by the Blackfoot sweat lodges. They were truly miraculous.

Old Jim nodded and turned to Persephone. "You missed the Sun Dance, but we figured on it, and we planned something special for tonight, since the spirits said this was your last and all."

Busybodies, Hermes thought. When the native spirits gossip that their Greek goddess neighbor is returning to hell according to a date on the Christian calendar, you knew the cosmology was all tangled up.

"So, youse two comin'? Got plenty room in my truck."

Hermes turned to Persephone.

She shrugged.

***

They drove through twilight away from the mountains, the valley opening into a wide over which the stars were out in mass. Old Jim parked at the edge of a tribal gathering, where a collection of trucks and a few beat-up city cars were scattered across the field. They were greeted with smiles and hugs by Blackfeet tribal members, families Hermes and Persephone had known since the mothers and fathers were children themselves. White cone teepees formed a half-circle around a bonfire that was just getting going. A pile of shipping pallets and beat-up furniture waited nearby as extra kindling. A twelve-year-old boy did the honor, squeezing an inordinate amount of lighter fluid on the whole thing until the pyro's father—a round man in his early thirties with a ponytail, who worked in a nearby mine and came home every other weekend—quickly won control of the matches.

Persephone sat in the grass with a group of women and their infants. Someone handed her a platter of barbecued chicken and coleslaw. She let the wash of reservation news fill her. Her smile returned with ease. She loved it here among the high plains people and their glorious heritage.

Modern life, however, was never far away. In the distance, lights twinkled from the community center (two double-wide trailers raised several feet off the ground) and a few tribal municipality buildings. Unseen was an underfunded community college, the struggling pencil factory that provided the main source of employment, and the reservation town where most residents lived below the poverty line and faced an insidious veil of racial and economic segregation. But here, tonight, the Blackfeet welcomed this goddess of a people they had never met, who existed a world away and generations under the Earth.

Hermes joined a game of touch football while the sweat lodge sweltered to the proper temperature. The traditional lodge, made from woven willow saplings and covered in hide, looked like a large turtle sleeping beside the river. About an hour later, just as the mortals were finished losing, Old Jim emerged from the lodge and called the game. The fragrance of burning sage invaded the valley. Hermes dispensed high fives as he headed toward his ceremony, his eyelids heavy and his heart light as the cleansing smoke doused him like water.

Old Jim hunched over the river, filling two plastic milk jugs as he blessed the water. Outlined by the glistening stream, his voice undulated with his people's sacred song. Hermes listened from the lodge's entrance, a slender neck extending from the base of the dome. The Blackfeet's traditional story said the lodge was designed to resemble a pregnant woman on her back, with her belly facing the sky. Hermes liked the symbolism. He liked to think he was returning to the womb.

Hermes crawled inside the darkened passageway, dry sage crunching under his hands and knees. He maneuvered around a post with a buffalo skull skewered on top, both altar and safety precaution, meant to keep the entrant from falling into the fire pit. Moonlight spilled in from an oculus, and a red glow pulsed from super-heated coals, licked by slender blue flames that reanimated the buffalo hides with the pallor of flesh and blood. Three men already sat lotus-style around the pit. One of them whipped a small mallet against a drum, a syncopated heartbeat rhythm meant to lure them into a trance.

Hermes took his place in the circle, and someone tossed a bundle of sage onto the coals to perform the ritual bathing in smoke. A burst of fresh air parted the pungent gray clouds as Old Jim entered from the tunnel with the river water.

"Robert, take this," Old Jim said, still on his hands and knees, as he passed the jugs to his youngest son. Robert, barely eighteen and trying to grow a mustache that looked like a rat's tail, eagerly took the blessed water.

"The stones and water are blessed." Old Jim turned to one of the two men not beating the drum, who bore a striking resemblance to his father. "Young Jim, close the flap."

Young Jim, Old Jim's eldest son, his long hair tied back in a ponytail, obeyed his father, and soon the lodge was plunged into near-total darkness, the coals flaring with each trepid exhale, casting fleeting red shadows across their faces. Both sons were in training to carry on a tradition more than a dozen generations deep.

Old Jim filled a large pitcher with the blessed water as the drumbeat quickened. He joined the rhythm, speaking the language of his people—a prayer to call forth the spirits to guide them on this journey. The prayer surged through Hermes like a gust of wind as the doorway to another world cracked open.

Young Jim eyed the Greek god warily. Calling forth one's spirits was a powerful ceremony, the medicine delicate and chaotic, cathartic and burdening. The results were unpredictable even when initiated by the most experienced medicine man under the most controlled circumstances. Conducting the ceremony with a strange god among your circle was unheard of among shamans, healers, and mediators. Old Jim had never permitted his sons to join a journey with Hermes before.

Hermes felt somewhat responsible for their anxiety. He reached over and laid a hand on each son's shoulder, embracing the full presence of a god. "Thank you for sharing your people's gifts."

The boys swelled with pride. Hermes knew it would be a difficult path, keeping the ancient ways alive in today's world, but he hoped that the brothers would follow in Old Jim's footsteps.

"You don't have to be frightened," Hermes said with confidence.

The brothers shared a glance.

Young Jim turned to Hermes. "We're not frightened for us—"

"You're the one the spirits want to talk to," Robert finished.

Oops. Just when you thought you had the humans figured out, they go and flip your world. Hermes didn't like his world being flipped. Especially when he'd just strapped himself into a cosmic rocket ship. A tiny voice agreed with Young Jim: *Get out now! Don't let go! Don't let strangers take control of your reality!*

Hermes took a deep breath and swallowed the voice.

"Young Jim," Old Jim called. His elder son leaned into the pit to cleanse himself with the smoke, then moved clockwise around the lodge to sit by his father's side. He lifted the basin of water to his lap. Hermes watched, perspiring from the heat that had only grown exponentially intense with the five of them cramped in this small enclosure.

Old Jim began, "Attendant spirits, help us see clearly inside ourselves, and thus may we turn outward with an open heart and pure mind. Cleanse our bodies and take from us what you must, for we seek the vision of Nah-doo-si, Creator Sun." His voice dropped to a whisper to finish his prayer. Sweat rolled off his face and down his chest.

Using a wooden ladle, Young Jim doused the hot stones with the blessed water. Steam burst upward like a dragon taking flight. Old Jim resumed his chanting, each syllable stabbing the silence. The drummer lifted his instrument and pounded—harder, faster. The steam thickened into a cocoon, vibrated with the poetry, heightened his sense of touch, taste, smell, sight, sound, and the intuitive one that let him know the barrier between this world and the Blackfoot Spirit Realm had dissolved. They now existed within—and were themselves—the portal. He breathed deep, the steam an extension of his consciousness. His skin prickled as the air parted for the spirits now joining them around the fire.

His palms lay flat on his thighs, and his eyes slipped shut. Two hands gripped his, and he knew without seeing they weren't human. These hands were made of mud and grass and bone. Snakes slithered onto his legs like icy water trickling along his heated skin.

A voice hissed, "Moo-goo-waw. Moo-goo-waw. Moo-goo-waw."

Hermes' body locked in place. He shivered despite the oppressive heat. The steam coiled around his neck and began to choke him, snuffing out the world. Something had gone terribly wrong. This was not the way these ceremonies were supposed to go. He wasn't afraid, per se. Little could harm him on Earth.

But what if he was no longer on Earth?

"Show him," Old Jim said to the spirits from somewhere far away.

Suddenly, he felt his spirit tugged from his body like a joint dislocated from its socket. And then Hermes was falling. He fell from the sweat lodge, out of Montana, away from Earth—yanked from the current world and dragged into the Spirit Realm of the Niitsitapii. His sense of direction failed. Gravity reversed. He began to float. He no longer knew how far from the sweat lodge he had traveled. He looked around, but all was empty, devoid of light, color, shape. He raised his hands in front of his face and saw nothing. Perhaps he no longer had eyes at all. This was the place of visions; one did not need eyes to see.

Then, in the blink of a useless eye, he went from seeing nothing to seeing all. He inhabited a sea of grass bending in a breeze, the great boulders waiting patiently on the mountains, the deer grazing in the prairie, and the wolves hunting them. This is what it felt like to be a spirit god: to inhabit rather than exist, to be the sun rather than a single ray of light. The great interconnectedness of life. These gods were everything and nothing all at once.

The awareness overwhelmed him—and then vanished—leaving him back in his regular three-dimensional god body on a cold metallic floor. Having hands and feet and a body again suddenly felt so old school. His body shivered. The ground was not simply cold, it was polar. Returning to his traditional body also meant he had to do all those inconvenient mechanical things, like opening his eyes. And so he did. His analog vision adjusted to a faded yellow blanket with floral patterns. The blanket partly covered a soiled mattress. Touching the cloth, it cracked like thin ice over a pond.

Turning to his surroundings, he realized he was inside that container from the Ukrainian cargo ship. Everything was coated in frost, like a refrigerated truck. Each exhale left a frozen contrail suspended in the air.

White mounds like piles of melted wax dotted the floor. They were bodies wrapped in layers, but not enough to save them from the cold. A woman, her blue face frozen in despair, stared into her cradled arms. Hermes snapped off a piece of the blanket to reveal an infant sleeping eternally against her breast.

These were his worshippers, his souls to care for and to keep.

Suddenly horrified, he tripped backward over another body. An arm snapped off the corpse, veins of ice like coils of licorice. Though he was no stranger to death and carnage, the terror squeezed his chest. Hermes scrambled to find Wu, checking each death popsicle.

Delirious with worry, he bolted from the container and found himself inside Saint Peter's Basilica. A frozen Yuri clung to the metal door as if he had tried to shut it against a blizzard. Icicles hung from the cathedral ceiling. Frescoes entombed in frost. Snowdrifts buried the marble floors as wind howled like injured animals. In the distance, a small figure in a white robe knelt at the altar.

"Wu?" Hermes called as he ran down the endless nave. A blizzard fought his every step, ice and snow swirling around the dome, driving him back. He kicked off his sneakers, feet burning on the marble. He stretched his wings and propelled himself against the cyclone.

Hermes finally reached the apse, that small figure now buried. He frantically dug into the snow despite the stiffness in his joints and the frostbite blackening his fingers.

"HERMES!" someone shouted. Icicles crashed.

Hermes whirled toward Saint Peter's holy doors as the Archangel Gabriel exploded through their cement seal. His angel wings unfurled; he rocketed toward Hermes at a frightening speed.

Hermes turned back to the mound, where a single blue Baach feather now plumed the snow. It wasn't there a second before. He plucked the feather, and the pile slid to reveal black hair. A face twisted to him—

Lilith! Her eyes snapped open, sapphires pulsating fear. A hand breached the snow and grabbed him in a grip that burned like dry ice as she pulled him to her frostbitten cheeks.

"I gave it to him," she whispered.

Powerful wings slapped the air as Hermes was suddenly hoisted away from Lilith. The altar receded. He was about to yell for Gabriel to release him, but Gabriel appeared below, watching his ascension in disbelief.

Gabriel tried to take flight, but his wings had been ripped from his back. The archangel fell to his knees in a rose of blood.

Blinded by the storm, a shadow carried Hermes up, shattering the dome as it escaped the Vatican. Fresco crumbled beneath his feet as the basilica collapsed.

Rising above the shrinking Holy City, the air warmed. Dust parted to blue sky. Suddenly, Hermes was flying. Instead of arms he had two great blue wings. Hermes had transformed into the Baach of the Yucatán. A sweeping jungle spread below. His long tail feathers were a rudder in the current as a mass of cold air collided with the tropical climate. His bird body rocked in the turbulence. The sky darkened as storm clouds followed him all the way south of the equator. The rainforest withered brown in the cold. Snow began to fall as the land shook violently, the Earth heaving upward as if some underground monster were trying to break its way free. Hermes spotted a cenote and instinctively dove. He smashed into a sheen of ice and his world went black.

A light illuminated a watery cave. Floating in front of Hermes was a single glowing egg. Its surface swirled like quicksilver. The egg was a seed, a small Earth floating in the primordial sea. He reached out to touch it. The egg seared his hand as he sealed it within his fist.

The light extinguished.

***

Hermes was back in the sweat lodge, drenched in a cold sweat that dripped off his face and sizzled on the stones. He felt weak, as if he had traveled a long way—and there was no one to say he hadn't. His fist was clenched around something hard and hot. He opened his hand but found only a coal from the pit. The portal had closed. His journey was over.

Through the steam, Old Jim watched him curiously. His sons took gulping breaths, their pruned skin making them look wrung. The drummer had passed out, leaving an empty silence.

Hermes exhaled, feeling unsteady. "That was interesting."

Young Jim extended a ladle with water. Hermes accepted it with a trembling hand before passing the water to Robert, who helped the drummer sit up and put the spoon to his lips.

"Does the phrase 'moo-goo-waw' mean anything to you?"

Young Jim and Robert turned to Old Jim.

"They don't speak the old language," Old Jim explained. "At least not fluently. Not yet. What was the phrase again?"

"Moo-goo-waw," Hermes repeated. "Sounds like something you order at a Chinese restaurant."

"Well, roughly translated, it means 'more than one' or 'more than one being.' And by 'being,' I would assume in the context it would refer to a divine spirit."

"Right," Hermes said, just to say something.

"Does it make any sense to you?" Old Jim asked.

"Not a lick."

"Who spoke these words?"

"Didn't catch a name," Hermes said.

"You can tell us what you saw..." Old Jim said gently, and Hermes half expected him to hold up a doll and ask where the spirit touched him. "Or you can keep the journey to yourself."

They leaned forward. The expectation was for Hermes to spill the beans.

"I fell asleep," he insisted. "That's all."

They shared a disappointed look, obviously not believing him.

"Whatever you do, don't push away a vision," Old Jim warned, using his wise sage voice. It was a tad cliché, but then again, clichés have their purpose. "It's dangerous to leave a quest unexamined. The more you resist, the more power you give the vision. And the less able you are to face its truth."

They really wanted to hear what happened. For humans, a sweat lodge ceremony typically led to dehydration and vomiting. Few experienced a bona fide spiritual journey. But even Hermes had to admit this trip was different. An ache in his bones wouldn't let up, and he felt a general unease, as if he awoke to a house that was too quiet. Perhaps it would help to untangle the dream with Old Jim. After all, what happens in the sweat lodge stays in the sweat lodge. The vision presaged some catastrophe, but to explain, Hermes would have to do a lot of contextual backtracking—the mishap at the Vatican, Lilith and the feather—details that could endanger Old Jim and his people.

Hermes rubbed his knees. "Seriously, total blackout. Anyone up for a beer?"

Post-ceremony, it was custom to bathe in the river. Not for any spiritual reason, just general hygiene. You tended to smell worse than a hippie after hot yoga. Old Jim and his sons scrubbed down with flat stones from the riverbed. The tribal bonfire outlined the embankment, separating these last moments of introspection from the conversation and laughter they would soon be expected to join.

Upstream from the humans, Hermes waded into the current up to his waist, eyes resting on the turbulent surface as his mind floated downstream.

More than one being...

His thoughts jumped to Lilith and their meeting at the lesbian bar. Did this obscure spirit-phrase mean there were other deities working with Lilith? Was there more than one religion involved? Involved in what? Hermes didn't know where to start and wasn't sure he wanted to. He didn't have any worshippers. *Well...like twenty.* Which only proved he didn't have a stake in this interfaith intrigue. Best to leave it alone, he concluded.

Finished exfoliating, Hermes dressed and joined the night's main attraction—a modified late summer Sun Dance in honor of Persephone and the end of the season. Summer was drawing to a close. The night humidity was now slightly less oppressive.

Moving through the tall grass reminded Hermes of the spirit realm, swimming through the vast ocean of knowledge that existed beyond himself. He let the blades run through his fingers and felt a growing anxiety in the plants. They too anticipated Persephone's descent and their inevitable withering. Hermes was exhausted by his immortality. Were the spirits as exhausted by this endless cycle of seasons—dying only to be reborn?

Back at the campfire, Persephone watched a group of tribesmen and women help each other don their ceremonial garb. Even by the dim light of the campfire, their robes were a riot of color. Feathered headdresses ran down their backs and bounced atop their heads like a rooster's crown. Streamers attached to the underside of their arms whipped the air as they moved.

Liquor passed hands. A few teenagers disappeared into the woods. The heavyset dad with the ponytail, now piss drunk, threw firecrackers into the bonfire, entertaining the younger kids by sending them running in a riot of screams. A row of elders in tailgating chairs watched helplessly, shaking their heads at the decline of the gene pool. Inspired, pyro son nabbed the case of fireworks, and while dad was rifling through the cooler for a beer, chucked the box into the fire. The following explosions sent everyone diving for cover as green and red rockets whizzed by like missiles. Pyro kid pumped his fists in triumph and then tossed a plastic lawn chair into the flames for good measure. The tribe scattered to put out the brush fires with blankets and help the elders back to their seats. Despite the near disaster, everyone laughed uproariously.

"What'd I miss?" Hermes said as Persephone brushed an ember off her dress.

"Just another night on the rez." She patted the ground beside her for Hermes to sit. Night-blooming jasmine blossomed around her, scenting the air with a sweet perfume. She watched dad-of-the-year retrieve the half-melted chair and then give his son a sideswipe to the head, which set him to crying. "Chubby's kid, the one he brought back with him from Boise—he nearly blew up the ceremony with fireworks and then tried to set the furniture on fire. The elders aren't happy. Shelly is mad at Eleanor for calling her fry bread undercooked. And by morning there will be at least three more pregnant girls."

"Humans."

"How was the sweat lodge?" she asked, noticing Hermes looked rather pale.

"We gave each other mannies and peddies and talked about fixing cars and manly stuff."

"Uh-huh."

"I'm radiating—can't you see it?"

"No."

"You're just jealous," he said, thrusting his chin in the air. "I look fabulous."

"Please don't ever use the word *fabulous* again."

She laughed, which made Hermes realize how much he missed that sound, nourishing as summer rain on a garden.

Her eyes narrowed. "So…nothing happened? No journey?"

"Nothing."

"Nothing happened here either."

"Good," Hermes said.

"And obviously nothing happened to you in the sweat lodge."

"Speaking of Old Jim…" Hermes turned to the medicine man, now dressed in a black robe with white feathers. He gave Hermes a charged glance before joining a group circling a massive powwow drum. All at once they began to pound out a rhythm on the buffalo hide that punched sound in the gut. It was time to initiate the powwow.

Da-da-dum, da-da-dum, da-da-dum.

Dancers gathered as the drummers began to screech, their voices stabbing the night. The screeching undulated, a discordant harmony. Notes stacked on top of each other until they broke under the weight and began to build all over again.

Hey-yah, hey-yah, eyyyh, eyyyh, eyyyh-yah eyyyh-yah. Hey-yah, hey-yah, eyyyh, eyyyh, eyyyh-yah eyyyh-yah.

The dance accelerated. Limber bodies hopped from one foot to the other around the flames, headdresses whipping the smoke into chaotic spirals. Sacks of loose pebbles and animal bones tied to their waists rattled like the cackling of the dead. The bonfire climbed to inferno heights. Shadows frolicked as the powwow surged to the level of a waking fever dream—an acid trip without the prerequisite drugs—designed to strip the varnish off the physical world. Persephone took Hermes' hand. Past the dancers silhouetted by flames, beyond the drummers, the teepees glowed across the prairie, a landing strip for the gods. The ground began to rumble. A second sun crested in the north over the distant mountains. Instead of rising into the sky, it spilled down the slopes and charged into the valley like a herd of buffalo. The herd folded into a single being of light that walked proud and tall toward the ceremony.

Naato'si, Creator Sun, had heard the call of his people.

Creator Sun stopped at the edge of the bonfire—a god of moccasins and bear claws and feathers, not manmade nylon and rubber—his angular face serious as an arrowhead. He looked to the stars. Galaxies swirled like cream poured into coffee to form Ko'komiki'somm, the Niitsitapi Moon Goddess, resting on a cloud, listening to her people chant. She rose and stepped down to Earth.

Persephone squeezed Hermes' hand, and the Greek gods left the powwow to visit with the Niitsitapi spirits, whose long black hair brushed the tall silver grass. Their age shifted in the night, youthful one moment, a wrinkled elder the next. They were divine holograms.

"Oki nikso'kowaiksi," Naato'si greeted, meaning "Hello, all my relatives." Hermes gripped arms with Creator Sun. "Oki nikso'kowaiksi."

"We've been watching you," Ko'komiki'somm said. "Restless, you leave no tracks. Hungry, you do not eat."

"Brother and sister should not fight," Naato'si added.

"How close have they been watching?" Hermes mumbled to Persephone and felt her elbow slam into his ribs.

"Close enough," Naato'si admonished.

"Hey, if we needed the family counseling—"

"Don't be rude," Persephone hissed.

"I'm not being rude." Hermes pivoted to his hosts. "Am I being rude?"

A tense silence followed.

That went downhill fast.

"We understand, Hermes," Ko'komiki'somm said gently, "that you had a difficult journey tonight."

"Journey?" Persephone turned to Hermes. "YYou lied to me!"

"Thanks," Hermes frowned at the Moon Goddess.

"Were you just not going to tell me?" Persephone asked, annoyed.

"I got distracted."

"Bullshit."

"It's my vision—it's my choice whether I share it," Hermes said, then turned back to the Niitsitapi siblings. "You guys suck at family counseling, by the way."

"Your spirit guardian has not been seen since your return," Ko'komiki'somm said with an expression grave as the winter to come.

"My spirit guardian? I was followed?"

Creator Sun was not moved. "Yes. We don't allow anyone, not even a god, to travel into the Spirit Realm unsupervised. We sent Eagle to watch over your journey. But Eagle did not return. We have never lost a guardian before."

Persephone looked to Hermes for an explanation, but he had none.

The Moon Goddess continued where her twin left off, as was their way. "You journeyed deeper into the Spirit Realm than any has ventured. Further than Napi, Old Man, who took part in the making of all. Beyond the Spirit Realm to…somewhere else. It is not understood how you survived. There are places even gods are not permitted. The vision is sacred. It demands introspection."

Introspection. Not Hermes' strongest attribute.

"We are the gods of the Earth," Creator Sun said. "We do not reign from a heaven or hell. Hear us, Hermes the Greek. We feel the gears—ancient, dormant—begin to turn."

Around them, the landscape vanished. They were surrounded by shooting stars. They floated in the void, toes dangling over the vast blackness of space.

Persephone grasped Hermes' hand.

"Mountains will break," Moon Goddess prophesied, her silver hair swirling like the rings of a nebula. "Worlds will shatter and be swallowed whole. This age shall end. And I cannot see what lies beyond it. God and goddess shall battle Chaos. You dream that dream, too."

All at once, they were back on the Earth, thrown from the spiritual merry-go-round.

Hermes stood, brushing himself off. "Well, that was dramatic."

Persephone sighed her disapproval.

Despite his Marlboro cool, Hermes reeled inside. *Chaos.* That word. Now spoken by Creator Sun. But what did it mean?

"What should we do?" Persephone asked.

"We don't know," Creator Sun said, suddenly dropping the mystical tone. "But our home is your home. Hermes, you are welcome to stay under our protection. We advise it."

It was a magnanimous offer.

Hermes hesitated. "Yeah, I'll think about it."

"What's wrong with you?" Persephone shoved Hermes, insulted on their behalf. Her no-good, family-pariah half brother on the run from the Catholics had been offered refuge, a home for the winter—and his reply was noncommittal at best.

"Nothing's wrong with me," Hermes said, aware of how defensive he sounded. He shifted uncomfortably, as if trying to squeeze into an ill-fitting jacket.

"We know you're being hunted, so consider our offer carefully. No one would find you here," Ko'komiki'somm vowed.

Hermes looked away. Clearly, no one understood his predicament. There was no place safe for him. He endangered them more than they protected him. Yet, it wasn't really that.

Persephone bowed. "You honor us."

"As you honor us." Ko'komiki'somm bowed her head in return. "With your residence, the harvests are bountiful and the game plenty."

"Harvests?" Creator Sun scoffed, shaking his head. "Our people eat potato chips and pizza."

"Amen," said Hermes.

And with that, the meeting between the Niitsitapi spirits and the Greek gods adjourned.

Hermes and Persephone walked home without uttering a word until they'd reached Persephone's cabin.

"I have to get a few things," she whispered hoarsely, passing him to enter her garden.

Every movement felt remote, as if her mind floated in a submarine at the bottom of the ocean. She gathered the few possessions she always took to the Underworld: toothbrush, clean underwear, and several books Hermes had stolen from a public library in Butte.

She stared at her lace underwear, rubber-banded around hardbacks, wondering how she got here. Persephone had enough self-pity to fill a reservoir, and every year, on this last day of summer, the levees threatened to fail. She forced her monstrous suitcase shut and buckled the straps.

By the time she reemerged on the porch in her travel yoga pants and hoodie, Hermes was gone.

At dawn, she reached the lake. With the snowpack depleted, the once majestic waterfall trickled down the granite into a muddy pool festering with moss. Persephone's private entrance to the Underworld gaped like an open wound. By choosing this spot to make her ascent and descent into the Underworld, Persephone made these woods sacred and therefore connected to her emotions. Aspens wept, blanketing the lake in a mosaic of yellow petals. Bluebells, poppies, and wildflowers that once trumpeted her arrival had shriveled to gray husks, mourning her departure. The world of green had ceded to autumn.

She found Hermes seated on a broken log, skimming stones across the lake, watching the leaves ride the ripples until he scooped a fistful of pebbles and pitched the bunch in a burst of anger. The lake churned from the scattershot. He silently trailed her around the teardrop pool to the mouth of the cave, shards of shale snapping underfoot. A stale breeze gusted out from the darkness, as if Hades had heaved a great sigh of impatience that traveled up from Hell. Before she could enter, Hermes intercepted, holding her in the sun.

"Not yet."

"I'm late," Persephone said.

"So you're late."

"Time moves slower down there. You know that. He's been waiting."

"I don't care about him," he shouted unexpectedly. Then he sighed.

"I know you don't care about him," she said wearily. "But I have to live with him...and his moods."

He opened her palm and pressed a small yellow daisy within. "It's the last of summer. A reminder of the sun."

"Come with me," she blurted, suddenly giddy. "There's nothing stopping you. We'll go together. Right now."

It felt like the first sunny day after a month of rain, and she was ready to burst outside and play.

"No," he said, extinguishing her excitement. "I don't belong down there."

"You belong with me. And wherever I go, you go. I'm Queen."

"And he's King. And I'm banned."

"He's likely forgotten. He's forgotten nearly everything else."

Hermes shook his head. "Hades never forgets an infidelity. Save his own."

"Please," she pleaded. "Just come with me. If you can trick the Vatican, you can trick Hades."

"It's not the same."

"You've disobeyed rules before. Why not now? Why not for me?"

"I can't," he said.

Tears spilled down her cheeks. "You mean you won't."

Hermes wasn't trying to be cruel. He couldn't follow her. There were no more answers down there than up here. Did he want answers? He didn't even want to know the questions. All he wanted was to sink into this depression, bury his face into it like a pillow. And all she wanted was to rescue him. He was almost grateful it was time for her to go. He was only torturing her with his uncertainty. Better to send her back to Hell. The quicker, the better.

"You push me away. I'm all you have left."

"That's not true. I still have alcohol, television, and masturbation," he said, and she laughed through a sob.

Never had a goddess looked so beautiful with a snot bubble.

"Don't worry," he reassured her. "I'll be fine."

She ran her sleeve across her nose, sniffled. "While I'm gone, please make peace with Gabriel."

His smile tightened more than a drug smuggler's ass at a Turkish airport.

"Hermes," she implored, "wave the white flag."

"I wonder if I can make a nun the pope."

"Very funny. I'm serious."

"I just need to lay low for a while. Let him cool off."

"Where?" Persephone said, sounding like a worried mom handing the car keys to her teenager.

He kissed her on the forehead. "I've got a place in mind."

Before she could ask him to elaborate, the mountain groaned. The cave split, a fissure opened; the stone cratered into a staircase. Hades was never one for subtlety.

Their eyes said their goodbyes.

I love you. I'll miss you. And I'll see you soon.

She sealed the daisy in her palm and turned as the rocks vibrated, the Underworld seething at her delay.

She crossed the threshold, into the mouth of Hell, and began to descend.

"I'll be right here when you get back!" he shouted. "Right here!"

She glanced back, and the portal slammed shut between them. Boulders and dirt scrambled to fill the cave. Two granite hands ejected Hermes with a backward shove into the lake as the portal sealed, an impenetrable slab of granite to rival the summit of Skolio.

Hermes lingered for a while, drumming his fingers on the stone.

No one answered.

CHAPTER SIX

THE NIGHT OF PERSEPHONE's return, Hades waited upon his throne. An old ritual. Her breath caught in her chest. A familiar dread. An inversion of the routine that announced her departure, she ceremonially approached her husband for him to reinstate his claim over her—his wife—his queen. *Fuck you* was all she ever thought.

He seized her supplicating, outstretched hand and traced her joints with his calloused ring finger, which had the sandpaper feel of a lion's tongue. Squint hard enough, she could almost see a god beneath the incontinence—noble, fierce, and gruffly handsome. Was that old abuser preferable to the new? She stood on eggshells. Which Hades was this? The senile Hades or the bastard Hades? The geriatric god could easily burn down his palace, either by accident or on purpose.

Hades abruptly released her and vacated his throne, shuffling past her like a defeated tennis player slinking off the court.

"Should we have dinner?" Persephone called after him, and instantly regretting it.

He stopped, turned, and faced her. His eyes radiated hope.

"That is, unless you're busy," Persephone quickly added. "You're probably very busy. I shouldn't have asked—"

"Yes! Yes. And yes again." Color flooded his stretched cheeks beneath the white beard.

My god, is Hades blushing?!

Flustered like a boy with a crush, he whistled for Cerberus and hurried from the room.

Persephone spent the rest of her first day in a whirlpool of regret. *Why did I have to open my big mouth?* She blamed Hermes for this dinner engagement. Entirely his fault. Without Hermes she was lonely and desperate and made mistakes.

It took her an inordinate amount of time to select her wardrobe. Something formal but not sexy, casual but respectable. Something that said she hadn't thought about it as much as she was thinking about it. She selected a red bodycon she'd discovered at a consignment shop on Earth, likely a prom dress of yesteryear. A lattice of straps made up the back, down to the waist, sure to ensnare any corsage-wearing teenage boy. Examining herself in the mirror, she realized she looked like a bottle of hot sauce.

If Hades got the wrong idea about tonight…

The tight, burning sensation spread from her chest to her throat. Her hands became numb. The horror of her early captivity flashed before her. The endless days and nights secluded with Hades. The constant dread. The humiliation. His mood swings she couldn't escape. Even long after she gained freedom to roam the Underworld, his volatility constantly threatened, like an avalanche poised upon the mountain slopes. She was trapped, unable to breathe in his presence. He infected her daily with a molten despair. It took centuries for her to harden herself against him, to insulate her heart. Despite her arsenal of coping mechanisms, Hades could still make her tremble with a single glance.

There are monsters in this world, and then there are *Monsters*.

Persephone wiped her sweaty palms on the red dress, balled it up, and threw it over her shoulder. Not in the next thousand years.

Hours and a hundred dresses later, she entered a parlor that would have made Marie Antoinette feel right at home, having selected a green toga fastened with a golden lace. Traditional. Simple. The hearth was damp and dark, stuffed with ash no one had ever bothered to clean. Yet the room was romantically bathed in candlelight. Hades was installed on a chaise lounge, sipping a cognac as he played a solo game of knucklebones. He used to spend ages in competition with Sophocles.

Thankfully, her husband had finally discarded the bathrobe for his old battle regalia. The armor was missing a few pieces so that he resembled an unfinished puzzle. A tie hung around his neck, a holdover from his own wardrobe indecision. It lifted her, knowing he cared enough to try.

She waited as he contemplated his move on the board. Somehow the strategy backfired, and he lost. Only after hurling aside the game did he notice her, his gaze clinical.

Hades motioned to an intimate dining table. A new game, it seemed— the board set for two. They took their seats, and a decrepit slave named Miklos emerged from a servant's door bearing a platter of foul-smelling pike, overcooked and oversalted. Miklos's age had shrunk him to the size and appearance of a roasted peanut. He shoved the platter between them, sending a vase of flowers crashing to the floor, then overturned a basket of half-baked rolls drenched in olive oil on top of the fish. Miklos was nearly one hundred when he died and was now Hades's last servant—too slow to flee with the others, too old to care.

Persephone helped herself to a bottle of bubblegum-colored rosé, pouring only for herself before allowing Hades to fill his stone mug (harder to smash during his drunken tirades). The fish was inedible. She marched her dinner around her plate, took small sips of wine. Equally wooden, Hades appeared paralyzed from the neck down, concentrating on his meal. The painful silence ended when Miklos dragged a chair screeching across the room.

"I arranged for music this evening," Hades mumbled.

Miklos unhooked a pan flute from his waist belt and made a sound somewhat like a baby blowing spit through a straw. To the ancient slave's credit, he did manage to turn the raspberry into a semblance of a melody.

Hades snapped his fingers along to whatever rhythm in his head accompanied the noise. Persephone hoped what he heard was better than this clarinet on life support. Miklos took another deep breath and nearly swallowed the flute. Persephone winced.

She turned back to Hades and searched for a topic. "So…how was your summer?"

Hades stopped snapping his fingers and fumbled about for words, settling on, "Quiet."

"And the Underworld?"

"Progressing." He gripped the table.

"Lovely." Persephone offered a faint smile and turned back to the concerto. They were just like a regular couple, married so long there was nothing left to talk about.

"The girls came to see me," Hades blurted.

Shit.

"They promised to visit soon," he said.

"Wonderful," she replied, wishing she could drown the rats that were his offspring.

The conversation reanimated him. His eyes traced the outlines of her toga.

"That color favors you. You look like…a Cyprus forest in spring."

Fuck. A compliment. "Thank you."

Hades frowned, his face darkening. "Nothing?"

"Nothing, what?" Persephone feigned ignorance.

"You've said nothing of my appearance this evening."

Word choice would be crucial here. "You look…" She couldn't say *dashing*—too strong. *Ridiculous* would be honest but unhelpful. "Formidable."

He leaned back and nodded before filling her glass, then his, which surprised her, as it was the gentlemanly thing to do. He joyously sipped from his mug, elbow on the table, regarding her with pubescent affection. Something shifted in him, the edges softening. "I've been difficult, haven't I?"

Persephone feared a trap. "No. Of course not."

"You avoid me. Ignore my gestures of entreaty. It's because of my moods, I know. I've hardly been a stable king to my queen."

Was that sincerity? Persephone's finely honed skills at reading her mercurial husband couldn't find purchase. Where were the hidden cameras? She prayed some TV host would jump out and shout *Gotcha!*

"Please, look at me," he calmly requested. She did. His eyes were clear and focused. "I've been a menace. Yes?"

"Yes," she admitted, utterly baffled. Her stomach felt queasy.

"How could you feel comfortable around me?" Hades admonished himself. "I'm not an easy god to live with. You've suffered immensely. For that, and more, and all, I am sorry."

Hades had apologized. This had to be some glitch in a software update.

"Sorry? That's it? *Sorry? Sorry* can't begin to encompass it—the millennia stolen from me."

Tears studded his eyes. "I know. But I will say it as many times as I must, sit here as long as you have words. Speak freely, hold nothing back. My apology is offered—a seed for the barren soil of our marriage, a spring to the endless winter of our union—if you will allow it."

If I will allow it? Persephone seethed. Even his apologies were weaponized. If she didn't forgive him, suddenly she was the monster. You don't get to behave badly for millennia and then suddenly offer one moment of remorse to restart the clock.

"I would like us to rule side by side once more. With love and respect. Think of the great things we could achieve together."

She nearly shattered her wineglass in her fist. To do something, she set it down. The glass tipped, and rosé splashed across the table.

"Think on it," he concluded, as if he had presented her a business opportunity.

She leaned over the tablecloth as it lapped up the wine. "Who are you? If this is some cruel joke—"

"The only cruel joke was the one played on you so many years ago."

"I…" Persephone struggled under the weight of a thousand horrid years of marriage.

He stepped into her silence. "I understand."

But how could he?

"Do you know what's happening in your kingdom?"

His brow pinched in confusion. Then he waved his hand as if to shoo a fly from his food, dismissing her question. An amused smile creased his beard.

"We receive new souls, Kharon takes his payment and ferries them across the river, they are processed and sorted, judgments ruled. The Underworld balances the power of Olympus. We help maintain order and rotation of the world."

The little speech boosted his endorphins. He stabbed his pike and shoved a large morsel into his mouth, masticating exuberantly.

Uh-oh. Persephone needed to tread carefully. "Not…exactly…"

Hades didn't hear her, lost in the fictional kingdom inside his head. She sensed the opening for this long-overdue reality check quickly closing. He stabbed again at the fish, and she stopped his hand before he could shovel another mouthful. "Have you noticed the state of your affairs lately?"

"The state of the state is eternal!" he proudly exclaimed.

"There are no more guards," Persephone pressed, determined to stop the charade of half-truths, no truths, lies, innuendos, and downright fictions. "There are no more petitioning souls. No courtiers or guests of the palace. No protocols. No worshippers."

Hades reached across the table to grab her pike and dropped it onto his plate. "Nonsense."

"Your daughters—they've been to see you? Why?"

He snorted at her ridiculous question. "Because they love me."

"They covet your power."

"NO!" Hades slammed his cutlery. Fork and knife quivered, half-buried in the table. She watched him sink back into the mist, eyes clouding, protecting himself from the reality that his empire was lost. The line between denial and dementia had blurred.

"Yes, of course. They love you," she said remotely.

"Yes! They love me! They love me dearly!" Hades raved. The mad god had returned. "Like all my subjects! Zeus and the others could not know such love. They are distracted by false admirers and sycophants pining for their attention, but it is subterfuge and insincere." The rage greased his wheels. He snatched the decanter to fill his mug but missed and emptied the contents onto the floor.

"Miklos! Quit that blasted noise!" Hades bellowed, though the slave had stopped playing some time ago and was asleep at his post.

A flushed Hades whirled back on Persephone. "What did you mean about my girls?"

"Nothing," she muttered. "I meant nothing by it."

Hades stood too quickly and toppled the table. "*Nothing* my ass. You meant *something.*"

He stalked the parlor, armor jangling like a tambourine in the hands of a toddler. "Nothing. Nothing. Always nothing. Nothing…"

Persephone held fast to her chair, exposed in the middle of the room with a wild beast. If she tried to escape, she would attract his attention. It was a risk worth taking.

She stood, and her foot disturbed a shattered plate. Glass crunched, and he spun to face her. His ferocious stare could cleave a mountain.

"Oh, so you leave me! Leave me like everyone else!"

She flung her gaze to the floor, her voice trembling. "No, my king… I'm simply attending to this mess."

"Then clean it!" The room shook.

On her knees, she gathered the broken glass and scattered remains of fish bones and skin. Suddenly, his hand was twisting her. He yanked her up with a wrench that ripped her toga.

"That will do. That will do nicely," he leered.

Something loosened inside her. She twisted to him, holding up the tattered dress with one hand, backhanding him across the face with the other. The slap was loud enough to wake Miklos.

Hades stumbled backward, stunned.

She was stunned too. Never before had she hit her husband—her king.

He recovered from the shock and grabbed her by the throat and squeezed. Her windpipe felt like a crushed soda can.

"Look what you make me do!" Hades roared, lifting her off the ground. Her toga fell away.

"My lord," Miklos squeaked.

Persephone felt her world dim.

"My lord!" Miklos squeaked louder. "Souls have gathered. They wait for you to ascend the throne. We shouldn't keep them."

Hades dropped his queen like a bag of trash. He cracked his neck and straightened his posture. "My souls await?"

"Yes. Many and more. Miles long they stretch," Miklos said, spreading his arms, with a glance at Persephone on the floor, coughing and gasping. She was grateful this tiny servant played his king better than his flute.

"Then what are we waiting for?" Hades clapped and bounded from the room. After the god's footsteps receded, Miklos grabbed a blanket from the back of a sofa and hurried to Persephone's side. He delicately covered her and then stepped away.

"Thank you," was all she could manage.

He bowed his head. She knew he risked his eternal soul with this act of kindness. "My queen. Shall I fetch anything else?"

Anything else? She wanted someone to say, *It'll be okay*, even though it would never be. She wanted Hermes by her side, even though he would never come.

"I'm fine." It hurt to stand. Persephone braced her hip against the couch and studied the wreckage of her evening. *Welcome home.*

That was day one.

CHAPTER SEVEN

HERMES STOOD ATOP AN eastern peak. Even when he said it in his head, he couldn't make it sound exciting.

Salt Lake City. Salt Lake City. Salt Lake City.

Nope. Nothing.

The City of the Saints sprawled along a valley like a bad rash, scratched and scabbed over. The actual Salt Lake pressed against the suburbs, looking like someone got bored with their coloring book and never finished filling in the blue. The year of their Lord, one-nine-seven-nine. That was the last time Hermes visited the Industry State.

Industrious? Yes. Clever? No.

Hermes sighed. This was his chosen purgatory.

A week prior, Hermes had crossed the Idaho–Utah border on foot, intending to lay low. The November air had turned crisp, and a hard, sleeted rain had soaked him through. Since leaving Persephone, Hermes had mostly stuck to the national parks. He could have safely traveled along the back highways, soiled a few cheap motel bedspreads, taken his meals at truck stops. He wasn't paranoid. He just wanted to be alone. Not think. Focus on the basics: hunt for food, make a fire, find shelter. None of the early nomadic humans needed a therapist. Granted, they died at alarming rates, and their life spans were minuscule, but damn if they weren't satisfied surviving the day.

So he kept to the routine, enjoyed the scenery, ate rabbits and venison. Tended fires. Shat in the woods. And walked. The routine had grown exceedingly old by the time he reached Utah with a long, scruffy beard, dirt under his fingernails, and an odor somewhere between bear urine and pine clinging to him. He was ready for a shower, shave, porcelain toilet, and a comfy bed. Hermes was more rough-and-tumble than the average god, but he still enjoyed some plush every now and then.

On the outskirts of Salt Lake City, he checked into a Motel 6—hardly plush—and hunkered down. December passed. Then January. He spent his days and nights pacing the worn shag carpet and admiring the odd seashell décor 834 miles from the nearest ocean. The self-imposed hibernation wasn't a total waste of time, though. He moved his stash of loot, quietly selling off the priceless Vatican artifacts piece by piece through a series of untraceable, clandestine exchanges that whittled away his profits. The underground economy thrived in the Mormon capital. The cash supported his vices—sports betting, booze, and casinos—till there was nothing left.

January rolled into February, and no, Hermes never made it to Sundance, although everyone claimed it was the "it" thing to do. Hermes had met Robert Redford once. They lunched. It was 1979, and Redford was researching a movie. Rich Hollywood types had a habit of buying access to the spiritual highway. After showing off their worthless crystal collections, they usually asked for some combination of eternal fame, fortune, and script notes.

Hermes, wrapped in a black pea coat and a pilling gray scarf, fondly remembered the Redford encounter as he stood in the parking lot of the Salt Lake sports arena. He blew into his hands, rubbing them together against the sub-zero temperature. He had courtside seats but, even in disguise, couldn't risk his mug appearing on ESPN. Instead, he watched the Knicks lose to the Utah Jazz on a Jumbotron overlooking the parking lot. And with their loss went his last ten grand.

Who the hell thought up Utah, anyway?

Oh, right. Them.

Them were always listening. Them had bugged every nook and cranny, every city block, fence post, and bathroom stall. The Mormons had constructed the most organized and efficient bureaucracy the world had ever known. When it came to policing their spiritual turf, they made the NSA look like a bunch of kids playing spy with tin-can walkie-talkies. Then again, Utah was a great place for a god on the run—a religious Switzerland. The Mormons staked their claim on the state and zealously guarded their holy ground against any incursion. Their fixation on the big boys made it easy for the small deities to slip between the cracks and nest under the Mormon nose. So long as they didn't interfere, the Mormons would look the other way. Their presence had the added benefit of irking the other superpowers. If it suited their interests, the Mormons would sell Hermes to the Catholics, but they were also his best customers, happy to purchase stolen Vatican loot, no questions asked.

"Oh, come on, play some defense! DEFENSE!" Hermes shouted as another three-pointer sailed past the Knicks' defense and the roar of Jazz fans pulsed from the arena.

A voice beside him celebrated. "Yes! Yes!"

Hermes swiveled to an obese black parking attendant in a puffy red ski jacket and thick oval glasses attempting a victory jig. The dance ended when he slipped backward on the ice. The impact to his ass was blunted by his airbag parka. He rolled like a turtle flipped on its shell and unable to right himself. A gracious loser, Hermes easily pulled the three-hundred-pound valet up by his polyester hood.

"Thanks," the embarrassed attendant said, brushing gray snow off his jacket. He straightened his glasses and pulled a wool cap over his shiny dome. "Knicks fan?"

"Not anymore," Hermes said.

The buzzer announced the end of the quarter—and that Hermes was officially broke.

The parking attendant shrugged. "They had a good run. Forty-two and ten, undefeated for a month…until today. Bad luck."

Luck. Hermes winced. On the Jumbotron, the Knicks' distressed coach broke a laptop over his knee.

The parking attendant tsked. "Bad luck. Like someone switched off the team's mojo. Strange, strange, strange."

"Don't you have cars to park?"

"Can't a simple human enjoy the pleasure of his hometown sporting team when they defeat their rival?" The man buried his hands in his pockets and rocked on the balls of his feet. "It's miraculous, almost as if the gods were tipping the scales."

"Are you fucking with me?"

The parking attendant studied Hermes like a barcode scanner trying to read a damaged can. "You dug yourself into a hole, didn't you?"

"I'm about to start digging a grave."

"Maybe this poor luck is somebody trying to send you a message."

Hermes did not want to hear another mention of the "L" word. "What are you, some Big Mac fortune teller? Spare me the calories of your wisdom."

The attendant chuckled. Hermes returned his scowl to the Jumbotron. The Knicks, with a forty-point deficit, lost the ball to the Jazz again. Their improbable downward spiral seemed to worsen by the second.

"What brought you to Utah?" the attendant asked, and when Hermes didn't answer, continued his line of questioning anyway. "Are you staying in Salt Lake City?"

"No," Hermes said.

"Off the 80?"

"Yes." Hermes wasn't even sure why he was answering.

A Jazz forward broke through the Knicks' defense.

Swish. Jazz 106. Knicks 14.

"That Extended Stay place?"

"No."

Swish. Jazz 108. Knicks 14.

"Where are you staying?"

Swish.

Swish.

"Motel Six."

"Ah. The *my-wife-caught-me-cheating-with-another-woman* motel. So your wife kicked you out?"

"No."

"Divorced?"

"No."

"Why are you staying there then?"

A three-pointer sailed into the net. *Swish.* Jazz 115. Knicks 14.

Hermes was ready to smite the man, so help himself. Yet his god anger simply slipped off the polyester uniform. The attendant's questions continued like divider lines on a highway. Eventually, Hermes wasn't even aware of answering them.

Where did he grow up?

What did he miss about home?

Where was he before Utah?

"Montana." The word slipped out before he could stop himself. Shit! Montana was Persephone's secret. Hermes snapped awake as if from a trance to a large, empty space he swore the parking attendant had filled a moment before.

The guy was too big to simply vanish, yet vanish he had.

An unsettling sensation trickled through his extremities that had nothing to do with the cold. It wasn't losing all his money. Money came and went. He could always steal more. The list of things unsettling him was long: his fight with Persephone, for starters. There was also the dream-quest thingy that seriously messed with his perception, the worshippers he was ignoring, that odd moment with Lilith, Eshu hating him, Gabriel hunting him, and the Knicks losing like they'd been cursed. Oh, and he was living in a fucking Motel 6. And now he had just aired all his dirty laundry, too. Maybe Persephone was right: he was the poster child for unintended consequences.

Perhaps it was Hermes who had lost his mojo. Hermes seriously needed a mug of strong Greek mead.

Unsettled, he hurried past a flock of parking attendants huddled around an electric furnace. All of them wore neon blue parkas. No red polyester in sight. The court buzzer blared like a tornado siren, ending the third quarter. A tang of bile burned the back of his throat.

Someone had tricked the trickster.

***

The Odyssey was a dive bar on the edge of Salt Lake, hidden in the basement of an old factory that never produced anything and yet persistently avoided the wrecking ball. The three-story building, with tall glass-pane windows, broken here and there by hooligans, abutted defunct railroad tracks that collected weeds, trash, and the homeless: the border between a daytime mugging and a ten-dollar cappuccino. Recently, a mix of art galleries, wine bars, and thrift stores had sprouted among the adjacent factories as a tide of angsty, semi-employed yuppies slowly gentrified the neighborhood. The mix of derelict and hip allowed the new residents to feel as if they were on the cutting edge of cool rather than displacing it.

Skinny jeans, dogs on leashes, smiles…

Hermes didn't like the transformation one bit. He turned a graffitied corner, and the traffic dwindled. Along the brick face, "JEBEDIAH'S WAGON WHEEL PARTS AND GENERAL GOODS" was still visible in faded white paint. The bony finger of the Salt Lake Temple loomed over downtown in the distance, a stern reminder that the All-Seeing Eye was watching.

Hermes avoided the used needles and stepped over an addict entombed in cardboard to access a set of stairs leading down to a passageway that ran below street level. An iron rail along the sidewalk kept the drunks from falling in, but not from using the walkway as an open sewer. Hermes stopped at a steel door. A waterlogged sign taped to the entrance greeted him with "FUCK OFF" in big, bold Sharpie. The Odyssey wasn't exactly keen on advertising. Hermes knocked.

A large, bloodshot eye filled a peephole. A deep grunt demanded the password.

"Buddha's Belly," Hermes said.

A latch slid on the other side. Password accepted.

The door screeched open to a dark causeway of steam pipes and coal chutes. A bullish frame blocked the way. Two large horns gouged the ceiling. The Minotaur threw out a hoof that clutched a metal basket filled with old flip phones and pagers and shook it impatiently.

Like everyone else in the bar, Hermes surrendered his phone. "I want that back."

Snort. The basket slid into a cubby.

"Facial recognition. Don't even bother trying to unlock it," Hermes added as he squeezed past the bull.

Minotaurs were well-known video game addicts.

The Minotaur thrust a torch at Hermes, since all the lamps were busted. A certain someone's horns were to blame. Not long after entering the tunnel, he heard the Minotaur roar in frustration, thwarted by the biometric security.

Hermes hit several dead ends while traversing the labyrinth—it had been an age since his last visit. The old pantheons still had a thing for mind games. Passé. By the time Hermes found the bar, he was desperate for a double. Effective.

The Odyssey—no brothel or dungeon of depravity (though Salt Lake had plenty of those)—had always been a stop on the underground transport for those seeking asylum in the New World: mythical refugees uprooted by monotheism and science and fleeing the march of conversion. Hiding had always been a way of life for nymphs, fairies, and other magical odds and ends; now it was their identity. The worst off were the beasts driven from their woodland homes by suburban sprawl. Now that the humans had conquered the dark forests and filled in the maps, where was a centaur or troll supposed to go? They had to wind up somewhere. And somewhere usually meant a bar like the one Hermes now entered.

Next to the entrance, a map of the world was stuck with pins marking the locations from which the various mythical patrons had fled. Hermes snuffed his torch in a bucket of water and unwrapped his scarf, spitting out a few balls of fluff. Hopper windows allowed postage stamps of daylight to checker the floor. Nicotine-stained columns lined walls decorated with grimy Etruscan mosaics and ancient posters of pay-per-view fights. The place was going for a distinct Hellenic vibe. A high ceiling allowed equal access for the larger patrons, like the day-drunk ogres hunched over the wood tables that ran the length of the room. An employee-of-the-month gallery chronicled the cyclops bartenders going all the way back to a daguerreotype of Celtus, son of Polyphemus, father of the Celts, who became the Irish—aka bona fide bartending lineage.

The Odyssey's midday drunks ranged from humanoid to bizarre. Most lurked in the shadows. Some dropped the pretense and took up permanent residence, curled under blankets in corners. Hermes aimed for an open stool at the olivewood bar and settled in. He attempted to flag the cyclops bartender, currently twirling the hair on a hideous-looking creature from the bogs of Scotland. The lass wore the soiled petticoat of an eighteenth-century duchess who happened to picnic in the wrong spot. A ragged bonnet rested on a mass of oozing black hair. The bartender whispered sweetly in her ear. She giggled, dribbling dark sludge.

Unwilling to wait for Cyclops Casanova to seal the deal, Hermes whistled impatiently.

The bartender's one eye swung to the interruption. He threw down his rag and sulked over, wiping sludgy palms on a filthy apron.

"I'd skip the condom and go for a hazmat suit," Hermes suggested.

The cyclops glared.

"Mead," Hermes ordered. The cyclops grabbed a casket-sized urn and filled a clay kylix, the traditional Greek mug, which he slid forward, sloshing nectar onto Hermes' pants. Anticipating another summons, the bartender slammed the entire urn on the bar for Hermes to refill himself. It wasn't the greatest service, but it wasn't the worst either. This one-eyed beast knew his clientele. Hermes handed over his American Express, and the cyclops returned to his impatient ghoul.

The first sip burned sweet and spicy. Divine. He tipped back the kylix until his nose touched the bottom. Setting the bowl down, he was disgusted to find his likeness painted inside, dressed in battle armor, muscles bulging, beard flowing, wings out, staff high, sword drawn—vintage Hermes memorabilia.

Hermes searched the bar for entertainment. The few nymphs tucked into a corner booth seemed half-asleep (hardly living up to their names), and the pool table was occupied by a group of rowdy woodland fairies being hustled by the Monster of Ravenna. Nothing interesting. Helping himself, Hermes seized a truly rare artifact from behind the bar—the Zenith remote—and began to channel surf. On local news, ornithologists were baffled by eagles hibernating in trees, the rodent population out of control, and never-before-seen yada yada. Boring. Next channel.

A blurry basketball court filled the boob tube. Knicks players hugged and celebrated. Commentators commented on the impossible comeback—a fourth-quarter, hundred-point turnaround. Something about a stroke of—

"LUCK?!" Hermes shouted, drawing unwanted attention. There was still a bounty out on his head, after all.

"What?" Hermes challenged the stares.

Patrons shrugged and returned to their own problems.

Except for one.

At a nearby table, an old hag slathered in rouge and stuffed into a tattered pink camisole drilled him with her dead, gray eyes.

Hermes raised his kylix to her. "To the Knicks. And their luck."

Her stalker stare continued, mouth slightly parted. A fly landed on her upper lip, but otherwise, no vital signs.

The uncomfortable gaze finally ended when she uncoiled from the bench. Her reptilian half swept through crushed peanut shells and pull tabs as she slithered for the exit.

Hermes snorted into his mead. "Clearly you missed the irony."

Turning back to the television, he drowned his portrait under another refill.

CHAPTER EIGHT

A DEEP, THUNDEROUS LAUGH woke Hermes. Peeling his cheek off the bar, he found himself hemmed in by empty urns. Two more cyclopses in white and black cocktail uniforms struggled to keep pace with the flow of orders. Hermes swiveled around on his stool. The Odyssey had filled with customers. The hopper windows were dark, and some late-night show played on the Zenith. The sketch involved a Black man on the roof of the Sistine Chapel waving rainbow smoke at Alec Baldwin playing the pope. Chuckles rose from behind the pottery.

Curious, the Trickster God parted the kylixes to find two more figures made of clay. The first golem towered above Hermes as if he'd run afoul of a rolling pin. Beyond him, a second profile laughed uproariously at the television. The companion was short and stocky with doughy cheeks. Both could pass for brothers, sculpted from the same copper-hued Danube clay, wearing matching trilby fedoras and ruffled suits from the back rack of a consignment shop. They overwhelmed the neighboring conversations with loud Czech accents, thick as borscht. Most golems—made by Kabbalah mystics to protect the Jewish ghettos of Europe against pogroms—were docile (until provoked) and obedient (if not prone to taking orders too literally). Once magicked to life, they were tethered to their maker and adopted their maker's personality. Those makers were typically elder rabbis with reams of wisdom, stern gazes, and a jar of candy ready for the kindala.

"The real one was funnier," the little golem said to the boob tube.

Pilsner dribbled down the taller golem's chin as he cackled. "Call Murray, tell him to watch."

"A bunch of goyim. Feh." The short one slapped the air with his hand and discovered Hermes. "The vampire wakes. Look at that."

The large golem lurched his stool toward Hermes like a semi trying to make a tight turn. Hermes finally got a front view of the giant: disproportionate features, a misshapen face, as if their rabbi only took one semester of pottery. Still, the Jewish Michael Jordan was an impressive-looking guardian.

The short golem addressed Hermes. "You heard about our Catholic friends?"

"Yeah, I've heard this and that," Hermes said.

"If only I could have been there," the shorter golem said wistfully. "First the feygele priests, now this. Not a good year to be drinking the blood and eating the body."

The tall golem tried to shush the short golem, but he wasn't one to be shushed. "I'm allowed a little schadenfreude." He pivoted to Hermes. "Do you kiss the ring?"

"Kiss whose ring?"

"The pope! Who else? You a Catholic?"

Hermes shook his head.

The small golem gazed up to his mountainous friend. "Then what do I care that he hears me?"

"Celibacy," the tall golem harrumphed.

The short golem agreed. "You should be able to schtupp. Too pent-up. The source of all their problems."

The two switched to Yiddish before bursting into laughter again. Once the short golem collected his composure, he translated for Hermes. "My friend says: *Why can't I be the pope? I'm made of clay. Mold me! Mold me!*"

They laughed again.

Jolly creatures, Hermes thought. Several thousand years of oppression had its advantages: humor and resilience. The tall golem clapped Hermes on the back with the force of a wrecking ball and poured out an extra mug of mead for their new friend.

The golems raised their beers. "L'chaim!"

Hermes saluted back, warming up to the two weary travelers.

"What about you, mister?" the short golem asked Hermes.

"What about me?"

"You have a lost puppy look about you. No, that's not it." He held up his large clay mitten of a hand and thought about it some more. Hermes inched aside on his stool, ready to make a quick exit should he be publicly outed in the bar as a fugitive god. "You're searching for something."

Hermes swiveled back on his stool. "Okay. I'll go with it. What do my tarot cards say?"

The short golem swiped the air. "Tarot cards? Do I look like I care about baseball? What's your point?"

The tall golem leaned past his short companion. "I like baseball. Go Yankees!"

"No!" The short golem had his answer. He wagged a finger at Hermes with a scholarly eye primed behind it. "You're looking for something you already possess. That's it...that's it."

The idea caught in the back of Hermes' throat, but he washed it down with mead. "Okay. Thank you, Confucius."

"Who's confused?" The short golem turned to his tall friend. "I'm not confused. You?"

"What about you? Where is your master? Aren't you searching for him?"

"Dead. Feh," the small golem said with a big shrug. His gaze slipped to an empty corner of the room and lapsed into a sorrowful silence Hermes recognized. Painful memories. Maybe the golems played a role in the rabbi's death or simply failed to prevent it. The big guy began to grumble angrily in Yiddish.

"My brother doesn't think too kindly on our former master," explained the smaller companion.

"Nor would I, if I had a master," Hermes said.

"The master part we didn't mind; it made things simple. And Rabbi Yehuda was kind. That's not why he's upset. But you wouldn't understand. What are you? Blond-haired, blue-eyed—"

"Nobody."

"Oh, a nobody! Yes, of course," the short golem scooted his stool closer, which forced his big friend to do the same, and dropped his voice to a whisper. "The old man burned it all. The spell books. Scrolls. Everything. Decided he didn't have the right to create a 'monster.' Only Hashem. But then, I guess, he felt he didn't have a right to destroy them either, since he left this world without unmaking us. Left it on his terms, if you catch my meaning. That is why my brother here does not think so kindly of him. Our master was always conflicted, too conflicted for a man dabbling in such powers. All day and night he fretted. Kabbalah this. Kabbalah that. Do I cast this spell? Do I cast that spell? Am I even allowed to cast a spell? If God created magic, were humans to use it? Do I make a golem? Do I unmake a golem? Do I buy milk or do I buy eggs? White or rye?"

Hermes cut him off. "The spells are lost forever. Got it."

"Would not matter in any case," the tall golem said.

The short one nodded. "The children today, they don't want to learn. It takes a year to summon one runty demon. Why bother when they can make one on their video games?" He threw up his arms. "Who has ten chickens to sacrifice? Who? And what's a Reform Jew? I don't understand."

"Are you searching for a new master?"

"We're headed west. A friend has a job for us. Antique shop. Fairfax Boulevard. You know it?" The short golem smiled eagerly.

"No," Hermes replied, and the golem's smile ebbed. Golems were proud creatures, and it must have stung to go from protector of the Jewish people to night watchman at the strip mall. Hermes sympathized more than he would admit.

The tall golem slammed down his drink. "Much rather guard a synagogue. But all the Jews have Merkavas now."

"How can clay compete with a tank?" the short golem muttered.

"Try email." Hermes raised his glass. "L'chaim."

The three lost souls raised their mugs. "L'chaim."

They were about to toast when the roar of an enraged Minotaur echoed down the labyrinth. Chandeliers swayed. Dust shook from the rafters.

"RAAAIIIIIDDDDD!!!!"

The bar's entrance exploded into splinters.

A flock of angels in riot gear breached the bar in tactical formation. Patrons fled or flattened to the ground—hands, hooves, or claws behind their heads. The deadbeats of the spirit realms escaped by vanishing through the walls, while ghouls and giants continued to drink, unbothered—semi-interested in the unfolding drama (anything beat listening to a jukebox that only played two Joni Mitchell songs on loop).

With nowhere to run, Hermes concealed his face in his elbow. The golems sensed his distress and shot up from their stools, closing ranks to block him from view. Master or no master, their protective instincts were still intact. Through a narrow gap between their torsos, Hermes spied a pair of Yeezy sneakers crushing the peanut shells that littered the bar's floor.

Who could have such god-awful taste in footwear?

"Nobody move," Gabriel commanded the room, then ordered his assault team to check each miserable face. The angels fanned out in pairs, batons at the ready, checking each patron with a special flashlight designed to illuminate any magical concealment. A particularly aggressive angel yanked back a red hood to reveal a less-than-cooperative ifrit. The fire demon latched onto the angel's bulletproof vest and attempted to melt its way through the Plexiglas visor. It took three angels with fire extinguishers to subdue the minion.

"We're after a fugitive," Gabriel trumpeted, quieting the commotion. "Greek god. About six feet tall. Blond hair. Blue eyes. No one has to be in trouble here."

A conspiratorial silence met his declaration. There were all manner of monsters in this bar, but no rats. Even if they personally hated Hermes, they hated Gabriel and his arrogant ilk more. Behind the golems, Hermes smiled at the uncivil disobedience.

"Mmmm, he sounds sexy," cooed a drunken woodland nymph with long hair the color of kelp. She unspooled from a poker table and fell on Gabriel. "And you look delicious. Would you like to taste my cheese curds?"

Gabriel shoved her into the arms of an angel who zip-tied her hands behind her back. She purred at the rough treatment.

"Fascists!" the tall golem cried out, drawing everyone's attention.

Great. Hermes crouched lower. *Perfect time to speak up.*

The short golem snuck Hermes a thumbs-up and whispered, "Don't worry, they can't kill us."

"That's nice," Hermes muttered back, unsure how helpful these new-found friends would be.

"Surrender," Gabriel shouted. "We know you're here!"

Hermes was trapped, a predicament worse than the six-hour creative meeting that led to those detestable sneakers the archangel now wore. Maybe it was the booze, but Hermes suddenly felt more invincible than usual. His idea would be a bit of a stretch…a leap, really.

Hermes vaulted onto the bar and sprinted for the hopper windows.

"Stop him!" Gabriel thundered, and a barrage of gunfire threw the Odyssey into pandemonium. Almost immediately, Gabriel recognized his mistake. The golems charged into the fray, furiously swinging their massive arms, swatting angels like gnats as their clay bodies absorbed the bullets. Meanwhile, the bog monster attached to one of the fascists with her ice-pick teeth, zip-tied fairies bolted for the exits, and the monster of Ravenna ducked into the bathroom with a nymph for a quickie.

Urns of mead exploded around Hermes and soaked his runway. He slipped on a puddle of beer and belly-flopped behind the bar. So much for the high jump.

"Hold your fire! No! Stop shooting!" Gabriel admonished his over-zealous hit squad, slapping down their rifle barrels.

The bar shook. The golems drew closer. The angels closed ranks to protect their leader but were knocked down like pins by a pair of bowling balls.

"Erech apayim, golem!" Gabriel commanded. The golems instantly froze a foot from him, and their faces went blank as lumps of clay.

The rest of the patrons lost their will to fight. Hands rose around the saloon, except for the bog monster, which straddled an angel while gnawing on the poor guy's helmet. Gabriel unsheathed his sword and thumped the creature in the head with the hilt, knocking her unconscious. Black sludge pumped from the bog monster's forehead as the bloodied soldier crawled out from under her gelatinous body and retched up his holy lunch.

Hunkered in his foxhole behind the bar, Hermes studied the silence.

"You have golems fighting your battles for you?" Gabriel called out. "Did you forget? I'm older than Catholicism. I know the Hebrew spells. I can send them after you!"

Hermes thumped the back of his head into the wall. Rookie move.

"How are you going to explain this to the Mormons?" Hermes shouted back. "Disorderly conduct? Spilling blood? Worse, how are you going to explain this to your brothers?"

A loaded silence followed.

Hermes smiled. He knew all the sore spots.

Then Gabriel spoke, his voice measured. "Haven't you put enough lives at risk? How many friends must be sacrificed to save Hermes?"

Hermes knew the playbook the archangel was following. It was a literal manual, hidden within *Corinthians*, that only angels—and one enterprising Hermes—could read. And read he did. Gabriel was stalling for time.

On the other side of the bar, Gabriel motioned for the rest of his angels to fan out. They took up an assault formation aimed at the bar.

"Is every religion just a pawn in Hermes' big game?"

Hermes grimaced and dug his knuckles into shards from the urns. Gabriel had a point. It wasn't like Hermes was trying to make things worse; the religions just kept getting tangled up in his personal problems. He had some personal reflecting to do—but not right now. Right now he had to get out of this predicament.

At the other end of the bar, a single eye glared through a haze of gunpowder and tobacco smoke. A stream of liquor dribbled onto the head of the cyclops bartender. Not a happy camper.

The eye rolled up, directing Hermes to the angel wings massing in the cloudy, bullet-marked mirror above them. Then the one eye rolled back to Hermes and narrowed.

Hermes frowned and removed his left sneaker to shake out two small diamonds tucked under the sole—an in-case-of-emergency stash left over from the Vatican heist. The cyclops eye widened greedily. For a monoculus, he was certainly expressive.

The cyclops attempted to snatch the diamonds, but Hermes swallowed them in his palm.

Two diamonds for an escape route.

The cyclops nodded and quickly crawled past Hermes. His one eye indicated a wood panel behind a crate of corks, and he pried open the secret entrance to a former coal chute. It was a way up to the surface, he indicated. But then he blocked the way, thrusting out his hand for the payment. Hermes begrudgingly obliged and handed over the diamonds.

He squeezed into the lift, and the cyclops sealed the opening. Halfway up the brick tunnel, Hermes heard the muffled assault: boots pounding, wings flapping, and angry yelling.

They would realize Hermes was gone in *five…four…three…two…*

"He's not here," an angel announced. Gabriel flew over the bar in one flap, landing on broken pottery. Three Cyclops bartenders cowered beneath the cold judgment of rifle-bearing angels.

Gabriel snatched the nearest Cyclops by the lapel. The one-eyed beast radiated defiance. "Where is he?"

The Cyclops clenched his jaw.

"Anyone who doesn't share information will be treated as an accomplice!" Gabriel threatened the room, and then, searching the debris around him, snatched a bar spoon. "Speak, or I'll scoop out your eye and serve it in a martini."

The Cyclops stared at his reflection in the silver and swallowed hard. Gabriel watched two small diamond-shaped lumps travel down his throat.

"What was that?"

The Cyclops laughed, and the archangel shoved the spoon into the base of his socket.

Headlights pierced the dirty windows. Gabriel whirled to the sound of screeching brakes and loafers filling the alley outside the bar. The Cyclops stumbled backward, shielding his face.

A megaphone squealed to life. "Gabriel! You have thirty seconds to exit this establishment and surrender!"

"Mother Mary, not them." Gabriel vibrated in frustration.

The bartenders used the distraction to flee while the voice behind the megaphone began counting down from thirty.

Gabriel turned to his flock, primed for a fight they would now be denied. They wanted Hermes just as bad. Mission unaccomplished.

"Stand down," he ordered. The hit squad obeyed, lowering their rifles and cutting the zip ties off the wrists of the ill-mannered creatures around the room. Then the angels filed behind their leader. They made their retreat through jeers and cackles and globs of phlegm spat at their feet.

A woodland nymph barred the door in front of Gabriel. Gabriel raised a fist, signaling his angels to wait. The nymph's eyes sparkled, gloating as she held out her zip-tied hands. Gabriel unsheathed his sword and hacked at the plastic, severing the ties with such precision she didn't even feel the blade pass between her wrists.

She rubbed the raw skin where the cuffs had chafed and then stuffed a dollar bill into Gabriel's belt. "Buy yourself a drink, asshole. You'll need it before you deal with them."

Insult to injury.

Gabriel crumpled the dollar bill and dropped it at his feet as he exited the bar. Since when was Gabriel the asshole? Since he started kicking down doors in the middle of the night and roughing up a bunch of sorry-ass refugees, that's when. Gabriel wasn't used to being so hated. He blamed Hermes. The Greek god had gotten seriously under his divine skin.

***

The brick tunnel through which Hermes wormed was about as wide and filthy as a chimney. Soot coated him from head to toe, and his hair crawled with spiders. The passageway split; one tunnel angled up, the second down. Grunts and angry voices echoed from tunnel number two. It sounded like some angels were roughing up his Minotaur pal. He squeezed inside and rocketed down the chute, using his elbows to batter through the metal grate.

Two angels had the bouncer perp spread against the wall, rifle barrels pressed into his spleen, when Hermes dropped headfirst from the ceiling like drunk Santa. The startled angels spun around as the fugitive they had come to capture rose unsteadily to his feet.

Hermes raised his fists. "Hey, pigs, why don't you pick on someone your own size?"

That would have meant someone considerably smaller.

The Minotaur roared, and before the angels could realize their mistake, the half-bull, half-man gored them with his gargantuan horns. Their riot helmets shattered against the wall.

Hermes held out his palm. "Phone."

A snort.

"Hand it over. And you're welcome."

The Minotaur grunted again, dug into the basket of confiscated devices, and slapped one into Hermes' palm. The battery only had twenty percent left. Someone had been playing Angry Birds. "No wonder Gabriel busted the place."

Another snort, this time dismissive.

"Thanks, chief." Hermes got a helpful boost from the Minotaur and disappeared back into the chute.

***

Beneath a high-profile Escalade, a manhole cover shifted, sloughing off bits of trash as it lifted several inches to reveal a flop of golden hair.

Hermes peered above the rim to survey his odds of an escape. Through a curtain of exhaust fumes, he saw the alley in front of him was barricaded by a vehicle directly above and two more SUVs at the other end. He heard car doors open. Several dozen loafers and snakeskin boots surged past, stopping within the headlights to crouch into an offensive posture. The odds weren't looking good.

Hermes craned his gaze past the chassis and clocked sculpted shadows perched along the rooftops, with hemp nets stretched between them to prevent any aerial escape.

So the gaggle of Mormon angels wasn't here for Hermes.

Hermes watched Gabriel climb up the recessed stairs that led from the Odyssey's entrance, hands above his head, followed by the rest of his flock, and smiled to himself. *Serves him right.*

The Knights of Joseph, as they were known on the streets, surged forward, hemming in Gabriel, high beams glinting off their bolo ties, their hunting rifles locked and loaded. Pocket protectors and bike helmets never looked so intimidating.

At the other end of the alley, a tall, handsome angel stepped in front of a custom gold-plated Caddy grill. His salt-and-pepper hair soaked up the LED glow. A megaphone hung at his side like a gunslinger's pistol. He had an old-school movie-star quality that could make the early-bird gals go weak at their arthritic knees.

"Tsk, tsk, tsk," the dapper figure said to Gabriel. "An archangel. Trespassing. On Mormon territory. You should know better. You're risking war."

That's when Gabriel noticed the Greek god peering out from under the souped-up Escalade like a curious sewer rat.

Hermes flashed his enemy a thumbs-up: *You're doing great!*

Gabriel lost his cool and lurched forward, wings unfurling in anger, and the Mormon steel jerked up in response. The Catholic hit squad sighted their rifles. It was a biblical standoff. Hermes lingered under the gas guzzler to watch. This was some serious West Side Story drama.

More religions all tangled up thanks to yours truly.

Hermes knew Gabriel would do just about anything to drag him out into the open and beat him senseless—except start a war with the Mormons. The tease was made for relishing, the prize catch dangling the hook in the angler's face before diving back into the great big ocean.

The megaphone crackled to life again. "We counted two hundred K new souls, Q1. How about you?"

"We lost count," Gabriel shouted back, not breaking his glare from Hermes.

"You never stop counting. We never stop counting," the Mormon blasted back. "Does the number of souls converted have any bearing on aim? Does a Catholic shoot straighter than a Mormon? Those are the sort of questions that keep me on my knees and my palms pressed tight. But in the end, it really comes down to one thing: who has more pull up there? Peter or Joseph?"

The megaphone squawked. "So I guess you just gotta ask yourself one question…Do you feel blessed? Do ya?"

Hermes rolled his eyes. *Cowboys.*

Even from across the alley, Hermes could hear Gabriel's teeth grind harder than a garbage disposal fighting cutlery. The archangel was in a serious bind. As a sacred emissary, he had to de-escalate the tension. Or else…the *else* being war. And the wrath of Michael. The unholy ruler to the holy buttocks.

Hermes offered an apologetic shrug.

The Mormon gave a last warning: "You fire the first shot, I will fire the last."

Gabriel wrenched his attention away from his target and twisted back to the Mormon commander. "No one wants to go to war, Moroni."

Moroni—the angel who spoke to Joseph Smith, who protected the Golden Plates, and set the whole Mormon religion in motion. Yeah, that Moroni.

"That so?"

"We're lowering our weapons. I pray you'll do the same." Gabriel gave the signal, and the scopes behind him lowered from so many sapphire pupils. The gesture of peace did little to quell the bloodlust. Lethal glares shot back and forth across the alley.

"You're searching for a fugitive. Care to state the name? Make an official request of the Council? It's only a bit of paper. Then we can help you save face in front of your brothers."

Hermes beamed brighter than the headlights. His adversary was most likely under orders to keep this abduction off the books and therefore was himself in quite the pickle. The last thing the Catholics needed was for the Mormons to offer Hermes asylum, which they would gleefully do. Check. And mate.

"Apologies. But this has nothing to do with the Latter Days," Gabriel said diplomatically.

"If you're in Utah, it most assuredly does. Do you think you can just invade our sovereign soil with impunity? That we'll all bow to you and your billion worshippers? That's the problem with you Catholics…you think you have moral authority over the whole world."

Gabriel groaned.

Hermes almost felt sorry for the archangel. Listening to Moroni's grievances would be his penance—and the rest of his night.

Good luck getting out of this one.

The Greek god transmorphed into a homeless woman and crawled to freedom.

*　*　*

The night was young, and a dusting of virginal snow coated the quiet downtown sidewalks. There were no after-hours parties, club scenes, or bar crawls—just sobriety, chastity, and propriety—things that made his Mediterranean skin crawl.

Watching over the land of the well-mannered was the Salt Lake Temple, a towering molar in a toothless smile. The Mormon Mecca drew Hermes to its gravitational center with a conveyor belt of worship, a spiritual highway created by a density of focused prayer. Having never officially visited Mormon HQ, he decided on some last-minute sightseeing—a detour to pay homage to the Latter-day Saints, who'd inadvertently saved his backside from the wrath of Gabriel's ruler. He hopped a metal fence—very un-Mormonlike—and entered Temple Park.

Lit against the high desert night, the great Salt Lake Tabernacle looked like a fairytale saltine castle. Hermes half-expected a photo op with Mickey Mouse and Donald Duck. Years of toil and devotion filled each brick, men yearning to erect a holy phallus vigorous enough to pierce the clouds and inseminate the Heavenly Father with their love.

He stopped at the front door and stared up between the belfry towers. Atop the steeple, a golden statue of Angel Moroni sparkled. The icon held a baroque trumpet pressed to his lips, ever poised to signal the end of days.

"Taking requests?" Hermes called up. "'Chattanooga Choo-Choo?' 'When the Saints Go Marching In?'"

The golden Moroni didn't respond.

Suddenly weary, Hermes folded into the powder and wondered what had happened to his new golem friends. He hoped they would find their place in this world—a world that had no place for the old.

"Hey, you!" A well-dressed, overly armed mall cop hurried across the stone plaza. It took Hermes a moment to understand why the security guard looked at him like he was a dog turd smeared on his precious white marble. He'd forgotten he was still disguised as a homeless woman.

"You're trespassing. This is private property," the guard said without an ounce of irony. He had a military buzz cut and very red ears from the cold. A cross tattoo stretched over the knuckles on his right hand, which hovered at a holstered gun. In his left hand—the hand of judgment—he brandished a can of pepper spray. "Let's go, get up! Up!"

Hermes lifted onto his knees and assumed the position of pious supplicant. "I've come to pray."

The guard was not amused. "This isn't a homeless shelter. Pray somewhere else."

Several hours later, just before dawn, Hermes tripped over a lawn chair outside his motel room and dropped two brown bags filled with liquor. The bottles shattered, sprinkling the icy pavement with glass and vodka. Where did those come from? Right! Hermes had robbed a liquor store. The contact high from the Mormon Tabernacle was hitting him hard.

Fumbling inside the motel room, he crossed the shag carpet, crawled onto an orange floral bedspread, and instantly passed out. Winter curled up beside him. He hadn't even bothered to close the door.

CHAPTER NINE

HADES SHUFFLED ACROSS HIS bedroom, deep in concentration, hands clasped behind his back, bearded chin burrowed into his chest. His robe caught on trays of rotten food and dragged them across the floor behind him. All three of Cerberus's heads followed the laps from her doggy bed. Decades—nay, centuries—of disregard for basic hygiene had left Hades's personal quarters stuffy and cluttered. The only light came from a single candle burning atop a mountain of wax. The marble columns were stained from nicotine and wine and scarred by violent tantrums. A drained jacuzzi served as a receptacle for discarded recyclables and a pen for the domestic slaves who ran afoul of their master.

A massive obsidian desk dwarfed the slave Miklos, slowly tapping out a decree, one letter at a time, on an old Malling-Hansen writing ball. The strange typewriter, a hand-me-down from Friedrich Nietzsche, consisted of brass keys protruding from a hemisphere, like a mental patient forced to wear a helmet for some terrible electric shock therapy. Miklos's crooked, arthritic fingers were ill-suited to the secretarial work. Streaks of ink stained his beard from stress pulls. On a good day, if his arthritis wasn't acting up, the slave could clock half a word a minute. Today was not a good day. The cold, damp fume Hades preferred only exacerbated the ache in his joints. Worse, his master had been particularly needy since Persephone's return, in one of his manic moods. After several nights of ceaseless demands, Miklos now kept nodding off during Hades's dictation. Still, Miklos labored to faithfully commit every word to parchment.

Hades reached a wall and turned back. His sleeve dipped into the candle's flame and Miklos winced. Hades reeked of the grain alcohol he drank ceaselessly. It was a miracle he hadn't ignited.

"Fifth," declared the king, as Miklos searched the tiny knobs to find "F," the letters blurring.

"Fifth," Hades repeated, and Miklos's eyes snapped open. "As Queen of the Underworld it is your duty to service, comma, in all manner, comma, the needs of her king. Period." Hades grunted in satisfaction. Number five was his favorite so far, especially since he no longer remembered the previous four points. No matter—Miklos was taking it all down.

Hades enjoyed spitballing. The ideas were flowing, and Miklos would edit later. Right now, he just needed to get it all out. It was liberating listing his frustrations, sifting through his catalogue of resentments, pulling out one old slight after another. He would fashion this into doctrine.

Persephone would have to listen. It would be official. On parchment. Wax sealed. Notarized.

"Six." Hades slouched on the edge of his bed, a monstrosity of dirty silk covers, moth-eaten veils, and frayed shrouds. Six required his full concentration. "Love should be reciprocal. No matter the nature of its inception… or the manner in which the relationship was conceived. Period."

Number six. Nailed it.

Hades searched for Miklos.

The slave's bald, sun-spotted head poked like a pimple over the barge-like desk.

"Read that last bit back to me," ordered Hades.

Miklos lifted a magnifying glass to the page.

Derest Wafe Perspon,
One. Yo

Miklos quivered, cleared his throat. Then cleared it again. The only thing between him and a good mauling from Cerberus was the possibility of Hades suddenly deciding on a seventh proclamation. He cleared his throat again.

"Well, get on with it!" barked Hades.

The bedroom doors burst open and Hades's three bastard daughters—the Furies, Hell's Mistresses of Torture—marched inside.

Miklos sighed in relief, then promptly cowered.

The youngest, Megaera, was the embodiment of Jealousy; Tisiphone, the middle daughter, tall and slender, represented Murder and Retribution; and finally Alecto, the patron of Fury itself, was the oldest, quiet, calculating, and ever implacable. They were the spitting images of their father, in that they were butt ugly. They had leathery, batlike wings. Snakes nested in their matted, greasy hair and burrowed into their flesh through the incisions they compulsively cut into their skin. Serpentine outlines slithered and roiled their flesh, causing their bodies to ripple even when they stood still. Their resplendent white robes were perpetually splattered with gore, and wherever they tread, their sandals left bloody footprints.

The sisters surveyed the room as if they owned the place—and they kind of did. A moment after, their demon entourage encircled the room. The retinue had once been Hades's royal guard, the finest trained soldiers in the Underworld, and as part of the Furies' recent modernization efforts, were now armed with the oddest assortment of decommissioned weapons salvaged from Earth, from Soviet Kalashnikovs to Civil War muskets.

"I should describe her beauty, don't you think?" Hades, still composing his letter, asked Miklos, who'd hidden behind the typewriter. A frisson of joy swept over Hades. He stared past the demons and his daughters into some alternate reality. "I must write about her hair, the color of a ripe red apple, her evergreen eyes. And her small hands. They're so small. The smallest fingers you've ever seen."

The Furies passed one another looks of disgust.

"I almost forgot. Almost. Ha!" He wagged a finger playfully, then turned back to the desk where Miklos was hiding. "Did you get that? Miklos?"

Tisiphone impatiently stepped forward. "Father, the realm requires your signature."

She shoved an official scroll into Hades's face, startling him. Meanwhile, Megaera rifled through her father's personal effects, opening drawers, sniffing at various powders and creams on his vanity, and generally not minding her own business. Alecto simply observed. She was always observing. Cold. Calm. Unnerving.

A confused Hades struggled to unfurl the decree across his lap. The scroll kept rolling back up until he finally tacked it with a knife to his headboard. The penmanship was terrible, like a child learning their letters. Hades donned a pair of spectacles without lenses and squinted.

"What is this?"

"The new list of reincarnations, and changes for processing. There's a backlog," lied Tisiphone.

"Backlog?" Hades rolled the word around his mind. His daughter was not making sense.

"Yes, Father. This allows us to expedite matters. Elysium is far from your palace and influence. The nymphs have become lazy. And there are certain infrastructure improvements required."

Miklos's eyes darted between the Furies and Hades. All those heavily armed demons were beginning to feel extra ominous, while before, they were just standard ominous.

"Where are these improvements needed?" Hades questioned.

"The river." Tisiphone's voice quivered with anger. She preferred to do the interrogating.

"Which one?"

"All of them!" she shouted.

"I see." Hades nodded. He didn't see at all.

Miklos grunted. Then grunted again, like an old car with a faulty ignition. Tisiphone reached across the desk, fit his face in her palm, and shoved. Miklos disappeared with a thud.

"You have much to attend, Father," said Alecto, her voice sweet as corn syrup and just as poisonous. She then flashed a disapproving stare at Tisiphone and her notoriously short temper. Yet again, Alecto would have to seal the deal herself.

Alecto crouched down in front of Hades and laid her hands on his knees. "Father, let us help you with your heavy, heavy, heavy burden."

Hades smiled at his eldest, most dangerous, and therefore favorite daughter. It drove the other two girls to fits of jealousy that he lavished all his attention upon her—not that he cared. In fact, he preferred it that way. He returned to the scroll, still not sure what he was reading or what they wanted from him, when Alecto motioned to Tisiphone, who slid a pen into his hand and guided it toward the space left for his signature.

The title beneath read: Departing King, Underworld.

Hades wavered.

"Father." Alecto sat beside him, the mattress sighing and blood dribbling onto the sheets. Pythons slithered from the hem of her gown. She gave his shoulder a playful bump, as if this were just a normal, heartfelt father-daughter bonding moment. They could have been sitting on a park bench to feed the ducks. "Do you not want what's best for your kingdom? There has been too much neglect. I fear the Underworld will soon turn its back on its king."

The thought of losing his treasured subjects filled Hades with dread. His kingdom was all he had left.

"They need your strength," Alecto pressed. "They need your signature."

He nodded vigorously, and then affixed his signature.

"That's it...that's all..." she gently cooed. "Yes. Such a good king you are."

The ink glowed, reflecting in her greedy eyes and filling the bedroom with a golden light, before the document turned to stone.

Hades had just signed over his kingdom.

***

Beyond her private quarters and the botanic comforts of the greenhouse, Persephone sought refuge in the solarium. She spent hours, days, weeks under the glass dome, enveloped in a tapestry of stars. On Earth she would often lie in a meadow and stare up at the night sky. Here, an accurate recreation of the universe rotated around the goddess, placing her at the center of the cosmos. It was an illusion, of course, but a glorious one.

The sun, churning with anger and gas, floated in the middle of the dome. Directly beneath the celestial body was Earth. Persephone stood over the globe, watching an intricate tapestry of magical gears shifting and clinking as they tracked, in astronomical time, the progression of the seasons, and therefore her imprisonment. Akkadian symbols represented the calculations for temperature, wind currents, and weather patterns. Currently, great storm clouds rolled across the plains of North America. There were no other models like this one, a wedding gift from Atlas. She lost hours in its slow rotations, the clock inching toward her freedom.

"You're always here," Megaera suddenly interrupted, jarring Persephone from her daily meditation. The youngest Fury circled the edge of the solarium like a wild bird introduced to a cage.

"What does it all mean?" Megaera asked, eyes mapping the heavens. Persephone knew her stepdaughter wasn't remotely interested in the answer.

"Time," she said curtly, not caring to hide her displeasure. "It counts time."

Megaera's lips curled in distaste. "It's almost spring. Same every year. Over. And over. And over. You just can't wait to get out."

Megaera disappeared behind the eastern hemisphere of Earth. The girl could have been beautiful, Persephone thought. Beautiful in her power. Hades spoiled that too. The dungeon was their nursery, and Hades weaned his children on pain until they were addicted to it—an insatiable appetite for suffering and violence worse than the Americans who lined up outside Walmart on Black Friday.

"Tell me what it's like," Megaera purred, sending a chill down Persephone's spine. "Spring. I want to hear about spring."

"I told you so many times at the beginning." Persephone stepped around Earth to find Megaera fiddling with the delicate dials.

"That was thousands of years ago. I forgot." Megaera began to pout. "Please, I so want to hear about the buds and the morning dew and fawns and chicks and Easter."

Once upon a time, Persephone would not have doubted her stepdaughter's sincerity. In the early years of her reign, Persephone would wake to Megaera crawling under her bedcovers, wet with some stranger's blood. The young and budding torturess would keep the Queen awake all night with questions of life above the Underworld—questions she could not ask in the presence of her older sisters or father, who considered her curiosity a weakness and any topic related to Earth or mortals vulgar.

Persephone shook her head sadly. "You've changed so much…"

"We've all changed." Her eyes resembled lumps of coal. "Tell me again."

Persephone was more annoyed than afraid. She had few places in Hell that were hers and hers alone, and Megaera was defiling the one refuge she considered sacred. "It would be like describing air to a fish."

"You insult me."

"Where are your sisters?"

"With Father."

"Doing what? Taking advantage?"

"He's not fit to rule. Half the time he forgets to wear pants."

Persephone couldn't argue with that.

The ambition of the Furies was no secret, and Persephone often wondered what damage they inflicted when she was on Earth. Lately, she had noticed them strutting around the Kingdom as if they'd secured the ultimate power of attorney. If they shoved Hades into a nursing home and took up residence in the palace, there was little she could do to stop them. She shuddered to think what would happen to her and the Underworld if that day arrived. She would pray to stop it—but pray to whom? Her prayers would be directed to Hades, and he wasn't picking up the phone. By transitive property she would then be praying to herself, and that just felt masturbatory.

"Why do you keep torturing your father? Do what you like with the Underworld, but leave him be."

Megaera clutched her heart theatrically. "How touching. Does that mean you're going to stop torturing him too?"

"I do no such thing."

"You know he loves you. Yet you reject him, spurn his affections. Is there anything worse? Certainly nothing we do could hurt him more. You break his heart on a daily basis."

"And what about my heart?" Persephone felt herself being pulled into the trap. The more she resisted, the more she knew she would be dragged deeper into Megaera's mire—and yet she had to fight back. "My being imprisoned isn't enough? I must give him everything?"

"Poor Persephone. Locked away in her fairytale prison, deprived of her sun, deprived of all her pretty flowers. But in the end, she always escapes. And she's always loved."

Persephone wanted to leave but knew better than to turn her back on a Fury. "Why are you here?"

"To visit with you, like we used to visit."

"Except you're fully grown now and don't need to sleep with me in my bed. You're not afraid of the dark. You are the dark."

"Does that make you the light? Is that what you think? It would make sense. You always thought you were better than us. You rubbed it in our faces: your free pass to Earth, how much Earth needed you, how beautiful it was, how beautiful you are."

"Doesn't it get old? Singing the same tired song?"

"I can't believe I once admired you. You privileged bitch."

Persephone broke the cardinal rule and turned away from Megaera, her eyes landing on Mars. She wished Ares were here right now to put this girl in her place.

"How perfect that the Goddess of Spring will finally reap what she sowed."

"What is that supposed to mean?"

In the silence that followed, the ticking of ten thousand copper dials echoed across the solarium like Father Time's factory.

Megaera smiled. "It would be like trying to describe sight to the blind. Best that you find out for yourself."

Persephone tried to step back from Megaera but hit Mars. The planet's mechanical gears dug into her spine. She promised she would never let the Furies see her afraid. Nevertheless, her pulse pounded along the side of her neck.

Megaera advanced. "Tell me, what does a peach taste like? A fresh-picked plum?"

"It would not taste the same to you. It would rot as soon as it touched your lips."

"Exactly." Megaera sidestepped Persephone to focus on Earth. She twirled one of the seasonal dials around its axis, forcing the gears past spring, summer, through fall and back into winter. The delicate instrument protested. Persephone wanted to order her to stop—explain that the model was rare and sacred to her—but didn't dare.

"I wonder if it could be spun back?" Megaera dragged a clawed finger through the frosted northern hemisphere, leaving a streak of destruction, and then looked up at Persephone, now frozen with dread. "You're probably the only one who could. Have you tried?"

"Why?"

"To show them we're still here!" Megaera exploded.

"Leave her alone," whispered Alecto.

The eldest Fury stood in the doorway with Tisiphone by her side.

Megaera dug her toes into the ground and innocently twirled a snake nesting in her hair. "We were just talking, is all."

"Reunion's over. Leave our Queen alone." Alecto was the only one who could control the other Furies. Her word was final.

Megaera scowled, turned back to Earth, and snapped off summer's golden dial. "Oops, it's broken." She dropped the instrument on the floor and then stormed from the solarium, plowing through her sisters on her way out.

A simple twitch of a finger from Alecto and Tisiphone turned on her heels to follow. Before she left, Tisiphone made sure to toss an arrogant smirk at her stepmother.

Persephone's heart raced faster than it had in centuries, and now she was alone with the deadliest of her three stepdaughters. The Furies had never challenged their Queen so openly, and Persephone had never lost her nerve so totally. Firsts abound. She was determined to regain her footing and hold her ground. True power was quiet, and humble, and didn't go parading itself around.

Neither spoke, staring over the wreckage of Earth. Alecto probed for any hint of emotion in her stepmother. Once they found a crack, they burrowed in, then festered. The only defense was to empty yourself, Persephone knew. Give nothing. Even so, Alecto happily took that nothing, ate it up, and after a minute that lasted an age, she bowed and took her leave.

A moment later, Persephone buckled, hugging Earth for support. Her body ached. Hot tears ran down her cheeks and onto Africa, feeding life to the Sahara. She prayed Alecto hadn't seen them coming.

***

The end of winter couldn't come soon enough. Persephone passed through her waterfall, cleansed in the spring snowmelt, and waded into her glacial lake ringed by ponderosa pines. The clear freshwater basin dropped precipitously beneath her soles, and as she swam she appeared to fly. By the time she reached the opposite shore, her body began to register the cold. She shivered with disappointment, holding herself while searching the empty forest.

For the second year in a row, Hermes had forgotten.

Persephone entered her woods alone and distracted by worry. If only Hermes had kept his promise. If only he had stayed at her cabin and out of trouble. If only he had welcomed her home at the shore. If only.

If he had, perhaps someone might have witnessed the horde of Underworld demons that spewed from the mountain cave the moment after Persephone disappeared down the mountain path. The six-legged, spider-like creatures swarmed over the cliff in a large, writhing mass. The mountain tried to seal the gateway, but their numbers were too great.

They were willing to sacrifice as many of their own to hold the portal open. Escaping the sun, poisonous to creatures of the deep, they filled every crevice and crack, and became the shadows.

CHAPTER TEN

On an old, bulky television set, a blurry Sunday televangelist mesmerized a packed house. The bent antenna atop the boob tube—like the TV preacher—was only for show. A nest of jury-rigged wires disappeared into a hole in the floral wallpaper. But the gospeler didn't care about illegally boosted cable, so long as his gift-shop redemption found its way into all the sleazy motel rooms in America, just the sort of 5:00 a.m. target audience he aimed to convert. Morning-after guilt: the perfect wallet laxative. Motel Bibles had his hotline number written into every dedication page. Gather all ye signal stealers and pious subscribers, for all need to hear the Word of God.

The preacher preached his sermon on the mount, striding metronomically across a shiny stage so large it hosted its own bandstand. This was not one of those old-school Tammy Faye and Jim Bakker churches with pastel carpet, sofa chairs, and plastic palms. If you wanted true old school, there was the plain podium on a platform, the soapbox tent revival, or the simple rock-in-the-desert variety. This was a megachurch with Jumbotron screens for parishioners in nosebleed seats and a fancy broadcast control room. The futuristic spaceship-Christian rocker extravaganza boasted the production value of a U2 concert, with an LED backdrop that twinkled like the heavens and was no doubt designed by creative consultants previously employed by that den of sin…Hollywood. The house band of twenty-something skateboard-magazine models run through a car wash, sporting trim goatees and Noah's Ark tattoos, waited for their cue to rock out for Jesus.

A camera soared over the crowd on a trapeze contraption. The preacher shrank to a grain of rice. The feed switched to carefully curated close-ups to demonstrate the power of the sermon: worshippers with teary eyes, hands waving, or that old faithful heart-clutch to say, *I'm overcome!* (Somewhere in the collective unconscious was the codex for devotional gestures.)

The feed jumped back to the too-handsome televangelist and his carefully groomed soul patch, his sleeves rolled up just enough to reveal an arm tattoo of a heart superimposed on a cross, all wrapped in barbed wire. *The bad boy who found Jesus* look.

Except this preacher had never been a bad boy. His parents sent him to Jewish Country Day School (Jesus Camp was summer detox) before he attended Exeter Academy, where he majored in business with a minor in guitar and sign language—because, sure. The grunge-gone-straight look had been honed by a PR firm on retainer for various shell companies and behind-the-scenes billionaires who profited from the merchandising, TV licensing, franchises, and ancillary deals. This was the almighty intersection of capitalism and religion, the longest-running cross-promotion deal on Earth. Even the Delphic oracles had once been in on the game. Want your troops to believe God's on your side? Pay up, nobles. No one wrote in the rulebook that you couldn't profit from a bit of prophecy. No one could be bothered to do more than pick on the Jews and money lending.

Loopholes, Hermes thought in an unholy loop as he sat cross-legged on the motel bed, transfixed and befuddled, rubbing a scruffy beard that resembled an out-of-control chia pet. Even wearing clothes had become too much of an effort. Hermes stared into the miracle of public access television. The preacher continued preaching to the choir, voice rising and falling as if he were strapped into a roller coaster.

"And God waaaarrrrned the Israelites against false iiiiidoooools. Foooouuuuulllll paaaagan godsssss, in leagueeee with the Devil." He abruptly switched his cadences, the rhythmic equivalent of a student driver with his foot rubber-banded to the brake pedal. "So what do we see today? What? Do? We? See? Today?"

The crowd leaned in with yearning desire. Hermes unconsciously mirrored them, the glow of the television irradiating his face.

What do we see today? Tell us. Tell us.

"The rise of an unholy spirit walking amongst us."

Preach it, brother!

"People coming to our shores to infect our holy way of life with ungodly notions." He stopped; a dramatic pause ensued. "Is it the woke Marxists? What about the infiltration of the radical Islamists, building mosques next to our schools and in our neighborhoods?"

Shouts rose. Angry faces. The mob stirred.

"Whoa, whoa, wait a minute," he said, pulling the reins on his crowd. "Wait one minute. Not all Muslims are terrorists."

A true pro. Make 'em angry, then scorn their temper. Spin 'em around. The Pied Piper was a master of his fiddle.

"Can't do that. Can't generalize. Demonize." He took a deep breath and hung his head, as if the next words would be difficult to speak. "There's a more insidious element that's crossed the border. And no, I'm not talkin' 'bout the illegal immigrants sneaking up through the desert or down from Canada. This is even more treacherous than the Muslim terrorists or the liberals preaching their atheism and critical race nonsense to our children."

A hush descended.

"Their god. Our God. No god. No." He stomped his foot. "No. No. No. No." Big stomp. "No."

Hermes twitched. The preacher turned to the camera as if to speak directly to any Greek gods that happened to be tuning in. "I'm talking about an old virus. Old with a capital 'O.' One that would send us *aaalllll* the way back. A return to the Dark Ages." The camera slowly dollied in on his face until it filled the frame with his whole-milk wholesomeness. "A return to *you*."

He stabbed his finger into the camera lens, and Hermes flew into the backboard as if hit by Zeus's lightning bolt. Unable to catch his breath, Hermes scrambled to the TV cart and flipped the monitor backward. The domed screen burst against the daisy wallpaper with a loud pop and went dark.

The room was too small. The world was too small. He didn't fit anywhere. Somehow, he was screaming. Screaming at the top of his lungs. Screaming at no one. Screaming at everyone. In the unleashing of his primordial rage, he never heard his cell phone vibrate. The magical device buzzed across the nightstand until it tumbled onto the carpeted floor that muffled the call.

The underside of the bed glowed with Persephone's name.

***

A distressed Persephone paced the length of her porch, trying Hermes' number for the fourth time. She normally wouldn't worry; Hermes could take care of himself.

Something's wrong.

It was intuition—an intangible, irrational, but wholly plausible thought. Hermes wasn't just hiking out of cell range. With dark thoughts clouding her mind, she didn't pay much attention to the actual dark clouds spreading across the horizon. A spring storm mushroomed over the mountains, swallowing the sun before spilling down the peaks into her valley. Bands of rain swept across the prairie, curtaining the landscape as they gusted toward her cabin.

The line rang and rang and again went to voicemail. Hermes' pre-recorded message started again: "Hi, this is the Son of God—"

Persephone hung up and instantly dialed again.

"Come on. Come on."

Veins of lightning skittered through tumorous clouds. A blast of thunder rattled the windows. The sky churned, a sick green tinge. Her soul trembled. This was not a natural storm.

Her wind chimes rattled chaotically. The wind blew the cabin door open and extinguished the lights within.

Persephone reached Hermes' voicemail again and again.

"Hi, this is the Son of God, in whom I am well pleased. If you'd like to leave the Messenger a message...(Pause) No, the other Son. (Pause) Of course. I get it, you're looking for someone else. (Pause) No, I don't have an attitude, you have an attitude. (Pause) Go—"

BEEEEEPPPPPP...

"It's me. Call back."

A floorboard creaked. Persephone whirled to an empty doorframe and sensed a presence in the darkness watching her back.

"Show yourself," she commanded, stepping closer to prove she wasn't afraid—though she was very much afraid. "I won't ask again."

Silence.

The tempest reached her garden. Sleets of rain pounded the roof. Wind howled. Adirondack chairs blew across her porch and crashed into the railing. Her cabin shook as if a giant were trying to rip it from its foundation. Soaking wet, Persephone quickly retreated inside.

Rain streamed down the windows, marbling the light like a deep-sea cave. Strobes of purple lightning stretched the shadows, sending them rearing across the ceiling.

A strange flower lay on the floor in front of her hearth, the size of a small teacup. It had not been there before. Another stroke of lightning returned color to its yellow petals. Her body seized with terror. The narcissus blossom seemed to blaze in the dark, filling the whole room, displacing the whole universe. It was the same blossom he'd used to trick her all those eons ago, that ruptured the ground beneath her, plunging her into Hell—the symbol of her eternal imprisonment.

"Hades?" She spun frantically to the empty room. The walls groaned and warped as the storm slammed against them. "Hades, are you here?"

Her cabin wasn't empty. It didn't feel empty. But all she saw was shadow.

The past came upon her fast and violent. The room dissolved. She was back in a meadow that smelled of honey and barley, high above the Aegean Sea, under an eternal summer sky. The young goddess innocently reached for the stunning white and yellow blossom floating atop the amber grass like a jeweled pendant. A butterfly landed on the back of her hand. Dampness between her fingers, she pulled on the stem. The roots resisted, the ground bulging beneath her knees. Then she felt herself falling—and his rough, calloused hands as he seized her. Hands that slid in and out of her dress, a caress the opposite of love. She was a catch, snared off the land, his prize. The ocean opened, then sealed above them.

Darkness. Paralyzed with fear. His humid, heavy breath on her neck as he pressed himself against her. Naked. The Furies' gutting laughter.

He found me. He found me. He found me.

She backed away from the cursed narcissus, the wood floor creaking, the Navajo rug bunching up until she tripped and reached out—nothing and no one to catch her. The contents of her stomach rose into her mouth. Her home, her refuge, defiled.

"Hermes?" Persephone desperately called, scrambling up off the floor and retreating to the tempest that raged as ferocious as the one within her. "Please. This isn't funny."

Her back pressed against the porch rail. She clutched the wood like a raft tossed by the waves. The wood cracked as she strangled the beam.

"I am Persephone, Goddess of Spring." Speaking steadied her. "I am Queen of the Underworld. Heir to my mother, Demeter, Goddess of the Earth and all that grows…"

Through the doorway to her cabin, she caught a shadow slip off a lampshade. Maybe it was a trick of the lightning and the rain, but Persephone tracked the shadow as it slithered over furniture upon its own volition, crawled along the wall. The shadow detached from the ground, rising into three dimensions—a man with six spider-like arms. Two pearls blinked from the hollow void of the shadow demon.

"Who permitted you to leave the Underworld?" Persephone demanded. "I am your Queen. I command you return to Hell!"

The void's face ripped into a smile.

Another shadow rammed the porch behind Persephone and scurried beneath her home. Another crash echoed within her cabin. She whirled back to the sound. The first shadow demon had vanished from the doorway. Her terror ratcheted up another level. The sound of breaking glass and tumbling pots sent her darting along the porch to the kitchen window. Inside, shadows squeezed between the floorboards into her home. Everywhere she looked, the shadows came alive—writhing, separating from the walls, the furniture. An army assembled from the darkness. She couldn't breathe.

The cyclone strengthened to unimaginable decibels, stripping buds off her trees, ripping them up by the roots and hurling them about. The only escape was into the storm. She fled back to the front of her house, to the porch steps that now disappeared into a lake of mud.

Through the rain she glimpsed a flash of color bounding across the prairie toward her. Bright orange eyes, then gold fur. Four muscled legs moved with unnatural speed, faster than the wind, graceful and dangerous.

Persephone's heart soared.

The female mountain lion vaulted over her garden fence. In three strides it closed the gap, baring rows of sharp white fangs, its war cry joining a roll of thunder as it soared over Persephone and connected with the first shadow demon. The two creatures—one from Earth and one from Hell—crashed through the cabin, a tangle of claws and fangs, nails and teeth, gnashing, biting. The mountain lion pinned the dark shape. The shadow demon dug its six clawed hands into the lioness's back and raked. She screeched and buried her muzzle into the demon's neck. A wave of blood fanned the air.

Shadow demons peeled from the walls and descended, butchering the lioness. The animal's last scream jogged Persephone from her shock in time to dodge an iron spear as it sailed past and smashed through a wall. She grabbed the nearest demon and pounded its ugly face against a post. The pop of its skull was the most satisfying sound in the world. It was as easy as cracking open an egg. Hot with fury, Persephone embraced that most ancient and primordial part of her god DNA: the thirst for war.

Four demons unfurled a net of woven metal between them and rushed her. She turned her head just in time to avoid losing an eye, the wire cutting into her face, small barbs clinging to her flesh. She snatched the netting—a thousand tiny razors biting into her palms, though she was too high on adrenaline now to feel any pain—and reeled in the four demons. Her hands found the first two necks and squeezed. Bones snapped. Sinew turned to pulp. She felt their lifeforces slip back to the Underworld. Around her, the shadow demon swarm continued to infest her home, scaling the exterior walls, oozing from the mud beneath the foundation.

Persephone grinned.

***

On the roof of the cabin, a shadow demon crawled beneath a shingle. For weeks it had followed Persephone's scent through dirt and rock. Among thousands of its brethren, it wormed its way through the barrier between the Underworld and top world. They were so many the soil churned like liquid and sent the earth trembling. It had been millennia since they had been sent to feast. Yet their orders were to take the Goddess alive.

This particular shadow demon had never been to Earth. Stories were told of a great orb of pure, unfiltered light that shone upon it. The Sun. It was called the Sun, and it created a climate unacceptable to a being whose sole constitution was darkness. Their new general promised them a storm that would blot out the wretched light. The storm would be their signal to attack.

Now the storm raged. The shadow demon heard the first cries and thumps of battle as it slipped down the shingles of the little wood cabin, through cobwebs and grime. Darkness was its home. It was darkness. Unable to contain its hunger, it shuddered at the thought of finally tasting the Goddess. In excitement, six arms disgorged from its shadow. It had a body, glowing white eyes, and a pronounced overbite. Through the pouring rain it beheld the ugly landscape of trees and mountains. Soon all of Earth would be their domain—a world of shadows. Pride. Pride filled it. It was among the first. It would not be the last.

Its pace quickened down the wet slope, shoving aside its competition. With a flourish, it clung to the ledge and flipped over to finally—after so, so long—face its prey…

***

Persephone stared into the upside-down face of a particularly ugly shadow demon smiling stupidly through an overbite. She poked her fingers through its eye sockets, ripped the idiot off her cabin, and hurled it into the storm.

Ear-shattering screeches erupted from the sky. Owls, hawks, crows, eagles, starlings, every type of bird, from near and far, burst from the clouds. They dove at the demons. The porch filled with wings. Claws raked. Beaks pecked. Those glowing opal eyes were perfect targets. Blinded shadow demons tumbled from the roof. The demons snatched birds from the air, biting off their heads. The ground was quickly littered with dead fowl.

A demon rammed Persephone off the porch. She landed in the mud, her head thumping the ground with enough force to momentarily stun her. Six hands gripped her neck and squeezed. The lack of oxygen worsened the ringing in her ears. She struggled to wrest the claws from her throat when a pack of mountain lions and gray wolves joined the battle. A wolf lunged, clamped its jaws around the demon on top of her, and wrenched it back, violently shaking the creature.

Persephone gasped, holding her neck as she lurched up from the blood-soaked earth.

The battle between Earth and Hell intensified. Two large black bears charged from the woods, announcing their entrance with a roar. They skidded to a stop at Persephone's side, and their wet snouts dug into her back, nudging her toward the trees. Persephone immediately understood—they had been sent by her Blackfeet friends, Creator Sun and Moon Goddess.

Her new guardians urged her to move. Her home was lost.

There was no time to mourn. Persephone fled through her trampled garden, flanked by the massive black bears. A pack of shadow demons gave chase, propelled on their six arms. Their speed was exceptional.

One of the two sows pivoted onto her hind legs and bared her teeth, emitting a growl like a jet engine. The enemy would have to get through her to get to Persephone. The demons obliged. The sow was swallowed by shadows like a burst lightbulb.

Persephone started to go back to help her guardian, but the second bear insisted otherwise, jamming her into the forest. They lost sight of her cabin in the thrashing pines. The bear galloped ahead, keeping Persephone moving. Away—only away. The storm crashed against the cries of the battle. Persephone could no longer hear anything.

They ran for what felt like an age, the storm never letting up, until they hurtled out of the forest onto a vast prairie. The whole world had turned gray. Her remaining guardian abruptly dug his claws into the wet earth. He stopped to sniff the air. Catching some foul scent, he began to whimper.

Across the valley, a single aspen set on a small hill whipped from side to side. Something about the way it moved transfixed Persephone. The tree's branches began to shred from its trunk, sucked up into the sky.

A funnel cloud descended, and the rest of the aspen was ripped to shreds. Her guardian bear bellowed in terror.

There was nowhere Persephone could run. She wondered what Hermes would do.

She boldly positioned herself to challenge the force that had sent this tornado to destroy her beloved meadow. "I'm here! Enough!"

Strobes of lightning scorched the sky. The earth trembled. A crack split the prairie. The ground began collapsing around them like a lung pierced by a dagger. Instinct took over, and the bear bolted.

But there was nowhere to go. Persephone shouted after him.

The ground gave way, and her bear tumbled out of sight with a last horrified cry. The sinkhole spread from the base of the tornado, devouring the grasslands. A swollen creek drained over the ledge. Persephone's heart sank, knowing the pit extended all the way down past this world and into the next.

And then the tornado abruptly dissipated. The thunder stilled. She felt a cold wind gust up from the void. The temperature plummeted. A crust of ice instantly formed atop the prairie, smothering the infant plants. A tremble rose through her breath. A cloud of steam hovered across her vision, through which she watched the earth freeze.

A noise echoed within the pit, sounding oddly like a breeze rustling the leaves in her garden. The sound rose, churning the frosty air—a clarion call of carrion wings.

It's them, she thought, her mind suddenly calm. Because this was her fate.

A moment later, demons erupted from the pit, infinite as ash from a volcano. They spread across the sky like an oil spill, their wings drumming a dirge.

All Persephone could think was how very much it looked like the lid of a tomb sealing her in.

CHAPTER ELEVEN

A PALE, ETHEREAL LIGHT penetrated the frosted windows of Hermes' trashed motel room. Trashed, as in a heavy metal rager would seem like Grandma's morning bridge club, trashed. The furniture was mashed to splinters. The carpet had been stripped, with a mosaic of shattered glass embedded in the foundation. The floral wallpaper had been singed by at least one flash fire. A mountain of takeout containers incubated a jungle of bacterial cultures that could either cure cancer or wipe out the human race. Pilfered pharmaceuticals covered the mattress, sorted by color and size. Management would have to tear the place down, burn it, and salt the earth.

Hermes stirred in the bathtub, having passed out beneath empty bottles. Yawning, he stretched, his hands and feet finding the cracked tile, his wings twitching from the cold. He nodded with approval as he took in his motel room. Blue ribbon for self-destructive behavior.

Something purred beneath the recycling. Confused, he scooped bottles aside to unearth a prostitute drooling on his chest. She had reddish-brown hair sticking out at crazy angles from the beehive hairdo advertised in her online profile. She had been described as full-bodied, and that body was now awkwardly contorted, her face lopsided from too many pills and smushed against the drain. All that aside, Hermes considered her an attractive specimen. She had been listed as twenty-three, but he knew she was really twenty-nine years, two months, and twelve days old.

Careful not to wake her, Hermes maneuvered out of the tub, causing the girl to sink beneath the remainder of the bottles with a loud snore. He winced as several displaced bottles crashed onto the floor. It would be a couple of hours before she came back to Earth.

Hermes relieved himself in the general direction of where the toilet once existed. Porcelain crunched under his feet as he left the bathroom. Hermes welcomed the pain. The pills from last night hadn't been strong enough. They never were.

"Betty," he suddenly remembered. Or at least that was the name she gave him. The quaintness of a prostitute named *Betty* made him smile. Not too subtle. There were odder fetishes in the world than wanting to be fucked by a First Lady cosplayer. Still, Hermes simply wanted company.

He tapped the broken television with his toe and it toppled off its cart, loose bits jangling inside like all the bracelets Betty had worn as she pounded on his door the night before. Now, the feeble morning light filtering through the windows made it hard for Hermes to locate his last joint, lost somewhere among the wreckage of his motel room. It wasn't under the mattress, nor behind what was once a nightstand. He sifted through debris, the glass on the floor; he even checked inside the busted television. Nope. Hermes always lit up in the morning. It took the edge off existence, and this morning, the anxiety of being him was off the charts.

He was about to crawl out of his own skin (which he could totally do) when he noticed Betty's purse beside the door, just begging to be searched. He ripped open the Velcro clasp and began poking and prodding through that most holy of holies, which was, disappointingly, filled only with condoms, makeup, and sundries. Then Hermes found an alligator-print spectacle case. Betty didn't wear glasses. *Jackpot.* Inside was a little baggie of coke, several twenties, and two perfectly rolled joints. He took one—no need to be greedy—slipped a hundred into her roll, and returned the case.

Hermes ripped open the door and stepped outside into the whitest white, forced to squint at the blinding glare that ricocheted off everything. It wasn't just his hangover, the whole parking lot was covered in sparkling snow. The typically congested highway that ran past the motel sat littered with abandoned cars, recognizable only by their shapes. The local mountains, bleached with ice, encircled a smoldering Salt Lake City. Black smoke swirled into an otherwise clear arctic sky. The silence took a moment to absorb, oppressive for the modern world. It reminded him of that nursery rhyme: 'Twas the night before Christmas, and all through the Motel 6, not a creature was stirring, not even a prostitute. *Something like that.*

Hermes couldn't remember the last time he'd been outside. Food delivery apps were a godsend for the clinically depressed. He exhaled, basking in the peace and quiet. Everything was blissfully mute, and soon all the pesky thoughts in his head would be too.

A convoy of National Guard trucks obliterated his meditation, urgently rumbling toward the city. He put one and two together, got three. Salt Lake City was on fire…

Matches! I don't have any matches.

He trudged down to the motel office in a pair of frayed boxers with a pattern of summer strawberries and watermelon slices, and his coveted Converse sneakers (the one and only 1984 Olympic Fastbreak Mids worn by Michael Jordan himself; only cost him the Holy Grail he stole from the Vatican, which was totally worth it). The office door didn't budge. When he rubbed the frost off the front window, he could clearly see people huddled inside. Hermes yanked at the door. Ice snapped off the hinges. Little bells jangled.

Behind the counter, an old man and woman were swollen to twice their size, mummy-wrapped in scarves and jackets. Only their eyes and lips were visible, frozen to the weather forecast on a small television hanging over Hermes' head. A beleaguered reporter tried to make sense of two continent-sized storms swirling over his map.

"Still no sign of the jet stream moving back north. Reports expect another five feet of snow across the Southwest and into Baja, Mexico. Another jet stream is bringing that southern polar air all the way up to the equator. With crops obliterated across North and South America, we'll start to see major food shortages across both hemispheres. National Guard ration distribution sites will be set up…"

The old woman noticed the half-naked god and nudged her husband.

"Mister, you must be frozen out of your mind," said the bundle that was the man.

"Matches?" Hermes inquired.

"Don't give him any, Harold," shrilled the female bundle. "He'll burn down the motel!"

"He's not going to burn down the motel," Harold grumbled.

The woman's gaze honed in on the joint pinched between Hermes' fingers. "You gonna share?"

"Not if I can't light it."

A few minutes later, Harold's wife was taking an inordinately long drag. She glanced at the television and exhaled forcefully. "Fuck Armageddon."

The smoke plumed from her scarf like a chimney with a clogged chute. Relaxed, she passed the blunt to her husband and offered Hermes a knitted Christmas quilt. Hermes took it with a token nod and draped it over his shoulders.

Hermes left the office with a box of matches, puffing away on the roach. Without the clutter in his mind, he could enjoy the snow beneath his feet, the sight of his breath hanging in the air in front of his nose, the cold sting on his cheeks.

His thoughts slowed to a molasses drip.

She had said winter was so beautiful it made her sad.

Hermes recalled it was a summer not so long ago—July 1953, to be exact. He had arranged a field trip, schlepping a resistant Persephone to the lower altitudes of the Himalayan range. Only two months before, the world had been captivated by the first two humans to summit Mount Everest. Hermes had long thought alpine mountaineering to be a ridiculous human endeavor—except for the fact that it gave him the brilliant idea to introduce Persephone, at long last, to winter. A court-mandated snowbird, Persephone had never actually experienced one of her winters.

The impetus for the field trip was a dramatic change in her mood that had occurred over the last few summers. She'd been prone to fits of random tears and long silences, obfuscations when pressed for answers. Other than diagnosing her with inverse Seasonal Affective Disorder, Hermes hadn't a clue what was wrong.

The mountains huddled around them like a gathering of elders to play mahjong, shrouded in shawls of snow. Secretly, Hermes had hoped this majestic place of a thousand peaks would begin a process of healing. He eagerly shook a pine tree to imitate a snowstorm. The flakes stuck to their hair, melted down their necks. She shivered, and her expression seemed to reanimate. Except her emotion wasn't the delight he expected, but exasperation.

"What's wrong?" he had asked, trying to suppress his irritation.

"Nothing," she said.

He raised an eyebrow, unconvinced.

"All right," she huffed. "It's beautiful. But it's also sad. It's a beautiful sadness."

"Why sad? Why would beauty be sad?"

"I dunno …it just is. And quiet. I didn't expect it to be so quiet." She touched the frosted bark of a pine tree and listened. "Their pulse is faint. The forest sleeps …"

Her eyes traced a slope to a snow leopard perched atop a boulder, nearly invisible against the white. It flicked its tail and bowed to Persephone. Their gazes remained interlocked, leopard to goddess. It was like they were having a private conversation in a language Hermes couldn't speak. It was rude and made him stew further. His special outing was not going as planned.

"Sad? You finally get to see winter for yourself and all you can say it's sad?"

The snow leopard leapt off the rock and vanished.

Persephone frowned. "I also said it was beautiful."

"Yeah. But do you mean it?"

She threw up her hands. "What do you want me to say? Do you want me to say it's great? It's great. It's also cold. Snowflakes are really fascinating. Happy now?"

Hermes kicked a pile of snow and turned his back on her. "Great. Yeah. I'm happy."

"I don't want to fight!" she yelled.

Hermes crossed his arms with a huff. "I don't want to fight either!"

"You want me to thank you…? Okay. Thank you for bringing me here."

"Your tone sucks," he said.

"I could have come here on my own if I wanted to."

He turned around. "I'm trying to show you winter isn't a curse."

"Sure. Not for you, playing with your snowballs."

"Real mature."

"Look who's talking."

He balled his fists. "Every year Earth survives, it comes back renewed. Can't you see that?"

"Yes. I know full well how the seasons change. I'm the one causing it. It's miserable."

"Oh, please. Like you're the only one who suffers."

"I thought you dragged me here to show me the Earth doesn't suffer?"

She had him dead to rights, which only frustrated him more. "Yes! That's what I'm trying to show you! Can't you see how magical this is? It's a miracle! It's fucking sublime, goddamnit!"

"Great. Snowmen and snow angels, ice skating and hot chocolate. I'm so grateful I can provide humanity all the jolly memories. Actually, I'm lying." Her stare was like an icicle. "I don't care about your winter wonderland, or the cycle of seasons. Fuck Winter. Fuck Spring. Fuck Summer. Fuck Fall. Fuck you! How's that for cyclical?"

"Fuck you too!" he shouted back.

She sighed and looked away at the frosted landscape. Her voice was hoarse with despair when she spoke next. "I know it's not a curse."

Hermes felt his anger thaw. "Then what's wrong? What's been going on with you?"

"Maybe I'm lonely. You're the only one who wants to be around me since I became Queen of the Underworld. Otherwise, I'm goddess-non-grata. It only takes a kidnapping by your uncle to find out who your true friends are."

"That's old news. Why would that be bothering you now? You've been moody, not yourself. Not for the last few years. Frankly, you're no fun."

"Fun. Yeah. That's what you care about." She made a noise somewhere between a scoff and a sob, then abruptly punched a pine tree, knocking loose an avalanche of fresh powder. Hermes was shocked. Persephone rarely resorted to violence. Perhaps winter had inadvertently become exposure therapy, allowing her to unburden and find acceptance. A tree wasn't the best substitute for a bataka, but it would have to do.

Well done, me.

Hot tears rolled down her frozen cheeks. "I'm a symbol of death and despair, harbinger of the long, cold night. I am the gray, the white, and the withering. No one wants to be around me. Even Mother has left me."

At that, Hermes nearly fell over. "Wait. What about Demeter?"

"She's gone."

"Gone? What do you mean?"

"She just left …crossed to the nothing, left me her responsibilities. I don't know why."

The revelation caught him flat-footed. Hermes wanted to give his half-sister a great big hug, but he was too shocked to comfort her. "When? When did this happen?"

"About a decade ago. I returned from the Underworld and she was simply gone."

"Persephone …this is the mother of all bombshells."

"A pun? You're going to use a pun right now?"

"It wasn't intentional," he lied.

"After I stopped panicking, I thought maybe it was a test. She'd come back next year. But then the next summer she was still gone, and the next, and I realized she was really gone. Now every time I come back to Earth, I keep thinking: who else? Who else is going to leave me? How could she do this? Why? All I have are questions, and I dread summer now. I dread it, Hermes."

She took deep, gulping breaths, and Hermes finally held her. The intensity of her moods, the sullen trail she carved through summer, suddenly made sense. The strength required to carry such a burden both impressed and shattered him. He wanted to blast off to Olympus and ask their father a thousand questions of his own.

"I'm sorry," was all he could manage. It felt so inadequate.

Her sobs subsided, leaving a shell of despair tucked against him in the cold.

"Maybe her leaving is a gift," he offered.

She lurched away, obliterating the snowman he had built that morning when she refused to participate. "A gift? My mother's vanishing?"

Hermes nodded, finding the conviction as he spoke. "Yes. It's the ultimate gift."

"Oh, please explain how."

"You'll preside over the harvests, over the living and the dead. You bring change and are change. You are Winter and Summer. You are death, but also rebirth. She wants you—only you—to have that. Without you, the world wouldn't turn."

"Bullshit. They have meteorologists and ten-day forecasts. The *Farmer's Almanac* has never mentioned Demeter once. She gave up. She left. And she didn't even say goodbye."

"It hurts. I'm not denying that. But what if she had come to you first? What would you have said? You would've insisted she stay. She's gifted you purpose everlasting."

"Did you just use the word *everlasting*? I can't—I can't even …I can't accept it." She looked away to hide the fresh tears icing on her cheeks in the frigid air. "I don't want to."

"You have to. You don't get how lucky you are. It's not fair, really, not to the rest of us. And then you reject it? Seriously?"

She sank into the snow. They spent the next several hours sitting with the silence of winter and mourning the death of Demeter. He had hoped she heard him.

Just before nightfall, he sensed her soften beside him and heard a loud sigh. She rose, walked several paces, and declared her intention to move on. Just like that.

Hermes beamed. *Nailed it!*

Then he pelted her with a snowball.

"Ow!" she cried. "What was that?"

"That, my beloved half-sister, is what I've been telling you about. A snowball."

He hurled another at her, and she ran screaming for cover behind a tree.

A quick learner, she mashed together one of her own. Without warning, she pelted Hermes in the head. She formed another and lobbed it at him. "What an invention!"

Hermes ducked the missile. "This is called a snowball fight!"

"If only we could fight all our battles this way!" Persephone shouted back as she molded an arsenal. Her cheeks were flushed. "It does inspire joy!"

"Doesn't it!" He launched his counterattack as Persephone's snowballs crashed around him. He was relieved to see her having fun, though he still wanted to curse Demeter for abandoning her daughter. The selfishness. It was so typical of a god. But that would be for later.

Right now, they were having fun again—a perfect Hallmark Christmas movie moment. His heart soared knowing he had cured Persephone of her inverse Seasonal Affective Disorder. He knew it in his bones.

***

The cherry on his roach blinked out in the icy wind that scorched his face like a blowtorch. Hermes struggled to rub feeling into his hands. All he needed was enough dexterity to light a match. He just about had the fuse lit when another arctic blast ripped the salvation from his lips.

"Damn." Hermes stared into the ocean of white. "Damn."

No more pot for Hermes. Recognizing defeat, he retreated to his motel room, pushing against the blizzard. He fumbled with the Swiss-hole plastic key he'd kept tucked in the band of his underwear. It took a bit of magic to get the door open. He stomped the snow off his sneakers and basked in the blessed radiator warmth when—

A hand smacked Hermes sideways into the wall. Blood rushed to his numbed cheek and a bright red blemish spread along his good side. The slap stung like a motherfucker.

"I usually don't go for foreplay," he said, massaging his jaw.

"Funny, since you're the one with all the time," the Archangel Gabriel replied, shaking out his sore hand. Slapping a god hurt.

Hermes racked his blurred vision to the three-angel hit squad standing behind the archangel, each dressed in puffy white parkas with wide neon ski goggles that made them look like dragonflies. Angels were always runway ready, this time for an Alpine fashion show.

Hermes figured it was best to skip to the end. "I don't have your treasure. I sold it."

Gabriel was too busy sanitizing his hands with the wet wipes he kept in the leather murse along with his trumpet. The crisis elevated to panic mode as he noticed a smear of a mustard-like substance on his boots. Hermes waited patiently as the archangel yanked out a string of moist towelettes like a magician drawing scarves. He finished scrubbing his shoes, careful not to contaminate any more of himself, and then searched the room in disgust. There was nowhere to dispose of the soiled wet wipes.

"Just drop it anywhere," Hermes suggested.

Visibly distressed, Gabriel crumpled the wet wipe and tucked it in Betty's purse.

"Are we finished?" Hermes asked.

"Hardly."

"I'm a bit short at the moment. What do you use? PayPal? Venmo? Zelle?"

"No."

"Neither do I. If you want the rest of your stuff, you'll have to track down Eshu."

"Is that so?"

"Jungles, kids with AKs, malaria, and tsetse flies—good luck with that."

"No luck required," said a familiar voice that stunned Hermes a second time, no slap required. Eshu stepped through the door in a puffy black and red ski jacket, looking like an inflatable tire advertising a service station.

"Good to know how long it takes you to sell out a friend," Eshu said.

Hermes felt his cheek out of habit. "Look who's talking. I'm not the one riding with the crusader and his white knights."

Eshu peeled off his gloves and entered the motel room. Streamers of pink insulation dangled from the ceiling around him like jungle vines. He shook his head at the sorry sight of the place and glanced at Betty, snoring away in the bathtub.

"That was you at the Knicks game." Hermes jolted forward aggressively.

Three manicured hands reached for the 9mm submachine guns strapped in the shoulder holsters beneath those expensive white jackets.

Hermes froze in place.

Angels were a quick draw. It was a *Vogue* spaghetti western. All they needed was a white tiger and a couple tumblers of Glenlivet.

Eshu smiled, his features flickering between his own and the parking attendant—a disconcerting party trick that gave Hermes the willies and caused Gabriel to risk going cross-eyed. "The Utah Jazz crush the Knicks in the first quarter …had to be divine intervention."

"So, you have the Christians protecting you now?"

Eshu dismissed that with a scoff.

"It was you that led them to *The Odyssey*. That's two betrayals. The African god of Mayhem—I should have known better."

"They let me keep the staff. And as a sign of good faith, they returned everything that was stolen from my people. They offered. I did not have to ask."

"It's true—" Gabriel began, but Eshu shot him a thunderous look. This was an argument between tricksters, and tricksters alone.

"What would Olódùmarè have to say about your betrayal?" Hermes scolded.

"Please. My Supreme wouldn't waste breath on you. Besides, you would have done the same."

"No." *Yes.* Hermes probably would have made that deal. It was a very good deal.

"I didn't have a choice," Eshu insisted, pregnant with regret.

"The god of Crossroads, who presides over the intersections of life, didn't have a choice?"

"I would have been cast out! Banished!" Eshu lost his cool. And when Eshu lost his cool, it was not a pretty sight. More than a mercurial god, he was borderline Borderline. "Not just denied the worship of my people, but scorned, spurned, erased. I would have been less than a human. You know this."

"Well, I'm just happy your people got to keep their toys."

Eshu sucked on his pipe, and Hermes braced for the explosion. He really wished he was wearing pants.

Gabriel cleared his throat. "Stop this. You're both acting like children."

Neither trickster was prepared to back down.

"I'm not here for what you stole," Gabriel said to Hermes, then pivoted to Eshu. "We agreed."

Eshu emitted an aggrieved grunt and relented, blowing his magical vape out the side of his mouth into an air vent. He sank on the soiled mattress, brushing aside random narcotics left over from the night before.

Hermes uncoiled his fighting stance and addressed Gabriel. "You're still sore about the pope. I get it."

"Livid, but that's not why we're here."

"You don't get it, not by a mile." An itchy Eshu launched up from the mattress and yanked down the window curtains, flooding the room with a pearly glow that gave the West African god a distinctly angelic appearance, more than the actual angels lurking in the shadows.

"What am I looking at?" Hermes asked, staring at the ice crystals shielding their view of the parking lot.

"How long have you been holed up here? What month is it?" Eshu asked impatiently.

"What month? What the hell are you getting at?"

Eshu and Gabriel exchanged a weighted look that filled Hermes with a sense of dread.

"Well, that's foreboding."

"What month?" Gabriel repeated.

"Help me out here. Was I in a coma? Take some bad LSD? If this is some cognitive test, we're in Utah, some asshole is president, and today is Tuesday."

"It's Saturday," Eshu corrected.

Hermes threw up his hands. "Saturday. Whatever."

"How? Long? Have? You? Been? Here?" Gabriel could barely contain his temper.

Hermes shrugged. "Couple weeks. Maybe."

"Five months," Gabriel answered his own question. "You've been here five months."

"Do the math," Eshu said.

Hermes counted the months on his fingers. "March. April. May—" Hermes stopped counting, his mouth suddenly filled with cotton. His palms went sweaty.

"Keep going," Gabriel commanded. Hermes' stomach plummeted all the way down. Down, down, down. Down to the furthest it could go. Down to the Underworld.

"June." Adrenaline rushed into the void. It felt like a woodpecker on speed was trapped inside his rib cage. "July!" Hermes couldn't breathe. "Oh god!"

"Oh, Persephone," Gabriel corrected. "To be precise."

Hermes punched a hole through the frosty window, letting in the ice and snow and cold and winter. Winter. The arctic end of days. It could only mean one thing.

Hermes bolted for the door, but Eshu was not hungover and therefore a fraction of a second faster. He cut off Hermes and blocked the exit. Without thinking, Hermes nailed him in the ear with a powerful right hook. Now it was Eshu's turn to stumble. Gabriel and the angels grabbed Hermes. Fists and elbows filled the room. A neon ski goggle cracked. Hermes fought like a madman, screaming and punching, shouting Persephone's name.

"Stop fighting and listen, you idiot," Eshu roared to get his attention.

"If you're a part of this, I swear—" Hermes growled, pinned between angels.

"Swear to whom?" Gabriel interrupted. "Swear to Zeus? Hera? Some good that'll do you."

So much for soothing the savage beast. Hermes lunged. This time, Eshu intercepted. The two god besties wrestled. The building shook as Hermes slammed Eshu through a wall. One of the angels put Hermes in a chokehold while the other two locked his arms behind his back.

"Traitor!" Hermes spat at Eshu.

"Let me go!" He practically moaned with desperation.

Eshu disentangled himself and dusted the asbestos off his jacket. "Fool. You've always been a self-absorbed fool. This is bigger than any one religion, new or old. Winter has fallen on my people too. I found Gabriel—yes. And I told him where to find you—yes. But only after it was apparent something was wrong. And something is wrong. Horribly wrong, Hermes."

Hermes struggled, but the angels tightened their hold. He finally submitted. "Why didn't you just come to me directly?"

"You need to ask?" Gabriel indicated the motel room. "This isn't so much a symptom of your disease—it's a reflection of you. You're one of the oldest beings in existence, yet you behave like a child."

"She's my sister! Did you think I wouldn't care?"

"Here we are, and it's July. The month, but not the season," Gabriel forecasted. "Once there was eternal summer. Until the spoiled and promiscuous Persephone had to taste the cursed fruit of Hell. Then came the division: summer, fall, winter, spring. Seasons—our collective punishment for her folly."

"I was there," Hermes seethed. "It was a dirty trick. You and every religion and every human who has and will ever exist owe her everything!"

"Of course it wasn't her. Or you," Eshu said to diffuse Hermes.

Gabriel pressed on. "While you've been wasting your days, the world's suffered. Crops wither. Creatures perish. The humans revert to barbarism, fighting like animals, killing one another to survive. Their cities burn and countries fall. And all you had to do was look out a window! If Persephone doesn't return soon, there won't be another spring. The Earth will die. As will humanity. That's not good for any of us. Snow covers Saint Peter's tomb, and the priests pray on their frostbitten knees to a god they think has forsaken them. Their blood turns to ice and they wonder why. We can do nothing."

A calmness washed over Hermes. "But I can do something."

"Don't worry, we didn't mistake you for someone important. You just deliver the messages."

"In a manner."

Gabriel scratched the side of his chiseled jaw. "Obviously, Persephone's domestic history gives us a pretty good idea where she is. But we can't enter your Underworld."

"You need my father's permission."

"That brings me to my message—and my deal with you to deliver it. You run to Daddy. Get Zeus to strong-arm Hades or have him open the gates of your Hell, and we'll drag her back to Earth ourselves. We don't particularly care. You do that, we absolve you of your sins."

Hermes stared at his winged feet. Any desire to throw the offer and an accompanying insult back in Gabriel's face was curiously absent. Only one thing mattered now—more than his pride or the prospect of absolution; more than the Vatican treasure; more than his wings, worship, and freedom—and that was his sister.

Gabriel motioned his angels, and they warily released the Greek god of Luck and Mayhem and no pants. First things first. Hermes recovered his trousers from under the mattress.

"One more demand," added Gabriel. Hermes paused, one leg in the cuffs. "Discretion."

And there it is. Hermes savored the irony. "Mortals knowing you're not the only game in town…that would be really inconvenient." He stuffed his other leg into his pants and zipped up.

Eshu grinned. "Monotheism's a bit more pluralistic than we all thought."

Hermes grinned right back. Bros for life. BFFs.

Gabriel wasn't amused. "Don't think you're our first choice—or even our last choice. There just isn't anybody else."

Hermes found his golden high-tops inside the busted television set and started to slide the first shoe over his wings when he stopped.

"I have a condition of my own."

Gabriel frowned. "You don't have the leverage."

"Oh, but I think I do." Hermes laced up his sneakers and stood face-to-face with Gabriel. "The day I was sacked, I was put on the no-fly list. Clipped. I need my wings."

CHAPTER TWELVE

FRIGID AIR SWEPT ACROSS the desert highway, a long silver ribbon stretching into winter's ever-widening oblivion. Orange lane dividers flashed between gusts of ice like lights on a runway. Hermes stood at the center divider, his back to an embattled Salt Lake City. Pillars of smoke obscured the downtown. The scrubland and farms on either side of the road were buried under Persephone's lament. Carcasses of frozen cattle littered the gulches and fields, butchered by caravans of humans searching for a land untouched by snow, their spirits fading with their odds of survival.

How could he have been so blind? So self-absorbed? He'd failed Persephone, the only being he cared for between Earth, Heaven, or Hell. Now, the one fate he had sworn to protect her from had happened again, and on his watch.

This swarm of remorse and self-reproach had circled Hermes since he sealed his bargain with Gabriel. Yet somehow, he managed to scrape off his stubble, shower, and iron the last clean shirt he owned. He laced up his lucky Olympic high-tops, shrugged into a stained Goodwill peacoat, and stood before the cracked motel mirror. His broken reflection stared back, small and uncertain.

Hermes had bummed a grand in cash from Gabriel and left it as a tip for Betty on the bed. His note to her read: *You're not dead. Thanks for the company.* He almost added, *Follow your dreams,* but that would have been tacky.

Gabriel and his angels were clustered in the motel parking lot, anxiously watching Hermes like new pet owners allowing their dog off leash for the first time. Would Hermes obey—or run?

Eshu must have felt his friend's turmoil, because the God of Crossroads suddenly appeared beside Hermes. Wind whistled through the frozen power lines and tugged at their coats.

"I've been trying to decide if I should say something sarcastic and witty, or profound and sincere," Eshu said, blowing into his hands and stomping his feet.

Hermes peeled his gaze from the horizon. "Which way are you leaning?"

"Whichever way will make you hurry the fuck up. I'm freezing my divine balls off out here."

Hermes chuckled.

"What's wrong?" Eshu asked. "You've been standing here for hours."

"I haven't been to Olympus in ages. And I return with my tail between my legs to beg my father for his help, so that he can berate me and tell me I'm a screw-up."

"You are a screw-up. But a lovable one. Sometimes."

"Thanks. Always a messenger, only a messenger. Now for the Christians…"

"You are a lion that's burrowed itself inside a turtle's shell," Eshu said.

"Is that supposed to motivate me?"

"It's an observation."

Hermes looked to the angels shivering in the parking lot, then back to the highway. They were waiting for him to blast off for Olympus. It wasn't the subzero temperatures that kept his winged feet planted on the ground. "The Vatican job was stupid and reckless," he admitted. "I put you and your people in danger."

After a silent moment, Eshu rested a hand on his shoulder.

Hermes exhaled, his breath swiftly stolen by the blizzard. A feeling of catastrophe had shadowed him since his journey into the Spirit Realm during the sweat lodge ceremony. "I don't think this winter will end."

"You don't think she'll be found?"

Hermes didn't know how to answer.

"Your love is the strongest power you have," Eshu said. "You will bring her back."

"I hope you're right. But I can't shake the feeling that this is a piece of some puzzle. More than one…" Hermes echoed the line whispered to him in the Spirit Realm.

"More than one what?"

Hermes felt afraid, but he wasn't sure what exactly he feared. "I don't know."

Eshu glanced over at an increasingly impatient Gabriel, who motioned him to hurry the fuck up. Their wings fluttered, shaking off an accumulation of snow.

Turning back to Hermes, Eshu grasped his friend by the elbow and raised himself up. "From the Old World to the New, the Yorùbá to the Lukumi, I am Eshu. God of Crossroads. And I stand here for a reason."

His benediction carried the weight of a proud and ancient people. A confidence stirred within Hermes. Although the road ahead was straight and narrow, Hermes did indeed stand at a crossroads—the intersection of many things seen and unseen, past and future, the world as it had stood and a world unwritten. Sealing his eyes, he absorbed the blessing Eshu bestowed upon him. When he opened them, he gazed down upon his most sacred sneakers …his lucky sneakers.

Hermes drew a switchblade from his pocket. The blade snapped open like a military salute. Eshu stepped back as Hermes steeled himself to make the ultimate sacrifice.

He took a deep breath and kneeled.

"Goodbye, my mint condition friends."

The switchblade plunged into the rubber, and he repeated the sacrilege until all four of his wings unfurled through gills in his one-of-a-kind sneakers. They were worthless now. The deed was done.

A warm smile spread across Eshu's face, and his eyes danced with mischief rekindled. His friend—the Messenger of the Gods—had returned.

Hermes knelt like a runner at the starting gate and whispered her name, "Persephone."

He went through his preflight check.

Wings? Check.

The road narrowed before him, and he remembered that day on the Himalayas, her laughter experiencing winter for the first time.

He would do whatever he had to do. He would bring her back.

"Persephone," he shouted into the wind.

At some point, his feet left the ground and everything became a blur of white, impossible to distinguish the Earth from the clouds.

Hermes was going home.

CHAPTER THIRTEEN

HERMES ARRIVED AT THE base of Mount Olympus with a heavy heart and a soul-crushing sense of déjà vu. A layer of frost dusted an expanse of Naxian marble leading to a bronze garden gate framed between two laurel trees pruned into elegant topiary spirals. A small sign hung on the fence simply stated, "No humans—dogs welcome."

The latch had been left unlocked. Hermes swung open the gate and stepped into heaven. His gaze traveled up the mountain path ahead, until the trail disappeared into cumulus folds of opal, coruscating faintly against the pink stratosphere.

No time like the present.

Without golden trumpets, heralds, a chorus of maidens, or grandeur of any sort, Hermes began the laborious ascent. His sneakers traced the polished divots worn into the steps by the countless pilgrims who'd once commuted between Earth and the Pantheon. A sheen of ice made the stones extra slippery and slowed his climb. The absence of a funicular or ski lift was most definitely intentional. Once, the lines could snake all the way to Olympus, taking weeks to make the journey. Entrepreneurs often sold food and wine to those stuck in the traffic jams. The stairs today were relics overgrown with weeds, winding through more relics. The lonely squeak of his soles echoed among looted treasuries once grander than Delphi, squelched through deserted villages and silent tavernas carved into the cliffs, chirped past the second palaces of the gods, and traveled noisily above the condo subdivisions and low-income housing erected for the demigods and their families.

The stairs deposited Hermes in a sparkling, snow-brushed peristyle courtyard framing a fountain of four lions, their expressions representing sadness, mirth, anger, and pride. Jets of ice connected each gaping mouth to a frozen pool. A grove of thousand-year-old olive trees typically provided a canopy of shade against the brunt of Helios, but under duress from the unnatural cold, they were shedding yellow leaves like a depressed parrot plucking out its own feathers. Apparently, Olympus had lost its landscaping crew.

Dry leaves crunched as he rounded the fountain, crackling like bones left among the ashes of a funeral pyre, recalling so many battlefields in the days of old when his duty was to collect the fallen souls and ferry them to the Underworld. Never did he think he would be reminded of death on Olympus.

Across the courtyard, a modest wooden door was set within a wall of pink marble. Hermes knocked twice. No one answered.

No sooner did he turn the knob than Winter gleefully blew open the door and let itself in. The vacuum of the palace sucked in the frigid air, snuffing out the oil lamps and plunging the sepulchral hall into a smoky gloom. He stepped across the simple threshold and had to throw his weight against the door to seal it behind him.

Trepidation fluttered through his body. The grand seat of Greek power seemed to expand before him, and yet the walls pressed in. A forest of Doric columns vanished into the invisible rafters, each one larger than Earth's greatest sequoias. The throne room was vast—far larger than he recalled—but maybe that was only because there was no one else here. Once upon a time, he would have been greeted by music and laughter, boisterous debates, thronging crowds, and a crush of commerce. The gallery celebrated all the might and creativity of his religion, no room for humility. A surge of pride would propel him, strutting like a peacock, into the great theater of the gods.

But this was a mausoleum.

Other than the haunting emptiness, nothing else had truly changed. Nothing. Even the air was stale. Some gods hold on too tightly. Hermes felt it in his bones. He heard a slosh of water and the slap of a wet cloth on the marble floor. Halfway down the hall, a golden automaton was on its hands and knees scrubbing an elaborate mosaic map of the ancient world. Forged by Hephaestus to serve the gods, the automaton was as lifelike as a high-end sex robot. Some of them even had feelings, which was more than Hermes could say for the divine beings who ordered them around. Hermes stopped at the edge of its chore and cleared his throat, yet the automaton gave no indication it had noticed the prodigal son returned.

"Hey. Tesla human…" He tapped its water pail with his foot.

The automaton paused to roll its copper inlet eyes up toward him.

"Do you know who I am?"

Its face was expressionless. It blinked once, then threw its cloth down, splashing Hermes' pants with suds, and resumed scrubbed away. So much for trumpets and lyres, bowls of grapes and dancing nymphs.

"Were you manufactured in China or something? Answer me. Where is my father?"

The automaton continued polishing Babylon.

Annoyed at the golden slave, Hermes plowed across the area it had just cleaned. Its gaze never even strayed from the floor.

The massive circular chamber known as the Pantheon held the twelve thrones of the Greek gods arrayed like a lollipop. Ten thrones flanked a walkway, five on each side, leading to a set of seven steps and a bema that hosted the thrones of Zeus and Hera. Their thrones were made of yellow Egyptian marble and were the largest by far. Size mattered. Hera's seat was just a fraction smaller than her husband's. Each successive throne got progressively smaller and further away. Hermes' throne, the smallest, sat next to the entrance for the latrines. Hierarchically speaking, it may as well have been in the parking lot. The gods had practically invented the corporate pyramid. The more absolute power one had, the worse the pettiness became. Immortality allowed plenty of time for bullshit.

Drop cloths hung over the furniture as if the gods had simply moved to their summer residences. Demeter's throne was shrouded in black. It was the first time Hermes had been back since Persephone's mother had permanently recused herself from the game—aka committed herself to the void. He wondered if Persephone had ever come here to pay her respects. Why had he never asked her?

Hermes stopped at his throne. He could almost smell the shit and piss from the latrines. Persephone should have sat beside him, but she'd never been granted an official place among the council, unfairly tainted by her husband. So when the dodecagon met, Demeter insisted her daughter share her seat.

He tugged off the cloth, kicking up a cloud of dust. His red throne was cut from a single uncomfortable block, the arms carved to look like two ram heads, the seat made of woven goatskin and fleece—a definite plus for comfort (try plopping your ass on a curb for ten hours).

He sat in the chair for old time's sake. After two thousand years, his cheeks still fit perfectly into the marble. *Thank you, pilates.* Dionysus used to sit directly opposite him, the god of frat culture. To survive the long and boring council sessions, they would drink wine and play chess by whispering moves through a giggling Ganymede, Zeus's male lover and cupbearer (having also been kidnapped, the mortal had a special affinity for Persephone). Inevitably, drinking to excess and highly competitive, they would forget about discretion and start shouting their moves over the proceedings. Zeus would then order their removal.

At least there were one or two pleasant memories…

The silence felt strange. There was never silence on Olympus. A single word uttered in this hall could change the course of history. *Maybe I should pray.* The thought amused him. Hermes drummed his fingers on the armrests and shifted to the great bema. A familiar pit churned his stomach. No good memories there. Every summons by Zeus used to twist him into knots.

Hermes ejected himself from his throne and hurried down the colonnade, head lowered in submission for old time's sake. So many empty rituals. Their time had come and gone. And somehow, that was comforting. Blocks of stone. That's all it ever was.

Hidden behind Zeus's throne, a small passageway led to the private chambers, where the gods could retire from the political theater and unwind in debauchery. Hermes passed through a series of ornate marble foyers, locker rooms, vomitoria, and drained bathhouses. Room after room, and still Hermes saw no one.

Eventually, Hermes emerged into a tranquil Mediterranean garden of ancient olive groves, paths lined with lavender, and reflective ponds terraced into Mount Olympus and overlooking Earth, which orbited below like a NASA gift-shop postcard—only Earth was smothered by the churning storm clouds of the apocalypse. Other than that, everything else was peaceful. The galaxies swirled above him in the endless ocean of space.

And then Hermes found them.

Scattered among the deck chairs that lined the lower terraces—one slumbering god after another—soaking up the sun as if they were on a cruise ship, nothing to do but let the world drift by, undisturbed by the frantic billions crying to the heavens for a savior. Only these gods weren't on any call sheets. No one would pray to them. They would sleep on in peace until the end of days. And by the looks of Earth, that day was nigh.

Hermes fixated on an ostentatious cabana set upon an exclusive prow that exuded a familiar privilege. A mane of uncombed, silver hair floated ethereally in a gentle breeze above the back of a chaise lounge. It was either Gandalf, Bernie Sanders, or Zeus.

His legs weighed more than steel girders by the time he reached the pearly gazebo with its unobstructed command of the sun setting on the end of days. An unnatural drowsiness settled upon him. The thin atmosphere on Olympus typically made him lightheaded, but this felt as if someone had pulled the plug on his sense of urgency. He resisted the warm and pleasant apathy spreading through his body. His purpose was too important. He had a message. The most important, and perhaps the last, he would ever deliver.

Persephone. Remember, always, Persephone.

"After all these years, do you want to know what I've learned?" The famous tenor rippled like distant thunder. A familiar lightning bolt of terror shot through Hermes. Zeus didn't wait for Hermes to answer. He never did. His voice dropped into a hoarse whisper, as if the King of the Gods could only muster enough energy for one bombast. "No one's chosen. It's all of us or none of us."

He sounds tired.

It had been nearly a thousand years since father and son had seen each other, and Zeus couldn't even be bothered to turn his head and greet Hermes. Vengeful, strict, and quick to anger, Zeus was a master of intimidation. And no matter what feats of greatness the Messenger God accomplished—from battlefield heroics to successful quests—Hermes could never meet his father's lofty expectations. Hermes had long stopped caring whether his father approved or disapproved.

And yet…

A hand lined with sunspots, purple veins, and battle scars softly patted an open cushion beside him. Hermes immediately obeyed. His heart pounded as he entered the gazebo and sat on the lounger beside his father. A side table between them held a pitcher of wine, a tray of dates and grapes, and a loaf of hard peasant bread. *Is Ganymede nearby?* Hermes wondered and hoped. The purdy prince turned divine boy-toy cupbearer was always good for calming his tempestuous father if things went south, as they inevitably did between them.

"Out there…" A long, bony finger stretched toward Earth. Michelangelo's depiction of Creation oddly came to mind. *A Greek god unconsciously chooses Christian iconography. Hermes would have to analyze that later.* The muscular arm that once hurled lightning bolts looked brittle as a twig with its loose skin draped over bones. "Out there," Zeus continued, "the humans fight just to hold on. But hold on to what? To their claim over Armageddon? The Rapture? The End of Days? The Rising? Muslims, Christians, Jews, Buddhists, Hindus…" Zeus sighed, and his breath rippled through the clouds.

Hermes faced an aged and frail Zeus, entombed by cushions and swaddled under blankets. His left eyelid drooped as if he'd suffered a stroke. Time and ambivalence had eroded him, scouring away the king who once commanded armies, inspired gods to sacrifice themselves in battle. Where had the mighty Zeus gone? His father looked small, and Hermes wanted to cry.

"Hello, Father," he said instead.

"Speak up! You're a god. Don't mumble." His energy rebounded in criticizing his son.

Chastened, Hermes turned to the apocalypse and enunciated his reply. "Yes, Father."

Zeus lifted his upper half from the lounger and leaned over the side table to inspect his son, wheezing through the whiskers that spilled from his nostrils. His lip, splotched and cracked, quivered from the strain. Despite the gauze-like film layering his gaze, Zeus detected his son's discomfort. "Are we so strained?"

"There's no strain."

"Then why must you look away? Is it easier to behold the end of Earth than your father?"

So the bastard knows about her kidnapping.

Zeus grabbed his wrist. "Is something wrong with my appearance? You can tell me."

"You look good."

"Are you sure? Do I upset you?"

"You do not."

"This is the way we are now, Hermes."

Hermes turned to Zeus, if only to prove he could.

Zeus caught his reflection in his son's disappointment and wilted a little more. His gaze fell to the ground like raindrops down a windowpane.

Hermes whispered, "Tell me what to do."

Zeus rolled back into his cushions with a satisfied sigh. "Maybe it's for the best."

Forgetting himself, Hermes catapulted to his feet, fists clenched at his sides. Zeus would not—could not—save humanity. Hermes suddenly wanted the god that thundered and raged and ruled with an iron fist. He wanted Zeus to hurl insults, to be ruthless and mean. He wanted to scream at Zeus, and for Zeus to scream at him. He wanted anything but this. "Don't say that! You can't do nothing!"

Zeus closed his eyes, and for a moment Hermes thought he drifted off to sleep.

"Demeter left years ago," Zeus said, eyes closed. A puff of air escaped his lips. "The rest of us, we stay. Waiting. For so long I don't even believe in myself anymore."

Loser, Hermes wanted to shout. *Weak.*

Zeus smiled. "Her exit was glorious."

Vainglorious, narcissistic asshole.

"She broke Persephone's heart," Hermes said.

"She gave Persephone such a parting gift." Zeus opened his eyes and for a moment they blazed like lightning. "Relevance."

The sorrow hit Hermes all at once, nearly buckling him, but he held firm the way Zeus always demanded of him, while tears streamed down his cheeks. *Why did I come here?* Hermes desperately wanted to run away, to go home. But where was home?

Home was Persephone. And where was Persephone? Gone.

Hermes couldn't return to Gabriel empty-handed. He hadn't even delivered the message. Unofficially, Hermes had his answer: Zeus wouldn't demand Persephone's return because there was no more Zeus.

Zeus smiled again. "You have a message to deliver. I can tell. You look constipated."

"I do have a message."

Zeus patted the side of Hermes' leg. "See, we're not all useless."

Then he waved dismissively at Earth. "Regarding this?"

"Yes. It's Persephone. She's been—"

"No," Zeus interrupted.

"No?"

Zeus lifted a hand. "I don't want to hear it. Later."

"You'll listen now," Hermes commanded.

"How dare you," snarled Zeus. He tried to sit up but collapsed back into his chair. "How dare you…"

On the second attempt he managed to prop himself sideways over the armrest. He tried to hide a tremor in his left hand, balling it into a fist and wrapping it in his right.

"I came all this way, Father. You'll listen to me."

"KING! Not father. And I don't need to hear it." Spittle flew from his mouth with each word. "I know what it's about."

"Then act. You must do something." Hermes stood over his king, no longer intimidated.

"I must nothing."

"You are my father! HER FATHER!"

The other gods now lifted their heads from their loungers, their glazed eyes searching for the disturbance.

"Right. I am. And do you think I haven't seen this a thousand times before? That I know not what's best?" Zeus shook with fury. The tremors spread through his body, impossible to hide.

"Do nothing then. If that's what you think is best. We'll do nothing and no one will help Persephone."

Zeus suddenly deflated, exhausted by the outburst. "Why must you rush? Wait. Just wait. Please."

"When? When is the right time to care?"

Zeus stared up into the galaxies beyond Hermes' shoulder, his trembling hands slowly lowering to his sides. "It doesn't matter."

"It matters to the humans, to Persephone, to me."

Zeus gritted his teeth like a stubborn mare and refused to speak. It was pointless to argue. The stress had taken its toll. Zeus sank into his pillow and his preferred state of inertia.

"So you won't help?"

Zeus exhaled. "What good would it do?"

***

Hermes left the garden. He stormed back through the council chambers, past the thrones and the courtyard with the four-faced fountain, resisting the urge to smash off each lion's face. Only when he reached the edge of Mount Olympus and the stairway down from Heaven did he stop.

He gripped the trunk of an olive tree and released the sob that had been lodged in his throat. His gods were gone. Heaven was gone. Persephone, the only one who understood him and cared for him, was gone. He lost his world several ages ago, but all the time since, he had successfully distracted himself with tricks and heists, other vices. There were no distractions left. Hermes was alone. For the first time, he was truly, utterly, completely alone.

Fate laughed in his face.

But who pulls the strings of the ones who pull the strings? Am I the arbiter of my destiny? Is my fate written or transcribed? Who ordains the gods?

Sickly yellow leaves hung around him, distorting his vision. He stared blankly through the lattice of branches.

Humans have the gods to pray to, to curse, to love, to blame, to celebrate…Who do we have? The gods have no one.

"Am I an atheist?" he asked no one and everyone.

Perhaps the silence was the answer. A sharp pain radiated from his heart. The frozen McMuffin he ate for breakfast threatened a defrosted encore. It was a dangerous question—the most perilous a god could entertain. Atheists could be the most enlightened beings. They rely on no one. *Maybe I should choose to believe in nothing.* But that was not atheism. Atheists did not believe in nothing.

He willed his mind to join the silence. A moment of blessed silence.

"*I am a god. And there are no gods. All humans are gods. All gods are human,*" spoke a Voice from within. But it was not any voice he recognized—certainly not his own. Hermes whirled to the empty courtyard.

I am a god. And there are no gods. All humans are gods. All gods are human.

Hermes shot forward through the screen of branches and nearly stumbled off the mountain. Before him, the endless winter storm pressed against Olympus. *Who was the Voice?* He dug the sole of his sneaker into the gravel. Gripped the olive trunk. Beneath the bark, he felt its pulse, aching, like him, for Persephone's return. He hadn't hallucinated. This was no dream.

Hermes lingered upon Heaven's ledge for what felt like an age. But the Voice never spoke again. Behind him, the olive tree's heartbeat continued, feeble yet obstinate, tapping out its own Morse code: *I will bear fruit.*

Zeus may have lost faith, but not Hermes. Hermes believed in Persephone. Her goodness. Her compassion. Her capacity for love, for hope, and most importantly, for renewal.

Right then and there, Hermes swore an oath to himself. Then swore to whatever or whoever presided over his fate, that he would do whatever it took, travel to the depths of Hell to find Persephone and bring her home. The journey had been ordained. He knew Persephone believed in him.

And that was enough.

Perhaps Fate smiled from beyond, because at that moment, Hermes decided to believe in himself.

CHAPTER FOURTEEN

HERMES HAD A HISTORY of playing with fire. Now, he was playing with lava. Gods weren't meant to be free agents. There existed clear lines of delineation for a reason. Overly complex dogma and doctrine …for one particular reason: chaos.

Chaos didn't matter to Hermes. If chaos were the true force of existence—if all things being equal, and equal equals chaos—then what was the fucking point? Why must Hermes be bound to the rules of a game the Greeks no longer played? The band had broken up. It was truly a brave new world. This was how Hermes chose to interpret the oblique message of the disembodied voice, and by embracing this convenient explanation, his uncertainty cleared. From now on, Hermes would deliver his own messages, and if there were to be any consequences upon his return from Hell, he'd face them like a god—blow a raspberry and proclaim, "Boo-fucking-hoo."

Hermes slogged in the general direction of Persephone's cabin, thankful for the nifty snowshoes he'd stolen from a corpse, as his wings were no match for the blizzard's unyielding brutality. Snowdrifts topped twenty feet, transforming the Montana plains into a bowl of whipped cream. The days were white, the nights Stygian. Sometimes the storms screamed; other times, large, feathery flakes cocooned him in a silence as profound as the Spirit Realm. Every step risked peril, and even with his headlamp, he often couldn't see past his frostbitten nose.

Hermes felt as if he were trapped in an endless sensory deprivation chamber. For any human to survive this winter, it would take a miracle. Indeed, miracles were all they had—deployed by all the religions still worshipped—a spiritual triage that would only buy Hermes time. Humanity was on life support.

Hermes didn't have time to sleep, only to keep trekking, warming pads shoved under his armpits. His breath left a trail of steam like a locomotive plowing across the tundra. Only the tallest pines huddled together had managed to claw out from the drifts. And soon, they too would be buried.

Three days after crossing what he suspected was the state line, a sense of revulsion spread from his toes to the back of his throat. He knew he was close. When demons visited Earth, they left a trace, like the smell of rotting corpses. Humans often reacted to their presence with a crushing depression or flu-like symptoms. Some humans were drawn to it—serial killers, sociopaths, and freaks who huffed glue. For Hermes, the stench turned his stomach.

The vast white became a canvas upon which every memory of death was projected. Hermes snowshoed through ancient battlefields as carrions feasted on what the treasure seekers left behind. But Hermes was no stranger to death. It was loss that haunted him. This had once been Persephone's home.

Below him, he knew, existed a vein of hope pushing back against winter's despair. Spring's revival. The power to bring forth the bulb and open the new leaf, awaken the hibernating bear. It only required Persephone to unleash it.

Hermes wished Creator Sun would descend from his sky perch. Yet this winter would have put Creator Sun and the rest of his kind into a deep freeze. Even Old Jim and his pickup would have been a welcome sight. His mind drifted to the revelation of chaos, his inadvertent journey into the Spirit Realm, and the voice on Mount Olympus. They were connected somehow.

Hermes was tempted to return to the Spirit Realm and find out. The Spirit Realm held many answers—all the answers, actually—if one knew where to look, what questions to ask, and possessed the right frame of mind, meaning you couldn't be an obnoxious, impatient, arrogant shit. Aka Hermes. He required handholding. The Spirit Realm was the Collective Unconscious on steroids, and there were many skills a god had to master to access the infinite data contained in its infinite spaces without going mad. Even if Hermes were successful in retrieving the answer to this riddle, the next problem would be finding his way back and then interpreting the cryptic dream. Most crucially, Hermes lacked the proper consent. To trespass into the great mystery without permission, without the guidance of the Blackfeet gods or its other guardians, could prove disastrous.

Fuck it. If Hermes truly wanted to turn over a new leaf and be a free agent, there was no time like the present. This was the new Hermes. And the new Hermes didn't ask permission. The new Hermes was a doer. He drew in the icy air and focused. The world around him blurred. He closed his eyes and let go—and fell backward through consciousness. He fell and fell, until he fell apart. His self expanded, and then dissolved into infinite pieces.

It was then that Hermes joined the Spirit Realm, opened his inner eye—

And started to suffocate.

The sound of a cannon blast thundered. Hermes felt himself falling.

Something's wrong!

He struggled to pull air into his lungs as if a pillow were pressed tight over his face. His body burned from the cold. In his panic, Hermes somehow managed to fling his spirit back into his god body. Everything was white and motion. A roar enveloped him with the fury of a thousand spears striking shields in the first confluence of battle. He accelerated. Whole forests were ripped out by the roots and joined him. Trees twirled like propellers, churning and snapping.

An avalanche!

A chunk of rock smashed his head. Hermes lost the horizon. An ominous hiss rose within the roar. Past his feet, a large object parted the avalanche. He threw himself toward it and was slammed into a tree wedged into a boulder, its bark scored off.

Stronger than a stampede in Mecca, the avalanche ripped him down the slick trunk until the stub of a branch jammed into his spleen. Hermes wrapped himself around the lifeline, head tucked into the crash position as a mountain collapsed upon his back.

The wave eventually thinned, leaving Hermes dangling over nothing. A calm dusting of snow swirled around him, catching the first golden rays of morning light to create a sparkling mist over a chasm that stretched across what was once Persephone's valley. Hermes rested his cheek on the wet pine to slow his racing heart. Death couldn't come for him in this world, but it could take him in the Spirit Realm—and that was a close call. Closer than he'd been in a long time.

The old Hermes would've laughed it off. The new Hermes, gripping the icy trunk, required new underwear.

He pulled himself upright on the pine to get his bearings. The tree extended over the void like a broken bone that had pierced the skin. The remnants of the avalanche sank into the black abyss like clouds drifting across the night. Down. And down. And down.

It would look a lot like winter, Hermes imagined, when the snow finally settled upon Hell.

***

Hermes stood atop what must have been the outer border of her garden. There was no trace of Persephone's cabin. Her beloved orchard and plants were all entombed in snow. No corn stalks, beanpoles, purple eggplants, or trellised tomatoes—their colors as varied as the sunset. Everything Persephone had cultivated with such care was smothered. The Spirit Realm suffocated. Earth slowly buried alive by Winter.

It took nearly an hour of furious digging to carve a tunnel into the hard-packed snow. Eventually, Hermes broke through into an icy cave, falling onto Persephone's front yard. The glacial cavern glistened like crystalline marble. The air was strangely warm, insulated and protected from the wind. He peeled off his gloves and goggles, unraveled his wool scarf, and lit a flare.

Phosphorus dripped and sizzled on the frost. The furious glow exposed the cabin's cracked walls and broken windows. The demolished porch swing had become a mobile of splinters, slowly twirling in the arctic air that followed him through the chute. The icy ground was streaked red and black with blood—animal and demon. A massive bear slumped against a post, frozen in mid-growl. Everywhere he looked there were owls with their heads bitten off, shadow demons with gouged sockets, a mosaic of carnage. One demon, felled between its physical and shadow form, looked as if it had melted halfway into a puddle of ink.

Plumes of feathers scattered as he climbed the front steps. Broken beams creaked in protest. Hermes abruptly stopped. An ache filled his chest.

Lying upon the cabin's threshold, as if left to mark a grave: a narcissus blossom.

His skin burned.

Cursed god. Evil god.

If Hades had lingered at the crime scene, Hermes would have torn him apart—rewritten the rules so that a god could die on Earth. No matter. Hades will die in Hell. He stuffed the bouquet in his pack. He looked forward to tossing the flowers on Hades's corpse.

His first stop was the wine pantry. During the days of Siberian drudgery, he had held out hope, but it was all savagery. Only a few bottles remained undamaged. He rescued those he could.

In the great room, the Mountain Lion Queen had managed in her last act to drag herself to the hearth. Hermes knelt beside her scarred body, shredded by the demons strewn around her. Her road to the afterlife had been painful—a sacrifice for Persephone. It would be improper not to mourn. Hermes lit the kindling in the fireplace with his flare, placed a palm over the mountain lion's heart, and offered a prayer of gratitude. She had done what he had not: come to his sister's aid. So had the others. He would honor them, restore Earth and the Spirit Realm, make what was broken whole.

As Hermes finished his prayer, the darkness at the corner of his eye began, ever so slowly, to shift. He pretended not to notice the burgundy shadow slither up the wall. It stopped, and Hermes lunged. The injured shadow demon scurried off, knocking a painting to the floor before slipping into the rafters. Frightened gray eyes peered between broken beams. A steady drip of demon blood pattered and pooled on a rug. It was trapped.

Good. One lived.

Hermes kicked forward a couch, climbed up, and yanked the squealing demon into its physical form, violently slamming it to the floor. The demon wore an old trench coat, shielding its face behind three arms; its remaining three arms lay crumpled and broken from the battle. The maimed demon was clearly in pain and had been abandoned to fend for itself.

"Speak," Hermes commanded, pressing his diamond-patterned sole into the demon's chest until he heard ribs crack. The demon clicked its tongue and wriggled in agony.

"Where did Hades take her?"

Hermes eased the pressure to let it speak. The demon gasped, and its purple lips parted into a smile.

"You think that's funny?"

Hermes ground his heel down again.

A dagger suddenly flashed in one of the demon's hands, pulled from beneath the coat. Before Hermes could stop the creature, it jammed the long poker under its chin and up through its brain. The demon twitched beneath his shoe like a cockroach sprayed with insecticide. Blood gurgled from the hole under its chin, its face contorted into a wicked smile.

Then it stilled.

***

The temperature dropped so low it couldn't snow. Every gust of wind was a razor dragged across his skin. Hermes arrived at the lake that shielded Persephone's entrance to the Underworld, solid ice from the surface to the bottom. The waterfall was now a sculpture of crystal. To reach the cave he would have to chisel through.

"Persephone…" he stuttered, face numb. "I'm coming."

Even his icepick had frozen to his pack. He ripped it loose and struck the first blow against the waterfall. A chunk of ice the size of a sedan skidded across the lake. He struck again.

"I'm coming."

He swung again.

"I'm coming."

He punctuated each strike was his new mantra.

"I'm coming."

Strike.

"I'm coming."

Strike.

Icicles crashed around him like a storm of arrows. The waterfall calved and crumbled, revealing the mountain's granite face. Hermes tore off his glove and slammed his bare palm into the barrier. The cold seared his flesh and yet he persisted, skin to stone, demanding entrance to the Underworld.

The mountain shuddered in response and finally yielded. Granite splintered beneath his hand. As the wretched cavern opened wide before him.

"I'm coming."

Hermes plunged into Hell.

CHAPTER FIFTEEN

THERE WAS NO SOUND beneath the earth. Descending and descending and descending. It was the silence that bothered Hermes most—a silence different from Mount Olympus, which had a particular retirement-home-at-naptime *je ne sais quoi*. This silence had the ring of nightmares and the buzz of danger. The coil before the snap. The cloud before the burst. It didn't help that the stairs were endless. There was no sense of time, just the slow descending and descending and descending into the Underworld.

Hermes had never taken this route. The long, slow, laborious service entrance was considered beneath the gods. Not for Persephone, though. No. She chose the stairs—every goddamn year. Down. And up. Good cardio. Hermes would have never been caught dead taking this entrance into the Underworld, which was ironic when he thought about it. Nothing was beneath him anymore...except for Hell, and soon, not even that. In the old days, he would breeze through the barrier between realms, noisy and flashy, on brand.

For once in his existence, Hermes wasn't after the attention.

He slipped in and out of time and consciousness, snapping awake whenever he happened to trip over a step. The stairs forced a state of self-reflection whether you sought it or not. Another of Persephone's annoying designs. At some point in the descent, Hermes went on cruise control, deeper and deeper, his mind free to wander. And wander it did. He revisited the last months with Persephone, returned to their argument last spring. It felt as though an age had passed. He saw how childish his behavior had been—cruel and vain, indeed deplorable. It would have to change once he arrived in Hell.

Self-control.

He paused somewhere between Earth and Hell to pat himself on the back for all this self-reflection. Then he self-effacingly acknowledged that the self-congratulating was more self-aggrandizing than self-aware.

Progress!

Eventually, Hermes reached the limits of self-reflection. His ears began to pop and his knees ached. How had Persephone managed this climb twice each year?

Descending and descending and descending.

Note to Persephone: Install a damn elevator.

At some point, he noted a reek of mildew and laundry exhaust seeping through the stone. The walls became damp. His frustration reached its zenith. He cursed the corkscrew.

Descending and descending and descending.

And then he wasn't descending. Level ground came unexpectedly, and he face-planted into Hell. His headlamp smashed on the ground, which was slick with a mucus-like algae. He dug into his pack and struck a flare to illuminate a forest of stone. The fire ignited a gas vent beside him, and from there the flame went on to spark another, and another, like the passing of the Olympic torch—until a constellation of ten thousand torches lit across the roof of the cave.

Jules Verne, eat your heart out.

Silence and gloom. Plenty of silence and gloom to go around in the Underworld. Hermes entered the maze of stalagmites leading to the palace grounds.

It wasn't long before the long-heralded decay and blight came into sharp relief. Like Mount Olympus, there was no one to welcome Hermes. No hosts of Hell. No guards. Hermes arrived unacknowledged, free to stroll through the imposing royal gates, which hung open.

The way to the palace led through the king's private orchard. A faint smell of mint permeated the stale air. Wild asphodels pushed up between the pavestones and the pulverized bones that the palace used instead of gravel. Husks of dried-out pomegranates dangled from petrified branches. Each fruit he brushed wheezed a poisonous silver mildew. Many of the long-dead trees had fallen over, while other sections of the orchard had burned in some past blaze, leaving charred stumps like tombstones. He nearly missed the clue of two branches delicately braided. Her pruning was masterfully done. It was ages ago that Persephone had carved a hidden tunnel through the shrubs. He waited several minutes to make sure he wasn't being followed, then abandoned the path and followed their old trail.

It was one of their secret spots. Hermes and Persephone used to picnic beneath a cinnabar canopy of pomegranate blossoms, entertained by iridescent hummingbirds pollinating the next crop—all before his banishment from the Underworld, of course. Those days were bliss, yet they were as hard to remember as the terrible days, of which there were also many. He knew he was only torturing himself revisiting the past. But that's all there was in the Underworld. Every step echoed with his former life, and the striations of memory pressed upon his chest. There would be no peace for Hermes in Hell.

Hermes lost the path in a confusion of thorns and dried fruit until he spotted a flattened husk within a footprint, too large to be Persephone's. Someone else had visited here recently. Someone else knew about their secret garden.

He pressed on, deeper into the grove, following the trail, catching glimpses through branches of something green. Something alive. He stepped into a clearing and found a small, thriving garden. Hermes half-expected (half-hoped) it was marijuana. Again, no such luck. It was a field of narcissus, grown in tidy rows. The nearest cluster was missing their blossoms. White sap still oozed, cauterizing the wounds. A recent harvest.

The narcissus Hermes found at Persephone's cabin must have been grown here—that was clear as day, even though it was eternally night. It was a message. Any place sacred to Persephone would be defiled, turned against her. Hermes pushed back the way he came, plowing through branches. By the time he rejoined the grand mall, he had found welcome purchase with his anger.

The remodeled palace reared over the horizon, ugly as Persephone had described—if not worse—somewhere between a botched facelift and a boxer after ten rounds. Hades was the master of poor taste. If Heaven held on too tightly to the past, then Hell was a midlife crisis.

A promenade led Hermes to the knockoff Versailles. Every palace window was dark and lifeless. He kicked in the front doors—why the hell not—and drew the same Remington pistol he had smuggled into the Vatican.

The hall had been hewn from a single slab of rock. A pile of coal smoldered in a large pit, wheezing black smoke that stained the rim of a large oculus. At the other end, Hades's anthracite throne was lit by a single exposed bulb on an electric lamp tethered to a dozen extension cords.

A monstrous bark loud as a cannon blasted his right ear. A half second later—ear ringing—Cerberus was on him. The massive three-headed hellhound pinned him to the floor. His Remington handgun skittered across the hall. Hermes blocked his face behind his forearm. Three sets of teeth tore through his impenetrable god skin, as if he were a mortal. Indeed, in the Underworld, he may as well have been.

The old bitch still had bite. The middle hound clamped onto his arm and shook. His elbow bent backward with a sickening pop that sent him roaring in pain.

The two remaining muzzles went for the kill, but their snouts collided. After the shock, they lunged at one another, dousing Hermes in slobber. Hermes attempted to twist free as the siblings fought; her grip was too tight. Cerberus began dragging him toward her doggy bed, festering with corpses and feces. His rubber sneakers squeaked and squealed across the stone.

Hermes reached behind him for the backup pistol he had packed just in case he ran afoul of any three-headed dogs. Cerberus sensed the threat only when his muzzle smashed into her muzzle. Hermes didn't want to put the old girl down, just stun her.

Brain circuitry exploded and her jaw loosened enough to pull his arm free. The two heads that had been fighting cocked to the side in confusion as the middle mutt flopped forward, a flaccid tongue draped out the side of her mouth like a crooked tie.

The other two pups sniffed their stunned, conjoined sister, then began whining and licking her wound. Hermes looked on sadly. He used to enjoy playing with Cerberus and giving her belly rubs. Why hadn't she recognized him?

The girls began to growl. Four cataract eyes pivoted to Hermes.

He slowly backed away. "Good girl. Who's a good girl? You're a good—"

Cerberus pounced. The left muzzle grabbed him by the waist and flung him across the room. He slammed into Hades's throne, smashing it off the dais.

Puppy charged, her middle head flopping between her legs and leaving a trail of drool. Hermes recovered, snatched the lamp, and thrust it out like a spear against a cavalry charge. The broken socket sent 230 volts surging into Cerberus like a shock collar. She howled and ran in circles, tripping over her middle head.

Time to put Lassie down. He took aim, hating himself for what he knew he must do.

"CERRY! HEEL!"

Cerberus instantly obeyed, skidding to a halt.

Hades strode into the hall, bathrobe open, rocking a pair of silk Disney pajamas—vintage merch from a *Hercules* movie. He approached Cerberus with a stern finger raised. "Lie down."

Cerberus cowered and spread-eagled on the floor.

Hades tussled her three heads. "Good killer. Good killer. Good killer. Now go to your bed."

Cerberus whimpered her way on arthritic legs into the soiled doggie sofa. Satisfied, Hades turned on Hermes with a stare as hard as an anvil and veins of coal bulging in his neck.

Then the blacksmith of the gods staggered forward into the light, dropped to his knees, and begged. "Find her! Find my Persephone!"

Hermes didn't understand. Was this another trick?

"She's gone. Something's happened to her. I know it."

"Damn right something's happened to her. Where is she?"

"Yes! Where is she? You must save her!"

It was like they were speaking two different languages.

"Where did you take her?"

"Take her? No. No, no, no, no, no…" Hades began rocking back and forth. His sunken eyes swept the cavernous room before returning to Hermes. He grabbed and pawed at his nephew. The calluses on his hands felt like pumice. "You must find her."

Hades moaned like an abandoned cub. Tears paved through the dirt and ash that coated his silver beard. "I miss her. I miss her so much!"

Hermes looked to the sky for a Hail Mary. "Jesus."

"I know she tells you everything."

Hermes nodded. She had told him of all the torture and suffering by her husband's hand.

"Then you know I love her!"

"You don't love her," Hermes spat. "You don't know how to love."

"I forbid you to say that!"

Hades flew from the floor, his hands suddenly finding Hermes' neck. The old god reeked of cabbage and sour milk. Hermes easily threw him off, and—unable to control the fury—stuck his Converse in his uncle's chest and kicked him onto his back.

That was for Persephone.

It brought him no satisfaction. *Well, maybe a little.*

Cerberus leapt up, hackles raised, and growled, but Hades threw out a palm from the floor. "NO! STAY!" He turned back to Hermes. "You all think I'm heartless. I have feelings, just like the rest of you."

"Where is she?"

"I told you, I don't know." Hades pushed himself off the ground and rubbed his brittle elbows. "I can love. I have dimensions. Layers. All sorts of sides you don't know about. My internal life is rich. Did I not give Orpheus his wife?"

"And take her from him again."

"He knew the rules!"

Hermes had been there when Orpheus was allowed to lead his wife out of the Underworld. Only, Hades added a catch. Orpheus could only have the love of his life returned under the condition he never look back to see if she was behind him—not until they completed the agonizingly long journey to Earth. Of course Orpheus looked back. Another one of Hades's cruel games. "You used his love against him."

Hades waved that off. "It's not my fault he couldn't follow simple instructions. Love is faith. He wasn't worthy."

"Love is love!"

"Orpheus came to Hell. Entered my realm!" His tone abruptly softened. "Did Persephone tell you how I've tried?"

Was the bastard seeking compassion? When he had none to spare for his wife? The god had no shame. Hermes towered with disdain, burying Hades in his shadow. "She did. Every insult. Every act of torture."

"Torture?! She said I tortured her? With what? Flowers and gifts? Go to Zeus. You tell him I didn't do this." Hades patted Hermes on the chest like he was Cerberus.

"Zeus didn't send me."

Hades blinked, utterly confused. "Then who did?"

"No one sent me."

Hades smiled; his eyes cleared and sparked with pride. "Let me pour you a drink."

It wasn't an invitation. Hades turned and swayed precariously, suddenly unsure, as if a breeze blew the thought from his mind. Then he walked away.

A skeptical Hermes retrieved his gun and followed.

"I need a damn drink!" Hades bellowed into the air.

Hermes trailed his uncle in disbelief. Persephone hadn't exaggerated the deterioration. Rooms were abandoned halfway through renovations. Trash lay in piles, halls sealed off with plastic, furniture covered in mildewed sheets. All the while, Hades rambled, half of which Hermes couldn't understand.

Hades thrust open two gilded doors and glided into a murky ballroom, the diamond-studded dance floor coated in dust, save for a well-trodden path to the bar.

"Just one drink won't kill you. Nothing can kill us!"

Hermes hesitated on the dance floor, his distrust of Hades as deep as his disdain.

One drink.

A cheerful Hades slipped behind the bar and smiled as Hermes leaned against the marble banister. Cheerful? Hades was especially mercurial this millennium.

Stone mugs cluttered the bartop, chipped and broken, as if Hades had recently entertained a gathering of boisterous gods. But there'd been no guests. Hermes pictured his uncle hosting cocktail parties where he drank with imaginary subjects. Were the voices comforting to the Mad King? Did he reenact his glory days and tell the same stories over and over? Had Hades slipped eternally into the fog?

Hermes squirmed, eager to continue his search. The King must know something about his kingdom, right? He willed patience. Persephone was here somewhere. Winter on Earth could only mean she was in the Underworld. The idea that she was being held captive in some other realm was possible, if illogical and utterly terrifying. No, she was here somewhere, a prisoner in her own home, which was also a prison. And who placed the narcissus in her cabin? Who secretly cultivated the blossoms in the orchard?

Each clue screamed Hades, whom Hermes watched search his stash, the lack of booze agitating him and making his movements jerky as he slammed one empty bottle down after another. Glasses trembled and crashed to the floor. It was a sad, disconcerting display.

"Damnit!"

"I'm fine," Hermes said with a wince.

"I'll find it, I'll find it—not to worry."

After a tense moment, his shoulders rolled and Hades came back to life. He plucked a dusty bottle from a dusty shelf and wiped the grime off the label. Alcohol gleefully sloshed within.

"Ah-ha! A fine vintage. Adequate. The Aztecs call it *te-quail-la*." He overturned two large mugs and poured liberally. The King then closed his eyes and drained his tequila while Hermes pretended to imbibe. Hades sighed with satisfaction. "Not divine, but close. So very close."

"You know," Hermes said, leaning over the bar, "Hell has really gone to hell."

"All the good help is Catholic these days." Hades shrugged. Tequila splashed over the bar as he refilled his mug and then topped off Hermes, whose cup already overflowed. "I heard a line recently: 'Better to reign in Hell than serve in Heaven.' Ha!"

"John Milton."

"Yeah, well, fuck this Milton. What does he know?"

"It was about Satan, not you." Hermes worried he had inadvertently entered a geriatric time suck. Yet how to escape without reigniting the god's temper? If Hades began opining about his golf swing, fixing cars, or prostate issues, Hermes was determined to make a run for it.

"Satan would never have said that." Hades downed his shot and promptly refilled their mugs, not realizing—or perhaps forgetting—that Hermes still had not touched his drink.

"The story is fiction," Hermes explained. "A poem."

"A poem? That's not poetry." Hades enjoyed holding court, unfurling his opinions as fact. And in this realm, they were. "Satan was and always will be a sore loser. Spends all his time trying to overthrow Heaven. Him and Priapus with their eternal hard-ons—it's unbearable. You know, I could never understand the lechery and the sin part. What's sin? What constitutes a virtuous soul? How the fuck should I know?! What a dull job it is to judge others. It's beneath a god to sit in judgment. Let the humans do that to each other. They are experts at it, after all."

After listening to Hades, Hermes finally needed that drink. The tequila was nearly divine.

"I always wished we were as clever as the Egyptians," Hades bloviated. Hermes tried to jump in with his planned interrogation, but once Hades was on a roll, there was no getting a word in. "Maat's feather—what a revelation! That's a policy we should have instituted right from the start. Weighing the heart—so eloquent. And simple! I always admired Anubis. The whole battle over the soul, Satan and his war of Sin—it's ludicrous. So focused on ambition he lost sight of what truly matters."

Right when Hermes was genuinely interested in what he had to say, Hades lapsed into silence. A vacant look drained his face, spaced out like a politician with a blank teleprompter.

"Yes?"

Hades startled back, not realizing he had drifted off. "Yes, what?"

"You were going to tell me what truly matters?"

"What matters…? What matters…? Truly, what matters…What truly matters!" Hades poured himself another drink, clearly stalling. He took a slow sip. Apparently what came next required lubrication. "What truly matters is…balance."

He wobbled unsteadily then set the mug down sideways. It rolled off the bar and onto the floor. "I don't want my brother's throne. I don't need it. Everyone thinks I am set on it, that I am some Satan progenitor. I am not. I serve here—that is enough for me. So why must I be demonized? Because I rule over the dead? What's the problem with that? It's because we all fear death, even us immortals. That's what this disdain is—it hides their fear. I've made this place my own and cared for it. The rules are the rules, and I'll be damned if anyone breaks one of my rules."

He swung his gaze to the empty dance floor as if the music still played. "We are not the only eternal beings. Thoughts, ideas, words, misconceptions, are eternal. 'Nay, seek not to speak soothingly to me of death, glorious Odysseus. I should choose, so I might live on earth, to serve as the hireling of another, of some portionless man whose livelihood was but small, rather than to be lord over all the dead that have perished…'" Hades released a melancholy exhale. "Now that is poetry."

Hermes recognized the recitation. The words were spoken by Achilles to Odysseus in the Underworld so many eons ago, immortalized by Homer. If only Homer knew how much those words would haunt the ages.

The Hades before him still cut a mighty figure, but his stare betrayed the weight of a weary soul.

"Ajax would rather be the lowest among humans than I. And that's only one passage. So many condemnations of my reign and of my realm. I have heard and read all of them. I remember every insult, every detestable line. Are they not unfair to me? These poems and passages and plays ripple through minds, infecting mortals and gods. I ask you: did Zeus ever hear me? Did he ever seek my counsel as he did the others? Why was I not granted a seat among his twelve? Am I so worthless? All the ages I've wished to know, and now it appears we are past answers, and I can't face another eternity in such unknowing. There are so many eternities." Tequila dripped down his beard. "But I will play my part, as I have faithfully thus far. The counterweight. I serve that almighty antidote to Chaos. I serve Balance."

Some battles never end.

Almost effortlessly, Hermes dredged up a poem of his own: "'But Hermes met me, with his golden wand, barring the way—a boy whose lip was downy in the first bloom of manhood…so he seemed.'" The simple passage had haunted him for over a thousand years, recalled at each of his innumerable failures, every time he had been scorned and dismissed.

Hades had been listening intently. "Literary assassins."

"We both have a beef with Homer," Hermes said, and after a moment of silence, Hades burst into laughter that shook the room. Hermes momentarily forgot the animosity for his uncle and joined in the catharsis. United in grievance, underestimated and marginalized. They both wore the same chip on the shoulder.

Hermes sobered and pushed his tequila away, blaming the spirits for this detour. "Why hold onto the past a moment longer? What would be the point now?"

"Right," Hades boomed, confiscating Hermes' drink. "What would be the point? Nobody worships us anymore. The coffers are dry. I don't know what's going on up there."

"The real question is, what's going on down here?"

Hades peered frightfully over the rim of the mug. "I don't know."

"Hades doesn't know?" Hermes mocked.

Hades growled back like Cerberus. "I. Don't. Know."

"You're Hades."

Hades downed the shot, started to pour another, when Hermes flattened the mug with his hand. *Wham!* Tequila and stoneware exploded across the ballroom. The assertiveness stunned Hades, who studied his ruined drink to avoid the accountability that now bore down on him in the form of a rogue nephew.

"I…I've lost control."

"And there it is." The truth he'd avoided for so long. Hades lifted his heavy gaze to Hermes. A fog rolled in over his damp eyes, dimming any wits behind them. His countenance diminished, an exhaustion that mirrored the realm. Hermes witnessed the waning in real time and realized he would soon lose Hades to the gloom, and then the King would be worthless.

"Zeus?" Hades searched Hermes. His eyes brightened, a ray of joy piercing the clouds. "Brother! Welcome! What brings you here?"

Great. Now Hermes had to deal with a full-blown senior moment.

"I'm not Zeus," Hermes attempted to redirect Hades, but it was too late. Hades was already rummaging for another bottle and another set of mugs. The tape was stuck on loop.

"I'll pour you a drink. You'll tell me everything—everything of Heaven and Earth." Hades, who secretly worshiped his older brother Zeus, had the insufferable excitement of a superfan meeting his idol. "The dead speak so little to me and I'm hesitant to ask them of life. I mean, who wants to be that guy?"

Hades stopped to give an overeager chuckle. It was objectively pathetic, and despite the geriatric-response training he received that one summer holed up in a Des Moines nursing home, Hermes had to intervene.

He reached across the bar and gently grasped his uncle's hand. The touch froze Hades in place as if by magic. His eyes widened with shame; his bottom lip trembled. Hades struggled to understand what was happening to him.

"Zeus?"

"He's not here. It's Hermes."

"Hermes?"

"Yes."

"You…" Hades snarled. "What are you doing here?"

"I'm here for Persephone."

"Of course you are…you…you incester mongrel."

Hermes yanked back his hand as if he had mistakenly grabbed a hot pan and shot up from the barstool. It had been an age since anyone flung that insidious rumor at him. Hermes was sorry he ever felt sorry for the monster.

"I banish you!" Hades screamed.

"You already did that."

"I did?" Hades quieted. "Why are you here then?"

"I'm here for Persephone," Hermes repeated.

That jarred something loose. Hades again looked out on his ballroom and sniffed the air. "Her scent lingers. Honeysuckle…jasmine…she was here. I remember."

Hermes disregarded the insult. "Wait. She was here? You saw her then? Where?!"

But Hades wasn't listening. He swept around the bar and across the ballroom.

Finally. We're going nowhere but getting somewhere.

They hastily descended into the catacombs, which had been spared the many palace remodels. The hem of Hades' bathrobe swished in the dark. Hermes followed the ghost of a god. To find his way, Hades ran his fingers along the wall until he came upon a large switch, which he pumped several times. Miner lights crackled to life over an earthen vault supported by great stone ribs. The naves between each column displayed skeletons of long-slayed monsters. Hades charged after the current into his museum of unnatural history.

This causeway was actually a bridge. The trophies rose from a chasm on either side. Hermes struggled to identify some of the fearsome and legendary beasts once commanded by the Titans, vanquished in the Great War over the Universe.

The bridge led them to a small ledge chiseled into the side of an underground mountain. A rectangular opening—dark and oozing serial-killer vibes—was cut into the stone. Hades gestured toward the entrance with a look of pride that begged for recognition. The sound of dripping water echoed off the cliffs. Hermes no longer feared a trap, but he wasn't on board either. All of this could end with Hades showing Hermes his toenail collection. For all his doubts, however, it would be counterproductive to turn back now.

Hermes plunged inside.

It was a literal man cave, complete with a frayed leather La-Z-Boy and a shag rug. Olympic memorabilia, old posters, framed proclamations, and laurel wreaths decorated the walls. Scrolls and old newspapers buried a battered billiard table. Several skeletons had been repurposed to hang coats and hats, while a monster's horn dispensed toilet paper. A weary bottle of hand lotion Hermes wished he could unsee rested on a side table with a pallet of moisturizer nearby.

Hades moved about the cave lighting oil lamps.

"Very nice," Hermes forced out the compliment. Because it was all just so awkward, he turned to the rabbit-ear television set. "Do you actually get reception down here?"

"Intermittent," Hades said as a flame singed his beard. "Marvelous things. But I didn't bring you here to watch my programs." He purposefully approached a large stone ark, muttering random syllables to himself, sounding like a car engine refusing to turn over.

Hermes had failed to notice the cabinet when he first entered, but now it was impossible to look anywhere else. Dominating the man cave, it appeared to be made from a substance both liquid and metal, soaking up the light from a single candle flickering at its base while radiating the most exquisite glow. Hermes kept his distance. Who knew what the master hoarder kept locked within?

The ark may as well have had a neon sign that said: REALLY VALUABLE DIVINE SHIT. It spurred Hermes to reexamine the room. A violent tapestry of dismembered thieves was strung along the walls, impaled by a series of booby traps. More dismantled snares were piled behind a pinball machine. Back at the entrance, a perfect rectangular block of stone stood ready to seal the exit. Hell forbid that. Before Hades had turned this bit of real estate into his clubhouse, it had apparently been a vault—a well-protected one at that.

Hades loudly cleared his throat, drawing Hermes' attention back to him. This was the denouement—the reason Hades brought him to his holy of testosterone holies. Cracking his fingers for dramatic effect, Hades shoved his weight into the ark.

With a coital exhale, the ark's twin doors spread open. An overzealous golden light flooded the cave. It was a tad much. Textbook cliché. Even so, a classic was still a classic.

Hermes let out an audible gasp. Hades stepped aside like a game-show host to fully reveal the illuminated face within the glow.

The Thracian helmet was cast in bronze. Shields swept across the cheeks, eyes delineated by a slender nose guard. Every part of it contained intricate reliefs carved by the most exquisite of craftsmen—hands blessed by the gods. A metal stallion leapt from the helmet's crown, bucking into the air. It was the most valuable treasure Hades owned—other than Persephone.

Every Greek, divine or not, knew of this armor. There were few items as coveted.

Hermes' jaw was embarrassingly slack with awe. "The Helm of Darkness."

Hades puffed out his chest, pulled his shoulders back, and stood tall. "For you," he said.

"You're…you're granting me your Helm?" Hermes practically did the pee-pee dance, but he had to act cool.

Like, pretend it's no big deal.

"Yes," Hades whispered dramatically, carefully hoisting the Helm from its berth. He slowly rotated to Hermes, a majestic moment that demanded slow motion, and spotlights, and soaring orchestral music.

He relished theatricality. Then Hades opened his mouth. "You're either on a quest or royally screwed. I think both."

Hermes frowned. "Thanks."

"I believe I let you borrow this helmet once before, and you wore it to slay some giant for me..."

Hades continued, "Yes, it was quite the plan I devised...so you know what it does."

Of course Hermes knew what it did. Otherwise known as the Cap of Invisibility, the Helm's divine power would enshroud its wearer in a mist of darkness, blinding all enemies but leaving the wearer with perfect vision. Forged by the same ancient Cyclops that created Zeus' famed lightning bolt and Poseidon's trident, this helmet was the divine symbol of Hades and his power. At times, he would permit other gods and demigods to wear it, but only for occasions of extreme significance or battles of an epic nature—and certainly with strings attached. Hades was extremely picky when it came to lending out any of his divine stuff.

Hermes had indeed "borrowed" this helmet once. Although *borrowed* might be too generous a word. Hermes had sort of taken it without permission to slay Hippolytus, a murderous old giant who had long avoided slaughter after the downfall of the Titans. To be fair, he only nabbed the precious Helm after learning that Hippolytus was plotting a sling-based terrorist attack against Mount Olympus. Hippolytus never saw Hermes coming—literally.

Hermes became an instant celebrity for the victory, fatefully embarrassing Hades in the process. It was on Mount Olympus, during the celebration in Hermes' honor, that the much younger and cockier god arrogantly decided to return the stolen Helm to its rightful owner. Hermes should have known the warning signs when Hades accepted the Helm without incident, a slight, amused smile curdling under his beard.

Hades had whispered to Hermes, "Don't worry, my most beloved nephew, I will help you carry the burden of this sudden, unwanted fame."

Without warning, Hades shunted Hermes aside and addressed the crowd of gods, demigods, mortal poets, and philosophers, taking it upon himself to recite the tale of how Hermes felled the giant Hippolytus. It went something like this:

On the eve of the Anthesteria festival, Hades summoned Hermes to the Underworld to share some dire news. Based on a rumor gathered by his agents of the Underworld, Hades feared an impending assault upon Mount Olympus and his oblivious brother Zeus. He ordered Hermes to travel to Earth and the realm of the giants to discover what foul plot brewed among that bitter race of monsters. The ever-obedient Hermes dutifully did as instructed, and while hiding inside the giants' privy—amid a mountain of shit (such was the Messenger's dedication)—Hermes overheard the devious scheme. Posthaste, a devastatingly pungent Hermes returned to beg the magnificent God of the Underworld to save his father and the Heavenly Realm. The wise and cunning Hades formulated a strategy to slay the dangerous giant, presented Hermes with his sacred Helm, and with a few words of paternal wisdom and a blessing, sent the Messenger off.

With that, Hades wrapped his arm around Hermes and proclaimed him hero (lowercase *h*). In the ruckus of toasts and thunderous applause, Hades turned to the boy-god with a private, wicked grin that could have slain the giant on its own.

"You'll always be just a messenger. Henceforth, it'll be my name chiseled first on this legend. Be grateful you didn't have to fly into the sun to learn the lesson."

Now Hermes relived the moment, the rage rising anew, as Hades polished a spot on the helmet's crown with his robe. Once finished, Hades thrust the Helm at his disobedient nephew.

If only it had been this easy last time.

The urge to rub this moment in Hades' face subsided. It was strange to keep finding common cause with someone he despised.

"I'm sorry there's no ceremony," Hades said.

"I don't need trumpets."

"Once, that was all you craved. You're not a messenger anymore."

"Guess not." Hermes unceremoniously stuffed the Helm inside his backpack and started to leave—only something held him back.

"I can't forgive you," he said to his uncle.

"No one can," Hades said. "Use my Helm, do whatever you must. Find her. Bring her home. Her home, wherever that may be on Earth. Home is not…here."

Hermes slung the bag over his shoulder and was stopped a second time as Hades grabbed him by the elbow. When Hermes looked into the god's eyes, Hades uttered the one word he had never spoken in his immortal life: "Please."

Hermes nodded. And Hades released him. And that was that.

Blessed by the Lord of the Dead, Hermes swiftly departed. As he passed over the great bridge, a strangled cry echoed out from the man cave and halted Hermes mid-step. Hades' voice rose in a wail, calling for his imaginary guards. His precious ark was empty, and something very important had been stolen from him.

Hermes pressed on, up to the palace, never once turning back.

In the Underworld, one never looked back.

CHAPTER SIXTEEN

The Olympians are Luddites compared to Hades.

Garish fluorescent tubes flickered on over the royal garage. Hermes grinned. Sometimes you had to bow—and indeed he gave a little flourish to acknowledge the King. Hades knew how to travel in style.

Pack-rat Hades was an avid collector of anything transportation. It was one of his minor infatuations, more favored than his collection of antique chamber pots but less than his instruments of torture. Before him, Hermes had his choice of Viking ships and chariots, American muscle cars, and everything in between. The collection was helpfully organized between land and sea (it was still a sacrilege that the humans could fly), and subcategorized by purpose: war, pleasure, or more war. His reflection leapt across waxed hoods as he strolled through the age of gasoline. An important part of any quest was the steed.

Grave robbers had pried open several of the garage doors like the lids on a tin can and had pilfered and looted to their hearts' content. Mostly they stole chariots and carriages. Not many souls were in possession of a driver's license, and certainly none could operate a tank. Earlier, Hermes was sad to have discovered the royal stables emptied. Every one of Hades' prized black stallions had been absconded with. Now that was a shame.

Fortunately, Hermes was left a considerable number of options. Besides, who wanted to gallivant across the lands of the dead in a chariot? Not Hermes. The frigates and triremes would be ostentatious, not to mention impractical. Hermes needed something with speed first, class second. Quiet would be ideal. The roar of a Mustang would turn too many dead heads, so would a motorcycle or tank.

Hermes settled on the Bentley GT convertible, a corner office suite on wheels. Call him childish, but he liked the logo of two little chrome wings on the hood. Color? Black. *Duh.* Hades only rolled in black. Red-accented gray interior. Classy. He retrieved the key tucked under the rim of the driver's-side tire and savored that heavenly new-car smell.

His tushy was caressed by a gentle vibration in the leather. The girl longed to run. Happy to oblige. Hermes slammed his foot on the pedal, roared out the garage and down the path of crushed bone, letting the Bentley's gears work up a nice sweat.

The back gate to the palace parted courteously, and Hermes floored it onto a road that plunged under a canopy of stone. In the rearview mirror, the palace sank behind plumes of calcium. He took one last look and felt, in his very whole bones, he would never see that nightmare again.

***

Hades wandered onto the dreary veranda in time to watch his Bentley peel through the palace gates and out of sight. *Odd*, he thought, not recalling any visitors. Something wet and salty dripped from his eyes down his cheeks. He looked up, wondering if a bird had shit on his head.

Instead, he caught a kestrel shape soar over the roof. His daughter.

Megaera landed gracelessly on the driveway like a drunk girl coming off a keg stand. Her clawed toes dug into the ground as she took a moment to absorb the pain imprinted onto each skull, femur, and fragment of bone when she helped pave this road in misery. Her leather wings folded like an accordion into her bloodied dress and she spun to the palace.

Hades ducked inside through a pair of French doors, hoping she hadn't seen him, and frantically scanned the vast hall for a place to hide. The crunch of bone from Megaera's uneven stride gave way to a sharp drumbeat of claws on stone. He slipped behind his toppled throne and peered out to watch her storm inside like she owned the place—and she very much did.

Cerberus perked up, her third head still unconscious, tongue lolled out.

"Someone stole Daddy's car…and hurt poor Cerberus. I wonder who it could be?" she called out in a sing-songy voice that echoed menacingly through the hall. One wicked look at her father's beast and the bitch whimpered in submission.

There was a chance he could make it to the doorway that led to his private chambers. It was only a few short steps, behind a column, then he would be free of his damnable daughter. The moment she looked the other way, he darted out from behind his throne.

She caught the swish of a maroon bathrobe out the corner of her eye, and his poorly obscured outline behind a candelabra. In one gust, she parted from the ground and cut him off mid-escape. Hades spun left and right like a rat trapped in the corner of a maze. Time to face the offspring. He tied the sash on his soiled robe, straightened his posture, and swung his chin at his daughter.

"Megaera," he said officiously.

Her gaze raked over his wild hair, the permanent twelve o'clock shadow, and puffy, bloodshot eyes. She sniffed and caught a whiff of remorse.

"Daddy, we never approved a visitor."

Hades flinched at "we." *The girls. My girls. My once-precious girls. Monsters, always. Once they were my monsters. And they adored me. Now they were uncontrollable monsters.* And that was a problem. Sometimes he was aware of that fact, sometimes not. Sometimes he still thought of them as his little Angels of Death, jumping into his bed to share with him their latest exploration—how they discovered a mortal would scream a new octave if you pulled out its fingernails or how they could bleed out in five minutes if you cut off its genitalia. He was so proud of them. He spoiled them, mistakenly.

Then there were the lucid moments like now, when he saw them for the cruel usurpers they had become, and it rocked him with despondence and outrage. Unfortunately, when those two emotional ingredients combined, they produced a toxic sludge of frustration and impotence. He couldn't bring himself to raise a hand to his own children, even in self-defense.

Spare the rod…the rod will be fucking used against you.

Hades was being bludgeoned to death by his own mint-condition, out-of-the-box, untouched rod.

"Daddy, you're not answering me. Why is there a visitor?"

"Visitor? I've received no one."

Hades himself wasn't entirely sure whether he was faking the dementia or truly couldn't remember, but either way, it was throwing his daughter off-kilter.

"Then this 'no one' just drove away in my birthday present."

"I don't understand…"

"You promised me the Bentleys. And someone just drove one off the palace grounds. There isn't a soul who can drive manual."

Her cotton-candy voice made him nauseous. Enough was enough.

Hades puffed out his chest. "What are you and your sisters up to?"

Megaera pressed forward. "Who was in the car?"

"Damn you, Tisiphone and Alecto! I'm tired of your disrespect. You covet my shit and conspire to take my kingdom from me. This is regi-patricide. It's treason. You'd piss on my corpse if you could kill me! But you can't and won't and you'll get nothing!"

Megaera stepped away, aghast. "Father! How could you say such cruel things? Your thoughts are corrupted, so I'll forgive you." Concern plastered her face. "I think it's time for bed. I'll put on the television for you."

"You speak slow, as if I'm a child. I'm not blind to what is happening."

In the flip of a switch, her smile vanished and her face hardened. "But you are blind. And slow. And withered. But you mustn't blame yourself."

Hades balled his fists and shook with rage. "I have been absent. No longer."

"Yes, Father. I'm sure. Now, who came to see you?"

Her black pupils were windows onto a freak show. For the first time, Hades clearly saw the full scope of their insurrection. His daughters rampaged freely as the plagues of Pandora (which, incidentally, worked for them).

"What have you done?"

"I don't like your tone."

"Tone? I'll show you more than tone if you don't answer me."

"ANSWER ME—"

Hades slapped his daughter. The shock of the blow lasted only a second. Then the Fury of jealousy and grudges drew a snake whip from her belt and cracked it across her father's face, ripping a diagonal gash from brow to cheek.

"I can't see," he cried out. His hand covered the injury as golden ichor bloomed, filling his right eye and drenching his bathrobe collar.

Cerberus bolted to protect her master. Megaera whirled around and unleashed the braids. The whip snapped over her muzzles. She squealed and cowered. The pain delighted Megaera, and she followed the crippled dog, lashing again and again.

"STOP! STOP!" Hades shouted in horror, running at Megaera to save his sweet Cerberus.

He grabbed the corner of her wing. It was slick with her sweat. Megaera twisted and seized Hades by the throat, marched him backward until he tripped and fell into his toppled throne.

Megaera had never raised a hand toward her father before. Never. She never knew she could. It was liberation. Did she feel remorse? Could she feel remorse? Remorse served as much purpose as a tonsil—in the way and prone to infection. And Hades knew his daughter especially delighted in yanking out tonsils while her victims squirmed beneath her.

Hades blinked away the ichor, his vision of Megaera gold and blurry, and his heart leapt at the beautiful and hideous thing that was of his flesh. He reached out to her with so much love it almost hurt.

She batted his hand aside.

"No, Daddy. You answer to me."

***

The universe began with a single thought, a simple *oh, hello, existence* that soon expanded—gently at first, then uncontrollably—moving inexorably in all directions and dimensions, giving birth to creation itself. Persephone exhaled, embracing the solitary part of her solitary confinement. Only thoughts mattered, and she painted the darkness of her cell with them. Otherwise, despair was eager to fill the void. Hope was but a faint flicker, a flame on a distant mountaintop.

Chains secured Persephone to the stone floor, constrained her movement. She had read the ground with her fingers, fashioning entire novels from the braille of its imperfections. Where was she imprisoned? The universe was a very large place, and the Underworld could extend beyond the physical and into the infinite world of nightmares. She could just as easily be shackled to a dream as to a cell.

The odor of rotting food clung to her clothes, which draped loose upon her emaciating frame. Occasionally she heard a guard enter the pitch-black cell to set a platter of food on the floor. Persephone knew better than to eat: a wicked trap she vowed never to fall for again. The shadow first deposited a stew of chicken baked in pomegranates, then lamb with pomegranate, quail with pomegranate, fish with pomegranate, pomegranate seeds over fruit, over everything—eventually pelted at her petulantly, kernel after kernel, because she would not yield. Every morsel was poison, meant to finish binding her to the Underworld for the remaining nine months of the year. When serving her winter sentence, Persephone could partake in the abundant, all-you-can-eat feasts of Hell. If she arrived even a minute early, or stayed a day late, the detestable rules reapplied, and the consequences would be disastrous. Eternal winter. In this void of a cell, Persephone had been stripped of her one ally in the Underworld: time.

How? The question roiled her mind. How could Hades do this to her again? She reviewed every encounter and argument, exhausting herself in speculation over which action, gesture, or word pushed Hades to revenge. The victim recast as the perp. That was life under Hades.

Hunger wrenched her body. Her muscles staged a revolt against the deprivation. She slipped her hand into a hidden pocket sewn along her waist seam and removed the last daisy given to her by Hermes. Kept close to her body, the flower had stayed vibrant as the day it bloomed. She plucked a petal and set it on her tongue, fooling her stomach for another day. Her stomach released its grip, and she settled onto her back, the daisy resting over her heart like she was a corpse.

Her fingers retraced the edges of the blossom. To survive, she would have to ration further. But for how long? Would anyone find her? What if no one was looking?

No. No, Hermes is looking. Hermes will find me.

Moaning and writhing in pain, she plucked another petal, set it on her tongue, and stuffed the flower back into her dress to prevent further temptation. The taste of summer allowed her to regain control. She rolled over and focused on that meager glow of hope.

No. It wasn't hope. It was movement. Somewhere in the dark. Her god senses felt the molecules part. Then footsteps, loud as a giant tearing through a forest.

"I hear you." Her voice was hoarse.

The intruder stopped.

She listened. A ruffle of clothes, a silk gown, a leather belt. Skin rubbing against skin. Then a scrape of metal. Flint on steel. Her guess was rewarded with a spark that burst into being like the primordial beginning. It vanished in an instant. Black again. More frustrating scrapes, as if God were cranking a gas-powered generator to kickstart creation. Where the fuck was Prometheus when you needed him? Sparks exploded and a teardrop of light tossed into the air. And over the flame appeared a pair of eyes.

"Hello?" There was only enough slack in the chain for Persephone to rise onto her knees. Her legs throbbed with cramps. She broke out into a cold sweat.

"Who are you? Speak."

"Shhh. I'm here to get you out," the darkness replied in a familiar voice.

"Hermes?!"

"Shhhh!"

Her heart fluttered uncontrollably. Freedom. Home. Summer. Sunlight. Warmth.

The flint struck again, and this time a torch exploded to life. Colors danced across her vision and she sealed her eyes.

"Hermes, it's too bright…"

Silence.

Incrementally, she peeled open her eyes, squinting through her fingers. Red and orange frustrated her ribbed vision. A silhouette shimmered within a glow radiant as the sun. Hermes had his back to her, shielding the flame. Only—his frame was too slender, too short. Crooked and unnatural. A marionette with too many joints.

The figure that was not Hermes but spoke with his voice slowly turned.

A nymph. The fire burned in her open palm, cupped as if she had rescued a baby bird, flames curling through her fingers. She was somehow impervious to pain. Her body was divided down the center—half of her charred meat, black and pink folds, no hair or lips, and a nose melted into putty, while the other half preserved the angel she had once been: face like a crescent moon, pale and angular, a countenance to grace billboards and sell perfume.

She was a before-and-after poster: hideous and beautiful.

Persephone gasped. Her chest shuddered with dread. The chains jangled as she recoiled, pushing herself farther into the prison, into the dark. But there was no way to escape. This was the monster that lurks under the bed.

"Melinoë," Persephone choked on the name.

Melinoë, Harbinger of Nightmares and Madness, smiled like a Girl Scout with a box of Thin Mints and a credit card processing machine. "Hello, Mother."

She sealed her palm into a fist and extinguished the flame—and with it, all hope.

***

A stone bridge arched high over the River Cocytus. The Bentley's tires thumped arrhythmically over the uneven cobblestones, and Hermes rolled down his window to let in the stale air. A ceaseless wail rose from the current below, where the dregs of humanity clung to the riverbanks like mollusks lamenting their fate. There was no toll to cross the first river, simply an honor system. Pay what you please. Drop a coin, begin your journey through the Underworld.

On the other side of the bridge, Hermes pulled into an abandoned service station to refuel. The pump, operated by an old-fashioned crank, tapped directly into the source. While waiting for the tank to fill, he watched the shore of the Cocytus churn with those miserable souls violently ripped from life. Unable to overcome their traumas, they had reached this first river and simply collapsed, adding their wails to the endless dirge. Sadly, they would never move forward into the afterlife.

The smell of gasoline jarred Hermes from the river. The tank had overflowed, fuel spilling down the side of his car like a child wetting his trousers. Hermes admonished himself—he couldn't afford to forget the danger here. Their grief was hypnotic, inviting him to wallow. It was the first of many tests to come. Hell was all about the tests. Tests and traps. It was very annoying. He quickly capped the tank and slipped back into the car, rolling up the windows to dampen the despair. Sure, Hermes had plenty of grief, but no time to indulge it.

Back on the road, Hermes discovered his GPS didn't work for shit. Thankfully, the Underworld had only one road. A single, unbroken strand of concrete unraveled before his headlights. The Inter-Hell Highway (the IHH) was a marked improvement over the footworn pilgrim paths that had once crisscrossed the realm. But among the lower classes, the IHH stood for Inter-Hell Hypocrisy, since most souls were still forced to trudge along those old dusty trails, which now doubled as a gutter. The highway existed for one reason: to let Hades and his consort glide between palaces unmolested by the sight of any wretched human.

It was the Lone Star rule: whether in Hell or Texas, cross as fast as you can.

His Underworld road trip was officially underway, and the mood thus far could only be described as morbid. By cosmic decree, a road trip required tunes. He tried to turn on the radio, but the damned touch-screen must have been designed by NASA engineers. He finally shouted "Radio," and the console woke with a friendly chime.

A woman with a British accent plush as 22-carat toilet paper answered, "How may I help you?"

"Radio," Hermes wearily commanded.

"Radio on." A dial appeared on the panel, allowing Hermes to scan through a narrow range of static-prone frequencies. Every station broadcasted the same crackly Jack Benny record until a disc jockey interrupted to announce they were in the middle of a spring pledge drive. An ill omen? Perhaps. What luck. Hermes nearly phoned in a contribution to ward off the bad mojo. Plus, for a donation of four diobal—or just one obol a month!—he could score a personalized tote bag.

"Radio off," Hermes ordered, resigned to let silence ride shotgun.

The first signs of (after)life crept over the landscape like a bad case of acne. Ramshackle cinder-block homes and roadside *tavernas* sprouted off the original pilgrim trail, remnants of that humbler time when devotion was about putting one foot in front of the other, not pedal to the metal. During times of war or famine, the route would be congested with souls ten across, shuffling for decades in the traffic jams, border crossing to border crossing. The trail was empty now. Occasionally, Hermes glimpsed a frightened soul scurry out of sight into the scrub.

Why frightened? he wondered.

The boonies soon morphed into suburbs, and then into a full-fledged exurb sprawl at its worst. Slums sprouted on either side of the highway in precarious, overcrowded termite mounds of insufferable humanity. The Underworld had a habit of mirroring earthly trends with the desperation of a wannabe influencer. It was a permanent side effect of being dead: a longing to be alive. And like those influencers, they could never quite get it right.

A growing rash of homeless camps slowed Hermes, forcing him to weave through clusters of souls huddled around dumpster fires. Envious glares floated through his headlights, their own progress stymied for a thousand years. At last, the highway crested a hill, and the full spectacle of Hell's first ring unspooled: the garish slums of Acheron City, a mass of tangled streets and crumbling, faceless tenements, twinkling like a circuit board. The Acheron River—otherwise known as the River of Pain, the second of the five river crossings—sparkled like a string of stolen diamonds across a hobo's neck, delineating the ugly metropolis from a vast nothingness beyond.

The River Styx had become the most famous of the Underworld's tributaries, but it was the least important. The meandering Styx started on Earth, delineating the realms before it circled through Hell nine times. No soul was ever denied passage across the River Styx. She was shallow and easy, and it had been Hermes' job to deposit the shell-shocked dead on Hades' doorstep. Once past the Styx, there was no going back. The newly departed souls could wait years to receive the ceremonial "howdy" from Hades and a half-second photo op before they began their descent into their appropriate level. The Acheron and its two sister rivers—the River Lethe and the Phlegethon—had their own stories to tell.

After a soul got the proverbial blessing from their indifferent overlord, they proceeded down the pilgrim's path to the various crossings, each requiring payment. Of course. Can't pay? Can't cross. From the swell of humanity bunched up along the Acheron, the financial burden appeared too much for the average Greek citizen. That wasn't Hermes' fault.

If you did have the proper coinage, you faced a whole host of other obstacles, boring stuff like judgment and the final decision to erase the memory of your former life—that last one guaranteeing your entrance to Paradise. Each river required that you surmount an ever-higher bar of self-awareness and self-reflection and—surprise, surprise—humility. Demonstrate those qualities, plus the coin, and you could pass to the next level. Too arrogant? Hell would put you in your place. Too certain? Hell would spin you right around. Too combative? Hell would flay your insolent ass. Wherever you failed, your journey ended. Purgatory was nothing more than the end of your line.

"Know what you don't know," was how Hermes began and ended his preflight speech to every mass of confused and frightened souls awaiting departure. It was the only bit of free advice they would receive. Most souls were too terrified to realize he was speaking the same language, let alone offering a golden nugget worth more than the loose change and lint their family provided for the afterlife.

Know what you don't know.

Know thyself muscled to the front of his mind. *Know thyself.* Hermes now wondered upon his return to the maze, not whether he could heed his own advice, but whether his advice was incomplete. *Know what you don't know…Know thyself.*

The leather steering wheel creaked under his grip. He swerved around an elderly farmer shuffling a wooden cart across the highway. What did Hermes not know?

Know thyself. The mantra of the judged and soon-to-be judged. Eternity rested on that very phrase.

Could he pass a mortal's test?

Once upon a time, Acheron City thrived, an important cog in the great industry of death. The Underworld was a series of colanders, progressively sifting the worthy from the unworthy. Now the system was broken, a clogged sink backed up with poverty.

The highway narrowed, hemmed in by shells of factories and burned-out row houses like rotten teeth in a meth addict's smile. Hermes struggled to recognize the city within this postindustrial nightmare. The trees that lined its wide boulevards had long been chopped down for firewood, and the stately apartment blocks had been subdivided into tenements. Banners of dirty laundry flapped over his sunroof. Acheron's architectural marvels once rivaled Athens and Palmyra, but now sat eroded by indifference and tagged by graffiti.

The proximity to the Acheron River made the streets dank and humid. He entered downtown and immediately found himself stuck in traffic worse than that time he accidentally blew out Manhattan's power grid. Except this jam was more zombie apocalypse than poor urban planning. Souls clogged the roads, aimlessly dragging their dead weight like lost sheep that had strayed from their pasture. He inched forward hopelessly.

"Dammit." Hermes leaned on his horn, but the dead refused to budge. They slowly turned and flipped him the bird. It didn't make sense to them that anyone would be in a rush. Who in their right mind, in this city, had a destination?

A rap fell upon his window. A woman of the night in a tight green sequin dress pressed her body against his door. Her long fingernails scratched the glass like a kitten clawing for attention.

Let me in. Let me in.

Hermes lowered the window and her dolled-up face wedged into the gap. A pair of dead eyes gleamed beneath a century of makeup. She dropped her hip back, elbow on the doorframe, to give him a good view across her breasts.

"Hi, méli, how you doin' tonight? I'm just looking for some coin to cross the river. You wanna have some fun?"

"Fun? What's fun these days?"

She cocked her head. "You new or something? You can't be new—ain't nothing or nobody new here in ages."

"Then consider me something," Hermes said.

Her heel lost its setting, and she toppled sideways, catching the side mirror before she could hit the ground. She recovered with a sexy hair flip worthy of a runway.

A crowd of beggars and prostitutes was gathering, ogling his car. Desperate to cross to the river, they could smell money. Hermes needed to hurry this transaction along.

"Where can I find a guide across the river?"

"A guide? You mean Kharon?"

Of course. Kharon.

The less Hermes appeared to know about the Underworld, the better. Gossip traveled fast in Hell. What else were the dead to do? If he turned the radio back on, that disc jockey was likely reporting on his Bentley causing a scene in Acheron.

"How'd you die?" she asked suspiciously.

"I didn't."

Her eyes swelled with greed. "You're alive?"

He watched her calculate how best to exploit him. She was as easy to read as a pop-up book. Her cleavage only accented the point. "Longer than you've been dead."

"It's been an age since I fucked anything with a pulse."

"Sounds like you should be paying me," he said.

"You got money?"

"Enough."

Her nails chittered on the window. "Enough, as in…?"

"As in enough."

She tugged at her hair and bit her lip. "Four obols. No, five."

"This an auction?"

She grinned and leaned in. "Six obols."

"Six obols?" Hermes whistled.

"Yeah, Mr. Something, that's my price."

Peasants. One obol equaled a dime, maybe less. She was haggling over pocket change. Nevertheless, he would give her the satisfaction of a victory. Why spoil it for her? He pretended to hem and haw.

"Okay," he fake relented.

"You're my lucky man! Living man!" She beamed and held out her palm. "That's three centuries off my timeline outta here."

Three centuries to make sixty cents? The poor girl. He didn't want to think how much longer this nightmare would last for her. Still, loath to reopen the bidding, he kept his heavy sack of coin out of sight.

The surrounding herd milled anxiously in the shadows, sensing a deal, as he deposited six obols in her palm, which she promptly slotted into her bra like a bouncy ride outside a supermarket. He quickly covered her mistake by placing his hand over her heart, making it look like just another indecisive customer waffling over the product.

A shudder ran through her. "Your hand…it's warm."

"You have a good soul."

To her surprise, he wedged another coin into the nape between her breasts like a magician performing a sleight of hand. The flush shined through all that makeup. She pulled out the drachma and began to hyperventilate. A drachma equaled six obols—another three centuries off her wait.

Hermes eyed the horde. "Keep that somewhere safe."

He didn't need to say it twice. She shoved the coin into the back of her mouth and swallowed. A tender kiss on his cheek followed. She used the moment to whisper in his ear: "North crossing. There's a little shack under the bridge. Don't like the dead much. So you won't find him in Acheron. Be care, that beasty's got bite."

Same old Kharon.

"Thank you."

She nodded and undocked from the Bentley as he shifted into drive. Tough afterlife.

"Anything you want, honey, you ask for Daphne!" She purred it loud enough for the rest of the street beggars to hear.

He cranked the wheel and scattered the other souls like a flock of pigeons, clearing a path for her as much for himself. In the rearview mirror, he glimpsed Daphne attempt to run in her high heels like a wounded animal. Moments later, the feral mob swallowed her. Her screams echoed after his taillights.

"I'm rooting for you, Daphne."

He sighed and turned his attention back on the boulevard of tree stumps and broken dreams. This was where he would usually shove the poor soul out of his mind as if she were last year's iPhone, but he couldn't bring himself to detach and filed the image of Daphne's gratitude away.

***

The Red-Light District hummed with greed and vice, drug deals and drunken brawls, bouncers ejecting rowdy patrons onto the street, everyone looking to lose a few minutes, hours, days, weeks, months, years of eternity. Hermes knew that routine. Putting down roots in Acheron was like spending an eternity stuck in a Vegas airport terminal. Neon flashed outside the clubs like bug zappers drawing in their victims. Limos dumped VIPs, women in fur coats and cheetah-print gowns, men in expensive coats and ridiculous hats. The lesser patrons queued miserably along the sidewalks, their cigarettes twinkling with each anxious breath.

So on Earth, as in Hell.

That oldest principle of the haves versus the have-nots would never fail. But when the elite were bottom feeders, where did that leave the rest?

Past the neon landing strip were the truly poor souls, the schmucks and schmoes who foolishly spent and gambled their coin before they had reached the crossing. Their shame burned brighter than any neon vice. They crawled into gutters and tucked into shadows, praying their loved ones would not see them—the same loved ones who placed the coin on their eyelids when they died. They had watched their family pass through Acheron, surrendering their chance for that long-awaited reunion. Sometimes a spouse refused to leave without their soulmate. The rare, touching love story. But it never lasted. Not for long. Not in Hell.

It was the wealthy of Acheron who intrigued Hermes most, the souls who chose to be the king of the garbage heap rather than cash in their coin and be a pauper in paradise.

"Better to reign in Hell than serve in Heaven," Hermes repeated. "Hades, you were right. Fuck John Milton."

A club flung open, spewing revelers into the rowdy street. Their faces were stretched in ecstasy, arms draped over one another, drunk on champagne and high cocaine. They boisterously sang Journey's "Don't Stop Believin'."

They reached the chorus and bellowed the song into the air: "Their shadows searching in the niiiiiiigggghhhhhhhht!"

CHAPTER SEVENTEEN

By all epical accounts, this was shaping up to be a bona fide journey. Though Hermes was neither a small-town girl nor a city boy from south Detroit, he was truly living in a lonely world. Oh, and his Bentley could be considered a midnight train...but not an express. More of a local. One that made far too many stops.

And the next stop was one he particularly dreaded.

Hermes exited the turnpike and dipped below the streetlights and the gloom to the underbelly of the underbelly of Acheron. The concrete dissolved to gravel and wound its way toward the shore. Behind him, the city faded into the mist. Once upon a time, the crossing was made by a punt barge anchored to a simple wooden dock on the mighty Acheron, as insignificant as a popsicle stick pasted onto the shore of the Mississippi. An expansive concrete bridge now shoved into the fog above his sunroof. Mud fanned out from the tires as Hermes rolled up on Kharon's tiny wooden shack on the shore and parked between the monstrous pylons. On the surface, the Acheron looked calm, but she cut fast and deep and could pull you under in a flash.

As was the nature of pain.

Kharon's shack, the last vestige of Hell's humble origins, sat directly beneath the bridge that replaced him. The cranky river lord had been the last holdout in the great redevelopment, refusing to budge from his bit of fetid real estate. The cabin was a pincushion of rusty nails expunged from warped planks, the exterior painted black with mold. A few shutters hung from crooked windows too covered in grime to provide a view of the glittering river. At some point, the shack had slid off its foundation and come to rest in the shallows. A dinghy beside the front door was filled with beer bottles, and another skiff tapped against the submerged side of the cabin. The place looked unfit for even the most miserable of Acheron souls, but Hermes knew better. This was just the sort of place Kharon would call home.

Hermes kept his headlights bathing the shack to assist in the snooping. If anyone had intel worth investigating, it would be the fish-and-gossip monger, Kharon. No Underworld dweller was more plugged in than the recluse. Though he hated everyone and anyone—dead or alive, god or human—he got his beak wet off their secrets. Information held value. Value meant coin. And Kharon loved coin. Ferrying souls across his river apparently didn't pay the bills. His day job put him in a plum position to pick up juicy details, news from Earth and the comings and goings of the gods. Kharon pried every morsel he could from his customers, who had no choice but to spill the beans (not the canned beans in his cabin, mind you), then sold that information to whomever was willing to pay his steep price. What he did with all that side money was one of the great mysteries.

Hermes was always down for a bit of breaking and entering, yet he felt a pang of guilt at the prospect of invading the privacy of the Underworld's most notorious loner. All the same, the door practically flung open for him, banging against the wall like a welcoming committee. Kharon's home consisted of a single room, with the kitchen resting in the river, water sloshing over the linoleum. Hermes nearly slid across the canted floor and into the furniture that had been propped up to account for the tilt. On the dry side, a pile of human, animal, and fish bones ringed a soiled mattress. As if there weren't enough signs of emotional instability, Kharon was a night-eater. There was a single chair, one table, stacks and stacks of newspapers, and a tower of canned beans—basically the Unabomber checklist. Other than everything, the cabin was cozy.

A flash of red light caught the corner of his eye. A modem blinked inside the fireplace, and Hermes traced an Ethernet cable to a corner of the room and under a mildewed sheet. He ripped off the duvet to find an ancient Gateway computer. He clicked and shook the mouse, bracing for some very specific porn to appear on the monitor. The desktop struggled awake, and Hermes sighed with relief: the browser window contained an application for a boating license from the Florida DMV. Hermes decided not to check the search history, but if Kharon was connected to the internet, he probably had a cell phone.

He held up his own phone. His bars switched from *No Service* to *Searching*.

Hermes stepped back outside and was teased by a single bar of reception. He walked to the shore, then to the car, where his phone lost signal again. Finding service of any kind in the Underworld was torture. There had to be a hotspot somewhere. *Hotspot.* Technology was godlike in the way it changed the definitions of so many words. To burn always meant to destroy.

The screen brightened under the immense shadow of the overpass.

The bridge! Hermes was bound to get service up there.

He hopped back in his Bentley and reversed up the driveway to rejoin the tangle of city streets, hitting a dozen dead ends and a thousand roundabouts before he found the right on-ramp. A large *Acheron River Crossing* billboard, Swiss-cheesed with bullet holes and tagged in graffiti, stood at the beginning of the bridge. Over the river, the thick fog shrouded the Acheron below and the road ahead.

"Brights," Hermes ordered his vehicular assistant.

High beams illuminated the sudden absence of road ahead. Hermes slammed the brakes, screeching to a stop several feet from the end of the bridge. His phone flung out of his hand into the dash, cracking the screen.

That was close. Hermes exhaled. "Old fashioned. Make it a double."

"I'm sorry, I can't help you with that," the Bentley answered.

Worth a try.

He retrieved his phone from the floor and exited the car, which was precariously perched at the ledge. The Acheron slithered down below, its diamond surface shimmering through the dark. The missing section of the bridge had been hoisted above, supported by four towers where anchor chains connected to the winches. A tollbooth the size and shape of a coffin stood empty. Someone with a sense of gallows humor had spray-painted *payment in cash, plastic, or blood* on the front.

No job security in Hell, Hermes figured. He felt sorry for his former pal.

His palm suddenly glowed, and Hermes grinned as he checked the screen. One bar! He paced the width of the bridge. The phone returned to *Searching…* Two steps left. *Searching…* Ten paces right. Two bars! Good enough. He punched in a text:

Delivery in. Toll unmanned. Need a ferryman. WTF LOLZ HKHK XOXOXO

Send. That ought to do it. The hugs and kisses were just to fuck with him a little. The clinical term was *haphephobia*—the fear of touching or being touched—though Kharon was a-okay in the physical intimidation department. Half-a-phobia.

A true pal, Hermes enjoyed tormenting Kharon, driving him up the homophobic, genophobic, whatever-phobic wall. Not his problem if Kharon was a nine-foot-tall, bat-eared neurotic. Hermes had once chased Kharon around the palace butt-naked after the river lord had walked in on him doing the dirty deed. Hermes had insisted he just wanted to give Kharon a hug. Kharon and his chubby dragon legs had never moved so fast. Persephone later chastised him for being juvenile and terrifying the curmudgeonly beast, while Hades was furious that Hermes had ruined Kharon's fearsome reputation for a millennium. *I just wanted a hug!*

Hermes stared at the screen with the impatience of a teenager firing off a text to a girl right after the first date ends. If only he could will a response. Unfortunately, Kharon moved for no one.

***

Kharon—official Ferryman of the Underworld, inspiration for the Grim Reaper (his protégé, little-known fact), who once led souls in his barge across the Acheron River—leaned back in his skiff and readjusted the wool fisherman's cap on his watermelon head, tucking his pointed ears under the rim to keep them warm. He wore a large and weathered mackintosh coat, not because it was fashionable for those who trafficked in the morbid, but because it was damn nippy working on the river. A lantern hung off the prow of his flat-bottomed skiff that drifted directionless down a wide, marshy stretch of the Acheron, where it converged with the Styx. Reeds infested the banks, and patches of black silt shifted with the currents. White crows nested in the thicker groves, while owls claimed a copse of oaks—the two competing clans battling to feast on the dead. Kharon wasn't a bird enthusiast; he just liked conflict. At present, a murder of ghost crows flew in a halo over the marsh. He lifted his oars and made for their hunting grounds.

Business had been slow for the last few hundred decades. Those with coin to cross his river had done so. Which made it odd, Kharon had recently noted, that new souls were popping up in Acheron with cash. But what happened in Acheron wasn't his business. These days, his business was to stay out of business. He did as he was told, and he was told very little. Occasionally, while fishing his river, he would glance up to that monstrosity of a bridge and catch a few souls slipping back into Acheron City, accompanied by the Furies. Souls typically—exclusively—moved in one direction: toward paradise. They never used to go backward.

Let it be, he would tell himself. The Furies were no good and out of his jurisdiction. Kharon had the same aversion to curiosity as he had toward sweets—he partook sparingly, and only to satisfy a craving or fill boredom. Otherwise, he preferred the savory nights out on his skiff with no one to bother him. Boats were his refuge, and for too long he had to share them with whiny earthlings who talked too much, cried too much, wet themselves, or threw up, tried to bargain, tried to cheat. He shivered just thinking about the wretched centuries. The only downside to retirement was the lack of any Underworld pension plan or even a goddamn rec center. Hell did not have safety nets. Broke and irrelevant, there was only so much fishing and mending skiffs he could do before he got antsy. And Kharon was antsy.

He set the oars in the rowlocks and drifted. The crows cawed, angry at his intrusion. A bag of pebbles waited for the pests at his feet. He reached down, and more caws came in reply. They recognized his bag-o-pebbles and knew he could throw stones with speed and accuracy. Kharon nailed the first crow between the eyes. It plummeted like a jet shot down in a dogfight. The rest fled, wings beating loudly in retreat, screeching out, "Screw you, screw you."

Line hooked, no bait, Kharon tossed a nice cast, rested his pole, and settled back to watch the slack slither below the surface. Steam puffed from his bent nose. His rotten beard brushed the planks as he nodded off. Those heavy eyelids sealed shut like coffins. Great snores soon wheezed over the lake.

Right when he was getting some quality shut-eye, the bell on his rod suddenly began to jingle. His head jerked up as if the line had been tied off to his beard. The bell jingled a little more, then jangled, then erupted in a furious jingle-jangle. The prow of his boat turned to the shore, where his catch was headed. *A big one!* Kharon grinned lustily and grabbed his pole.

"Trying to swim my river, are ya? Not the Acheron, not Kharon's river!" he shouted down the lure.

Leathery, calloused hands ferociously reeled in the line—hands hardened by salt air and years punting his dinghy. Rope bunched at his feet until a bloated corpse flopped into the skiff. The dead man coughed up water and squirmed to dislodge the massive meat hook gored under his shoulder blade. His mouth opened and closed, but he was too frightened to make a sound.

Another soul foolish enough to cross my river without paying the toll. It took courage to attempt a subaqueous stroll, because the dead could feel pain. Trudging across the bottom of the marsh was nothing less than drowning—only you couldn't die again. Most who tried the illegal crossing this way failed, as an echo of self-preservation would inevitably kick in and the soul would break for the surface, where Kharon, or something worse, waited. Worse were the crows. Or owls. A.K.A. talons. They liked the eyes.

Kharon flashed a crocodile smile of coffee-stained incisors. "No one gets a free ride."

"I...I...have coin..." The corpse dug into a fanny pack.

Kharon swatted the man's waterlogged hand aside and yanked off his pouch to rummage for coin. The time for bargaining was past. The corpse scrambled for the side of the boat, but Kharon grabbed his slippery neck before he could leap overboard. Kharon hated handling humans.

BREEP!

The unwelcome buzz shocked his crotch. He twisted for his pocket and pulled out his BlackBerry. Could it actually be a text? No one texted Kharon. Other than *them*...Them. He shivered at the thought and prayed it was anyone else.

The BlackBerry was the size of a matchbook in his giant palm. While trying to unlock the blasted thing, his corpse slipped free and belly-flopped into the water with a sorry splash. Kharon didn't even register the escape.

Kharon hated his damn BlackBerry and its miniature keyboard. New technology was slow to hit the Underworld. The bottom of the river was littered with broken flip phones and pagers thanks to his temper. A vendor in Acheron City once tried to trick him into buying an "apple" with a fanciful story about touching this and pressing that, and Kharon had stalked away with the willies. *Nonsense, all of it!* BlackBerries, then apples. *What was next*, he harrumphed. Raspberries? Bananas? Humans made no sense.

The crows swooped in on the corpse. The marsh water roiled with splashing and annoying cries for help. Kharon turned his back on the noise to focus on deciphering the text message. The screens were so tiny. It was from *Delivery Boy*.

The Messenger God had sent him a text. *Oh, what irony*, he thought with a grin. It was like a symphony conductor going "fuck it" and putting on a cassette. Then the realization that he was texted by Hermes made him squirm with uncomfortable emotions. Kharon didn't like emotions. Was he supposed to respond? How should he respond? This was like deciding if he should attend his high school reunion all over again—and he never went to school! Kharon wasn't even a demigod. Immortal, yes. Strong, yes. Employed, kind of. Favored, no. Kharon was the bus driver everlasting, a minimum-wage, low-on-the-totem, blue-collar monster.

He took a deep breath and exhaled.

Why am I so riled? One text message throws me into a panic?

He stared at the cracked screen. The text was unexpected, though not exactly unexpected. He had been planning for and on Hermes' return. *Remember? Focus. Visualize. Never close an open door.* Kharon was an avid reciter of motivational psychology—bargain-bin self-help phrases to shore up his conviction. *Possibilities. Opportunities. Visualize.* The knot in his stomach loosened.

He smushed his response into the keyboard, cursing each wrong key-stroke, ignoring the desperate pleas for help off his starboard. A crow took off with an eyeball in its talons, dinner for the little ones. Blood dripped on his screen, and Kharon accidentally hit send before he could finish.

***

FUV U HEERM MET in doa

Either Kharon was being cryptic or he'd had a stroke.

Hermes started to reply when a foul breeze slapped his face with the stench of rotting meat.

Acheron mist whipped into fancy, fun curly-qs as Megaera landed on the bridge. Her wings immediately slurped back into her spine like eels into a den. Hermes acutely felt the dead end nipping at the heels of his sneakers, cornered on a diving board above the River of Pain. Her eyes slid over him and attached to the Bentley.

"Mine," she said, with the entitlement of a Beverly Hills teen at the dealership.

He squinted and wedged his hands on his hips with a smile. "My, my, my. Is that step-niece-cousin Megaera? Look at you. You're all grown up."

"Very funny. Must be Hermes. And that's my Benny. I see you've put a dent in the hood. You'll have to pay for that."

My Benny? He glanced back at the microscopic blemish just above the ornament. "I can buff that out."

Her upper lip trembled. "You don't take other people's stuff without asking."

"Funny you should say that—"

"I hear it's quite chilly on Earth these days." Her grin burned like acid. Hermes weighed whether this was just Megaera being her usual catty self or something extra.

"First the humans complain it's too hot, now it's too cold," he said. "They can't make up their minds."

"Yeah, well, they don't matter. Their brains are small. Why are you here?"

"House call."

"No one's home. So back to yours, go back to Earth."

"Earth isn't home."

"Then that's too bad for you. Because you're not welcome here." She snapped her fingers and the fog behind her ignited into flames.

Three empusai hobbled forward like walking tiki torches at a far-right rally. The androgynous demons had the legs of mares and their hair was braided with flames. The last empusa Hermes encountered had been stalking the Silk Road. This particular breed of demon had a thing for harassing travelers, disguising themselves as beautiful women to lure men into bed before devouring them.

Hermes was semi-disappointed they had skipped the seduction, but their presence had its desired effect. He suddenly became hyperaware of the distance between his hand and the holster hidden at his waist.

"You have the guards of Hecate," he said.

"They jumped ship," Megaera declared proudly.

"I'm only trying to pass the Acheron."

"Without paying the toll?"

Her empusai cackled as if she had just delivered the funniest joke. They gave their boss a fealty typically reserved for the campus queen bee, bitch supreme. Hermes didn't have patience for high school bullshit; he'd had enough of that on Olympus.

"Where are your sisters? Where is Alecto?"

The smirk vanished from her face. "Not here."

Like all younger siblings since time immemorial, Megaera was perpetually outshined and unappreciated. It didn't help that she was the embodiment of jealousy. Hermes liked ruffling feathers and pushing buttons—and, judging by her sneer, clearly had.

"So they sent you to check on me?"

"No one sent me. I can act on my own."

Sounds familiar.

"Yeah?" Hermes mocked. "On your own? Good for you. You're a big girl now."

Push.

"You're trying to rile me," she responded haughtily, pretending she wasn't bothered.

"And smart! All the best traits."

Push. Push. Push. Ruffle. Ruffle. Ruffle.

"Screw you, Hermes! And your sarcasm and condescension, and the rest of the gods too, while we're at it."

Her empusai flared on her behalf like novelty birthday candles.

Hermes had gone and done it. He'd pissed Megaera off. It wasn't hard. She was a grease fire in a fast-food kitchen. Angering Megaera, if he was being honest with himself, didn't really serve a purpose, except maybe for its entertainment value. He would have meditated further on his poor choices except a braid of flames suddenly whipped across his face. Those mare legs could really hoof it in a pinch.

An empusa pinned his arms back while a second wrapped around his neck. A headbutt sent sparks flying and the demon in his face crumpled with an indented forehead. Hermes flipped over the empusa behind him and kicked her spine like it was a door during a police raid. The demon folded and twitched hideously, hooves clopping on the concrete like a tap dancer hooked up to jumper cables.

The last empusa rammed him just as he attempted to draw his pistol. The gun was wedged between them, locked in place, as the force of her charge pushed him backward toward the ledge. His god-flesh sizzled. Her skull was a blowtorch, fusing to his ribs. He gritted through the searing pain and managed to shift the gun barrel just enough to empty the magazine. Each bullet rocked them as it exited the chamber and tore through her clavicle, until she finally extinguished in his arms. An acrid cloud of smoke billowed, smelling of burnt hair and meat. The final demon crumbled, and he swatted at the choking fumes, hacking up a foul black phlegm.

The smoke cleared and Megaera was gone. His eyes rolled up. She was circling somewhere in the mist.

Not good. Hermes raced to the nearest winch and ripped out the ratchet that held the gears in place. The braided cable snapped loose with a loud whir, the drum spinning wildly as the raised portion of the bridge fell. It slammed down like a hand swatting a bug, the impact sending shockwaves rippling through the bridge. The suspension towers buckled.

He darted out of the way as steel beams collapsed across the road and cascaded into the river. The Bentley's alarm bleated, headlights stuttering a frantic SOS.

A violent burst of air squeezed him from both sides like spikes driven into his eardrums. Talons latched onto his shoulders and yanked him off the bridge. Hell twisted around him as he fought a sickening wave of vertigo.

"You shouldn't be here!" Megaera screamed over the thunder of her wings. Serpents wormed out of the open sores along her legs, slithering down her calves toward him, hissing menacingly like burning coals doused in water.

"Grow up!" he shouted back.

At least a dozen snakes coiled around her ankles and reared to strike. Hermes dodged one and flung another into the fog. Megaera continued to climb.

"You had everything! We had nothing!"

Below his sneakers, the bridge was quickly receding, now just visible by the sparks of his flashing headlights. The car alarm was swallowed by the roar of wind. They were high enough to do a skydiving stunt—only he didn't have a parachute, and his tiny wings were built for running, not flying.

He sensed her weight subtly shift, readying to drop him. A snake struck his neck. Another set of fangs sank into the back of his hand. Their poison shot through his veins like liquid fire. He gritted his teeth and took the pain like a champ. The emptiness below his feet had snapped him into life-or-death focus.

Her talons loosened. He was ready.

The moment she released her grip, he grabbed her ankle. Every snake rushed him, going for any bit of exposed flesh, injecting him with venom over and over and over.

Caught by surprise, Megaera's primal instincts took over. She violently jerked and twisted to break his grip from her legs, then desperately pummeled the top of his head with her fists. What she failed to account for was the overdose of venom. It had unintentionally shorted out his pain receptors and thrown him into a godly rage. With relentless focus, he scaled her body. He reached her waist and drove his thumb into the pressure point where her wings fused with her spine.

The reaction was instantaneous. Her left wing collapsed like a folding fan. They stalled midair, locked in an awkward lover's embrace.

Then they plummeted, bouncing and spiraling as Megaera frantically beat her remaining wing. The bridge rapidly unfurled through the mist.

No safe landing. Only concrete and steel ribs. Hermes measured the collapsing distance as they fell and fell and fell.

At the last moment, he kicked off Megaera, launching himself toward the bridge and sending her hurtling over the river. He cratered the roof of the tollbooth as she vanished below the railing. The splash echoed over Acheron City like a wrecking ball dropped on a champagne tower.

Megaera's screams raked the silence, sharp and unrelenting. Hermes staggered out from the wreckage, dizzy from the carnival-ride fall. Shaking off pieces of timber, he peered over the side of the bridge.

Below, Megaera thrashed and wailed, which only made it worse. A trillion shards of glass shimmered and swept over her body, drawing her away in a current of melted silica. It was death by a thousand cuts, a torment Hermes wouldn't wish on anyone. By the time the river drained into the marshland, Megaera would be mince.

If only he'd spared her long enough to glean some information and then kill her.

A mercy stroke. Not this torture.

No, she would have preferred it this way.

Megaera was a Fury, and the Furies trafficked in suffering. It was only fitting she died the way she lived: swimming in immeasurable pain.

A burst of Bon Jovi echoed from his pocket. "Livin' on a Prayer" was his ringtone.

He shook off the horror and turned his back on the River of Irony to read the latest text.

Persps Grove. Hr.

Deciphering the message, Hermes deduced Kharon wanted to meet in Persephone's Grove in one hour. Normally, Kharon would have escorted him across his river, as he did with any VIP guest—a rule he enforced religiously. Permitting Hermes to cross his bridge untaxed? It would give him plausible deniability if any more shit hit the celestial fan. And meeting him at the grove? Perfect setting for a clandestine meeting—or an ambush.

He turned back to the Acheron, its polite clinking of glass so incongruous, like a thousand groomsmen competing for the first toast at a wedding. There was no sign of Megaera. Even without her confession, Hermes was certain she had played a role in Persephone's disappearance. Foul Megaera surely deserved to die. Yet he couldn't shake the aftershock of battle, a sour taste of guilt sticking to the roof of his mouth. He hushed the car alarm, sensing eyes watching from lofty perches and dark corners.

Don't be fooled by the sibling rivalry, he reminded himself. The Fury girls were inseparable. Once Alecto and Tisiphone discovered their sister's murder, which would be imminent, they would be honor bound to hunt him to the ends of the Underworld and beyond. To kill one Fury meant he would have to kill them all.

What fury hath Hermes wrought?

Hermes had no doubt: there would be hell to pay.

CHAPTER EIGHTEEN

THE GRASSY MEADOWS OF Asphodel rolled endlessly beyond the Bentley's headlights. White blossoms twinkled above the stalks, little starfish faces upturned, hypnotized by the eternal darkness. A scent of honey and lavender dripped through his sealed windows. Unambitious souls considered Asphodel the next best thing to paradise, and the desperate convinced themselves it was good enough. The neutral didn't have an opinion. Hermes didn't care for the bland, Zoloft canvas of Asphodel, but he had business there.

Hermes almost missed the turnoff among the monotony, steering onto a lonely dirt road, kicking up dust through the prairie. Eventually, a stand of poplars marshaled, swaying as he drove past like the criminally insane fighting against straitjackets. The once-magnificent garden Hades had commissioned for his new bride appeared almost like an afterthought. The roadside attraction had fallen into disrepair long before it was bypassed by the highway. It was not the Underworld's largest donut or the Museum of Boogers That Look Like Celebrities. Those were still visited by hordes of perplexed souls whose insatiable curiosity took them on the lengthy detour off their pilgrimage routes. Another fiendish trap.

Hermes parked outside the ornate iron gates that had been ripped from their hinges for reasons unknown. They now lay across the entrance, rusting into history. Unfortunately, Hermes hadn't brought his machete or bug spray. Weeds and vines had conquered the meticulous beds and footpaths, and no amount of glyphosate would turn back the insurgency now.

He bushwhacked his way through a seashell of petrified rose bushes that wrapped a parched fountain, cursing Kharon for choosing such a lousy spot for their clandestine rendezvous. At the center of the maze was the *pièce de résistance*, a large vanity sculpture recasting the moment of Persephone's abduction into a romantic triumph. A heroic-looking Hades had been carved galloping into the air as he cradled an adoring Persephone in one arm. The other arm was a broken stump. No wonder Persephone hated her garden.

A burble of anxious mumbling rose from behind a gazebo. Tracking the sputtering, Hermes unclipped his holster, primed for the draw. The threat slowly emerged from the dead topiary: an old soul in a disheveled, two-shouldered toga circled the fountain, compulsively tugging on his thick beard, hunched forward and resembling a teapot, hair frazzled and sticking out at all angles like the bushes from whence he emerged. The lack of spatial awareness and personal hygiene were the hallmarks of genius. The old soul had likely been a philosopher. Hermes withdrew his hand from his pistol. The ruminations persisted, even as the philosopher bypassed Hermes like Pac-Man gobbling up dots through a digital maze.

"Horses would worship horses. Cattle gods for the cattle." The philosopher abruptly stopped to angrily address a rose bush. "You've banished me, but you can't silence me! You'll be proven wrong. The whole hears. They all lead back to one God!"

He cackled triumphantly and lapped Hermes on another circuit around the fountain, making wild gesticulations while consumed in his ramblings.

"Yo, Plato!" Hermes jogged after the philosopher.

(He wasn't the actual Plato. Plato was likely in some cave smoking a bowl. It was more a term of endearment, really. Besides, one self-involved academic wackadoo with their head up their ass was like any other.)

"It is not enough to think. One must know. One must know. One…"

Hermes caught up to the philosopher and walked backward in front of him. "Where can I find the Ferryman around here?"

"One…the whole…cattle and horses…cattle and horses…cattle like cattle…let them paint, and you'll see."

"That all sounds fascinating. But I'm looking for Kharon. Big? Ugly? Bat ears? Ring a bell?"

"The cattle…the cattle…"

"Dude, you have the protector of herds right in front of you."

The philosopher excitedly shook his hands in the air. "Give them hands instead of hooves! Hands instead of hooves!"

Frustration mounted. "I'll get Prometheus right on that. Now, can you—"

"They shall draw for you! Draw their cattle gods. Cattle like cattle…"

It was pointless. Not even a god could break through his self-absorption. The rambling philosopher peeled away into the bramble. Poor bastard. Purgatory indeed.

A murder of crows cawed, circling the air in the distance. Hermes recalled Kharon's strong feelings toward crows. In that he hated them. And the crows hated him. The birds were perhaps objectively and collectively the smarter of the two species, but despite their mutual hatred, there was a certain codependency. The crows feasted on the flesh of Kharon's discarded souls, and Kharon enjoyed hurting animals.

Heading in the direction of the murder, Hermes followed a causeway flanked by dead poplars originally planted to symbolize Persephone's virginal beauty and growth into a queen. Dried leaves crunched like broken glass. In this part of the garden, an infestation of souls took advantage of the neglect to make Asphodel their eternal resting place. Shopping carts squeaked and squealed down paths. Every bench had become a makeshift bed. None of the vagrants made eye contact with Hermes, their blank stares searching, never settling. These souls led indifferent lives and were now cursed to a death of indifference. Asphodel was the black hole between the couch cushions of Acheron and Elysium. Those who rested here lived their short lives on Earth neither in piety nor sin. They were the silent ones who watched catastrophes from distant shores, who clung to the road as armies marched past to war, who refused to harm their fellow man but closed their doors on those in need. They stood in the middle, and because they neither inflicted harm nor spread virtue, their complacency followed them to the afterlife—no will to carry on further than the first crossing. So here they remained, in eternal drudgery, without desire. They wouldn't endure the danger of Acheron, nor reach paradise, or have the possibility of rebirth.

He finally found that overweight, unshaven Port Authority bus terminal of a beast seated on a bench overlooking his river, beer in paw, two six-packs by his paddle-sized boots, seven soldiers already drained. The collar was up on his dirty-brown mackintosh, half covering his oversized bat ears (which he was very self-conscious about—do not stare). His nostrils flared as Hermes joined him, and he scooted to the other side of the bench. Hermes was careful to follow Kharon's no-touch rule. No slap on the back how-are-ya, or handshake, or squeezing his scabby cheeks.

Kharon tipped his beer upside down to empty the dregs. In a ferocious jolt, he lobbed the bottle. It shattered against the head of one of the souls huddled by the shore.

"Fuck off!" Kharon shouted, and the pathetic vagrants quickly scattered, abandoning their possessions. The poor maimed soul struck by Kharon crawled away holding his bleeding head.

Hermes rolled his eyes. "Very nice."

"Like you care." Kharon grabbed another bottle and bit off the neck, sloshing beer down his coat. He chewed the glass with knobby teeth and spit out the green shards like dip. "Pests. They're just lookin' for handouts."

Hermes felt an unexpected surge of pity. "I think they're just looking."

Kharon grumbled. "Tuck 'em."

Hermes didn't understand what Kharon meant.

The beast aimed his surly gaze at Hermes' feet. "Those pixie feathers couldn't even pass for buffalo wings. Tuck 'em."

Point taken. However insensitively made. Hermes tried not to be insulted as he stuffed his wings back into his sneakers. "Where is she?"

The Ferryman smiled, wheezing as if it took a rusty boiler firing at full steam to cast more than a grimace. "No foreplay. Look at you—the Sundance Kid wants to be Butch Cassidy."

"I know she's here."

"Who are we talking about? Do you mean Lily? Big tits? Guiding virtuous souls to Paradise? I thought it was easy pickings up in the middle world."

Lily, formally known as Lethe, was also a ferrier of souls—but only across the Underworld's final river to Elysium. Oh, and once upon a time Hermes and she had a "thing." It didn't end well.

Dragging his ancient romantic history into this wasn't appreciated. Hermes shifted on the bench, allowing his jacket to part just enough to showcase the holstered firearm. The piece sobered Kharon. He held up a giant paw of a hand, eyes ever glued to his river.

"I wouldn't touch this if I were you. You've been seen. A god never travels unnoticed…"

"That also true for a goddess?"

"…most 'specially true for a god with a famous mug. One who's supposedly banished. Last I heard, Hermes isn't allowed to visit the Underworld no more."

"You're not answering my question."

"I don't have to answer your question."

"There's no summer. Spring turned to winter. Time's running out."

"Well, I've got all the time in the Underworld." Kharon rolled a slow, unhurried glance toward Hermes, lungs rumbling like pistons strong enough to crush a car. "Word spread someone killed one of the Fury sisters. The other two won't be happy."

"Megaera wasn't very helpful," Hermes said.

Kharon rocked between butt cheeks. "I may be a low Ferryman, but I'm not thick."

"Never said you were, friend."

"Huh. Friends. That what we are?"

"Depends."

"You know I require payment. And not Lily's kind, where you're on your back."

"You sure about that, big boy? Perhaps it's not Lily you're picturing on those dirty sheets of yours."

Kharon seized Hermes by the throat with fingers thick as sailor's rope, reaching all the way around his neck. Muscles and tendons creaked.

Hermes leaned into the chokehold and forced out: "She's…my…sister!"

Kharon snarled and released him.

Hermes stretched his neck and felt a few pops. "She never spoke a mean word to you."

"Irrelevant!" Kharon barked.

"She showed you kindness. You—a monster from the wrong side of the tracks; her—a goddess of the highest order—yet she treated you with dignity and respect, asked for nothing in return."

Kharon looked away, furious at his own emotions. "That she did."

"You're not doing this for me. You're doing this for her."

"These are meager times. No favors. No handouts. Not for a soul. Not for a god."

"So what do you want?"

Kharon turned back to him. "Topside access."

"No. For real. What do you want?"

Kharon grinned.

Fuck. Wouldn't matter if Kharon was the most pious little cherub in Heaven, only gods were allowed free rein to cross realms, and they did so rarely. Hermes was unique with his heavily stamped passport. And that distinction came from a job description. Celestial travel was heavily regulated as it inevitably ended in some disaster—earthquake, flood, war, unintended pregnancy. Beasts like Kharon stopped getting weekend passes altogether once the new religions butted in. The monotheists sought to erase the local mythologies and superstitions. At first, they prohibited their movements, then sought to eradicate their existence, relegate them to legend and bedtime stories.

Hermes didn't have authority to grant Kharon his wish. Nor did he know whom to ask. Gabriel? Fat chance. Gabriel expected this mess to be cleaned up with a wave of Zeus's wand (FYI, Zeus didn't have a wand). Yet again, Hermes was shit out of luck.

Nevertheless, he didn't blink.

"You sure you want access to Earth?" Hermes went on to describe the many failings of the modern world. "The humans kind of ruined the place."

"Spoken like a god who hasn't spent an eternity in hell. And I don't mind a bit of pollution. I want to roam free, see all the sights."

"A weekend for two in Las Vegas?" Hermes countered.

"I said Earth, not hell on Earth." Kharon sensed his advantage and held firm.

Hermes interlocked his fingers to prevent himself from smashing Kharon's nose.

"Oh, we got the inter-web now," Kharon said, amused to no end. "I've seen enough to know what we're missing."

"Then you also know that without Persephone, Earth is freezing to death. And this little problem affects all the gods."

Kharon held firm. "'Course it does."

"Topside..." Hermes repeated. "Help me, they'll pay."

"You mean all those fancy new gods? And I can hide in the shadows. I'm guessing they're the ones who've got your wings in a vice, probably sent down here to do their bidding. You got to sell out your own religion to save them from a bit of nippy weather, which only makes them look like fools for denying we exist. Never mind winter won't end. Right now I'm not seeing a problem. I help you, you rescue the Goddess of Spring, we're all still under their big-ass thumb. I never got any respect from my gods—why should I expect any gratitude from these strange, greedy new ones? Ugly old monster like me's got to look out for himself."

"Ah, Kharon, you're not ugly. You gotta stop selling yourself short."

"But..." Kharon held up a pudgy finger. "If I wait for this to play out, maybe I wouldn't need them or you? Maybe I could claim a religion for myself? That would be somethin', wouldn' it?"

"And rule over frozen humans?"

"They've got central heating."

"I don't care about the new gods, or saving Earth...I care about Persephone."

Kharon clutched his cold heart. "I'm touched."

"They didn't send me. Zeus is out. Hades is out. This is just me. Asking you."

Kharon spun on the bench to face Hermes, jaw ajar, the extortion momentarily forgotten. "Since when did Hermes go without a leash?"

"I'm a free agent."

"So you're delivering your own messages. Guess you think you're a man now." Kharon chuckled at his joke. "You think you can manage without Daddy's protection?"

"Since when did he ever intercede on my behalf? I've always been a bastard."

"I guess it was only a matter of time. Was it your insolence or your arrogance that did it in the end?"

"I wasn't excommunicated. There's simply no one left."

"Except your sister." Kharon took a sip of beer and lapsed into silence.

"I think I always knew, but I didn't want to see it. And now that I've seen Olympus—"

"The Dodekatheon disbanded. You know what? I think you're fright-ened."

Was it that obvious?

Hermes was frightened. He'd never been so scared in his immortal life. But he would never admit it.

Kharon shook his head. "We've been disrespected long enough, you and me. Good riddance. The new gods should be next—we should be so lucky. To whom should I offer my prayers for such an outcome?"

"Come spring, we tell them all to fuck off. You and me."

"A strongly worded message. Is that all? Is that all it takes?"

"You're forgetting how important Persephone is in this equation. She's my sister. I'm her brother. And you're—"

"—I'm your friend."

"Are you?"

Kharon scanned the park, considering the proposal. Hermes waited patiently, feeling his ass crack fill with sweat. He had just agreed to a price he couldn't pay. There was being a trickster and then there was lying—and for the first time it felt like there was a distinction. What other choice did Hermes have? Kharon and his realpolitik had forced his hand.

The Ferryman finally leaned over the bench, lowered his voice, and obscured his mouth as if there were someone who could overhear or read his lips. "You had a hunch to find your way to Elysium. They want to take her to Tartaros. You think Hades fucks hard? Try the Titans. That's as far's I've heard. Them Fury girls really got themselves a grudge. They got no love for their stepmom, and you're on your own down here. And when I say 'you're on your own,' I mean it. There's been grumbling for centu-ries—outsiders coming down here, spreading all sorts of talk. Talk about new beginnings…People down here've been listening."

Outsiders. Hermes recalled the voice from the sweat lodge journey. More than one.

"I keep to myself," Kharon added, anticipating his next question, "so I never seen them—him, her, god, goddess, whoever or whatever they are. No one has, truth be told. They comes around. They leaves. Sets all sorts of trouble in motion." Kharon tossed aside his warm beer and reached for a cold one. "And if I took Persephone, hypothetically speaking, I'd want to starve her first."

"Jesus," Hermes uttered, a verbal tic he'd picked up on Earth. He real-ly had to stop invoking someone else's deity. "They want her to eat."

"Kind of a waste to catch and release," Kharon said. "They get her to eat, they finish the job Hades started. No more in-and-out queen. A permanent resident."

"Anything else?" Hermes hoped not. He had enough groundbreaking revelations to last through Armageddon.

"Now that you mention it—since you need to cross the rivers—there's only one judge holding the keys to Hell. Whole checks-and-balances thing fell apart once old Hades was pushed aside."

The next stage in the Underworld after Asphodel was judgment. Hades despised the process of weighing sins against virtues. Too tedious. It was like solving math equations all day, except it wasn't five minus one—it was more like she saved five kittens minus that one time she fucked her sister's husband. Most human lives were boring. Occasionally, you got the juicy soul, a serial killer or a hero. Most of the time it was the court clerk reading out a grocery list of minor infractions, from stealing a loaf of bread to masturbating in a temple.

To make the judicial process fair, Hades instituted some sound policies, the most important and influential of which was his creation of a three-judge court to determine if a soul was destined for eternal damnation and punishment. No judge could rule unilaterally. The three judges, once mortal kings, were chosen to represent Europe, Asia, and Africa. Of course, Hades undermined his own system, picking two competent judges but falling in love with the most despicable despot in the ancient world and placing him on the bench.

"Minos," Hermes said.

Kharon beamed like a child staring down his birthday cake. "Your old pal."

From his seat of power in Persia, Minos ruled the conquered peoples of Mongolia, China, and beyond with an iron fist. A man of short stature, Minos overcompensated in about every possible way, even riding his battle horse astride an ingeniously designed bumper seat, giving him a generous height of six feet four inches—every inch was important. The armor-clad legs dangling down his stallion were filled with bundled silk. To preserve his impressive stature, no one was ever permitted to see Minos in private.

One day, as Minos observed a battalion practice maneuvers, he decided to inspire his troops. Yanking the mechanism that kicked his false foot to cue the mount, he cantered in front of his infantry wall. While riding the line, an archer—unaware of the royal interruption—accidentally loosed a practice arrow that hit the king's steed in the rump. The horse reared, bucking Minos out of his height contraption. The fake legs, still mounted on the saddle, had kept the steed in a steady gallop while Minos trumpeted orders into his horse's ass.

The soldiers made the mistake of laughing.

The entire battalion was put to the sword. One thousand soldiers, Minos' finest, beheaded for six days without pause. Minos commissioned a pyramid of their skulls. No one ever laughed at the king again. In fact, no one laughed ever again. Period. The army of Minos became so feared in part because, even when camped at night before a battle, his soldiers never made a sound.

No one understood why Hades chose Minos. The gods whispered that Hades was simply too embarrassed after parading Minos around Mount Olympus before all the dirty details came to light. Bad vetting. Instead, Hades doubled down and defended the tyrant as if he were an adopted son.

The other two judges—Rhadamanthys of Africa and Aiakos of Europe—were safer choices, kings who ruled with wisdom and justice and inspired their peoples to great heights of thought, literature, art, and music. Together, the three judges held the metaphorical keys to the realm. But there was an actual set of keys. Hades kept losing them, so he gave them to Aiakos. The master keys opened the gates on the next river Hermes needed to cross.

And now Minos had them.

Hermes sighed. "Great."

"He's still a laughingstock after the trick you pulled. Just not in public."

Why was all his past behavior coming back to bite him in the ass? After learning Minos had an aversion to public humiliation, Hermes just couldn't help himself.

"Minos hired the Keres to keep his new lot secure," Kharon said, continuing to string together pearls of bad news. "Doesn't matter if you're good or bad—for the right price, anyone can go to Paradise."

Hermes launched up from the bench, as if standing could somehow staunch the tide of shit. And the tide had most definitely risen over his head. He looked over the weeds and the lost souls. Part of him wanted to grab a soiled blanket, a few flattened cardboard boxes, and curl up alongside them. Zero-calorie paradise suddenly sounded satisfying enough.

"Hey, Sundance," Kharon called out, and Hermes turned back around to his old friend. Kharon flashed his pearly yellows. "Topside."

CHAPTER NINETEEN

Sometimes the body falls into pain like a pillow. Persephone wished that were true. Her screams pushed into the silk, filled its folds, praying this bed of knives would give way so she could tumble further into some other world—any other world. Her hands were pinned. Fabric strangled in their clutch. The word *nubile* gushed from coarse lips, and it echoed in her mind.

Nubile.

Hades's new favorite word, whispered a thousand times. All at once, the stabbing released. Hades appeared above her, his brute body a rope of knots, wiry beard braided with ribbons of coal that scored her back. A calloused palm ran along her cold cheek, then petted her hair, dragging across her skull. He lifted her to face him as if she were a doll. Fiery eyes. He took in his prize, all unwrapped beneath him.

"You are now officially my queen," he oozed, his hot breath sticking to her skin.

She was no one's queen.

Surrounding the king's bed, a ring of candelabras threw shadows upon a chorus of chthonian faces. Hades had gathered his slaves, attendants, and nobles to watch Persephone's great humiliation. She struggled to focus, ultimately finding purchase on three white gowns among a sea of black togas. Alecto, Tisiphone, and Megaera made glorious silhouettes, their hair tucked into laurel crowns. The eldest two glimmered with their father's triumph. Yet the small Megaera stepped backward into the shadow of her sisters, fear in the rapid rise of her chest. Persephone glimpsed a single tear spill down her cheek—the only one shed for her. Megaera instantly covered her face, at once ashamed and enthralled watching her stepmother suffer.

Persephone played the part: a doe felled, hoisted, and flayed. Every muscle in her body went limp. She felt nothing, severed as she was from her life by a poisoned arrow. She gave Hades her profile and, oddly, thought of an infant waking in an empty home, and no one to hear its wail.

"We must rejoice!" Hades erupted at his consort from some distant place where people still laughed, played music, and recited poetry.

Persephone's gaze moved from the Furies to a slender frame stepping into the room with the grace of a dancer. Her face was hidden beneath a saffron veil. Her feet whispered as she parted bodies like beaded curtains. She removed her hood to reveal dread incarnate.

Melinoë immediately sucked the oxygen out of the room. She was, after all, a walking nightmare. *But how was she here?* Persephone thought. Melinoë was not yet born, would not be conceived for another century, by another incestuous crime, by another heartless god—her husband's brother, her father: Zeus.

Persephone managed to look away. Her gaze landed on a pitiful woman, clothed in rags with matted hair and chained to the ground. This stranger was watching her. It took a moment for Persephone to realize the woman was no stranger, but an older version of herself. Not older, for Persephone never aged, but a Persephone wiser and more miserable than a goddess had any right to be. The chained Persephone had clearly suffered, but was not undone. Not yet. She watched herself watching her, and thought how strange to find a stranger version of herself—stranger yet, here.

As soon as the thought entered her head, the world around the two Persephones began to dissolve. The Furies, Hades, and attendants all vanished like smoke, leaving the two goddesses: one chained to her marital bed, the other chained to the floor. The younger Persephone on the bed lifted herself to speak first, to say hello to the older Persephone on the floor, both in such miserable states.

"What are you doing here?" the Persephone chained to the bed asked, and a moment later, she blinked out of existence.

The Persephone chained to the floor was all that remained now. She focused on the cuffs biting into her wrists and ankles. Pain was real. Pain and Melinoë. The rest was a nightmare. Pain kept her grounded, kept her sane. One after another, Melinoë brought those nightmares crashing down upon her—every past horror, each one an attempt to break her mother's iron will.

Reliving the trauma depleted Persephone in a way she had not felt since the day Hades destroyed her innocence. *It's only a movie,* she told herself. She could almost hear the film through the projector. *Click, click, click, click.*

No, the clicking was real. It was a hobble that favored Melinoë's left foot over her mangled right. Her daughter was pacing the cell. Something in the last memory had disturbed the harbinger of nightmares. Persephone grabbed at the lifeline, pulling herself out of the despair. *Click, click, click, click.*

"Melinoë," Persephone called out softly. "Melinoë. Are you all right? That wasn't easy to see. Do you want to talk about it?" Melinoë ignored her mother, busy whispering to a clay lamp hooked on her charred finger. The worthless artifact was shaped like a sparrow, but she clutched it as if it were a treasure. A blue flame quivered from the beak as Melinoë spoke to it.

This is my neglect.

Persephone, aching with guilt, watched her daughter pace. *Click, click, click, click.* The girl had spent her immortality channeling night-mares. Anyone would go mad. Meanwhile, Persephone had been absent, and no amount of family therapy could heal that wound. Melinoë would never turn to her mother. Their only miserable bond was a single night, and the rape that defined it from all the ages before and after.

But there was a second night: the night Hades discovered Melinoë's existence. The girl had been sheltered among the nymphs of Elysium, not because Persephone was afraid of her husband, but because she couldn't bear what her bastard daughter represented. Hades forced Persephone to witness as Melinoë was mauled by beasts and tortured, turned from mis-take to monster. Perhaps if Melinoë had known love from her first breath, it wouldn't have been so easy for Hades to push her from angel to demon.

Persephone was ready to accept the blame.

A surge of resilience and compassion lifted her onto her knees. *Click, click, click, click.*

"I'm ready," she said to her daughter. "Whatever you need to do." *Click, click—*

Melinoë shifted from the lamp to her supplicating mother and con-sidered the gesture.

Persephone closed her eyes and quietly braced for the next wave of vengeance.

Silence.

After minutes of silence, Persephone took a chance and peeled open one eye. Her daughter remained exactly in the same position, simply watching her. Perhaps Melinoë mistook this for another act of defiance.

Without warning, Melinoë jerked to life, folding onto the floor in front of Persephone, legs splayed at her side like a broken doll. She placed the little bird lamp between them and propped herself to favor her un-maimed half. Her deformed arm curled over her breast the way a bird held an injured wing. The wound was no weakness. One look into Melinoë's eyes could drive a man to madness.

"What shall we play for you next?" Melinoë asked in a hundred whis-pers, each a ghost from Persephone's past. "How about the night I was conceived? Your passionate affair."

"Rape," Persephone corrected.

"It's always rape with you. How about the night I was mutilated?"

"I don't think you want to relive that any more than I."

"How compassionate of you, Mother. Where was your compassion when Hades took me to the river's edge? When he pressed me into the flames?"

Persephone sighed. How could she explain what few could understand. "Any protest would have made it worse."

Melinoë threw her head back and laughed. "Excuses! But I like them!"

Her laughter rippled and multiplied, suffocating the room. Persephone heard Hermes and Hades, Demeter, and Zeus, and a thousand others join in.

"Please. Don't," Persephone pleaded.

The whispers ceased.

"He punished me for your crime," Melinoë said, speaking only for herself. Her voice quivered. "Mother…Mother…"

A surge of affection filled Persephone's heart. She tried to crawl to her daughter, but the chains prevented her. "Oh, Melinoë? What is it?"

Melinoë turned cold as winter. "You brought this on yourself."

Persephone recoiled as if her daughter were a viper rearing to strike.

"I vote for the day you abandoned your bastard daughter to your abusive husband. When he released the wolves of Hell to prey upon me." As Melinoë spoke, her dress darkened, blood pooled around her. The sound of howling wolves filled the cell.

"A gift, from one victim to another."

Four-legged predators stalked the shadows, circling beyond the light. Melinoë's blood crept toward the lamp, a black stain widening across the light. There was a ferocious snarl, and the wolves suddenly leapt from the darkness onto Melinoë, shredding her body.

"Mother!" Melinoë screamed. "Mother! Help me! Please!"

Persephone lunged to save her daughter. The shackles yanked her back, cut into her wrists and ankles. "Release me! I can help! Please!"

The screams intensified. Persephone pressed her hands to her ears at the sound of tearing flesh.

"Only you can stop this!"

"How?" Persephone sobbed, listening to the muffled carnage. "How?!"

A pomegranate rolled into the light and came to rest in front of Persephone. The cursed fruit.

Melinoë smiled between the jerking haunches, the wolves ripping her to pieces. "Are you ready to eat?"

The ghosts picked up the question and repeated it like a chant. "*Ready to eat? Ready to eat? Ready to eat?*"

Persephone reached out and took the pomegranate as if it were a live grenade. She shoved her thumb into the crown and squeezed. The shell crushed, purple juice exploded from her fist.

"Eat!" the voices demanded.

The wolves turned on Persephone and snarled. She hurled the pomegranate at them, and the nightmare shattered. The cell returned to mother and daughter.

Furious, Melinoë smashed the sparrow lamp with her mangled hand. The oil within splashed over her, and the flames leapt off the floor onto her skin. Melinoë jumped to her feet, towering over Persephone. The fire spread up her arm, engulfing the charred half of her face.

"You did this to me!"

Melinoë blazed like a torch. The light was too bright after so much darkness.

Persephone shut her eyes and burrowed herself into pain.

CHAPTER TWENTY

IT DIDN'T SIT EASY watching Hermes sink down the garden path into the eternal weeds. That's what friends do, right? Friends extort friends. The grouchy, reclusive river lord always fumbled the social game. If Hermes were indeed Kharon's friend, he was his only friend.

Kharon needed to escape this foul mood. Sulking when he had the upper hand and played it beautifully—what sort of Underworld beast was he? A low monster besting a god, now that was something to be proud of. Kharon lingered on the bench, hoofs swinging with pesky negative thoughts.

Kharon should be celebrating! He sold out the Furies for one hell of a deal. Miraculous, the way things worked out. *Earth! Visualize.* Now he intended to leverage that sweet deal for an even better one. Kharon mapped out his blessed future, what he wanted and how he would seize it. *Visualize.* Once that image formed in his mind's eye, he removed a little pocket notebook from his coat, which he had recently begun carrying with him at all times, and wrote down said mind-picture. This new habit had started after Kharon found a ratty paperback called *Mind Thought Power* propped atop a urinal in an Acheron bar, rabbit-eared for an inspirational thirty-second read.

Kharon's happenstance acquisition of this sacred earthly text was fate. The book contained a miraculous recipe for success. The reader needed only to envision what they wanted. Relieved at both ends, he emptied his bladder whilst filling his mind with dreams.

Kharon liked to take things that weren't his. Hence, he pocketed the book and returned to the bar, skimming through its pages over the next seven pints and three more trips to the restroom. The book promised the reader would become the world's best salesman, find a wife, and more—all of which sounded great—but sadly, it was the gods who controlled Kharon's fate.

Yet something in the author's persistence stuck like bones in the teeth. The author, Harold Shonda, said you could make millions through the power of thought. Money would simply come to you, such as finding it on the street or through a random job opportunity. Just envision it. Draw dollar signs on scraps of paper if it helped, which Kharon started doing on napkins until the bartender laughed at him and told him he didn't accept "crazy money." Kharon knocked in the corpse's teeth, stormed out, and threw the book in a dumpster. Not even a day later, Kharon found a stack of drachma piled on a curb as if it were waiting for him. Amazing in a city of beggars! So he scurried back to that alley and went dumpster diving.

Next thing, Kharon was alone in his cabin flipping to a mind-focusing exercise. With the book wedged under a lantern, he read the chapter six times, making margin notes, until he understood all the nuances. "What did he want in an immediate sense?" the book asked. Answer: a change in scenery. "Okay," said the author. "Choose a specific want, need, place, person, and focus on it. Visualize. See it in your mind." The author wrote like a psychologist moonlighting as a bar mitzvah magician. Kharon heaved a self-conscious sigh.

Where was a place on Earth Kharon wanted to go? Las Vegas? He liked the girls in those wild VHS tapes. Too many flashing lights—and it was a soulless city. New York? It had so many rivers, and Kharon liked crossing rivers. Too many humans. San Francisco? Homosexuals. Athens? Sick of Greeks. Paris? Indigestion. London? Too expensive. Berlin? Too German. India, China, Japan? More crowds. Africa? Ebola. Latin America? Catholic. Middle East? Oppressively…hot.

Then it hit him. One magical place he'd read so much about: Florida. Trashy and swampy. Plenty of fishing and future customers. Spread out and flat. Early bird specials. He liked scamming people, and apparently it was a scammer's paradise, where sulking was an official sport. So he focused on Florida, spent weeks studying Google Maps on his decrepit desktop, pushing his dial-up modem to the limits, thinking about Florida while he ate, while on the potty, while fishing, and while sleeping. He even found a town called Jupiter. It sounded vaguely Roman and therefore essentially Greek, so he browsed every street and read every Wikipedia page.

You know, research.

Florida, here I come.

So Kharon was thinking real hard about Florida at this bar—a different one, since he broke that bartender's face—and *wham*, some soul flew in shouting about Persephone's return.

But it's not winter.

The place started buzzing. More souls crowded the joint. Kharon almost left because there were too many sticky humans, but he was too intrigued. He let the dead bunch up around him when normally they'd steer clear. There hadn't been news like this in centuries. The book had insisted events would arise to support your dreams. Persephone's kidnapping couldn't be coincidental. The bar had hummed with speculation, theories, questions. *What's next for the Underworld? What's going to happen to Earth? Why would they want Persephone?* And then: *Will the gods try to rescue her?*

Kharon may not have been a part of the inner circle, but he spent enough time employed by it to learn a thing or two about the way a god's mind worked. And the one god he understood more than any other was Hermes.

Hermes would come. Hermes would do anything for Persephone... *FLORIDA.*

Did friendship have an expiration? Could a god count a low beast like Kharon as his friend? Too bad Hermes didn't want to stick around, kick back some mead, and give each other shit like the old days. Kharon missed his companion. *A companion? Get a dog.* He reached for another beer—only he had finished them all.

No more wasting time.

Lost in happy visions of Florida, Kharon stomped through the garden down to the shore, crushing the possessions of the souls who scattered at his approach. His boat was tied to a waterlogged dock, and by the time Kharon untied the moorings, he was downright nostalgic for the Underworld he would soon be leaving. Had Hermes ever noticed how the poplars listed to the faint gas flares along Hell's vaulted ceiling? How the leaves took on a viridian green in the gloom?

Kharon had noticed.

Stupid, stupid, stupid. Of course Hermes didn't notice! Hermes didn't travel to the Underworld to see Kharon. Hermes didn't care about Kharon. Hermes cared about Persephone. Therefore, Kharon didn't need to care about Hermes.

Simple math.

Kharon untethered the last rope from a piling with too much force, and the dock collapsed into the muddy bank. The boat squelched and rocked as he plopped his fat ass onto the bench. He pushed off with an oar into the gelatinous slime that passed for a river in Hell. Joining the current, Kharon planned never to set eyes on Persephone's Grove again.

Hours later and miles up shit's creek, Kharon was forced to drag his boat through a shallow canal by a towline over his shoulder. Eons ago, slaves dug this estuary to water wheat fields in a Stalin-esque collective farming experiment that Hades abandoned once he realized he really didn't care about feeding his subjects. All that remained was ankle-deep sludge and endless mosquitoes. The effort helped to work off steam. Judging by the soul-sucking silence, Kharon figured he was close enough to his destination and chained his boat to a rock.

Unlike the bogs of Acheron, this part of the Underworld was flat and dry, a whole lot of nothing and scorpions the size of rottweilers. A perfect location for the Fury Sisters to set up HQ. The Fury Sisters located their headquarters here, far off the inter-Hell highway, for its privacy. A desert colony for the depraved. Miles off, Kharon spotted the Friday night glow surrounding the open-air prison that marked their domain, impossible to miss in the dark wasteland. The hum of electric fences carried far over the flatlands.

Being away from his river made Kharon anxious.

And visiting the Furies?

Visualize. Palm trees. Jimmy Buffet. Florida.

Eclipsing the prison was the black frame of a hollow mountain honeycombed with chambers that housed the shadow demon colonies. Rumor said that if you abducted the shadow demon queen, you could control the whole hive. The rumor was recently revived when the Underworld witnessed those mountains belching up a biblical swarm like an oil derrick, plunging the entire realm into shadow as the demons surged into the hidden veins that led up to Earth. Kharon joined the rest of Acheron that day, eyes fixed earthward, watching the eclipse with utter dread.

What disturbed Kharon most was the lack of judicial review now that the Furies were in charge. Do what you want to the humans, Kharon believed, but only after they'd been appropriately judged. The Fury girls gone wild were trolling the Underworld at will, plucking souls—innocent or not—and subjecting them to their whims. The Underworld needed an overlord. Without Hades, things were getting out of hand.

Kharon avoided the pen where the Furies kept offending souls like livestock waiting for the slaughter and stuck to the shadows around the outer perimeter fence. The panopticon within was guarded by the Furies' preferred guards, the elite Cacodemons. Cacodemons were a rowdy bunch of Hell's angels, armed to the claws with hand-me-down Soviet weaponry. At the front gate, about a dozen guards were playing cards around a bonfire and, from their cackles and shrieks, piss-drunk to boot. The lax in security suggested a confidence that suggested an arrogance that suggested all the Underworld was under their dominion.

The laughter died as Kharon emerged into the firelight. A chain of solid white eyes latched onto him, glowing around the campfire like burning marshmallows.

Visualize.

Kharon tipped his cap and gave a congenial "I'm just another grunt" grunt. A series of grunts were returned, and then the cacodemons turned back to their card game. His knees almost gave out, and with a sigh of relief and a piece of nicotine gum, Kharon was on his way.

Fury Town was a desolate collection of boarded-up storefronts like a Hollywood Western at high midnight. Kharon nervously tugged at his beard, river galoshes clomping too loudly along the deserted main street. The only bustling came from a quaint boxcar diner called *Pleasantville*, the local haunt for the Underworld's torturers. A nauseating smell of burnt meat and grease wafted from the kitchen. His stomach rumbled despite his nerves. Outside the entrance, a coat rack bowed under the weight of blood-soaked aprons. Kharon popped his collar over his bat ears and lowered his cap past his eyes, hoping his odor wasn't stronger than the day's special mystery meatloaf advertised on a chalkboard sign. The mystery was human. Human meat. Demons crowded booths at the windows, devouring their not-so-mystery meatloaf, oblivious to the lone Ferryman so far from his water.

Farther ahead, a main square was filled with stolen possessions. Lobotomized souls waded among the loot, sorting and hauling away family treasures in ox-drawn carts. The main feature of the main square was a concrete municipal office, like a bouncer hunched on a stool during a slow night. Faded red banners draped from the cornices of Doric columns that graced the utilitarian façade. Torchlight flickered in the windows, menacingly proclaiming *we're open for business*. Kharon gulped in a truckload of air, plunged his hands into his pockets, and climbed the chubby steps. Time to see the mayors of Shitsville.

A revolving door vomited Kharon onto a linoleum lobby with a distinct medical complex vibe. A series of bulbs screwed into the green-tiled walls buzzed with static. The Furies had discarded the cheap stagecraft. No dungeons and fire pits here, just padded cells and waiting rooms. The banality of the Furies' palace—its *je ne sais bleakness*—was carefully curated by an expensive interior decorator. Pick a number; the girls will be with you in a minute to flay your skin.

A switchback staircase ended at the third floor, a pink hallway with white doors numbered by black Roman numerals. Each door leaked some disturbing noise—muffled, but only just so. Thin walls. They wanted you to hear, Kharon understood, as he passed a series of barely disguised horrors: an endless scream behind one door, a woman wailing from another, the sound of someone gasping for air, a man babbling, a child singing itself a lullaby, on and on. His goosebumps had goosebumps. His armpits squished with sweat, and his pace quickened.

Visualize, visualize, visualize.

The office of the Fury Sisters was fittingly located at a literal dead end. He wiped his brow with a massive kerchief once given to him by an old lady who had hung herself with the bedspread and had no more use for it, and stepped into the secretarial room.

On his way in, a heavily bundled woman bumped into him on her way out. The contact left a whiff of strawberry lip gloss as she stumbled past, briefly brushing his arm with an elegant gesture that said *excuse me, fucker, you're in my way*. In the fleeting moment, he caught sight of her bright fire-engine-red manicured nails, fingers festooned with rings adorned with owls. Her pulse fluttered on contact. His wide girth caused her to knock over a dead plant, spilling soil on the carpet. She didn't bother to set it right. And just like that, she was gone.

Her pulse.

She wasn't dead!

He hurried back to the doorway in time to catch her heels vanish around a corner. Kharon almost pursued, but oh how the Furies hated waiting. He turned back to the unmarked door from whence the mystery woman had fled. A portrait of Hades glared from behind the unmanned secretary's desk. Personal assistant to Hell's mistresses of torture—not many souls vied for the position. It chewed you up. Literally. Dread surged from his feet to his brain as he crossed the waiting room, gripped the doorknob, and froze.

Yank the door open. Step inside. Breathe. All there is to it.

Kharon kept his eyes down, focused on the single folding chair with a stained purple cushion, and promptly sat. The seat squealed with terror beneath him. The office was cramped. No windows. Three scuffed metal desks positioned in a U around him like an inquisitorial chamber. Oddly modest for girls with deiform aspirations. You would've thought they got shafted in the office lottery—except they owned the building, owned the whole damn realm. No one challenged the Furies.

Well…until now.

Alecto sat behind the desk directly in front of him, Tisiphone to his left. Megaera's absence practically reverberated through the room. He couldn't help a quick glance at the conspicuously empty desk parked on his right. Unlike Alecto's zen organization and Tisiphone's mess of scrolls and quills and ink, Megaera's desk was covered in novelty toys, bloodstained Beanie Babies, art supplies, and a framed collage of crime-scene photos. Abandoned crayons mourned Megaera's last, unfinished drawing: a little earth house in winter, icicles hanging off the roof, and naked corpses lying in the snow.

She had promise.

The impatient drumming of Tisiphone's claws snapped his attention back to the surviving sisters. Kharon's eyes darted between them, unsure whom to address. His hands felt out of place, so he folded them in his lap. He had an urge to ask about the woman who fled their office, but a jolt of good sense aborted the idea. All the while, the sisters kept him in suspense.

Tisiphone sniffed the air delicately. "You've been handling humans."

The middle sister had a bad habit of speaking first. Alecto's power came from hoarding silence, a whole ocean of it.

"Caught one this morning," Kharon said, struggling against a rip current of fear.

"You're a long way from the Acheron," Tisiphone said.

"Yes…yes," Kharon said to each sister in turn, wanting to show deference.

"Our sister was murdered. At your river. Drowned in pain."

"I can tell you where he's headed," he blurted out.

"We know," Tisiphone said. "And we know he killed our sister."

"Then what don't you know?" Only an hour ago, he arrogantly believed he'd come with all the cards, but not only was his hand worthless, it was on the chopping block.

Tisiphone leaned over her desk. "You think we don't know what's going on in our own realm? That we're so desperate as to pay you for your help?"

Kharon gulped. "My mistake, Miss Tisiphone."

"Queen Tisiphone," she corrected.

"Yes, my Queen." Kharon bowed and caught an eye roll from Alecto.

Tisiphone gave a Lady Windermere cough, signaling him to look at her. "Where he is now? That's what we don't know. Where he is. Right. At. This. Very. Moment."

Kharon's black lip curled into a grin. "Well, that's right impossible with me sitting here."

"It is," Tisiphone agreed.

They were throwing him a lifeline—but the rope could just as easily be used to hang him. Kharon had to tread carefully.

"He'll be at the River of Fire. Hermes will go to Minos to get the keys, then cross to Elysium. I know that. For a fact."

"That so?"

"Yes, my Queen. It's where I told him to go."

Tisiphone looked to Alecto, and her expression darkened. Alecto remained inscrutable, at least to Kharon. The sisters didn't need words to communicate. He wiped his wet palms on his pants and shifted nervously.

Tisiphone turned back to him. "We intend to dispatch Melinoë."

Kharon turned gray and shuddered. Every human, beast, and god got the willies from that girl. She was the death of every party and avoided like a plague. Not even the Keres, those walking petri dishes, could match the aversion awarded to Melinoë. Her very nature bothered Kharon, her ability to reach inside your mind, fish around, and use your own thoughts against you. Nevertheless, Kharon needed to get this negotiation back on track.

"I can track Hermes for you. I'm a good tracker."

"Your plan was to send Hermes to Persephone, then run to us to set it right—for a price."

Kharon felt the tightrope fraying. "I didn't know…not for certain…" he stammered. "Rumors, I heard. But if I knew, I would have sent him anywhere but Elysium. Would have sent him to you!"

"But you didn't!" Tisiphone shot out of her chair, rocking the much larger Kharon back in his seat. "We should flay your skin and—"

"What did he offer you?" Alecto interrupted, in the way a host might gently steer a conversation away from politics to safer waters.

Kharon needed a moment to compose himself. "Access to Earth."

Tisiphone began to speak, but Alecto silenced her with a withering glare and nodded for her to sit. With a scowl, she slumped into her chair, pouting like an executioner denied a decapitation.

"You understand Earth will be very different upon our ascending." Alecto intoned *ascending* like it was a brand of perfume. Her voice carried not a hint of Megaera's rage or Tisiphone's scorn. Alecto the spider wove a silk web and let you nestle in.

The firstborn, Alecto was always a perfect example of a Fury, never shying from a hard day's work. But unlike her sisters, she took special care to present herself as anything but a Fury. Here in her private office, Kharon could have mistaken her for some repressed schoolmarm.

"I believe it will be cold," Kharon said with a smirk, as if he were in on the joke. "But we're used to that down here."

"We are," Tisiphone butted in.

Alecto withdrew, aware of her younger sister's need to take center stage.

"The gods have a certain tolerance for one another that we never shared."

"Tolerance or arrangement?" Kharon added haughtily. "Seems like they've staked their claims and held the line. They arrived at a balance of power, and we're not part of it."

A glance at Alecto and her implacable bust gave him no hint whether he was on the right track or on a one-way train to torture town. Her skin writhed in the soft light of the oil lamp on her desk. The snakes that nested just below the surface were restless, wishing to be fed. She raised a fingernail and dragged it across the scars of her many self-inflicted wounds, opening fissures for the snakes to disgorge themselves. It gave him the willies.

Tisiphone stood again, casually this time, moved around her desk, and settled her tooshie on the edge. Though tall, she barely met Kharon eye to eye. Nevertheless, he reflexively shrank, wilting at her closeness.

"That's very astute of you, Kharon. How can we be a part of this arrangement? The balance of power rests on our shoulders. Our old ways hold up the new world and these new gods. Yet our gods are too distracted, too weak. They let these usurpers own the field, and we invented the game."

"The Earth will need a cleansing, reset the board," Kharon pronounced, feeling slightly more secure. One of the girls. Then he overstepped. "We'll make sure of it."

Tisiphone reached over and placed a hand on his inner thigh. "That we will."

Kharon instantly froze. Someone was touching him down there. *Was this how you got an STD?* Normally, he would remove the offending touch with maximum violence. But Tisiphone knew he wouldn't dare—not even raise a squeak of protest. Contact, flesh to flesh: nothing could be worse to the River Lord. His brain was screaming inside.

He forced his gaze onto Tisiphone, who was pleased by his discomfort. Alecto watched the torture with her trademark indifference, as if it were an old sitcom rerun.

"And what must come next, once these new gods are overthrown?" Tisiphone asked, jarring him back into his body.

"New ones will need to be installed." His voice croaked.

Tisiphone removed her hand and smiled.

"Our thoughts exactly," said Alecto as her serpents braided themselves into a choker around her neck. Their tongues flicked the air. The lamp seemed to flicker in response.

Kharon looked into her approving eyes, beheld by so many in the throes of agony, and suddenly relaxed.

The future looked positively lovely.

CHAPTER TWENTY-ONE

THE TOP OF THE five-story parking structure gave Hermes a commanding view of the challenge ahead. He rapped his knuckles on the hood of his car, parked beside a bevy of rusted chariots. Around him, corridors of glass architectural gems rippled with a golden-hour glow from the Phlegethon. Tamed into a concrete channel, the river of fire passed safely through the city while choking the air with toxic smoke. The smog was a kaleidoscope of pollution—coils of burgundy and black swirling up from the lava. Outside the city, the river of fire continued, scorching the horizon as if time froze at sunset. The infernal sight reminded Hermes of the sacking of Rome.

Minos had been busy solidifying his new authority. The city—which had no name, since it never existed during Hades's reign—had sprouted around the newly privatized judicial system. Preying on the migrating souls so close to paradise was easy pickings. They practically gave away their coin. All roads led to a glass honeycomb skyscraper better suited for a Dubai skyline. The *Tower of Babel* sequel was currently being built directly atop the Underworld's original white marble courthouse.

Hermes finally got to use his fancy pair of spy binoculars and aimed them at the construction pit that ringed the judicial erection. Slaves toiled away, hauling boulders like ants along ridges and scaffolding, excavating raw ore, smelting said ore into beams, and then lifting those beams by cranes up the side of the building. The top floors were a frame of girders that nearly touched the rim of the Underworld. Each time another floor was added, the *Tantalus* skyscraper sank a little deeper from its own weight and fell out of reach.

A line of souls zigzagged through the city, block after block after block—beyond the scope of what his binoculars could see—snaking down into the construction pit and finally ending at the courthouse. Countless souls queued for their chance to spin the wheel of judgment. They slept on the ground or in tents, played games of stones to pass the time, tended cook fires and pens of goats. There were no fast passes in Hell. The poor souls were forced to live their afterlife like a millennial waiting for Sunday brunch.

Hermes spent several hours studying the courthouse and deemed it impregnable. Cacodemons patrolled the ground while a swarm of Keres incessantly buzzed the perimeter. The Keres were a vicious breed of winged, vulture-like daimons that began pestering mankind when Pandora first released them from their box. They flocked to conflict and especially loved a good battlefield, where they rode men to their deaths with the excitement of a toddler on a coin-operated hobbyhorse. Ever wonder how a man could run straight into a pike wall? *Yippee!* They carried diseases, sexual and otherwise, which they eagerly transmitted—lick and stick. Of course, Minos had hired them. Hermes lowered the binoculars and paced the rooftop.

The golden keys were somewhere inside that fortress. Here stood Hermes, facing the prospect of another heist. The Vatican suddenly felt like a cakewalk in comparison. The only plan he had generated so far was to conceal his identity under his hoodie, cut the line, and pray for rain. Only it didn't rain in Hell. Once inside—presuming he made it inside—he would just…what? Wing it? Hardly a plan. Hardly a trick. Tricks were his specialty, the source of his pride. He could spitball a million ways to spin a human, fool a god, send religions crashing into one another. But the more he tried to squeeze out a plan on top of this parking garage, the more mentally constipated he became. Hermes was blocked when it mattered most. When the trick was not to boost his ego and notch another win. Why couldn't the messenger deliver?

"You're the Trickster God! Think of something!"

Even his pep talk felt like an acknowledgment of defeat.

He grabbed his bag and shook it upside down for a field check. The contents spilled onto the cement, covered in a sprinkling of lint and tangled up in ridiculously long receipts. Maybe there was some inspiration buried among his gear. His primary pistol was tucked into his belt, while his backup gun had suffered a significant mauling by Cerberus. He had thought to pack two additional Glock 9mm pistols, as well as twelve extra clips, the Helm of Hades, one bowie knife, his manly murse with his drachma spending coin, a second coin pouch for bribes, ChapStick, bottles of water (Hermes would consider product placement), protein bars, two packs of nicotine gum, two celebratory joints for later, three packs of cigarettes (because fuck the nicotine gum), Airborne in case of the sniffles, and six dozen travel-sized bottles of hand sanitizer, because he went to Costco.

He stared at the supplies and felt like a child who runs away from home and only makes it to the end of the block. Pathetic. He was pathetic. How was the Trickster out of tricks?

Burying the panic attack in his stomach and his fists in the pouch of his hoodie, Hermes settled on the original, unoriginal plan. He exited the garage on foot with his backpack and made his way toward the courthouse. The full-blown existential crisis would have to wait.

He didn't know what to expect of Minos' new domain, but it wasn't a spotless metropolis. An army of forced labor swept the gutters of ash; every pane of marble and glass was polished to a mirror finish. He had to hand it to Minos—the tyrant ran a tight ship.

Hurried profiles jostled past without a second glance. Souls he once guided to the Underworld surged past him like he was a boulder parting a river. They either didn't recognize him or didn't care. Hermes didn't know which was worse.

For two thousand years, Hermes had raged at every rosary, kippah, turban, burka, and hijab because it meant the human bowed before a different god. Humans worshipped technology and sports and television, lined up for phones and sneakers, could list every celebrity, musician, and royal—but didn't know his name. So he lashed out: pranks and hijinks, attention-seeking stunts, an endless campaign waged against irrelevance. And now in Hell, Hermes was just another dead man walking. Yet for the first time, anonymity was his friend.

One person seemed to notice him. A little girl ensconced in a lawn chair among the sorry line. She had a chubby pumpkin face, her arms crossed in boredom. Her family camped on the sidewalk around her. She emitted a low growl like a savage chihuahua, and her stare suggested he back the fuck off and keep moving, buster.

"Hey! No cutting," a voice cried out. Hermes whirled around to an old man with a mushroom nose sprouting off an indignant sun-splotched face, jerking a thumb over his shoulder. "Back of the line."

"What's the line for? There some new Apple product out?"

"Why would I wait a hundred years for a lousy apple?" The old man cleared his throat and thrust a crooked, arthritic finger at the courthouse. "New judgment."

It sounded like a bad Hollywood sequel. "What's new judgment?"

"Minos." The old man spat a wad of phlegm to show what he thought of the king.

A tug on his pant leg drew Hermes to a boy, maybe ten, with blond locks and a conspiratorial grin. "I know who you are. You're Her—"

Before the kid could finish, Hermes sealed a hand over his mouth and yanked him across the street, where the noise of chariot traffic meant they wouldn't be overheard. He took his hand off the kid's mouth once they were safely away from the line.

"You're Hermes." The boy beamed with pride.

"Okay. You got me, I'm Hermes. I thought no one recognized me."

"Oh, they don't. But my master worshipped you. I cleaned your temple every day, polished your statue. You once autographed my band."

The boy showed off a metal ring bolted around his wrist that signified his enslavement. Sure enough, Hermes had carved his signature into it. In hindsight, he maybe should have freed the kid.

"No one remembers the gods anymore, but the gods forgot us first." He gave an indifferent shrug. "No one cares anyways."

Hermes frowned. Well, that tracked.

The boy continued. "We hear you don't have power anymore. And we hear mighty Hades is mighty no more. That he forgets, forgets himself in many ways…and the palace reeks of urine."

Hermes had heard enough and turned to the souls in line all the way down the street.

"The line isn't for a new phone, so what's all the excitement about? Are they serving bottomless mimosas?"

"What's a mimosa?"

"You were born too soon. I thought everyone was already judged."

The boy's eyes widened in disbelief. "You don't know?"

"No, kid, I don't know."

"I've been waiting for ninety-eight years, ten months, and fifteen days, and I'm so very close now. Everyone's impatient. But not me. I have a plan."

Hermes realized this street urchin could be useful. "Why is it called new judgment?"

"Minos declared the last court was rigged. So everyone has to be rejudged. Minos prefers you pay for a favorable ruling—and pay in cash. No more merit, he said. I don't have any money, so I could be sent back to Acheron with the others."

So that's why Acheron was overstuffed with desperation. The empty spaces in the coloring book were starting to fill in. Hermes crouched down eye level with the kid, showing him extra favor, since a god would never stoop to a mortal's level.

"Tell me more."

The kid nodded vigorously. "He's searching for thieves and killers and liars. He rewards them. I'll tell Minos I was the greatest thief in Corinth, and that was why I was killed." He held up two palms marked by crucifixion, then lifted his shirt to show a giant gash. "And then he'll let me be reborn on Earth, where I can serve him."

"Smart kid like you, how'd you die so young?"

"Father sold me in payment for his land debt. After, I was a bed slave for Master Phalaris. I also rowed the pleasure craft and brought water in from the wells. General Sulla freed us with his army. Master Phalaris paid for the war against the Romans, so as punishment, Sulla nailed us to wooden crosses and slit open our stomachs."

Hermes sometimes forgot how much harder the humans had it in the old days. They lived short, painful lives, then spent an eternity paying for it in the Underworld. People today had some warped views of Ancient Greece: men in togas arguing over philosophy, thespians performing comedies and tragedies, the Olympic Games and pretty laurel wreaths, or the perfectly buffed Trojan ridiculousness that made its way into comic books. The reality was pretty miserable. The world had changed—from the Renaissance to the Enlightenment, the Industrial Age, the Digital Revolution—and Hermes had to admit, things were improving. In a way, the human capacity to evolve placed them above the gods.

Unfortunately, his religion was attempting to drag mankind into a new dark age.

"That is how I died. But no reason to despair. I prefer this afterlife and will prefer serving Master Minos on Earth. I hear Earth is very different now—no more suffering!"

Hermes peered over the boy's golden curly hair to the endless sunken faces, bored souls glued to the pavement, too afraid to abandon their place in line even for a piss. Peasants and nobles, farmers and philosophers, statesmen, musicians, actors, and…

Hermes was stunned he'd missed it before. "Where are the soldiers?"

Greece sent scores of its young men to die in battle. Yet not a single hoplite in sight.

The boy lowered his voice. "They aren't allowed judgment unless they can pay lots."

It made sense. Minos hated soldiers—macho guys with swords longer than his, who laughed at him and excluded him and teased him. Soldiers were also notoriously broke. The army was a career path for the destitute. With the Keres, Minos didn't need to hire the warriors for protection. Minos probably saw this as cosmic punishment.

"Where can I find Greece's fighting men?" Hermes asked.

"Sometimes they beg us, mostly they wander. They gather to the north."

Hermes gave the kid a grateful pat on the head and slipped him some coin from his manly murse. "Bribe the front of the line with this."

The kid opened his palm to find two dekadrachms, large silver coins worth ten drachma—probably making him the wealthiest soul for miles. Hermes waited for the praise, but the kid was busy studying Athena's minted profile, then scratching at the owl impression on the back. Satisfied the coin was legit, he stuffed the money in his pocket and extended a hand. The kid had balls.

"Name's Alexis." Hermes shook it. "And you're not Hermes."

"When you make it topside, look up a friend named Wu in a village called New York. I'll find you there." Hermes rotated the scrawny urchin around. "All right, Alexis. Go get reborn."

Alexis scampered off to the tower, which rose like a giant middle finger to the Underworld.

"Fuck you, too," Hermes said, and headed north.

***

Mercury vapor hung over a concrete wasteland and the huddles of Greek soldiers that made this mall parking lot their home everlasting. The cavalrymen, hoplites, archers, and infantry were marred by hideously fresh wounds, though they appeared to be dead of boredom. Their ragged uniforms spanned centuries, republics, and ranks. Behind the field encampment, the city skyline barred the horizon like a palisade wall guarding the gated community of paradise. Dwarfing all was the spire of Minos' vanity project, the needle on a sundial in a world of darkness.

Hermes generally liked soldiers and had interceded to help a few in his day. They were proud and boisterous, drank too much, pillaged too much, fucked too much, and generally lived as if there were no tomorrow—sort of like himself. Their current skid row vagrancy was a sorry state, but their loss was his gain. He jangled his bribing sack above his head. Soldiers perked up at the suppertime sound of loose silver.

"Soldiers of Troy, Sparta, Athens, Thrace, Macedonia, men of Ithaca and Sicily, of Greece and her greater lands!" His voice trumpeted over the disorderly battalions, easily lassoing their attention.

He grinned. "Who's looking for work?"

Jingle, jingle, jingle.

Men charged forward, hands waving. *Pickmepickmepickme!* Hermes was quickly cocooned by desperation. So many soldiers to choose from!

"Out of my way!" an irate voice pierced the commotion. A red plume bobbed over the crowd like raised hackles on an angry rooster. "Step aside! Barbarians! Fools! Make way!"

A scowling face like a purple melon wedged atop a bronze cuirass elbowed to the front, jacking soldiers aside with his wide shoulders. He was young for an officer and wore a smear of peach fuzz attempting to pass for a beard. Hermes knew the type: an aristocratic heir given the rank who saw in himself a protector. The earnestness practically filled the blackheads on his cheeks, an honest-to-gods patriot who took the band-of-brothers oath to heart.

"Hold! I negotiate!" His helmet slid over his eyes. He slammed it back in frustration and whipped his velvet cape with a flourish.

The cape embarrassingly caught on the armor of the tall hoplite beside him. The commander ripped his cloak free and used it to cover the hole above his groin where a lance had struck him down. Hermes also noted the guy was missing a sandal, likely lost in battle along with his life.

The commander faced off with Hermes and puffed out his bronze chest. The feathers on his helmet tickled the face of an archer behind him, who batted at it like a kitten. "I speak for these men—otherwise they'd sell their souls for a piece of hard crust. We're worth more than that small pouch."

"You're worth much more," Hermes agreed, throwing the commander off balance. A buzz of excitement rose anew. The ring of bearded soldiers, tattooed soldiers, child soldiers, and soldiers past their prime cinched tighter, their heavy breathing like dogs panting for treats.

The commander spread out his arms. His men would take any job, any payment, do it for free, if only to have a shred of purpose.

"Fairness for all hoplites and infantry," the commander spoke, stare aimed like a javelin. "That's what we died for, that's what we stand for. Equal pay for equal work. Enough silver for each man to cross the river despite Mad Minos. You don't provide, you don't get my men."

There was a collective inhale, and a dead silence followed. The soldiers sensed their commander had overstepped.

Hermes gave a nod of respect. "I should have enough."

"For how many?" the commander fired back.

Hermes counted in a circle—eenie, meenie, miny, moe. "Everyone."

The commander held out a hand with a gimme gesture. "Let me see it. I don't believe you have enough for my army."

His army, Hermes scoffed. This wasn't his army. This guy just had the chutzpah to seize control of the disbanded, unemployed troops once all the kings and generals fled to Paradise.

Hermes lifted his pouch.

"Nice murse," shouted a hoplite in the crowd, spurring a barrage of laughter.

Hermes glared. *No coin for you, asshole.*

Aware he was taking the bait, Hermes nevertheless decided to upstage the joker and filled the commander's hand with silver. A collective gasp rippled outward.

The stunned commander stared at the wealth, momentarily lost for words. "Who are you to have such coin?"

"Irrelevant."

"When it comes to my men and their afterlives, nothing is irrelevant. I would know this coin's provenance. If it is stolen, then its value will be stripped by retribution. This wealth could be worthless."

The accusation stung. "I swear by the gods it's not stolen."

(It was technically on loan from the Christians. Hermes had stopped at an ATM in the palace before beginning his journey. The exchange rate was definitely in his favor.)

The commander continued his interrogation. "Then are you divine? Fooling us with this schlubbish disguise?"

Who was he calling a schlub? Hermes had stolen his designer hoodie at an outrageously overpriced boutique on Melrose—the highest order of fashion—and his acid-washed, pre-ripped jeans were the hottest look of last summer (hopefully not the last summer). Not to mention, he had shaved and put on deodorant before leaving Salt Lake City.

"A second when the job's done," the commander countered.

Groans rumbled among the edgy soldiers.

"Just take the damn money!" someone shouted.

One word and Hermes could trigger a coup.

The young leader faced his kinsmen. "Enough for all of us, or none of us fight. We're not mercenaries. We're soldiers of Greece. And though we have fallen far from our homes and status, we still look after one another. A brother's soul weighs more than silver."

This man died too young, Hermes thought. Still, two bags of coin? It was a steep price. All Hermes had. The soldiers were left in suspense as he deliberated. No one breathed—which didn't matter, since they were already dead. Ultimately, it came down to his budding respect for this commander's fidelity and resolve. He could learn a thing or two from the officer.

"Done."

The tension broke and the soldiers erupted in cheers for the end of their purgatory. Hands slapped the commander's back, shook his shoulders, and playfully punched his arms. They nearly lifted him into the air, but he urged them to stop with a false humility. He was all dimples and teeth. Hermes had done right. Money well spent.

The commander suddenly remembered his obligation and knelt to swear allegiance. "By the goddess Styx, I grant you my loyalty and service."

An unbreakable oath. Not bad.

(It wasn't technically valid unless you swore it on the banks of the River Styx with Miss Styx present, but Hermes didn't feel the need to tell him that.) The entire battalion bent the knee next. Hermes breathed in the fealty with a surge of pride.

Pride and…

Why, hello, old friend.

That familiar euphoria. The best drug in the universe: worship.

Old habits? piped that pesky Voice.

Hermes shoved it down. Why couldn't he bask? What was wrong in a bit of basking? A teensy ounce of adoration never hurt.

In the middle of basking, one soldier refused to kneel. The soul was short, even compared to his kneeling companions, bulked with muscles forged in battle. He wore the white robe of a naval captain and an ornate breastplate. His auburn hair was flecked with sea salt and flowed in windswept curls past his neckline. He rested his hands on the wooden pommel of his sheathed sword. A yew bow hung from his back. His brown eyes challenged Hermes. The face was so familiar, but Hermes couldn't place him.

Almost as soon as Hermes had the thought, the sailor joined his comrades and took a knee, disappearing among the forest of bronze armor. He couldn't shake the sense he should recognize that man—like that actor in that movie who did cool stuff. The one everyone knows.

"Would you know my rank, sir?"

Hermes turned back to the commander staring up at him.

"Taxiarchos Aegos, sir. Infantry Commander. Felled in battle during the coup of Theramenes against the wretched tyranny of the Athenian democrats. Who fought for the enfranchisement of the soldiers of Greece. Lost to my family. No kindness paid for my afterlife. One thousand six hundred two years ago."

"Okay. Cool. You can get up now."

Aegos rose as instructed and tugged his cape from his crack.

"Aegos," said Hermes in his most officious tone.

Commander Aegos snapped to attention. "Yes, sir?"

"We have another coup to plan."

***

The soldiers moved with purpose and efficiency, transforming the mess of shanties into orderly rows of tents. Within hours, the parking lot became a proper military encampment. Campfires illuminated circles of infantrymen sharpening blades and javelins as a constant clang came from the blacksmiths beating dents out of the shields that had failed to protect these men the first go-around. Companies reassembled under new volunteer officers, once lifeless souls sparking with the prospect of glory. A new pride had been rekindled: the Underworld was preparing for war.

Inside the crowded commander's tent—a double-wide family camper nicked from Earth—Hermes and Aegos huddled over a map of the courthouse while a bevy of advisors encircled them. Looking up from the table, Hermes saw that familiar naval captain slip into the meeting behind an officer, as far from him as possible. The man had to have been one of Hermes' bastards, or the descendant of one, but an ah-ha moment of recognition remained elusive. They were connected in some genetic way, the most obvious being the naval captain's good looks. The man had died sometime in his fifties or sixties but had been blessed with a vitality that erased decades.

Hermes had asked Aegos about the man's identity before the meeting, but Aegos only knew he had drowned in a shipwreck and knew of no name. Not uncommon. Most soldiers suffered from severe posttraumatic afterlife disorder from those brutal hours, minutes, or even seconds spent on the battlefield. The trauma became a prison, erasing any remembrance of their lives before.

Aegos slid an oil lamp across the charcoal blueprint to illuminate another entrance to the skyscraper. "My men have successfully scouted the entire perimeter of the fortress, cleverly disguised as beggars along the line. They report each of the four main entrances are heavily guarded by Keres—large flocks, perhaps thousands strong."

Hermes cursed at the impregnability. If they stormed the courthouse outright, they would suffer catastrophic losses. Cosmic justice said you couldn't die twice, but you could feel pain. That frightened the humans more in death than in life. Worse, a wound suffered in Hell would not heal. There would be no end to their misery. "Any more bad news?"

"The souls choke each doorway while awaiting judgment. The line slows further as Minos makes every soul remove all metal, jewelry, and weapons before stepping through a magic archway that beeps and burns red or green. Then they go through another portal made of glass and raise their hands over their heads. From what my spies have gathered, this second magic device allows the cacodemons to look at their genitals. The perverts…"

An angry murmur rose through the officers. The Greeks weren't prudes, but everyone appreciated consent. Hermes decided it would be pointless to explain the machines.

The intelligence briefing continued with a report on the skyscraper's position within the ever-deepening pit. Scores of cacodemons patrolled the granite rim and harassed those in line. Cacodemons had nothing to do with chocolate. They were evil spirits most closely related to an ogre with a schoolyard bully complex. They were dimwitted and cruel, and the account from their spies detailed the cacodemons as mounted on screeching, two-wheeled horses. (After an awkward game of charades—more for his own amusement—Hermes guessed they were describing a motorcycle.) Hermes had the numbers and the spirit, but Minos held the high ground and had the superior arms.

Aegos finished his downer of a presentation, and the tent went silent.

"What does Minos want with all this coin?" Hermes posed.

Aegos could only guess and offered a shrug. "To build his palace?"

"I thought he used slaves?"

"He's always been greedy—when he was alive, and now that he's dead."

"And his collecting thieves and murderers? What do they have to do with Persephone?"

"Reincarnation," said a voice across the tent.

All eyes turned to the mysterious naval captain as he pushed forward to the map.

"He's reincarnating them. As to the connection between a madman's whims and your sister, I defer the puzzle to you."

"Half sister," Hermes corrected.

The captain bowed with a hint of a smile. "My apologies. I've angered enough gods."

A fresh uproar erupted. Hermes ignored the whispers and held the sea captain's weather-worn eyes.

"Do you remember your former life?"

"I try to forget," the man answered.

"Too painful?"

"Too glorious." The naval captain then pointed to the map. "May I recommend a solution?"

"Recommend away," Hermes said, enjoying this game.

"The tower rises higher by the hour. Never have I seen such heights." The captain gave a dramatic pause. Expectant ears hung onto his every word. The guy knew how to work a tent. Aegos seemed rather miffed; this nobody had just stolen his limelight.

"Claws lift more than men can carry on their backs, drawing the weight up impossible slopes. Moving mountains by a finger. The slaves must climb into contraptions. Spiders that slide up and down the wall."

"Elevators," Hermes chimed in.

"Elevators…" The captain savored the word as if it were an exotic fruit. "These elevators climb to the top of his phallus, which remains… incomplete."

"A vulnerability!" Aegos exclaimed, bursting with the energy of a class valedictorian suddenly faced with a rival. "We must exploit it!"

Hermes sighed. "Yeah, we know."

The attention stayed on the naval captain, sucking the wind from Aegos's sails. The mysterious captain proceeded to explain his plan: a division of troops would take the pit—a coordinated strike to create a distraction, allowing Hermes to hitch a ride up an elevator.

"Wise land strategy for a man who drowned at sea," Hermes said with a grin.

The naval captain played it coy. "Well, you know, a divine spark of inspiration whispered in my ears."

Hermes decided to test his hunch. "Who whispers? The Muses or Sirens?"

"I pray I would recognize the difference, should I ever face such a test."

"I believe you would. A gifted mind such as yours wouldn't give away strategy for free." Hermes removed a coin from his murse and flipped it onto the map. "Name your price."

The captain wasn't tempted by the money, his gaze stapled to Hermes. "Perhaps I did not drown at sea. Perhaps I received divine intervention once or twice and now owe the god a favor."

"Tell me about this plan of yours." Their flirtatious dance continued.

"The soldiers swarm. A surprise attack on the Keres is paramount to take out their aerial superiority. Meanwhile, you shall be dressed as a slave, which I hear you do well. I will deliver you to one of these elevators that you will ride up, then descend into the courthouse."

"A Trojan Horse? Don't you have any other tricks up your armor?"

"If it worked once..."

They broke into matching grins, smiling ear to ear.

Hermes thumped a fist on the map. "Why didn't you say anything?!"

"I'm a wanted man, Hermes."

A shockwave rippled through the soldiers at the mention of his name. The soldiers were at once awestruck and apprehensive.

Hermes ignored the reaction, rounded the table, and pulled the captain into a hug. "You're wrinkled—but that's well met. Means you died an old man. You just can't avoid exile, can you? What happened this time?"

"Minos despises my breed. Anyone favored by the gods or related to one."

Looks of bewilderment passed between the other officers.

Aegos raised a hand. "Sir Hermes?"

"Yes, Aegos," Hermes answered.

"What is going on here?"

"A family reunion. This salt dog is my great-grandson, Odysseus!"

Another uproar. This time the tent descended into teen-idol fandom. Aegos and the soldiers practically fanned themselves and dropped to their knees.

Aegos stuttered, "King Odysseus, we could not have known..."

Their reaction to Odysseus was decidedly and annoyingly bigger. Hermes should have been the A-lister. Instead, he felt like a B-, or heaven forbid, C-list celebrity at the movie premiere. All the fans wanted their selfies with Odysseus. He soaked up the glamor and paparazzi attention. As the golems would say, Hermes was chopped liver.

"Hold it!" Hermes shouted, stepping between Aegos and Odysseus. "You already knelt before me. No takebacks. No refunds. I paid cash. You're my army."

Odysseus shook his head. "I don't intend to lead."

Hermes pivoted to his great-grandson. "But I demand it."

The soldiers buzzed anew, swiveling between Odysseus and Hermes like spectators at a tennis match.

Odysseus held his ground. "You'll have my sword and my bow. Aegos is a fine officer." Then he cast his voice over the assembly. "I pledge my loyalty to Commander Aegos!"

Fists shot into the air with triumphant cries and shouts. The soldiers lifted Aegos and he surfed the crowd. The decision was made and sealed before Hermes could protest. He glared at his great-grandson through the celebration.

"Thanks a lot."

"You didn't ask what I wanted. I'm done leading men."

A conga line bumped past Hermes. "You're always stealing my spotlight."

The proud former captain and king of Ithaca stepped back, affronted. "I'm no larcenist."

Hermes dismissed him with a wave. "You've taken it wrong. Relax. Chill out."

"I shall not relax. I shall not chill."

The tent abruptly quieted and filled with tension as awareness of the family feud spread. Hermes took quick measure of the mood. It was clear he would have to swallow whatever remained of his pride or risk losing his army.

"It's a term of endearment on Earth nowadays. Means you're a rock star."

Odysseus clenched further. "Now you call me *rock*?!"

How to dig himself out of this one? "Not a rock—a rock star. It means you're cool beans. And not the legume kind...fucking colloquials." Hermes let out a sigh and forced a smile. "Are we good? Can we please be good?"

Odysseus eyed him warily, painfully stretching the moment, then relented. "Yes."

Still flustered, Hermes rubbed his hands together. "Great. We're good then. I'm just damn glad to find a friendly face."

Eager to turn the page, he turned to his troops. "Now! Shall we go to war?"

The officers straightened into clapboards and shouted a deafening *hoo-rah*. They beat their mailed fists and swords on their shields. Their army had a god and a varsity king on their side. Not unstoppable—but not destined to lose. That was something. Their hearts were full, fired up with the energy of a locker room pep talk, ready to reclaim Hell.

Cheers thundered on as Hermes and Odysseus shared a genetically linked twinkle in their eyes. The god clapped his mortal great-grandson on the back.

"The best part: you're already dead."

CHAPTER TWENTY-TWO

IT HAD BEEN A long time since Hermes wore a toga. He forgot how horribly they rode, and with the force of Quasimodo ringing the bells of Notre Dame, he freed the wool from his crack.

"Stop fidgeting. You look suspicious," Odysseus chided as they surveilled the courthouse tower rising over tents, camp chairs, and cook fires. They had entered the line a mere block from the pit, where one of Aegos's informants had saved them a coveted spot.

Long before Hermes had arrived in the Underworld, Aegos had strategically recruited resistance fighters throughout the endless line. It was his impressive network that allowed the soldiers to slowly infiltrate the queue over the last twenty-four nail-biting hours.

"How are Penelope and the children?" Hermes asked, to kill time.

"Also dead," Odysseus answered, not easily distracted.

"That's nice." Hermes stopped fidgeting with his toga as six Keres landed at the end of the block. Decked in black and silver camouflage, the buzzards were armed with Civil War muskets. They sniffed each soul for suspicious emotions: fear, anger, no emotion at all. The demonic fascists recalled a few neo-Nazis Hermes had encountered while traveling off the grid in Idaho.

"What does it say about humans when the evil spirits take their cues from the living?"

"Nothing good," Odysseus muttered.

A cloaked beggar suddenly rushed them. Hermes instinctively reached for his pistol, Odysseus his bow. Torchlight spilled into the stranger's hood and onto Aegos, his face wired with the panic of inexperience.

"Fool, you're going to get us found," Odysseus hissed.

"The Keres sense something amiss, and not all the men are in place!" Aegos warned.

Hermes and Odysseus glanced over at the patrol. The Keres had missed Aegos's reckless charge, but the souls around them stirred. They were friendly to the cause—up to a point. They would not permit anything to jeopardize their spot.

"I need more time," Aegos begged.

"You don't have it, Commander," snapped Odysseus, not used to playing second fiddle.

"Calm down, both of you," Hermes reprimanded. "You're both running hot."

At the end of the block, the Keres sniffed at the sky with reptilian nostrils and perked up as they identified a fresh scent.

Hermes, Odysseus, and Aegos quickly hid their faces. One of the Keres snatched from the line a blacksmith with large muscles and soot-blackened clothes. The blacksmith threw up his hands and begged for mercy. His daughter wailed, and his wife grabbed her husband, starting a tug-of-war with the demon. The blacksmith wrested free and sprinted for the courthouse.

Another Ker took flight, aimed its musket, and fired. The ball ripped a quarter-sized hole through the blacksmith's neck. The poor man flopped onto his face, instantly paralyzed except for his vocal cords, which screeched an octave Hermes hadn't heard before.

Aegos heaved a sigh of relief. "Oh, thank Zeus! He wasn't one of our men."

Thank Zeus? How refreshing.

Zeus was pretty much worthless, but Hermes didn't feel any need to tell them that.

The Keres had finished with the blacksmith and proceeded in their direction.

"Aegos is right," Odysseus said and cursed. "We have to signal the attack."

"No, it's premature." Aegos watched the Keres, his breathing rapid and shallow.

Hermes seized him by his armored breastplate hidden beneath the cloak. "Clear your head, Commander!"

The Keres drew closer, tearing souls out of line to sniff and interrogate.

"We're not ready," Aegos whimpered. "We must abandon the attack."

Hermes mustered his godliest god voice. "Close your eyes." Aegos obeyed. "When I met you, I met a warrior respected and loved. Fear is but the shadow of courage. Within you is the strength to confront your demons. I have seen it. You have…" Hermes faltered. "A glowing chakra."

Odysseus raised his eyebrows. "Is that supposed to inspire?"

Hermes shrugged. "It's the best I can do on short notice."

The Keres pivoted in their direction, locking onto the scent of fear oozing from Aegos's pores. They barreled through the souls like snowplows.

Odysseus discreetly moved his hand under his cloak.

Hermes needed his commander to give the command. "I'm going to count to three, and when you open your eyes, you're going to remember that your name…"

Hermes turned to Odysseus. "What's his name again?"

"Aegos."

Hermes shifted back. "Aegos. You're going to remember Aegos is the name of your father and your father's father, and your father's father's—"

"We get the point," Odysseus muttered. "Hurry up."

"This fight is for our lineage, for justice. Sound the charge. Inspire your men. Free these souls."

The commander's shoulders rolled into a battle posture. Hermes unholstered his pistol. Odysseus gripped the pommel of his sword.

"One…Two…Three!"

Aegos's eyes snapped open, beset with confidence. "See you in Paradise." He thrust his kopis blade into the air. "DOWN WITH MINOS THE CRUEL! FOR THE AFTERLIFE!"

The Keres screeched and took flight. Before they could aim their muskets, a hoplite hidden in line threw off his disguise and speared one of the demons with a javelin. Ten more soldiers immediately ambushed the patrol. Taken by surprise, the Keres opened fire, expending their single-shot muskets. Gunpowder smoke filled the sky as the line dissolved into panic.

Aegos sprinted for the Ker that had felled the blacksmith, and in an agile dance, ducked a bayonet and skewered the creature through its ear. Battle cries joined Aegos. Each of the four lines was a Trojan Horse, carrying the soldiers to Minos' front door. Companies formed and field officers directed their separate attacks.

Hermes felt the joy of a perfectly choreographed trick. "Shall we?"

Odysseus grinned at his great-great-grandfather of a god, and together they charged into chaos. They careened through baying livestock, knocking men and women aside. Odysseus took the lead. White fletchings poked up from his quiver, shimmying over the panic.

At the edge of the construction pit, they entered a warzone crackling with gunfire. Overwhelmed by the Greek surprise attack, Keres had taken flight and scattered, firing madly in all directions.

The sound of bullets smacking into metal spun Hermes and Odysseus to a Ker hovering over a group of soldiers pinned under their shields. The Ker unleashed buckshot from a 12-gauge shotgun. An infantryman was struck and fell from the circle in terrible howls. Hermes aimed his pistol and picked off the Ker with a single crack shot. The Ker dropped onto the shields, and the soldiers quickly hacked it to pieces.

Odysseus chopped down his gun. "Fool! Don't draw attention to yourself. Their sacrifice isn't for you to play hero."

Hermes bristled and holstered the weapon. It was open season on his ego. They raced down the switchback, fighting the souls fleeing the gorge. Bullets rained from the sky. Bodies tumbled and pinwheeled off the ledges when struck. Slower souls were trampled in the stampede, their cries silenced once they had been stomped to a pulp.

Just ahead of Hermes, a Ker dove from the sky and plucked an archer like an arcade claw snatching a prize. It swooped up, then released the archer, who plummeted, screaming, to land on soldiers below.

"This is worse than Troy!" Odysseus shouted.

"Would you rather try another siege? Only took ten years for your last one."

Odysseus shook his head. "No, thank you..."

In the construction pit below, the landlocked cacodemons were in full retreat behind a makeshift barricade of overturned chariots and re-bar. The Keres had regrouped, hovering in formation above to provide cover. Along the tower, office windows shattered outward as demons took up firing positions.

"We need to pick up the pace," Hermes said. A worried Odysseus nodded.

They fought their way to the bottom. Over a phalanx of helmets, Hermes spied Aegos facing off against the demons blockading the west entrance. Aegos shouted and a storm of javelins whistled out, impaling demons to the courthouse. A row of archers popped up next and loosed arrows at the Keres above. The Greeks had a three-thousand-year technological disadvantage, but Aegos compensated with superior discipline and tactics. His pregame nerves had given way to a fierce warrior keeping Minos' minions occupied.

The distraction worked. Hermes and Odysseus headed to the north side, now deserted thanks to Aegos focusing his attack on the south, east, and west. Frightened slaves peered out from behind pyramids of stacked pavers.

"Fight! Come on, take up arms!" Odysseus bellowed, but the slaves only cowered.

"Leave them," Hermes said, heading for the construction lifts. The nearest elevator opened, ejecting a pair of cacodemons carrying four rifles apiece.

Hermes shoved Odysseus behind a crane as the demons opened fire. A bullet grazed Hermes' elbow and ichor splattered the gravel. A steady *pock, pock, pock* of metal punching metal chased him as he dove for cover. "Odysseus—"

He whirled around, but Odysseus was gone. "What the hell! How many times can he get lost?"

Another round of bullets answered. Without warning, a cacodemon toppled off the roof of the cab above Hermes and landed in the dirt, its throat slit. A few moments later, the gunfire abruptly stopped. Hermes peered around the crane to find Odysseus yanking his blade from the second demon's chest.

"What took you so long?" Hermes teased.

Odysseus scowled and wiped his blade clean on the demon's uniform.

Across the yard, the slaves warily emerged with power tools, axes, and pieces of rebar.

"Come on," Odysseus urged. "Join the revolt! Earn your freedom!"

Emboldened, they did just that and charged a cacodemon attempting to escape in a lift. The demon manically pressed the up button, but the doors didn't close in time.

Hermes joined Odysseus above his kill. "I thought we weren't showing off."

"Not everything is about you." He saw the blood dripping down Hermes' arm. "You're hurt?"

Hermes hadn't even noticed. "A scratch."

They jogged toward a service elevator not currently occupied by slaves hacking apart their former demon overlord. A round of gunfire echoed behind them and bullets whizzed past.

"Move!" Hermes barked at the slaves and returned fire over his shoulder. A dozen cacodemons scuttled for cover. He managed to pick off two before they disappeared behind construction equipment.

Odysseus threw open the gate to the service elevator and entered first as Hermes backed in, scanning for any demon that dared show its face.

"What are you waiting for? Hit up!"

He glanced over at Odysseus, who was overwhelmed by the buttons.

"We're doomed," Odysseus muttered.

"Up. Press up!"

The cacodemons took the opportunity to advance. Bullets ricocheted off the cage.

"For god's sake!" Hermes shoved Odysseus aside and smashed the "up" button with the fervor of a gamer on cocaine.

The elevator lurched off the ground as the cacodemons swarmed below. Their curses and gunfire pinged harmlessly off the reinforced floor.

A horn bellowed in the distance, and Hermes and Odysseus pressed against the grill to watch Aegos leading a tidal wave of soldiers at the demons. The first part of the plan was a success.

"Doomed, huh?" Hermes scoffed. "There are only two buttons: if one doesn't work, you press the other."

Odysseus huffed. "I want nothing from the modern world."

"Shame, you'd love GPS."

"What does that do?"

"It shows you how to get home." Hermes winked.

Something abruptly slammed into the elevator and sent it swinging like a carnival ride. A massive Ker clung to the cage, beating its double-wide wings. The lift cables groaned.

"It's trying to pull us off the building," Hermes realized.

Odysseus notched an arrow. The elevator rocked him off balance, his head slammed against the control panel, and he crumpled in a daze. The Ker clawed and tore at the cage with its fangs.

Hermes surfed the turbulence and aimed. "Cover your ears."

Odysseus slapped his hands over his ears as Hermes unloaded his weapon. The Ker screeched and took flight. The elevator resumed its typical rumble up the tower, and the sounds of battle faded. They had made it out of harm's way—for now. Hermes slid to the ground opposite Odysseus. It might be their only chance to rest for a while.

"I had him," Odysseus said, wiping blood from the back of his head.

Hermes slapped a fresh magazine into his Glock. "You can't always be the hero."

"Since when? I've been dead over three thousand years."

"Doesn't matter. You're a celebrity, more famous than the gods." Hermes pointed to Earth.

"What is fame-ousse? How would I have more of it than the gods?"

Right. Hermes often forgot how much had transpired among the humans—how far they had traveled since the days of antiquity, when their pursuit was reverence and comprehension. Now the humans understood everything and revered nothing.

"Fame, celebrity...it's..." He puzzled. "You remember when I was worshiped? It's like that, but for a living human."

Odysseus burst into a hearty laugh, like the good old days on Ithaca when he was the golden boy racking up championship trophies and bedding cheerleaders. Hermes didn't know whether to be insulted or to join in.

"Why would they do that? Why should I have this fame?"

Hermes sighed. "Everyone knows your name and your deeds the way they once knew me and recognized my statues and temples. They can't get enough of you blinding Polyphemus, battling the Sirens. I'm forgotten, left out of your story altogether. Makes it simpler, more heroic that you did it on your own."

Odysseus turned incredulous. "But I didn't, and that's absurd! I am not a god. I'm only human—and dead, for that matter."

"But you do sell movie tickets and action figures."

"Is this Homer's doing?"

The god turned to watch the lights from the skyscraper roll past like a carousel. "What do you think? The asshole only cared about his sales. But I'm not sore."

The silence that followed said otherwise.

"Our roles were different back then. I was the one adrift, trying to find my way to Ithaca. But I had a god watching over me. Who can you put your faith in, great-grandfather?"

The question unsettled Hermes. "Dealers shouldn't use their own supply. And gods don't have faith."

"The gods are supposed to drive our destiny and the world's. Yet here you mope as if you have no control over any destiny—not even your own. The grand order is broken."

"Is this supposed to inspire?"

"It's the best I can do on such short notice."

Whole ages of experience and history separated them across the elevator. They shared a fleeting smile.

"Tell me a story," Odysseus said.

"About what?"

"How about the truth of Minos and the pigs, since we're about to face the judge. I've heard many versions, but none from the source."

"I have you to thank for the trick."

Odysseus sat up. "Truly? How, perchance?"

"It was your run-in with Circe. If she could turn your crew into swine, why not turn swine into men…dead men."

"Which you delivered to the Underworld?"

"Straight to Minos, along with some half-baked cover story…something something…they overthrew an Asian king."

Odysseus nodded. "Sure to anger an ex-king of Asia."

"Nothing frightens a monarch more than rebellion."

"Agreed."

Hermes continued, "Minos brought his whole court to witness his judgment. He would grill them—in the literal sense. He wanted everyone to see how his court handled instigators and ideologues."

Odysseus chuckled.

"Since he heard I'd brought them down, Minos kept embellishing their crimes. Anyway, the day comes, he has the guards drag them in for trial. A big show. He lectures and lectures from his dais and then begins the prosecution. But when he questions them, the rebels only grunt or snort, which he takes as offense. 'Insolent humans!' So as a lesson for the Underworld, Minos orders them tortured in the courtroom…burned alive. The squeals were terrible, but the bacon was delicious!" Hermes delivered the punchline, and they burst into laughter.

"Persephone wouldn't speak to me for three months."

Odysseus wiped away happy tears. "Because you made a mockery of her court?"

"No, because I hurt innocent pigs." His laughter faded. "She loves pigs. Thinks they're cute."

It hurt to think of Persephone.

Is this what losing someone feels like?

Odysseus stared at him curiously.

Hermes was embarrassed to show his emotions like this. "Hey. Maybe we should star in our own reality show? We can both be famous."

"Reality show? Another strange combination of words."

"It's what they call life now. But on television. People can watch us living together, overcoming obstacles, finding love…"

Odysseus placed a comforting hand on his knee. "You'll find her. You're Hermes."

"Am I?"

"Are you what?"

"A god. Am I even a god anymore?" Hermes looked up at Odysseus, who couldn't even wrap his mind around the question, let alone articulate an answer. It wasn't fair to ask a mortal to address a god's pain. That wasn't how the world was supposed to work. And yet here they sat.

Ding! The elevator jolted to a stop.

"This is us," Hermes said.

"Indeed."

A battlefield was one thing, an emotional minefield another. Thankfully, they had an actual war to fight.

Facing the grate, Odysseus drew his bow, arrow notched, impatient to release. Distant pops of gunfire echoed far below. The other side of the elevator remained eerily quiet. Hermes yanked open the grate to a maze of crisscrossing girders and oil lamps dangling from rattling chains. They crept over a black chasm on a steel beam that connected to a slab of concrete. Directly above, they could nearly touch the bottom of Earth.

Odysseus gazed up in awe. "It's the end of the world."

Hermes perched on his toes and, just as his fingertips brushed the stone, the building rumbled and sank away from the roof.

Odysseus nudged Hermes to a staircase and they quickly descended through hollow floors, not a soul in sight, until they reached a nearly completed level. The paint was fresh, and it had a new carpet smell. At the far end of the office was a solitary door to the next stairwell. The two

Keres stationed to guard it were glued to the windows, gazing down at the battle below.

Just as the Keres noticed a reflection in the glass, a plume of feathers exploded from the throat of one. In a single graceful motion, Odysseus notched and loosed another arrow. The second Ker stumbled forward, an arrowhead piercing its chest like a medal. It spun around to catch a second arrow between the eyes.

"Big deal." Hermes let out a pfft. "They weren't even moving."

Odysseus retrieved his arrows. "What next, great Trickster?"

"This is as far as I got in my plan."

Odysseus frowned. "Figures…"

Hermes ripped open the stairwell door and found two barrels pointing at his chest. All four of them froze in shock.

"Any of you seen a goddess named Persephone?" Hermes asked.

The demons exchanged a confused look, and Hermes yanked Odysseus from the doorway as a spray of bullets tore through the space they'd just occupied.

A series of banshee screeches resounded from the levels above. The gunfire had alerted a hive of Keres to their intrusion. The alarm had sounded.

As soon as the demons inside the stairwell reloaded, Hermes sprang into action, snapping their demon necks like Pez dispensers.

"Grab a rifle!" Hermes ordered, snatching one himself.

"I'll stick with my bow, thank you very much."

Hermes cursed the king's stubbornness as Odysseus vaulted past him down the stairs. Moments later, they heard the crash of the Ker swarm entering the stairwell.

They sprinted past floors—118, 117, 116…—bullets zipping down. Odysseus launched several arrows upward. The frenetic beating of wings sounded like a rookery disturbed by a fox.

"I'll lead them away. You get to the courthouse," Odysseus directed, grunting with effort.

"Fuck off," Hermes said. The last thing they should do was split up.

"Find Persephone. That's all that matters. This is your odyssey. You have to travel it alone."

"I hate that rule!" Hermes shouted over the angry screeches as he exchanged gunfire.

114…113…112…

"You're telling me! Who came up with it, anyway?"

"The voice behind the gods, behind everything." Hermes nearly slammed into Odysseus, who had planted himself on the landing outside the door to floor 111.

"This is you." Odysseus saluted, pounding his fist into his chest. Hermes pulled his great-grandson into a hug.

"If my journey taught me anything," Odysseus said, "no parting lasts forever."

Hermes released Odysseus. "You're still my hero."

"That was horrendous. Now go!"

Hermes saluted back. Odysseus gave an exuberant war cry and plunged down the stairwell to lead the demons away. Hermes quickly entered floor 111. The door sealed, instantly extinguishing the sound of the unevenly matched battle.

Alone again.

Hermes slammed the pistol's stock on the door handle to jam it shut. He turned to a honeycomb of cubicles, desktop computers, and piles of paper. At least in Hell, they called you what you were: desk slave. Hermes was struck by the sophistication. Screens tracked live maps of Earth cities. Slaves wearing headsets dictated messages. Something was cooking, and Hermes doubted Minos or the Furies had the brains to organize it.

A hush fell over the office as the soulless eyes of souls landed on Hermes. A slave pushing a coffee cart froze with an outstretched Starbucks cup in hand, gaping at the god. A stream of coffee suddenly spurted from the green mermaid's face. The slave looked down at the hole that went straight through the cup—and into his chest.

Shots pierced the stairwell door. The Keres had wised up to Odysseus's diversion.

Hermes shoved the coffee slave aside and sprinted into the cubicles. The door shattered, unleashing a swarm of Keres. Hermes wove through the honeycomb, wishing he could grow a pair—of wings.

Not these buffalo wings…

Slaves scrambled for cover beneath their desks as the Keres flew overhead. Their talons shredded any scalp foolish enough not to duck.

Hermes fired over his shoulder. A Ker crashed through the office like a downed airplane flattening the suburbs. Gunfire wildly strafed the office, rifles dangling from their claws. Computer screens and paper exploded. Hermes threw up his elbows and tackled a cubicle festooned with "World's Best Dad" cards, sticky notes, and *Dilbert* cartoons. Using the partition as a shield, he blasted through a glass wall onto a walkway around the tower's atrium.

On his back and covered in shards, Hermes faced the office. The Keres gathered into a V-formation to attack. Another swarm landed on either side of the walkway. Every route blocked. Behind him, the atrium burrowed through the center of the skyscraper, lit up like an acid trip in shades of neon.

One. Two…

"Persephone, you owe me."

Three!

Hermes lifted the cubicle and dropped backward like a diver off a boat. The office vanished. His stomach felt as if it had stayed on the landing. Floors whizzed past. Hermes flipped the cubicle wall over and surfed the air resistance. Of all his stupid ideas, this took top prize. If only he'd brought the flying carpet from the Vatican.

Keres dove off the floors as he passed them—beaks down, cheeks rippling. Demon missiles, and Hermes was a great big bullseye. He leaned hard to one side and capsized the cubicle just as bullets hammered it. Past his feet, a stained-glass dome bulged as he rocketed toward it. At the last second, Hermes flipped the cubicle upright and slammed through the dome.

Stained glass rained onto a courtroom and the crowd of eager souls that had finally reached the end of their wait. Riding serious G-force, Hermes landed on a steer, flattening the livestock and spraying meat across a stereogram marble floor. It was meant to be sacrificed anyway. The force of the landing bounced Hermes off the cubicle wall like it was a trampoline and sent him crashing through courtroom benches. The marble felt marvelous beneath his ass, but its dizzying optical pattern didn't help the vertigo. The clack of talons signaled the arrival of Keres. The world was still spinning as Hermes pushed himself upright, shaking off glass and debris. His arrival was met by the ominous *ca-chunk* of chambering rounds.

Pandora's vultures circled.

"Let me see him!" a shrill voice cried. It could only be Minos. "Move aside!"

Hermes smiled at the pestilent spirits. "Looks like I'm about to have my day in court, ladies."

The Keres begrudgingly stepped aside.

Hermes strutted past the snarling demons. "You see what I did there? You can use that line in the movie trailer."

Moving beyond the Keres, Hermes turned his attention to the courtroom, enlarged to fit the mad king's ego. At least a dozen cathedrals could fit into the grand space, Hermes noted on his stroll down the nave lined with soaring Doric columns, between which oxen and goats were tethered and munched on hay. In the Underworld, equality under immortal law meant a soul couldn't change their judgment by tossing some coin or influence. Minos clearly had changed that tradition. Hell had finally caught up to capitalism. Those anxious souls that had reached the end of the line—only for their turn to be interrupted—cleared the dance floor for Hermes. Wealthy spectators rushed in to fill the gallery. The presence of a god promised far more excitement than the typical endless, droll proceedings.

Hermes reached the booster seat of a bench from which Judge Minos, flanked by columns that dwarfed his already short stature, presided. A stack of slaughtered oxen was piled before him as sacrificial offerings. Ghastly tapestries, sewn from human skin, hung over his shoulders and depicted the history of his reign, most notably his recent overthrow of the other two judges. In the center tapestry, the two deposed judges were wrapped in chains, reaching up to touch the feet of a heroic Minos. An homage to the *Last Supper* but with a bondage-fetish twist. An eyeball in the tapestry followed Hermes like a corny haunted house trick, though it wasn't a trick. The judges had literally been sewn into the banner.

Two seats had been left vacant on either side of Minos, a conspicuous reminder of who was the one true judge. Minos was the Cabbage Patch Kid of dictators—plump cheeks a grandma would kill to pinch. His heritage was faintly South Asian, and his seat was bedazzled with exotic jewels. He dressed in a blood-red robe, fingers encrusted with heavy rings, perpetually slouched from the weight of gold draped around his neck. Hermes quickly scanned for the keys to Hell but saw no sign of them.

Minos clenched at the sight of his nemesis. "You're banned!"

"I lifted it," Hermes said.

"You can't give your own orders."

"Apparently, I can."

Minos leaned forward. "You've done it now. You are above yourself."

"Funny coming from one man when there should be three."

"Hades granted me this post. By decree. All souls must pass through my court."

"That's bullshit, and you know it," Hermes said. The Keres chittered ominously. "I'm no fan of the abusive prick, but you know the Furies forced him to sign. You took advantage."

Minos dropped back under the weight of his jewelry. Gold coins rattled around his neck. "You've been away too long."

"No shit, dude."

"I was an emperor in life. A king in death. Never a dude," Minos declared.

"Well, you're certainly no god."

"And thank them all for that!" Minos rapped his ring-festooned knuckles on the marble. "I don't have to suffer your insults anymore. I'm in charge now. So...so...there!"

Hermes wouldn't have been surprised if Minos followed that up with a nanny nanny boo boo. Minos loved grudges, and Hermes had certainly given him plenty of opportunities to harbor them. In hindsight, he probably should have laid off poking his thin skin.

"You're a tyrant, at best," Hermes said, embracing his worst tendencies.

Minos vibrated with fury. "If I'm a tyrant then you're…you're a bully!"

"Am not," Hermes mocked. "I'm rubber and you're glue, whatever you say bounces off me and sticks to you."

Minos sputtered and spun to the courtroom. "What riddle is this?"

Hermes laughed, giving permission for everyone else. A round of chuckles rippled around the courtroom. Minos turned a bright scarlet. Nothing was worse to Minos than laughter at his expense.

"QUIET! STOP LAUGHING!" he thundered, which only led to more laughter. "You've set them all against me! With soldiers at my gates. You're trying to depose me!"

The courthouse doors shook from the roar of battle, which had broken through to the lobby. Minos finally had cause to be paranoid.

"Give me the keys. I'll call them off," Hermes lied, knowing Aegos would take the tyrant's head.

"Fuck you, Hermes!"

The pestilent Keres stirred with anticipation, sensing Minos was ramping up to one of his notorious tantrums—and that meant they would soon feast. Their batlike wings rustled and fluttered discordantly. A few hovered off the ground.

"They're mine! Go to hell!" Minos raged.

"Easy commute."

All four stocky feet of Minos launched up from the bench and he shouted: "DOWN WITH THE GODS!"

Hermes sighed, and the Keres unleashed their own hell. The brainless creatures had inadvertently formed a circular firing squad, cutting down many of their own. Hermes launched himself into the stack of carcasses. Rounds pounded the flesh as he fired back from the bovine bunker. The enforcers scattered, sheltering behind benches and columns.

The courtroom quieted with battle lines drawn. Hermes wedged himself into the cavity of an ox, shoving aside its stomach to tuck within the rib cage. It smelled oddly like spring meadow laundry detergent—oxen innards fresh. Despite the predictable predicament, Hermes did enjoy a good standoff. There was an art to getting out of messes of his own making. He shimmied off his backpack and rummaged for a fresh clip. Protein bar wrappers spilled out, and his fingers hit bronze.

"Hermes, I've told my Keres not to fire!" Minos called out cockily from behind his dais. He thought he had Hermes cornered.

"Very kind of you."

"The gods thought making me a judge was some sort of honor."

Hermes pictured a smirk on the small man's face. "You felt otherwise."

"Subordination is insufferable," Minos continued.

"I'm all about insubordination. Why don't you help me insubordinate the subordinates and hand over the keys?"

"Ha!" Minos cried. "I decide who passes through the Underworld and where. I alone. You're in no position to barter. The only outcome I'll accept is your abdication."

Hermes thumped the back of his head on a rib. Gods and mortals were so much alike. Everyone was after more and more and more—including himself. There was not enough to go around, and nothing was ever enough anyway. He was getting weary of it. "How did we all get so dissatisfied?"

Hermes heard Minos scoff. "The gods dissatisfied? How rich! You are unhappy and complacent. We had famine, death, heartbreak, and unanswered prayers, while you drank and fucked away immortality. Then you act surprised new religions claimed Earth. What did you expect? You lost the right to our worship."

Hermes sighed. "You're right."

Minos cackled like a hyena. Hermes hated that laugh. "Of course I'm right. And now that I've shrugged off this yoke, I'm well on my way to eternal satisfaction. You Olympians are reaping what you've sown. We control Hell. Earth next. Then Heaven!"

Heaven too. Huh. That's new.

Minos continued ranting away.

Hermes stopped listening. The time for negotiation had clearly ended. "Welp, time to do this the easy way."

Hermes burst through the oxen carcass like Marilyn Monroe from a birthday cake, surprising Minos and the Keres, fanned up his pistol, and fired a single shot. Minos squealed as a bullet grazed his ear and fell backward over his bench to a fresh uproar of laughter that included the sycophantic Keres. That shut Minos up.

A moment later, Hermes mashed the Helm of Hades over his golden locks. Fireworks exploded in his brain and his pupils burned as the god magic instantly did its work. All light extinguished inside the courtroom, blinding everyone but Hermes. The hall filled with terrified screams.

He watched Minos leap back up and whirl around, wildly swiping at the air. "No, it can't be! Hades gave you his helmet? Not fair!"

The Helm didn't just blind everyone who wasn't wearing it—it gave its occupant the vision of an eagle. The contrast and detail were astounding. Hermes loved his god toys. "Time to play."

He watched the Keres squeal in frustration as they stumbled over benches and groped about the courtroom. It was almost too easy to avoid them.

"Marco!" Hermes called, and Minos pirouetted in a circle.

"Her-her-her-mes," Minos stuttered, eyes wide and vacant, unable to find purchase.

"No, you're supposed to yell *Polo*," Hermes instructed. "I yell *Marco*, you reply *Polo*."

"Shoot him!"

Only Hermes could see the fluorescent streaks that blazed across the courtroom as the Keres blindly opened fire with their assortment of prehistoric rifles, felling terrified souls and their own alike. Bullets obliterated columns and hacked pieces from the marble walls. The scent of blood further whipped the demons into a frenzy until they finally forgot their orders, dropped their guns, and descended on each other like piranhas.

Hermes shimmied his way through the mayhem, avoiding snapping jaws, slashing talons, and tangled wings. Reaching the dais, he commandeered Minos' throne, propped up his feet, and lit one of his in-case-of-emergency joints.

"Nice to feel like a god again," he said. The weed wafted over Minos, who was crawling on all fours. The judge made it a few feet, stopped, then turned back.

The last two Keres rolled on the floor devouring one another. They simultaneously ripped out each other's throats, and the courtroom blissfully fell silent.

Minos stopped moving and looked up at nothing. "A cheap parlor trick."

Hermes leaned down and whispered in his ear, "But effective."

Minos leapt to his feet and ran straight into a wall. Hermes grabbed him by the scruff and ripped open the front of his robe.

The golden keys—one for each river—were fused to the judge's chest. Hermes grumbled.

"We're going for a walk," he said, and dragged the judge from his court.

***

Odysseus descended all one hundred and eleven floors unscathed. It seemed a bit perverse to do so without a scratch. But there was no guarantee he wouldn't meet catastrophe around the next corner. Literally Catastrophe—she was a Ker.

Instead, Odysseus sighted a sign for the courtroom, which, incidentally, was on the ground floor after all. In hindsight, Hermes should have continued with him down the stairwell, but Odysseus was never an ace at navigation. He hoped Hermes had found another one of those terrible elevators and rendezvoused with his target.

Odysseus sprinted through the judge's private chambers, decorated with homoerotic statues of Judge Minos' favorite subject: Minos. He skipped a visit to the bathhouse sauna, where his contemporary kings lounged with young harems slithering over their raisin bodies like pythons.

He stopped at an oval foyer of extravagant pink marble where two corridors intersected and froze with indecision. Which was the right way? The sounds of distant battle—cries, gunfire, clashing steel—rang from either side. A sense of doom crept over his shoulders and down his spine, landing in his stomach like food poisoning.

He slowly turned around and came face-to-face with Catastrophe. Like body spray on a teenage boy, she overdid it on the eau de doom. In hindsight, that sense of impending death should have been a dead giveaway. Catastrophe was one of the most powerful Keres, preferring the classics: spear and a spiked mace. Chain mail armor draped down to her talons, and her wings were stapled with razors. Behind her stood two stupid-looking cacodemons blinking excessively and clutching rifles from the Great War.

There was no time for Odysseus to notch an arrow, and his sword was sheathed and fastened. He closed his eyes and readied to meet his doom. Rather, he thought he closed his eyes—because the world went utterly, completely black.

Odysseus must have gone blind, overdosed on doom. Because his eyes were most definitely open, but he saw nothing. He crouched into a defensive posture and drew his sword, listening to a series of blows, screeches, and screams, intermixed with the crack of gunfire. The smell of gunpowder filled his nostrils. The clang of steel vibrated along his skin. Bodies thumped to the floor.

Then nothing.

"Hello?" Odysseus spun around to the blackness. He couldn't even see his blade. Catastrophe had plagued him with a second death: eternal darkness!

A hand suddenly gripped his arm, and all at once his sight returned. He had eyes. Arms. A body. He was still dead. Hallelujah!

Hermes—glorious Hermes—stood grinning before him, the Helm of Hades tucked under his arm. Minos was hog-tied and draped over his shoulder. Above them, a chandelier swayed madly as its bulbs sucked in the darkness like tar slurped through a straw. Bits of Catastrophe painted the marble walls like syrup on frozen yogurt.

Odysseus lowered his sword. "Look who's the conquering hero."

"I should've taken the stairs," Hermes admitted.

An orchestra of armor and sandals filled the west flank as Greek soldiers stormed the foyer. Aegos led the charge. Their shields were dented, splintered, or gone; swords broken; ammunition spent. Marred by wounds that would have been fatal and covered in demon blood, they were more alive than ever.

Aegos dropped to one knee in reverence, out of breath yet beaming. "We've taken control of the courthouse. We'll clear the tower, then regroup, march on the Furies, and free the Underworld."

The soldiers thrust mailed fists into the air and thundered their approval. The floor trembled under their triumph.

Hermes removed the coin pouch as promised and held it out for Aegos. "Fair is fair. But, uh, feel free to refuse the money out of pride."

Aegos stood, quickly snatched the coin purse, and stuffed it under his cape.

Hopes dashed. Or were they?

Hermes was several pounds of drachma lighter—and lighter still, because, strangely, he didn't care. Before he could ponder his turn of fortune, the commander interrupted.

"My lord, where would you like us to keep the prisoner swine?" Aegos affixed his bloodthirsty eyes on Minos, wiggling persistently on Hermes' left shoulder.

Hermes shifted the dead weight of the king. "No need. I have plans for him."

"Sir?" His lips pinched together, clearly unhappy with the arrangement. "I think—"

"You have your coin. Minos is mine." Revolution be damned, Hermes was a god and wouldn't bow to some human. He turned away from the commander. "Odysseus?"

The contemplative king didn't respond, lost in some important thought. Hermes snapped his fingers in his face. "Yo! Hell to Odysseus."

Odysseus blinked. "Yes?"

"Are you ready?"

"For what?"

"Pick another two judges—the job's yours."

The idea slowly sank in. Odysseus started to protest, then abruptly relented with a sigh and a shrug. "Yeah, sure. Why not."

"Not the enthusiasm I was hoping for…" *Enthusiasm*, derived from the Greek word *enthousiasmos*, meaning to be inspired or possessed by a god. It would have to do.

Aegos was affronted. "You're leaving?"

Hermes shifted the judge's dead weight. "Yes."

"But you can't!" Aegos stepped back like a man threatening to jump off a building.

All this melodrama was getting on Hermes' nerves. A god had no need to explain himself. And yet he felt compelled. "Hey, I'm no savior. I didn't come here to set things right. I came for Persephone. You have your coin. You've won your freedom. Seems like a good day to me."

Around the foyer, the soldiers mirrored their commander's disappointment. More than disappointed—they were crushed, abandoned, betrayed. They wanted their god to fight alongside them, as they had every right to demand.

Hermes hated awkward goodbyes. "Okay then. We're all set? Good."

No one said a word. Hermes scooched around Aegos, who refused to budge, and walked through the army toward the exit. Soldiers openly wept; it was a lousy parting.

The lobby looked as if it had been rocked by a cruise missile. Demon corpses had been stacked into a pyramid, while broken soldiers moaned along the ground. The pain would not leave them for a thousand years. They had given up their eternal rest to fight for Persephone.

No, not Persephone—for me.

Outside, the slaughter continued in every direction and into the city. Here and there, a Ker swooped down to feast on an injured soldier before being chased off by liberated slaves who now wielded spears and arrows.

Faith. Aegos had lost faith. Right in front of his eyes, Hermes saw it slip away. Only hours ago, the kid had worshipped him. So had his men. Hermes had dismissed it then, mistaking it for loyalty bought and paid.

Hermes had lied again—lied to Aegos. He did want to set things right. He cared. But he had a sister to save. Earth to save. Hell, this was Hell!

He couldn't sacrifice Persephone to rebuild the Underworld. Gabriel and Eshu were right: his religion was dead.

Hermes didn't feel worthy enough to be called a god. Hadn't in ages. He was no more a god to these soldiers than a dime-store televangelist claiming to be the Messiah preaching to a motel room at three in the morning. Severed from his terrestrial ties and detached from his celestial obligations, Hermes was supposedly free…

The tingling sensation started in his left pinky, quickly spread from nose to toes. A revelation was rising.

Hermes could not exist unbound and undedicated.

He required a new place in this new universe.

This role demanded transcendence, no ego, and promised a greater power—because it obligated him to serve a higher purpose. Hermes had to find Persephone. *Not because I love her. I have to find her to save humanity. Save humanity so that it can worship any and all gods. Save humanity so that it can worship no gods at all. Save humanity to advance knowledge and science, art and philosophy. Save humanity so the humans can travel to distant universes and overcome their limitations of mind and body—and the limitations of their gods.*

Wherever the humans went, Hermes instinctively knew, they would carry him with them, carry the whole extended pantheon, the library of knowledge and thought and spirituality gathered since the first spark of creativity erupted in that second great cosmic explosion.

Humanity had been writing a bible more expansive than any scripture recited by priests, shamans, rabbis, imams, on whatever day they proclaimed holy. Perhaps, he could help the humans inscribe new chapters and new stories in which he was not a character. He liked thinking of himself watching over their small, bowed, sturdy shoulders as they scribbled, replenishing inkwells, sharpening quills, and saving PDF files to the cloud.

It would be a grand library. And when they were off achieving greater heights, he would have the library to himself, even if for a microsecond—a microsecond that would span infinite time—and he would sit in solitude with the encapsulation of all that there ever was and would be.

There was a greater destiny for him. For the humans.

Hermes knew it…he could feel it…

Hermes had faith.

CHAPTER TWENTY-THREE

THE HORIZON BURNED A forever crimson, and for a moment Hermes felt calm. He dumped Minos on the hood of the Bentley and re-lit the premature victory joint while taking in the altered state of the Underworld. On the streets below the parking garage, Greek soldiers had set up barricades of burning tires. Strings of coarse black smoke bumped between the glass towers before congregating along the roof of the world. There were no more lines snaking through the city for judgment. News had spread fast of their victory (credited to Aegos) and the ascension of Judge Odysseus. Souls were flooding into the city by the hopeful thousands, eager to join the fight and end their purgatory.

Hermes had promised Persephone to lay low. That almost made him laugh.

The hood thumped behind him as Minos tried to wriggle free of the bindings. Instead, he wriggled off the car and smacked his face on the concrete. Hermes grudgingly flicked away his roach and propped Minos back on the windshield.

Ripping open his robe, Hermes found the keys had fused to his chest. It was a grotesque sight, in a botched-plastic-surgery kind of way.

Hermes scooped the rag from Minos' mouth. "Remove the keys."

Minos threw his head back and cackled as if this was the funniest damn thing he had ever heard. A wet stain expanded between his legs. So much for diplomacy.

Hermes shook his head and went to the trunk. Under a spare tire he found a crowbar. Minos immediately sobered as Hermes returned, slapping the claw edge against his palm.

"Wait! Wait—"

Hermes jammed the chisel between the keys and Minos' chest. The judge squealed. Hermes threw his weight into it, jimmying the claw as ribs cracked, but the golden keys wouldn't budge.

Eventually Hermes had to stop and catch his breath. Minos flopped forward and vomited a torrent of raw fish. Hermes barely dodged the wasabi slurry, though some of it splattered his sneakers. As an emetophobic, Hermes wanted to run for the hills, but he stayed put for the greater good. Thanks to whichever god invented benzos.

"Sorry, should have warned that was gonna hurt. Oh, and who the fuck eats sushi in Hell?"

Minos spat a piece of sashimi past his feet. "Don't judge me, it was all you can eat. And I was trying to explain, if you'd only allow me. That won't work because—"

"Let's try again." Hermes slammed the claw into Minos' chest and propped a foot on the tire for better leverage. The judge's eyes rolled upward as Hermes twisted and twisted, grunting from the effort, until the crowbar finally snapped in two.

"Guess we're going to have to get creative."

Minos gasped. "I swore an oath!"

"To whom?"

"Styx…Goddess Styx. Unbreakable."

Hermes grimaced. "Shit. Why didn't you say so?"

This complicated things. If Minos swore an unbreakable oath to the goddess Styx on the banks of her river, then there was nothing Hermes could do to remove the keys.

"What was the oath? Exactly. Word for word."

"I don't remember word for word." Minos sealed his eyes.

"Paraphrase."

"I'm trying! I'm not exactly of sound mind and body right now. What does it matter?"

Hermes flicked the half of the crowbar still wedged between Minos' ribs. Minos screamed again.

"Indulge me."

Minos slumped over. Air wheezed out from his punctured lungs through several holes. It sounded like a chorus of six-year-olds with recorders strangling *Mary Had a Little Lamb*.

"Hermes the torturer? No better than the Furies."

"Never claimed I was. Now talk."

"I swore I would protect the keys for all time. That…that only through me could you navigate the Underworld. Something to that effect." After some effort, he managed a droopy stroke-victim smile.

Hermes hurled the broken half of the crowbar into oblivion and paced through the Bentley's headlights, shoving his hands through his hair. "Moron, she tricked you!"

Minos shimmied off the windshield and onto his feet. "Explain."

"She made you the key. You are the key."

Minos began to cackle but instead hacked up half a lung.

This wasn't how Hermes had pictured his lone-wolf hero's journey when he was putting together his vision board. He may as well trade his Bentley for a minivan.

"I guess we're carpooling."

Hermes buckled Minos the corpse into the passenger seat. Safety first. The hand sanitizer came in handy to clean off the demon blood. He motioned for Minos to hold out his palms and squirted another dollop into them.

Minos stared at the gel. "What is this ritual?"

"It's called hygiene."

Minos sniffed the sanitizer, then cautiously licked his fingers. "Not bad."

The Bentley screeched down the corkscrew ramp. Minos cringed with each drop until they rocketed onto a street past a wall of flaming tires. Hermes floored his beast, running lights, weaving around chariots until the courthouse tower wilted in the rearview mirror like an old pecker after a cold dip.

Back on the highway to Hell, an orange curtain partitioned the landscape. Their next destination: the burning river of fire. In olden times, this was when the noble and virtuous had been whittled from the vast waste of humanity. They passed out of purgatory and started their final trek to Elysium. If you were only a tourist, you needed Hades' permission to travel, which meant you needed his keys. The Furies had a copy, but the keys attached to Minos were the master set that opened all doors in all directions. How exactly they would work fused to Minos, Hermes wasn't sure, but he hoped it would save him some miles and help him avoid bumping into Lily, formerly Lethe, goddess of the final river in Hell that bore her name. Though Lily was the goddess of oblivion, as an ex-girlfriend she never forgot, and she never forgave.

Hermes really wanted to avoid her.

Beyond the swampland of the courthouse district, the Underworld became a vast and barren salt flat with a cocaine-lab glow. No water. No life. Nowhere to rest your eyes. Boring as boring could get, and Minos wasn't much company, his arms petulantly crossed for the last several hours. Though, to be fair, that was partially to hold his ribs together. It would be a long ride.

For several hours, the only conversation came from the same radio disk jockey, now broadcasting the latest Hermes gossip. Hermes was responsible for the most action the Underworld had seen in centuries. Callers stacked the lines, and everyone had an opinion. Hermes couldn't have shocked a system more than if he'd strutted into a retirement home with strippers and bath salts. So far he'd killed Megaera—check; instigated a revolt at the courthouse—check; installed a new judge—check; and kidnapped Minos—check. But the most popular subject was Hermes' quest to find Persephone. Everyone wanted to dish on her abduction. Eternal winter: for or against? It was a fifty-fifty split. The latest caller was lamenting the messenger god's unwanted meddling. "Why doesn't that arrogant son-of-a-bitch god just butt the hell out of Hell!"

Hermes caught Minos nodding his head in agreement. "How about music?"

He switched to a random station. A swing band played a raucous melody. Minos bobbed his head enthusiastically with the song, much to Hermes' surprise.

"You like this?"

"It's boogie-woogie," Minos said, trying to snap his fingers along—hard when cuffed.

Hermes switched the station again to some Middle Eastern pop, a grating Arabic ditty with too many zithers and electronic beats. All they needed was a light cube and a belly dancer and this would be a real party. Minos soured. It was the music of his kingdom's enemies.

"Now this is boogie," Hermes said with a smile.

Minos studied him like a finger painting hanging in an art gallery. "I gather we're headed to the White Island"—Hermes turned up the music; Minos raised his voice—"to rescue the goddess. How virtuous of you."

Hermes flashed a look of warning. "You don't get to say her name."

Minos shut off the radio. Bold.

"You weren't listening anyway. You know, I've been sitting here... thinking..."

"Glad you decided to give that a try."

"What's your angle?"

The question threw Hermes.

"I mean, I had nothing to do with this predicament. Yes, I aligned myself with the Furies—hard to turn down the Mistresses of Torture. In return, they allowed me to reclaim my birthright. The Furies want revenge, ascension, a taste of the limelight. The shadow demons and the Keres—well, they want fresh blood, a little chaos and mayhem. We're all playing an angle. So again I ask, what's yours?"

"I just want my sister back."

Minos shook his head. "Hermes going out of his way for someone else? Without receiving anything in return? Doesn't make much sense to me. I've been trying to work it out for the last few hours, but I keep hitting a dead end. Everyone knows you're incapable of love. Gods like you have access to everything, the most exquisite food, but have no ability to taste."

Hermes kept his eyes on the brutally bland road. It was the only thing he could do to keep from chucking Minos out of the moving car.

Minos squished back into his headrest. "That's why you're hated. No... reviled. That's why the humans turned their backs on you. You demanded sacrifices, demanded worship and adoration. Then you offered nothing in return. We may be dead, but not on the inside. Not like you. The vainglory of immortality. You strut, Hermes. You aeolist. Only difference between you and Narcissus is a mirror. I fought for my place in history. The gods won't fault me for following my nature. Oh, wait! They honored me for it, remember? But you, hiding behind Persephone—"

Hermes slammed his foot on the brake pedal and Minos' forehead nailed the dashboard with a hard smack that sent blood gushing from a gash above his brow.

"Traffic."

Minos smiled at the empty highway.

***

The salt plains gave way to coal, a stark yin-yang, black-and-white-cookie divide. The wiper blades squealed as they pushed coal dust across the windshield. The dense smog was furnace red and sulfurous. They were close.

Crumbling factories sprung up along the road like warts. Smoke-stacks belched pollution while massive earthmovers plowed the black soil, drifting in and out of the smog like slugs. The highway widened by many lanes, though there were no other cars on the road.

Ahead, the road passed beneath a colossal statue of a centaur, its fore-legs thrust in the air as if to buck a rider, as this was their place of punish-ment in the Underworld.

"Where are the Centaurs?"

Minos chuckled ominously. "You'll see."

Hermes should have grown accustomed to the foreboding.

After passing beneath the centaur's hindquarters, they drove onto an immense suspension bridge unfurling over the Phlegethon. Flames shot up from the river, licking the sides of the highway. Hermes cranked up the AC.

Minos marveled at the magic trick, pushing his face in front of a jet of cold air. "The wonders of the gods never cease."

"Yeah, we have a few tricks up our sleeve."

Upon the far shore, a black fortress blocked the final toll road to Ely-sium. Gothic statues devoted to the minions of Hades decorated its many ledges. Another two marble centaurs stood at attention beside the fortress gate, their bronze spears raised in salute.

"You see, the centaurs are still here," Minos said with a snicker.

"You turned them to stone. Did you use Medusa?"

"We would have if someone could find her. Hades misplaced her head. The Furies had to do it the old-fashioned way—poured concrete over them."

"So they were alive when you entombed them."

"We tried gold, but it kept melting from the heat. And don't tell me you're going to weep for the pests. Their population was getting out of control anyway."

Centaurs loathed humans. And both gods and humans loathed centaurs. Their punishment in the afterlife was to carry human souls on their backs and ford the Phlegethon. Upon reaching the opposite shore, horrendously burned, they were allowed to drink only from a trough. The water would heal their wounds—but only so they could make the painful journey all over again. The whole thing was designed to be as degrading as possible.

"And Nessus?" Hermes asked. Nessus was the leader of the centaurs, slain by Heracles.

"Where he's always been." Minos directed Hermes to the rearview mirror. The large statue they had driven beneath was no roadside attraction. Hermes suddenly saw the striking resemblance to the king of centaurs.

"We poked a few holes for him to breathe," Minos said.

Hermes quietly seethed.

"What? It's an honor."

It was a punishment Hermes wouldn't inflict even upon his worst enemies—the kind of cruelty that was the hallmark of his pantheon. Nessus and the centaur race were guilty only of existing. Hermes wanted to crush Minos right then, but a line of headlights erupted in front of the fortress, spanning the width of the bridge. He hit the brakes, and they skidded to a stop.

Minos whistled mockingly. "Oh dear."

Engines revved as cacodemons kicked their military Harleys to life, with sidecars for second gunners. Since the demons had four arms—two for the handlebars, two for their rifles—they could multitask better than a college student on Adderall.

"What trick will Hermes pull this time? Better be clever, better be quick."

A female frame cut in front of the headlights. The glow from a phone illuminated half a face. The rest of her was shrouded in darkness. Hermes read her lips—"He's here"—before she hung up.

Minos practically bounced off his seat with excitement. "You're screwed, Hermes. Screwed!"

"Thanks for the encouragement." Hermes focused on the mystery woman. Her stare reached down the bridge and grabbed him by the throat with a thousand volts of fear. Images of frozen bodies flashed through his mind. He saw Lilith's frostbitten face in the snow, Saint Peter's Basilica, and those angel wings carrying him higher and higher…

The invisible fingers retracted and Hermes collapsed onto the steering wheel, clutching it like a life preserver. Chills wracked his body as dread coiled around his spine.

"It's Melinoë…"

"It's the end. Might as well embrace it."

Hermes shifted into reverse, threw his arm around Minos, and tucked his chin over his elbow. "Like hell."

Rubber squealed as they hurtled backward. The motorcycles shot forward. A swarm of Keres hidden in the keep rocketed down the bridge like missiles. Bullets crackled and pocked the car. Hermes steered toward the Arc de Nessus.

"Hold on," Hermes warned, and flattened the pedal.

Minos looked into his side mirror and squealed.

They slammed into a stone hoof. Minos' head ricocheted into the dashboard again. A perfect ten. The personal injury claim would bankrupt him—if he had any money left. But Hermes couldn't worry about litigation; there were enough demonic threats as is. He switched to fourth gear and twerked his bumper against the statue.

Minos pressed his knuckles to his nose to stem a tide of blood. "What are you doing?!"

A crack crawled up the centaur's stone haunches. Hermes kept the Bentley dry-humping against the concrete leg.

"This is embarrassing," Minos said, jerking in rhythm with each hump.

Hermes kept an eye on the demons hurtling toward them.

The trunk pancaked and the statue finally gave way. For a moment, they supported the centaur's weight.

Hermes grinned and shifted to drive. "Timber!"

The Bentley launched at the cacodemons as the statue pitched forward. Its shadow crested the sunroof, triggering the car's soft interior lights as a thousand tons of concrete threatened to crush them. Hermes gunned the engine. Bullets blasted his side mirror and battered the roof. He swerved between startled cacodemons now making hasty U-turns and veering out of the way. But they were trapped by flames on either side of the bridge. Hermes smashed through a sidecar, flattening a demon lassoing razor wire. The barbs bit into the grill, dragging the squished demon under the chassis, scraping and thumping and spitting sparks from the tailpipe. A few disoriented Keres splattered against his windshield like plump mosquitoes. They were almost at the fortress gates.

The massive monument crashed down, flattening the biker gang. The bridge pitched violently side to side, cables snapping and whipping through the air. Keres dropped like flies, snared in the metal or nailed by shards of cement. A wave of dust tumbled over them. Hermes hit the brakes, unable to see past the bullet-riddled hood.

Laying low yet again.

Behind them, the centaur statue had fallen on its side. Its concrete belly began to distend. A deep rumble emanated from within, building until the statue erupted in a violent C-section. Two hooves kicked through the stone. A savagely muscled stallion, capped by the torso of a Neanderthal, exploded from the prison.

Hermes had just freed the ferocious Nessus, king of the centaurs.

The colossal centaur dramatically whipped his mullet mane, shaking loose boulders from the knotted beard that cascaded past his stomach—a portrait of steroidal rage and five-time centerfold of *Bodybuilder Centaur Magazine*. Nessus roared like he was taking the ring at WrestleMania, shaking the Underworld with his fury. Grabbing chunks of concrete, he hurled the wreckage at the surviving cacodemons. Nessus was out for vengeance.

Minos grabbed the panic bar. "Oh dear."

"Shush," Hermes commanded, and adjusted the rearview mirror to watch the centaur rampage. Nessus bucked and trampled demons under his hooves, snatching Keres from the air with barbaric glee.

The dust finally cleared from the bridge ahead, and Hermes shifted into gear.

Almost immediately, Melinoë peeled from the shadows into the headlights. Hermes slammed the brakes, and they skidded into a face-off with his niece. You never wanted to find yourself playing a game of chicken with a nymph—especially Melinoë.

Hermes flashed his brights and honked, but she wouldn't budge.

"She's not a cow," Minos said derisively.

Hermes laid on the horn. *Beeeeeppppp! Beeeeeeppppppp!*

"Try flashing the lights again. That might work."

Hermes finally lost his cool. "I fucking invented music! I shouldn't have to deal with this shit!" With every word he punched the horn. "Does?" *HONK!* "Everyone?" *HONK!* "Have?" *HONK!* "To rebel?!" *HONK!* "Even! Persephone's! Daughter!" *HONK! HONK! HONK!*

The last punch went through the steering wheel, and the horn died like a tuba player shoved into a volcano. His cheeks were red, and he was embarrassed by the outburst.

"You act surprised," Minos said.

"Persephone didn't consent to be raped. She didn't want the child. She didn't want her power and status. She didn't want the responsibility— didn't ask for it. None of us did..."

He leaned against the broken wheel. Melinoë never strayed from the beam of light, eyes steely black, like a possum guarding a garbage bin in the dead of night. Meanwhile, Nessus had galloped off into the pollution, likely to free his herd. *Good*, Hermes thought, embracing the despair. *More chaos for the Underworld. Let it all burn.*

The sudden onset depression was Melinoë's doing. Hermes had no doubt.

"I guess some waves you can't see until they hit the shore," Minos said wistfully.

Hermes whirled on him, fist cocked, but there wasn't a smirk or excuse for a face-punching to be found.

"I didn't choose to be a king." His voice was tinged with sadness.

Intrigued, Hermes lowered his fist.

"I was born into it. Well, I also killed my father...but once I took the throne, I think I did some really great things. Conquered a few lands. And yes, I killed a lot of people. Made a few enemies. At the time, it didn't look so bad. How would I know? No one ever tells you the crown is poison. You rule over your people, but like a great big ocean, you never know what's going on beneath. One day, the water's receded and your pleasure craft is beached in the mud and a wave is barreling down on you and everything you built. Anyway, point is, some waves you can't see until they hit."

Hermes turned away and squeezed his eyes shut. Snowflakes danced behind his vision, darkened by mountain peaks.

"I once showed Persephone winter..."

"Why would you do something as stupid as that?"

"Her mother had vanished. She was depressed. I thought it would cheer her up."

"You thought taking her to the one place that reminds her why she is depressed would make her *not* depressed? Do you host AA meetings in a bar, too?"

Hermes opened his eyes and frowned. Minos wasn't wrong.

"She enjoyed it, I think. She saw winter wasn't so bad—the beauty in it. That the seasons need to change, and it isn't a curse. We made snow-men and had a snowball fight..."

Minos' face crinkled as if Hermes had let one rip in the car. "Sounds delightful."

Yet the memory suddenly didn't feel so rosy. Perhaps it was Melinoë's power, but Hermes wondered if he had been remembering it all wrong—doctoring the footage. It had always been the perfect winter's day with Persephone. Too perfect.

"It's the world that keeps changing. That's our curse," Hermes said.

"There are no more rules, and that frightens you—despite you being the rule breaker, or most especially because."

"Why do you say that?"

"Because rule breakers need to know where the lines are more than those who simply live within them. Now you won't know if you've gone too far—not until you've fallen off the edge of the universe."

"Feels like I've been falling."

"Best to embrace it then."

Hermes took a deep breath and turned to Minos, who held his gaze without judgment. "When you live forever it's hard to be perfect."

"A god confessing fallibility to a mortal. Interesting times."

Hermes nodded. "This doesn't mean we're friends."

"I would also despise such an outcome." Then Minos jutted his chin toward Melinoë. "Well, what do you want to do about her? Adopt her? Otherwise, let's boogie."

Hermes gritted his teeth and shifted to fourth. "Boogie it is."

The car lurched forward with drag-race propulsion. He centered Melinoë between his headlights like an ex in a crosswalk.

A smile crept across her face. She extended her arms to embrace the two tons of steel.

Thud. The grill punched slender Melinoë in the stomach. She folded over the hood then disappeared, swept under the wheels. The fortress gate loomed over the end of the bridge just ahead, sealed shut like gritted teeth.

Hermes thumped the keys with his fist, knocking the wind out of Minos. "Do you push a button? What do we need to do? It's not opening."

Minos gasped and filled his lungs. "You don't—"

A charred hand grabbed the roof, and Melinoë appeared at Hermes' window. Her face molted into an anguished Persephone—only the proportions were all wrong, and she had been burned, cheeks scarred and flabby like a rubber mask. She wept Virgin Mary tears of blood and moaned his name, pleaded to let her in. To save her. A trick. Hermes knew it was a trick. Yet he reeled as Melinoë's darkness crept into his heart. Despair was the only emotion left in the universe.

Persephone bent her neck back and smashed her brow into the window. Glass exploded into the car. Hermes lost control of the wheel as she squeezed inside, bones snapping, shards ripping through her nightgown and slicing her skin. The road ahead disappeared.

Persephone was on top of him. Her mouth gaped like a croaking marionette. The voice that spoke echoed like a chorus of witches chanting in the forest.

"Hermes, who comes to my temple, I oft doubt whether you are god or man. Hermes, who acts but does not think, you doubt whether you fight a war you want to win. Chaos reigns at the edge of your path."

She clamped her burning hands onto his face. "You don't want to save your sister."

Then her leather lips pressed against his, and Hermes felt his heart and soul—for whatever wither remained—go black.

Melinoë slithered into his mind, into his past. An invasive parasite. Hermes suddenly remembered every wretched moment in his existence. It were as if a tucked-away box forgotten on a shelf had been upended, raining memories and scattering them on the floor. He had to pick them up, put them back, frantically hide them away. But she'd already seen everything the instant she touched them. Read his nightmares like an open diary.

Hermes was helpless.

***

A boy stood while the gods sat. Splayed on silk cushions, they feasted—bodies polished with oil, draped in silk gowns and chitons. Platters were spread along the marble foyer. The first eleven lounged, sucking gristle off fingers as they dined on succulent lamb and pressed sun-ripened grapes to their lips, popping them between their teeth so the sweet, sticky juice dripped repulsively down their chins and beards to dribble on their breasts. A goblet fell and wine raced across the floor. They laughed and dragged their tongues through the ruby mess as sensually as if they were licking it off their lover's body.

The boy was so young. A mere messenger. He watched.

He watched Persephone, nestled beside her mother, a girl too old to suckle, and yet Demeter clutched her close like a doll. Young and beautiful and dotted and spoiled. She did not have to deliver messages nor fetch wine. She was not told she required patience. She ate, dainty fingers picking morsels of branzino, tasting and spitting out, choosing perfect pears and tossing them aside to burst upon the golden statues with perfect indifference.

He was told he was his father's favorite, and he was equal, yet they placed him in a corner. All day, he delivered their words. Ran until his feet bled and his wings lagged listlessly on the same floor they lapped with their tongues. He earned a bite. They promised him that. And more. Promised him the world. Promised him a spot at the never-ending feast. When?

When.

When he did all he was told. When he learned to be a god. When he listened to their bombastic sermons, withered at their roots, stating they were older and therefore wiser. When he learned his place was beneath them, even as they ordered him to act above them.

So he waited. Patient. Obedient. Repressed. And when he finally said, "Now, now I'm ready." When he arrived and asserted his right, they said, "Not yet," and "Wait," and "It's not time," and gave him their backs to gorge themselves until the air rang with bells of flatulence and they fell asleep with heads resting on the rims of their latrines. So he waited again. Did as he was told, was obedient. He told himself: *soon.* Still, they spat "Not yet," as if they had not even the time to consider his request. He stood his ground, and they caressed his face, said, "I love you" and "You mean the world to me," and then they tossed him scraps.

His lip curled in distaste, his eyes cold and mean. He screamed, "How dare you!" Screamed, "You devour indifference!" And they stepped away, aghast and betrayed, wounded and hurt. And he was confused. So very confused. And he couldn't speak. They stole that silence from him and twisted it as an affirmation of his guilt and banished him from their room of plenty.

So he no longer stood in the corner. He stood beyond the wall, listening to their muffled conversations. And he suddenly wished to stand in the corner. He mourned his lost corner. Just to be close. That is enough. Close to the intemperance and the vile smell of farts and wine. That is enough. His stomach rumbled for scraps. And his skin warmed. Then his flesh burned. His tears dried like sea spray on the sunbaked cliffs of Lindos. Rage engulfed him. His mind split like an atom. He punished his body as his fists pounded bruises on his chest like war paint. Hate nourished him. Filled his knotted stomach. He vowed revenge. He vowed REVENGE. Hermes vowed revenge.

He buried it in that box. That forgotten box. The box she found. She found it. She found his revenge.

***

Hermes snapped back.

Fake Persephone smiled. "You're ready."

Hermes released the wheel, embracing the old pain. Minos watched, baffled and afraid.

"I'm ready," Hermes said, and she pressed her forehead to his.

"Revenge. That's what you always wanted." She said it so softly it was almost a thought. But he didn't need her to say it at all. His lust for revenge had long been distilled, fused with his identity.

"Yes. My revenge."

"Yes!" she screamed, orgasmic.

His gaze rolled from her to the approaching gate. "It's time."

He gently placed his hands on her waist, and she buried into his lap like a cat. Then she felt his grip tighten. Past sensual. Melinoë, Harbinger of Nightmares, would finally taste her own medicine.

Melinoë was suddenly afraid. "But this is what you wanted."

"My revenge"—Hermes felt the strength of revelation, the truth as he said it aloud for the very first time in the whole of existence—"is to save them all."

He opened the door, and fake Persephone morphed back to Melinoë.

"I saw him! I saw the boy! I saw his bruises!"

Hermes shoved her out just as they slammed into the great iron gate. He expected a crash. Screaming metal, breaking glass, crushing steel— but they simply passed through the portal. The keys glowed an effervescent blue under Minos' robe.

The gate sheared Melinoë in half in a mist of ash and blood. Then she was gone.

The fever dream broke with the taste of bile in his throat.

The rest of the suspension bridge continued ahead, lined with an army of entombed centaurs. A tornado of Keres burst from the cables. They congealed into a murmuration and lunged at the car like a spear.

Hermes wrestled the wheel and pumped the brakes. Air hissed. The line had been cut by Melinoë. The Bentley finally revolted and swerved uncontrollably. He looked up—

The engine block flattened the stone railing. Momentum flipped them vertically over the side of the bridge. The river of fire appeared below, ravenous and blinding as the surface of the sun. Keres latched on to the airborne, cartwheeling vehicle, snarls filling the windows.

For a moment they seemed to float. Then the car face-planted, the hood stuck upright in magma. They were buoyant, but it wouldn't last. Everything began to melt. Hermes untangled from his seatbelt and crawled over his seat. The heat was unbearable. Sweat sizzled on his skin.

Minos struggled desperately with his restraints. "Don't leave me! Help!"

Hermes stopped at the back window. *Damn my conscience!*

He turned back for Minos and cut his seatbelt free. Lava oozed over the hood.

Suddenly, the passenger door was ripped off its hinges. Nessus bent into the car, his body wreathed in fire, yet his hate of Minos burned hotter than any flame.

"Don't! Please, it was the Furies who ordered you imprisoned, not me!" Minos scrambled to climb between the seats to Hermes. "I was just following orders!"

Nessus gripped him by the scruff of his neck.

"Help me, Hermes! We bonded!"

Hermes could only offer a sorrowful look back. "Guess it's judgment day."

"NO!"

Hermes winced. "You're right. That was terrible, sorry. How about: justice is served. No, that's not it either..."

"SCREEEEWWWWWW—" Minos' last curse died as Nessus wrenched him from the seat like a bag of groceries. The centaur slung the judge on his back and galloped into the smoke.

The car dropped, and lava spilled past the windshield, melting the dashboard. Hermes needed to escape this death trap. *Should have asked if there was room for two on that pony*, he thought.

Outside, the Keres circled as they waited for him to appear.

Appear!

Hermes suddenly remembered...

He whirled for his bag in time to watch the Helm of Hades melt into a bronze puddle. It was too late to save Hades's most prized possession— but not himself. He lunged for the back window and onto the trunk. Keres screeched and dove. Hermes took a more literal leap of faith and snatched one of the flying demons as the lava swallowed the last of the Bentley.

Hermes rode the Ker like a bucking bronco through the acrid smoke. A glimpse of the shoreline passed below his sneakers. He tugged on her wing. "This is my stop!"

The Ker swiped its talons at his head. Demons made the worst Uber drivers. "No tip for you then."

Hermes yanked harder and sent them crashing into a sand dune, blowing a crater into the shore. A loud snap—and he felt his nose crush into the dirt. He disentangled from a mess of wings, aching and bruised.

The riled Ker came to its senses and pounced. Only, its head had vanished.

The decapitated Ker collapsed on top of Hermes, knocking him onto his back. The wound was a clean cut, a death so swift the demon never felt a thing. Stuck beneath the corpse, Hermes heard metal scraping rock. He rolled the Ker off him to find a goddess dragging both sword and body down the crater toward him.

Lily moved like a mirage, a vague quality that made her simultaneously ubiquitous and unmemorable, a beauty both rare and replaceable, like a billboard fashion model. She was thin and pale as a wisp of smoke, as if she could simply trickle through your fingers. Faint as a daguerreotype and fleeting as a moment of inspiration. Her voice was the whisper tickling your ear, the white noise lulling you to sleep.

Lily was the goddess of the river of oblivion, and she lived in the shadows of time.

She was also his ex-girlfriend.

The stare she generally aimed at Hermes would normally drop men and women to their knees, erase any sense of time and place. Hermes had long since grown immune to it. Demon blood funneled down her blade, dripping in a sad little pool by her bare feet.

"Is it true?" she squeaked.

Here we go…

Hermes snapped his broken nose back into place. "Hello, Lily."

She made a little show of dropping her shoulders in defeat. "You're here to save her?"

She wiped the back of her hand across her brow, as if it took monumental effort to do so.

Most any response would upset her, so he settled on a nod. She took a moment, seemed to accept it, then slowly turned and walked away. No shouting or yelling or crying. *Okay…*he thought. *Progress.*

"Come on. Don't want to waste eternity," she called from atop the ridge.

Hermes stood, his legs unsteady. Perhaps it was the car crash or the flight across the industrial badlands or the instigating of a rebellion. He was spent. And Lily had a habit of drinking your last reserves through a straw and slurping the bottom so that you knew there was nothing left.

Silver sand dunes extended around him. Lily left faint footprints down the beach, a cute trail of depression and misery.

Hermes had no choice but to follow those tracks deeper into Hell.

CHAPTER TWENTY-FOUR

PERSEPHONE HAD WATCHED A green Shakra candle burn to the nub. This Shakra supposedly promised prosperity. The flame, ten feet off the cell floor atop a tower of melted wax, flickered fitfully about, as if it could sense the impending darkness. It did not want to go out. The darkness would not last long, though. Like clockwork, an oddly cheerful cacodemon with the disposition of a kindergarten teacher at story time would enter with a replacement. Sometimes the candles her cacodemon candle-bringer brought had little bits of personality, like the purple birthday candle in the shape of the number four, or the cinnamon-scented one. Hell's scavengers must have gone dumpster diving behind a mall with a Yankee Candle. Her excitement rose as the wax dripped down the slope. This was Persephone's one bit of entertainment in the deprivation chamber.

By the devotional light, Persephone rummaged into her secret pocket. Only two petals remained on her summer daisy. She plucked one and promised herself that she would have no need for the last—she would be free. The petal tasted of honey and a perfectly ripe cantaloupe. She let it sit on her tongue and savored summer, staring up at the flame's promise of renewal. Once back on Earth, she would carpet Montana in the blooms.

The glow dipped below the ridge of the peak she now called Mount Waxymus, and the door to her cell opened. Her heart skipped a beat, and her thoughts raced with possibilities—new colors and new scents—a new candle. It was the dab of a wet cloth on parched lips, and she would suck it for all its moisture.

Her favorite demon did not enter. Soft footsteps crossed the room. A hem brushed the mice droppings and rustled the bones that littered the floor. A new visitor. Alecto eclipsed the crescent of light, her face bronzed from centuries bathing in human blood. The princess had come to pay the queen a visit. *Queen no more*, Persephone reasoned. Maybe she'd get the title back. Maybe not. Who cared?

The snakes nesting beneath Alecto's skin squirmed impatiently, betraying her state of mind. Persephone's eldest stepdaughter was more Mount Vesuvius than Mount Waxymus, ready for its thousand-year eruption. It took Persephone ages to learn how to decipher Alecto's moods, a skill necessary to survive Underworld high society. Hades was never buffeted by Megaera's fickle winds or Tisiphone's one-note bluster. Alecto, however, was in a league of her own. She could bend Hades to her will with terrifying ease. One look from his eldest, and the next hour, day, or month could be a nightmare of Hades jumping to her psychopathic demands. Initially cowed by her stepdaughters, Persephone had slowly grown immune. Chained to the floor of this dank cell, however, the terror had returned.

The Fury's stare probed the room. Control was the game. Persephone knew Alecto considered humans and gods as pawns and playthings, slaves and sex toys. When Alecto's gaze settled on her, Persephone jolted with fear.

Alecto snuffed out the candle. The promised prosperity of the green Shakra was not to be.

Heavy footfalls joined them in the darkness. Whatever large beasts they were, they easily found Persephone in the pitch black and unchained her shackles. A lengthy, scabrous finger traced her torso. She sealed her eyes and stifled her outrage. There lived creatures in the Underworld she had never seen and wished to keep it so. The humans feared these numens so much they never wrote of them or produced any depictions. They existed only in the oldest oral histories.

Some monsters were best forgotten.

The mysterious creatures pulled her to her feet and forced her to march.

CHAPTER TWENTY-FIVE

"You're tracking in mud," Lily mewed as she padded into her exquisite Romanesque villa, leaving Hermes in the sandstone foyer. His sneakers were indeed caked in mud, feathers, blood, and all sorts of odorous matter, fecal included. Did he give a shit (other than what was stuck to his soles)? Not really.

Hermes followed her into the first courtyard, where a large urn burbled with water, feeding a small pool. His shoes deposited little presents along her mosaic floors, and he took juvenile pleasure whenever a foot landed on a tiled face.

The villa consisted of a series of courtyards, each serving a different purpose of pleasure, overstuffed with daybeds and creature comforts, feather pillows and silk sheets. If Lily had come of age today, the palace would be wallpapered pink, plastered with nauseating unicorn stickers and boy-band posters, buried under mountains of stuffed animals, all of them screaming *I have daddy issues.* Basins of oil burned along the floor and a heavy incense mixed with soft vapors from mineral baths. His eyelids drooped, body aching for a massage table.

Lily crossed another courtyard, this one filled with sex toys and swings. A third contained a garden of white roses and fig trees pruned into sensual, willowy curves, and a fourth was a Pilates studio. Lily had acquired a few odd modern-ish appliances: a TV, a VCR, and a stack of Jane Fonda workout tapes. His eyes followed the two half-moon curves of her buttocks, caressed by her turquoise gown that rekindled dormant desires. He couldn't remember feeling this aroused since he enrolled in a month of free hot yoga in Malibu.

They hadn't exchanged words since she ordered him to take off his shoes, which he still hadn't. The silence left Hermes dreading her inevitable explosion. She sashayed into a den and stopped beside a sunken pit layered with pillows. He forced his eyes up.

"You dyed your hair?" Hermes remarked. Her signature white hair was now black. Morose may be Lily's maiden name, but mourning was just a drag and bad for her wardrobe.

She rolled her chin over her shoulder, radiating disappointment. "Did you just notice?"

Her eyebrows arched and a curtain of jet-black hair shielded her face. "Wait here." Then she slipped down a hall.

Without a tushie to behold, Hermes turned his attention on the opulent bedroom. A bedroom he knew well. Too well. A series of columns opened to a painfully familiar view of the River of Oblivion (or River Lethe), the last Hellish obstacle for the weary, far-traveled soul. The river was wide and deep, more like a lake, and cloaked in an impenetrable, disorienting fog. The magic waters guarded the White Island of Elysium, the last refuge for the brave and virtuous few. You could call it the Grecian Heaven. Lily ferried the worthy souls to their eternal, deserved resting place on the golden shores of plenty and peace.

However—always a catch—there was one final test, a last act of contrition. Every soul seeking admittance to Elysium needed only to drink a mere handful from Lily's river. Imbibe, and off you go to Paradise.

Easy? Not quite.

One sip from the River of Oblivion would erase your Earthly hard drive. Data irretrievable. Not just the porn stash, the bad deeds, ugly thoughts, and shameful moments that weigh a heart. The sip severed all ties, erasing you from all that made you…well, *you*. Your mother's face, father's wisdom, childhood games, spouse's embrace, first child's birth, true loves and heartbreaks—all of it gone forever. To obtain passage on Lily's ferry, the only way through the mist, a soul must be willing to sacrifice its identity. If a soul were truly virtuous, he or she would be willing to surrender their ego.

Drink freely and be blessed with anonymity. Only a blank slate, ready to be reborn, could embark to Elysium. Refuse to drink, which many did, and you were forced to turn around. Souls traveled hundreds of years on foot across the Underworld to reach this shore, for this single moment, and often only made up their mind once they knelt at its bank. The journey—its self-reflection—dictated the choice. By the time you reached this innermost ring, the Underworld expected resolution. Many who arrived decided to turn back, having already reached Paradise. An inner peace needed no external dimension. The soul could wander the Underworld for all eternity, content, forever connected to the generations that flowed beyond them.

During his messenger days, Lily's villa was a last pit stop once his duties to Hades and Olympus were fulfilled. Their not-so-secret-secret affair lasted several centuries—on and off, off and on, again and again—fraught with drama and sex, jealousy and intimacy. He fed into her fantasies, let her play the bored, work-from-home single goddess with a secret thing for the hunky mailman. It seemed harmless then. Hermes never stayed more than a month. Never. The plush and comfort of Lily's villa was as dangerous as Venus's flytrap. Hermes always managed to escape before she could consume him whole. He would flee while she slept. A cruel gesture—his departures always left her reeling. Then the clock reset, and she would anxiously await his return. Lily was a caged exotic bird left unattended and ignored, plucking out her own beautiful feathers one by one.

Hermes stepped out onto the terrace. A path meandered down a stunted cliff to the water's edge and a white pebble beach. A small boat tapped doltishly against the end of a wooden dock, the only sign of a current. The tranquility was treacherous, tempting Hermes with the siren song of amnesia. His journey, like the souls that ended their long pilgrimage here, had been one of self-reflection. Could he call it a hero's journey? Most certainly not. Hermes was no hero. Not with a capital *H*. Screw you, Joseph Campbell. Sigmund Freud would have been more interested in how Hermes wound up on this netherworld veranda, hosted by his ex-girlfriend, as he searched in vain for his lost half-sister, with whom the history books had long insinuated some illicit affair. His turbulent sexual and familial history shadowed his mythic triumphs. Hermes was just thankful he never became shorthand for incest: *The Hermes Complex*...an overabundance of feelings toward a half sibling.

If he were to grade himself thus far, he'd give himself a C+, verging on a B–, with extra credit for overthrowing Minos. But his hero's journey remained incomplete. Somewhere in Paradise, Persephone was held captive still. The glassy river mocked; the mist swirled with visions of Persephone struggling against her shackles. Tortured, or worse.

Hermes had gravitated to this ledge in all the prior iterations of himself: as a boy of inexperience, as a god overconfident at times, lonely and frustrated at others—and now as Hermes, standing at a crossroad with no one to tell him which road to take. Resolute, he turned away from the Oblivion to search for his missing host.

Inside, he found Lily entering her bedroom carrying a stack of towels. Her eyelids drooped, eyes unanchored, her thoughts perpetually drifting downstream, the shore passing by without notice. She appeared grayer than usual, in a sickly sort of way.

"You're remembering..." she crooned in a socialite drawl with a pack-a-day habit. "From the waters of Oblivion. How ironic."

She deposited the towels and busied herself with an e-cigarette. He scrutinized her movements, forced in the way a drunk feigns sobriety. She struggled to fill the vapor capsule with tobacco oil, which she laced with a drop of some brackish liquid in a syringe. Once finished, she balanced the silver stick between her fingers.

"I got these new little things from Earth. So much better than smoking. Even with the lead. And look..."

She inhaled, and the tip glowed green like a lonely Christmas light. "Isn't that cute?"

"Yeah. Cute," Hermes said without a gram of excitement.

"Fuck you, it's cute." She frowned defiantly and sucked on her vape.

"Well, what are you waiting for? Clean up." She pointed her pen at his feet. "And thanks for not removing your shoes. I got to clean that shit up myself. On my hands and knees. So domestic." She exhaled, and tobacco vapor escaped her ears. "Use the salt bath first for the cleanse, then the mineral for your skin, and finish in the fresh water. You know the drill."

"I do," Hermes said.

"Actually…" She listed to one side. "Take off your clothes here. I won't have you making a worse mess."

"You want me to do a little dance for you, too?"

She shook her head. "Please. You're no surprise. If anything, you look like you've added a few pounds. Frankly, being among those dirty humans hasn't been good for you. If you think I want to see all…*that*…think again."

Hermes gave an uh-huh.

"Don't flatter yourself. I'll have you know I still get plenty. Plenty." Her gaze drifted away. "Plenty."

Hermes sighed and walked off in what he hoped was the direction of the salt bath. It had been a while.

The hot water felt fucking fantastic. Lily's little villa on the river of forgetfulness was better than any spa, bar none. Steam rose from an interior pool. The mosaics at the bottom featured an entertaining assortment of mermaids on beds of kelp in various acts of copulation. The underwater *Kama Sutra* was framed by images of fish, which Hermes thought had rather frightened expressions.

Hermes melted with relief, head nestled onto a warm obsidian ledge, resisting the urge to fall asleep. His wings soaked in the restorative water. The steam invaded his pores, made him woozy and drunk. He kept his guns in reach atop his towels, just in case. Lily had claimed his clothes for a tumble in her salvaged Betty Crocker–era washing machine.

Should I feel guilty? Hermes wrestled, trying to justify this bit of R&R, even though there wasn't anyone to judge—he had just killed the only judge and stacked the court with friendly ideologues. Hermes had been on the go for…God only knows how long. Which god kept track of the how long, he didn't know. Point being, he was tired and deserved a little break, if only to revive him for the mission ahead. Hermes decided to forgo the ten-dip bath and do only a strict four-dip treatment—no more, no less. Bones and bruises healed, he'd be on his way.

Underwater, he wiggled his pruny toes. His eyelids fluttered.

Maybe, like, fifteen more minutes. Twenty tops.

The last thing he felt was the water surging over his head.

***

He remembered her in splashes of color, fragments of time, like a book torn at the spine and scattered by the wind so that he raced to gather the pages. Healthy and vibrant, Lily ran around the pool in her villa with a stem of purple grapes, her tiny feet pattering through puddles. Her silver hair bounced down her back like a waterfall. Handpicked naked slaves, specimens of Aphrodite-level beauty, waited on them ceaselessly, offering their services in all manners of the flesh. When the humans weren't attending to whims, they affixed themselves like statues along the walls. Lily relished the Greek pantheon's ascension to the apex of celestial power. Such decadence. These were the good centuries, the years of plenty, without limit or self-restraint.

Lying on a cushion just out of the water, Hermes laughed as Lily twirled, eating grapes, popping the fruit into the mouths of her slaves. She stopped, flushed and silly, faced a younger male and female pair, and pressed them together.

"Eat more grapes. Eat more. Eat."

She giggled and wedged herself between them and their lecherous expressions, quickly aroused by Lily's passion.

A wave of warm, salty water splashed him. A mischievous smile crested the waterline. Persephone pushed more water at him and drowned a platter of dates and roasted quails. They were young. He was happy. She was happy. They were all so fucking happy.

He slipped onto a bench in the water and she nestled beside him. They watched Lily tease her slaves before they all fell to the tiled floor and began copulating in a jumble of limbs.

"Where have you been keeping her?" Persephone said, breathless and exhilarated.

"This is your kingdom. I haven't been keeping her anywhere. You need to get out of that palace."

"If I knew there was this much fun to be had…" She rested her head on his shoulder. "You always know where to find the fun."

"Maybe I just make everything fun," he teased.

She lifted away and stuck out her tongue. He gave her tongue a playful pinch and she punched him in the chest.

"Ow. That wasn't funny."

But it was. It was all so funny.

Hermes turned serious. "You need to learn how to live here."

"Duh."

Hermes nodded to Lily, absorbed in her current debauchery. "She likes you."

"Oh, please. She's in love with you."

Hermes shuddered. "Don't use that word."

"Ooh, Hermes has a soft spot. And I found it! I found it!" Persephone squealed.

"Cut it out."

"It's so tender. Love. Love. Hermes and Lethe. Are. In. Love. K-I-S-S-I-N-G!" She sang the schoolyard taunt.

"I am not," said Hermes.

"Oh, you so are."

"She's a good time. But I would never couple with her. Not celestially. She's too needy and desperate."

Persephone beamed. "With a fantastic ass."

"Yes. Divine," Hermes agreed. Lily had a Grade-A behind.

"When do I get nieces and nephews?" Persephone asked excitedly. "That would make the Underworld a home."

Hermes flicked water at her. "Now you're sounding ridiculous."

"So up until this very moment, I wasn't ridiculous. This is the line. Children. Which means you are in love with her."

"That doesn't make any sense." He splashed her again and she swam backward with an "oh no you just didn't" grin. A full-on splash fight commenced, sending waves of delicious water at one another until they treaded at opposite ends of the pool.

"Hermes doesn't fall in love. Hermes doesn't believe in love," said Hermes.

"Is that by intelligent design? Because it sounds more like a stupid guy thing. And convenient cover."

"And you're the expert?"

"Course I am. I'm the preeminent scholar on Hermes. I know you love. You're practically overflowing with it. Yet you consider it a weakness. Perhaps it's that great big chip on your shoulder."

She said it playfully and he smiled, but inside he was reeling.

"A chip on my shoulder?"

"I know you love, Hermes," she reiterated more forcefully.

"And how can you be so certain?"

Lily abruptly returned from her romp, tossing grapes into the water from afar to get their attention. They bobbed like buoys.

"Because you love me," Persephone whispered in his ear. She splashed him one last time and hopped out of the water, naked, to chase after Lily. Girlish screams circled the pool. Persephone caught Lily in the adjoining room, and they collapsed together into a pile of sheets with squeals of delight. Their wet bodies twisted around one another. Hermes swam to the edge of the pool and rested his chin on his arms, watched them make love until he let go and submerged. The pool was a womb—no sound, no thoughts. He held his breath for what felt like an age.

The womb thundered. A storm of bubbles cratered the still water before him as a naked goddess sank. Lily swam toward him, her dyed-black hair a tangle of seaweed, breasts undulating like jellyfish. Hermes pushed to the surface.

Steam filled the spa, again lifeless and cold. No Persephone. No slaves. No sumptuous feast. No debauchery. It was a memory inside a dream, Hermes realized.

Lily surfaced closer to him. This dark-haired Lily, goddess of loneliness.

"I'm sober now," she said, leaving her lips parted for water to fill her mouth. She stood, exposing her upper half. "I don't need mortals. Their love means nothing to me anymore."

What is she trying to prove? Does she want my approval? Recognition? Does she want me to congratulate her? Embrace her? Console her?

This is what Lily always did: shove into your life and throw you onto thin ice.

"I guess that's good for you," Hermes said.

Her arms settled on his shoulders, pressing into his most personal space. "It can be just us. That's all I need. We need."

She straddled him, knees digging into his pelvis, and rubbed her wet cheek against his with a feline hunger.

"I think you forgot why I'm here," he said and extricated himself from her. He exited the pool, quickly wrapping a towel around his waist. Lily stayed in the water, legs kicking in little bursts to keep her head above water.

"You understand, right? Tell me you understand. Or I leave now."

She nodded as she swam slow laps, like a tropical fish tracing its tank. Hermes retreated, exhausted but unable to rest. Not here, not in her villa.

He dried off and dressed in her bedroom, where she left his clothes in a wrinkled pile. Lily was not one for chores. The once-spoiled and extravagant Lily had been livelier than this impoverished one.

A fire danced in a pit. He warmed his hands over it. Lily strutted past without acknowledgment, wearing only a towel wrapped in a beehive atop her head. He suppressed a sigh and focused on the flames. Lily the exhibitionist. There was a staleness to her flirtations, and he merely felt sad. He wondered if this was how others saw him.

She peeled a lace robe studded with sapphires off the back of a sofa and shrugged it on, leaving the sash undone so the front parted like stage curtains at a peep show. Then she flippantly tossed another log into the fire pit and settled into a nest of pillows, her head in the cup of her palm as if she were posing for a portrait.

"Look…" Hermes began. The dreaded *look,* harbinger of bad news and piles of shit about to be dumped on laps.

Her eyes slid over to him and waited.

"Look," he repeated. "Thank you for helping."

Hermes instantly regretted the word choice.

Her gaze narrowed, fixed on him like the sight of a rifle. "You're welcome."

"I didn't come here to—"

"You don't want to fuck. Got it."

"I know how difficult that must be to hear."

She snorted. "You won't rail me. Watch me slit my wrists."

"I deserved that." He stared at the floor, afraid eye contact might prompt her to throw something. "I never called. Never sent a message, which I know I have no excuse for, seeing as I'm the Messenger God. But you know why I was banished. And you're…well, there's no reason to dredge up old history. I'll drink from your river and forget it. We're past it." Deep breath. "I'm sorry. So there."

"You're not supposed to say *so there* after you say *sorry.* It sounds punitive and negates the apology," said Lily.

"Jesus H. Christ. I'm sorry. No *so there.*" It was a marvel how quickly she could exasperate him.

"Sit," she requested.

It was a familiar trap. He acquiesced, sinking into a cushion at the opposite end of the sectional, as far away from her as politely possible. Her eyes measured the distance between them.

Yeah, measure away.

He protected his crotch with a pillow. "It wasn't a healthy relationship. I've come to understand my feelings better now—not perfectly, but enough to be honest. I hope you can respect that and not suffer your divine wrath."

"Honey, stop talking," Lily said, puffing away on her e-cigarette. She laid back to gaze up at the ceiling and blew a mushroom cloud of vapor.

"I go to these meetings. They help me accept truths." She rolled her head to look at him. "Difficult truths."

Hermes didn't like where this was going. "Are you insinuating I need help?"

"I'm trying to make you understand."

"Understand what?"

She smiled weakly. "I'm lonely."

Lonely and sad. He read it in every crease of misery on her face, lines absent all those centuries ago. In that moment, he saw that she'd grown old. Though they were eternal, they weren't immune to the ravages of time and heartache. Depression had dulled her luster.

"We're all lonely," he offered. Not much of a consolation.

She turned back to the ceiling. "You're not hearing me. Not in the deep way."

Hermes sighed. An old desire to placate her reared its ugly head; he should have fled when he had the chance.

"We all lived so large," she mused. "Everything was ours. And we took it all. No compunction. Why should there have been? We loved being worshipped. Their admiration, so sensual, so intoxicating. And then—"

"The addiction abandoned the junkie," Hermes finished.

She lifted her palm as if offering them up to the heavens—or for Hermes to take, he wasn't sure.

She smiled. "High and dry."

They shared this common ground, this validation. Be it on cloud nine or in the mud, Lily was happiest when she had company. And Hermes felt mud between his toes.

Lily leaned over to a coffee table and a silver jewelry box encrusted in diamonds with numerous tiny drawers. She opened random ones. Each drawer revealed a different narcotic. Cocaine. Heroin. Meth. Not what she wanted. She unfolded the top to a tackle box of pills, compartmentalized like a pharmacy on steroids—which she also possessed.

"You've got enough in there to tranquilize a sorority."

She flipped over the box, spilling it all onto the table. Every substance oh so familiar to him.

She sighed. "They're so weak. I feel almost nothing. Did you ever wonder how we came to be?" Her question caught him off guard. "Did mortals think us into existence, or did we create them? No one's answered that one for me."

"Who could?" Hermes said.

"And if the humans did think us into existence, if we're only here because one day some mortal philosopher took a shit and had a bright idea…then what are we now? When no one cares?"

"There are those left who still care. We are remembered."

She glared at him with a harsh reproach. "But not worshipped. What happens if the humans are all gone?"

"I suppose we stay, linger. It would be rather boring whether we're worshipped or not."

"Maybe it'll all go back to the way it was in the beginning. Full circle. Primordial Chaos. And all will be reborn."

There it was again, that word...*chaos.*

"Is that what you want?" he asked calmly. "Chaos?"

"As opposed to what we have now?"

"Which is?"

"Nothing. We have nothing, Hermes. And what could be worse than existing forever without purpose? Aren't you tired of it? The endless waiting for something to happen that will never happen? Why can't we let destiny take back the reins and restart the clock? Perhaps then we can return in ascension. If Jesus gets to be reborn, why not me? Why not you? Why not all of us? And without the humans to dictate terms. I don't like that they have all the say. Zeus and Prometheus made them. And now we must claw and pine for their admiration, weep and despair when their feeble and fickle minds find a new breast to suckle—for the consolation that their lives are utterly meaningless."

"Persephone has meaning and purpose. And that is worth preserving. Protecting."

She shook her head in disagreement. "With your own life?"

"Yes."

"You say that without hesitation. But what if you could see past your feelings for her?"

"And why would I want to do that?"

"Because she's in the way!" Lily shouted. "This is part of a plan larger than Persephone and bigger than the Furies, who are several votes shy of a quorum. By sacrificing her, they'll reclaim their purpose. All of us will reclaim our purpose. Even you, if you allow yourself."

Hermes was beginning to see the painting from the brushstrokes. "Eternal winter."

"Chaos." She let the word simmer on her tongue. "Us junkies really need our fix."

His head swam. He would sit if he weren't already sitting.

She feigned consolation. "Oh, babe, this has been a long time in the making. You showed up to the dinner party and everyone's on dessert."

Fury awakened inside him. She was fucking enjoying this.

"The Furies couldn't do this alone, you said it yourself. Who is supporting them? Who helped them kidnap her?"

"Oh, I don't know if they're working with anyone. I gather they're being played. Maybe someone set them up to it. I'm not important enough to be privy to the details. However, I think they're sincere in their ignorance. They mean business. But just because you can boil water doesn't mean you can cook."

She unraveled the towel, releasing her hair. Damp strands tumbled down her back. He waited as she dried the front of her body, unbothered and unapologetic, dabbing at the last droplets clinging to her pale breasts and stomach.

"The Furies. Well, the two remaining"—she shot him loaded look—"they've been reincarnating evil for the past three centuries. Noticed an uptick in wars lately? Terrifying new weapons? Death toll's really been racking up. Chaos spreading. That feeling of things spiraling out of control. Enough to cause any God-fearing human to lose faith. Perhaps question the very existence of a celestial power." Finished drying herself, she tossed the towel at her feet. "Well, the powers that be."

"Meaning the Christians? Muslims? Hindus? Who?"

She shrugged.

"Then what? Kill off most of Earth with winter?" Hermes asked. "Emerge and reclaim what's left? Humans flock back to the old religion, kick-start the Underworld economy?"

Her nightgown slipped off her shoulder as she joined him—closer than he liked—on the sofa.

"Don't you get it? They don't just want to play this game of gods. They want to win. Someone else set the board, whispered the moves. Persephone is their check. And mate. Only problem in that plan is you." She tapped his nose with her finger.

He felt lightheaded. Standing was a bad idea. It was all that time soaking in her mineral baths. She pulled his arm toward her, and he dropped like a stone. Lilac perfume clung to her gown. Raven-black hair draped over his face as their foreheads met. He practiced enough willpower to pull away.

"But if I save her," Hermes said, "it'll end."

She gathered her nightgown, sealing the curtain. "I doubt it. But you can try."

"I can try," he repeated, unsure if he was reassuring himself or telling her.

"Yes. You can try. But I wouldn't get involved. I just wouldn't," she whispered.

Soft fingertips traced his cheekbones to the lobes of his ears, then guided his head into her lap. He breathed in her intoxicating scent, felt the heat of her against his face. Her velvety fingers stroked his hair. At some point, he fell asleep.

***

Hermes was back in Persephone's cabin. Outside the kitchen windows, dusk painted the faraway mountains gold and purple. Persephone lay apricating in the prairie. Red poppies and blue lupine had blossomed around her like a spring angel. The scent of a sizzling pan drew him toward a feast of freshly harvested vegetables, roasted in offering to the vegetarian goddess. He grabbed a bottle of Assyrtiko wine and headed outside.

The sun had set, and twilight clung to the fingernail of a moon. He joined his sister to dine *al fresco*, warmed by a bonfire tossing sparks up to Olympus. A faraway owl hooted. All the while, his heart ached, knowing this was just a dream.

"I would do this every night and never grow restless," he said.

"You would stay here forever?"

He uncorked a second bottle of wine. "Yes. Wouldn't you?"

She watched him fill their glasses to the rim. "You're restless even now."

"Do I look restless?"

"A goddess knows. A sister knows."

"Okay. Illuminate my blind spot," he challenged affably.

She lay back in the grass and stared up at the sparks chasing the stars. It felt like an age before she answered. "You're searching for what you already have."

He set his glass of wine aside. "And what is it I already have?"

"Only you can answer that. But you won't find it until you let go of everything else."

"Everything. What do I have left? Everything's gone."

"Yes, but it left you. Now it's your turn. Cut the strings, release yourself. You have to mourn."

His chest tightened with doubt, that familiar foe. "What if I can't?"

"Then you don't get to grow."

He stood too quickly, dizzy from too much wine and prophecy. The world spun, the prairie swirling into the night sky into the cabin into the distant black mountains, like acetone erasing a canvas, leaving only Persephone's warning and its discontent.

A new dream slowly developed around him. He was now inside Lily's villa. Torches blackened the tiled walls, scorching the intricate mosaics. Hermes felt rumpled silk caress his skin, soft pillows filled with eiderdown. Worship electrified his rusty veins, unclogged his pores, heightened his senses. His wings shuddered. Colors were brighter. Sounds more intense. These were the glory days.

The sheets slithered beyond his toes, two lumps rising and falling under the covers. An overwhelming sense of déjà vu shuddered through him, warping his senses. The room itself seemed to hold its breath.

This isn't a dream…

This happened.

He peeled back the covers to discover Persephone and Lily entwined in passion. Mosaic voyeurs bore witness to the bacchanal, gazing down from the gilded walls. There was no shame in their pleasure. In fact, it had been his intention. Attempting a discreet exit, he edged away and knocked a chalice to the floor. The clatter echoed off the marble, breaking the love fest. He silently cursed his clumsiness. Lily untwined from Persephone, leaving the goddess panting and sweating, eyes closed in ecstasy.

She crawled to Hermes, languid limbs and wet, and begged him to stay. The torchlight kissed her chamomile hair. She ran her fingers sensually down his forehead and along his neck. "You're perfect. We're perfect. It's all so perfect."

Her touch felt hollow. She didn't excite him. He stared past Lily, watching Persephone's breathing slow as she sank into a deep sleep.

"I don't know. Maybe."

Persephone shivered. He maneuvered around Lily, his concern solely for his sister, and tenderly draped a fur blanket over her.

"I'm not enough…" he heard Lily moan behind him, her voice strangled.

He turned and found her now standing rigidly at the edge of the bed. A pained smile tore across her face, a smile wholly disconnected from her being.

"What am I missing?" she said.

"Missing?"

She turned and searched the room, as if lost on a street corner in a foreign city. "I ferry them across my river…"

"Is something wrong? Why are you upset?"

Her voice wavered. "The mortals. I ferry them to Paradise…to happiness."

She cycled through emotions at dizzying speed.

Elated one moment. Unhinged the next.

Ferocious. Wild. Broken. Desperate.

Hermes left the bed and blocked Persephone, afraid Lily might do her harm.

"They drink the water…" Lily mumbled. "Forget everything. No memories. A blank slate. Everything new…"

"Lily? What's going on?"

She didn't respond, but drifted onto the veranda and took in her river snaking across the night. She emitted a gasp, as if seeing the view for the first time.

"Lily, what are you doing? Come back to bed."

His plea drifted past her. Nothing could penetrate her madness. She swept out of sight down a gravel path, pebbles rustling under her bare feet, a white flame dwindling into the dark.

Hermes considered Persephone, still asleep, and followed his host.

The path zigzagged down a cliff of sharp, bleached coral. The cliff tightened into a slit of stone. He shoved himself sideways through the grimacing rock. Jagged coral scraped his arms before he finally emerged onto the shore, toes sinking into cold sand.

About a mile downstream, Lily knelt in the shallows of her river, palms hovering over the current as if lost in prayer. The water lapped at her stomach, her nightgown billowing around her like a jellyfish. The sand dampened his footsteps, masking his approach. Instinct pounded the inside of his skull, warning him not to approach. Yet he continued.

Her hands sank into the river. "You love her."

At that moment, Hermes realized her intention. He broke into a frantic sprint. "Lily! Stop!"

She glanced back. Something feral and unhinged in her eyes froze him mid-step. The water in her cupped palms glistened, as dangerous as a loaded gun.

"You love her. Don't lie."

"Yes," he answered truthfully.

"No. You love her impurely," she hurled at him.

What if she's right?

The question leapt from the darkest recess of his psyche and stabbed him through the heart. Her accusation would torture him for an age. He did love Persephone. But was it *eros* or *storge*? Incest was nothing new for the gods, but Hermes never cared for it, didn't partake. To each their own—their own not being his own. It had been bedrock that his relationship with Persephone transcended the tumultuous affairs of his kin. Now, Lily had thrown his world into doubt. And she did so easily.

She found where to strike.

"I knew it. I suspected from the first moment I saw you together," she said with glee.

"Careful," he growled. "Careful what you imply."

She drilled him, taking pleasure in the meanness of it all. "I imply nothing."

"I've never—"

"That's not what the humans will remember."

"There's nothing to remember, because nothing happened."

She shook her head. In her mind, the sordid tale had already been chiseled on tablets of stone. Her indictment picked up speed. "It's what they will recite in their poems, what the chorus will sing. Because I will tell them EVERYTHING!"

His heart pounded with a rage that was nothing compared to the geyser of fear beneath it. Lily was threatening to destroy that which he treasured most: his reputation. He always knew she was poison, but he thought he could manage her. How naïve he had been.

"They won't listen to your story," he said. "The bards will write of a brother who protected his sister when she was on Earth and when she was imprisoned in the Underworld. How he helped her pass the tedium with easy entertainment, finding her a pitiful, lonely river goddess that was an easy lay."

He instantly regretted the insult. The rejection trampled her soul. She turned back to the river water cupped in her palms.

"I think I'd rather not remember you at all."

She raised her hands to her lips and drank with the fervor of an alcoholic racing happy hour. Later, he would analyze and reanalyze this moment, why he never tried to stop her. Maybe he had wanted to see what would happen, if a goddess could taste her own medicine.

Ages passed as she stared into the mist, and he stared at her, until she finally lowered her hands to her side.

"My river betrays me," she whispered, voice raw and hoarse. "It won't let me forget."

His lungs expanded with relief. He hadn't realized he'd been holding his breath. "I suppose the rules don't apply to us."

She clenched her eyes shut. "I want oblivion."

He could not console her. Would not. She was the goddess of Oblivion, who wiped away the memories of mortals, and this was too fitting a punishment. Oh, the cosmic irony. Her suffering was to remember everything.

"It won't let me forget. I can't forget," she repeated again and again. "Where's my oblivion?"

He waded back to shore, leaving her to unravel. She pushed her face into her river, gulping down water until her stomach was grotesquely distended.

"I can't forget!"

It was easier than he thought, leaving her behind. He climbed back up the trail. Her cries echoed off the coral cliffs like a maimed horse desperate to be put out of its misery.

"I CAN'T FORGET! I CAN'T FORGET!"

The villa crowned the plateau with its columns and cornices. Persephone swept off the portico and into the garden, hugging the fur blanket he had draped over her before.

"What's happening? Where's Lily? Is that her shouting?"

He could only nod.

"We have to help her!"

She started past him, but he gripped her elbow, securing her to his side. "We can't."

"What do you mean, we can't?" Her expression darkened. "Hermes, what did you do?"

A second blow. "I didn't do anything."

"Then what's going on? You just came from the shore. That's where she is, isn't she?"

He instinctively looked up toward Earth. How to explain. "She accused us…"

The rest needn't be said. Not like he could say it anyway. Persephone read their fate in his tortured look and pulled her brother into a hug that felt like the end of everything. Her world was cratering for a second time. They listened to Lily's wailing reverberate endlessly off the crevices of the Underworld.

"Hades will hear this," he whispered. "It will reach him."

"I don't care. We stay together. He'll have to learn that I'm not his. This is supposed to be my home now. I'm queen, and I can make rules and edicts too."

"You know that isn't true. It can still get worse for you—much worse."

She pulled away and forced him to look at her. "Then I have a message for Demeter—and Hera."

"No, Persephone."

Her eyes narrowed. "Is the messenger of the gods refusing to deliver a message?"

"That's not what I'm doing, and you know it."

"Good. Then you'll do as I say and go to my mother. That's an order, *messenger*."

The blow hurt more than any from Zeus. He took a step away, unsteady and shattered.

This is how Lily must feel, he thought.

"I'm sorry, Hermes. I didn't mean it," she said and reached out to him.

He recoiled. How easy it was to return to privilege. Too easy. They would never—could never—be truly equal. It was his fault to have forgotten.

She began to panic on top of her panic. "Please. I don't want to lose you."

"I know."

"Then try! They listen to you."

"They don't!" His voice rose, raw with frustration and an anguish. "They listen to other gods, whose words I speak! I have no authority, no pull, none. I posture, strut, and boast…but I'm just a joke. Do you get it now? I'm a *nothing*, Persephone. A nothing."

He was the smallest god in the universe.

"You're not nothing. Not to me."

"I may have a seat among the twelve, but no voice, no say. And no one will speak for us—not with what Lily is accusing. It'll be too much. Hades will banish me."

"I won't let him," she said, though they both knew it wasn't true.

He squeezed her hand, choosing to forget, a small dose of oblivion to save the one relationship that mattered. "You have to go. Get back to the palace as quickly as you can. You can't be caught with me when he learns about this. Lily drank from her river, only it didn't work. She'll get her revenge in other ways."

"Why is she doing this?"

"Because…" He stared at their clasped hands. "She can't ever reach Elysium."

She squeezed his hand back, and he felt foolish to doubt their love, even for a second.

"We'll survive. We have no other choice," he said and kissed her softly on the forehead.

The villa behind Persephone began to melt. So did the trees and the cliffs. Globs of the Underworld dripped around them.

It was happening again…

Persephone didn't notice the world coming apart at the seams. Tears rolled down her cheeks, then her cheeks rolled down her face, and her face rolled down her body. She crumbled through his arms, joining a swirling tide of color as the memory dissolved, draining from his mind like sand through an hourglass.

CHAPTER TWENTY-SIX

HERMES WAS CATAPULTED FROM the dream, knocking a body to the floor. A woman. *Who is she? Why was she on top of me?*

His head pounded and his vision was blurry. He struggled to focus but the effort only worsened his condition. Was he conscious? Was this another dream? A memory?

He attempted to push off the floor, muscles burning as if he'd fallen asleep on a block of ice. His knees buckled. A stabbing pain tore through the crook of his elbow, a sting more ferocious than Zeus's cursed bee. There was a needle buried in his arm. A clear liquid in the half-plunged syringe.

He furiously ripped out the needle and willed himself not to panic. Panic would quicken his heart rate, which would only hasten the effects of whatever was injected into him. His thoughts moved like shadows sliding behind clouded glass. Mosaic eyes shimmered in torchlight, watching, unblinking. Murky vapor swirled above a black pool. Pills and drugs were scattered across a chaise and the ground, as if swept off a table in anger.

The woman…

He whirled back to the strange woman rocking on the floor, breath hitching between sobs. Swaddled in silk sheets and drenched in misery.

I know her. But how?

A name swam just out of reach, like a B actor passing on the street, from that TV show who did that thing. He watched her with a dull fascination. It required too much effort to be inquisitive. Anger seemed appropriate, but his emotions drained as quickly as they came. The woman moaned for someone named Hermes to forgive her.

Hermes. Am I Hermes?

The thought slipped through his grasp. Memories, dreams, faces—everything was fading. Fading to oblivion.

Who am I?

He blinked, felt his mind settle into a calm blank canvas. The yogis would be proud. He turned from the crying woman to a veranda. A vision of a goddess appeared.

Persephone. I know her.

She was radiant. Her smile warmed him like a perfect summer day.

Love. He felt love. The feeling lasted. Real. Solid. Sweet and thick as honey.

Hermes. I am Hermes. And who is Hermes?

Hermes was a god. *Holy shit.*

Quite literally. This was Holy Shit.

Hermes was finally having a goddamn divine moment. *So this is what the humans are always raving about.* Muhammad on the mountain, Moses and the burning bush, the Virgin Mary toasted on a grilled cheese. The experience was just as advertised. Celestial. Magical. A bit blurry. Tad smudgy. Too bad he couldn't put this on display and sell tickets, because he wanted this moment to last forever. To simply behold a vision of Persephone was a gift.

Or am I diminishing?

It was so hard to tell. His mind lost focus again. It was all so fucked up. The divine light faded too. *Who was that goddess in the window?*

He had known her only a moment ago. So familiar. He vaguely recalled that he loved her.

Did he love her? He...

What is it that I feel? Why is it so hard to remember?

Remembering. The question was the answer. The clarity became a rope. Fleeting clarity. But the rope was fraying. The strands snapping. He needed to pull himself out of the quicksand. Fast. Before his mind sank into the abyss. It took everything to cling to the revelation, to haul himself back to himself. *The River Goddess of the River of Oblivion and she poisoned me with the water from her river!*

He opened his eyes, and the blurry woman on the floor snapped into focus. "LILY!"

Lily wailed. "I'm sorry. I'm so sorry! I couldn't do it. I can't keep this sobriety."

"You tried to erase her? You tried to make me forget EVERY-THING?!"

Anger planted him. Firm ground. Even while the villa careened around him like a mental merry-go-round that wouldn't stop. His thoughts reordered. Lily. The poison. Persephone.

He needed to find Persephone!

He pressed his palms into his eyes. Stars exploded behind his vision while Lily babbled:

"They came to me, offered warmth and sunlight. A chance to be reborn. To be worshipped again. They wanted me to hurt you. But I couldn't. I thought...if you couldn't remember her, then they wouldn't care. You could come with me. You wouldn't care either, and wouldn't that be such a relief? You didn't love her, not carnally. I was foolish to be jealous. But that true love will only mean pain for you because there's no hope for Persephone."

She pulled at his legs, eager to explain. "I don't have a Persephone. I have only you. You couldn't possibly understand the loneliness. The utter absence—merely half a life. As if we can only exhale."

She clung on, shedding tears of joy and madness while preaching, "I'm bringing you relief. A chance to forget her, forget it all. We'll be worshipped again and beloved. We'll make our own paradise."

The poison continued its aggressive march. He twisted away from her and toppled.

She continued raving, her speech pressured and her eyes bulging. "Isn't this what you've been missing? I know you, Hermes. I've known all of you."

"Yes," he muttered, back on his hands and knees. Something glinted between the torches. Just on the balcony. Not so far from him. The light forged into a spear.

"You martyr yourself. For what, religion? There's no one left to build you any temples." She balled her fists and shook them in the air. "You feel it! You feel it! You feel it!"

"I do," he said. The poison retreated again. Enough to stand. Lurching. A stagger.

His feet steadied.

"Then why deny it?" She brushed against him, petted his hair. "Why should we all be left without worship? She hasn't shared any of it with you."

"She can't."

"Then let her rot in the dungeon," she snarled and spat. "Let the spoiled queen stay beneath the earth. Just let Persephone go."

Let go. Just let go.

The words burned through Lily's river water like spiritual Narcan. That night by the campfire—it all came back to him. Persephone lying in the grass, staring up at the stars.

"You have to let go," she had said.

Ages at sea, Hermes had been sailing to a destination that no longer existed, gripping the rudder so hard his knuckles had turned to stone. There was no Ithaca at the end of his odyssey. Humanity had moved on from Hermes. Hermes had to say goodbye, to mourn, to move on in turn. This was Persephone's prophecy. Lily's poison had inadvertently gifted him a miracle. It erased all he held sacred.

"I have to let go," he said. An affirmation.

"That's all," Lily purred, stroking his hair.

The light on the veranda swam into focus. It was no vision. It was steel. He shirked away from Lily, snatched her sword, stained black with blood.

"Where is Persephone?"

Her eyes raced up the blade. He had stature. And grandeur. He was a god. In a way Lily could never fathom, Hermes had been reborn.

"You don't need to play Zeus's messenger anymore," she said.

His grip strangled the hilt. He had forgotten the heft of a sword, so much more personal than a gun. "I am no one's messenger."

"You've been corrupted by Persephone. She's not innocent, you know."

"None of us are. You made a mistake trying to poison me. You don't even realize what you've given me. I don't fully know myself, but everything feels different now."

"Well, hooray for you," she said with contempt, and looked away, staring out at her river. "You love her."

"I love her more than devotion. Not for a billion worshippers would I give her up."

Lily doubled over, the heartbreak shattering her all over again. The Goddess of Oblivion who remembered everything. She would never have Hermes. Maybe they could be friends.

"Where is she?" he asked forcefully.

A distant crash echoed through the villa. Someone bashed down the front door. Lily erupted in a fresh wail as thunderous footfalls crossed the inner courtyard.

Hermes tossed the sword and darted for his pack. The iron door to Lily's bedchamber burst open with the force of a Black Friday mob gate-crashing Walmart.

The out-of-breath river lord stumbled into the crosshairs of his draw. "Kharon?"

Kharon threw up his hands. "Is that how you welcome a friend?"

Hermes backed up to check the portico while keeping the gun trained. No horde of demons swarmed the garden or circled the sky. There was only the soft lap of water on the shore and the tap of the dinghy against the dock.

"If I wanted to hurt you, I might've tried sneaking up on you. I came here to warn you."

Hermes returned to the bedroom. "Explain."

"First put down the gun, Sundance."

"How did you know where to find me?"

"Where else would you go? T&A. That's Hermes."

Lily's sobbing subsided. This drama was more interesting. She folded onto her legs to watch, her nightgown hiked up to her waist. Kharon ogled approvingly.

"Don't trust him," she pouted. "He's guilty as the rest of us."

Hermes pivoted between his ex-lover and his ex-pal.

Kharon sighed loudly. "She's a junkie. You know that."

"He's been tracking you for the Furies! How else was Melinoë waiting for you at the Phlegethon crossing, huh? That's how he knew you were here. He told me to pick you up." She glared at Kharon. "Explain that one, you great big river oaf."

Solid point, Lily.

The river lord grunted and turned back to Hermes. "I was fishing my river when you texted me. I pointed you in the right direction. I told you Persephone was in Elysium."

Solid point, Kharon.

Kharon shoved a fat finger at Hermes. "You took Minos. Once I heard you crossed the fire, it was obvious where you went. She tipped them off. Tried to drug you, too, didn't she?"

"LIAR!" Lily screamed.

It was a sociopath sandwich with Hermes in the middle.

"You'd trust the Grim Reaper over me?" Lily said to Hermes. "A soggy, overblown river rat, tollbooth operator. He loves coin, and only coin— would do anything for it. Not me. I love you, Hermes!"

"No, I love Hermes! He's my best friend!"

Now this is getting weird.

Kharon revved up, chest projecting out of his ragged mackintosh. "You think you're such a high and mighty goddess? You're nothing but a narcissistic, histrionic whiner!" *Heard that one before*, Hermes thought. "You've never worked a hard day in your life! Ferry one soul across your river out of how many? One out of every million? You sit in your pretty villa, high on your Earth drugs supplied by the Furies!"

Lily shot off the floor and snarled back, "You know nothing! I sift the worthy from the garbage you let into the Underworld. You beg for copper. I mine for diamonds!"

"Woe is me!" Kharon mocked. "You feast and complain. You fuck and complain. You complain and complain. You moan for someone to love you. Wanna know what your boy crush Hermes says about you behind your back?"

Lily pressed her hands over her ears, closed her eyes, and turned around in circles while Kharon howled with laughter.

"Enough!" Hermes commanded Kharon.

Lily lowered her hands and stared mopily.

"You were going to tell me about Persephone," Hermes said.

"Was I?" she squeaked.

Kharon chuckled and Hermes silenced him with a stare like a jack-hammer going to town on asphalt. "You were about to tell me what the Furies have planned. You said they would imprison Persephone."

Out of the corner of his eye, Hermes clocked the slimy beast shift—only just. A fist clenched, a single pulse. The flash of a snarl. Lily flinched. If he'd blinked, he would've missed it. It was some kind of threat.

"Well…yes. They would imprison her, wouldn't they?" Lily seesawed.

Hermes waved the gun at Kharon. "Is he making you nervous?"

"He always makes me nervous," Lily said.

Kharon grunted.

"If you ever truly cared for me, then tell me right now: Where is Persephone?"

Her eyes flicked to Kharon.

They're working together.

"WHERE?!" Hermes bellowed, startling her back to him. "I won't ask again."

She whispered something at the floor.

"I couldn't hear you. Say it again."

She looked him dead in the eyes and enunciated: "Kronos's tower. They're taking her to Tarta—"

A bullet slammed into her shoulder, spinning her. The side of her head slapped the tile. A moment later, the barrel of an old Remington revolver jerked from Lily to Hermes.

They exchanged rounds while diving for cover. Those buffalo wings gave him the edge. Hermes folded behind a column, facing Lily's garden. Kharon took cover at the opposite end of the bedchamber. Hermes could curse himself for this mistake—later.

A wail from Lily let him know it was a flesh wound, and she was milking it for all it was worth. Kharon and Hermes traded a second volley over the river goddess, until the senselessness of it sank in.

A metallic rattle echoed across the room as Kharon emptied his revolver, cartridges clinking to the floor. Hermes checked his own clip. One bullet left.

"Hey, Sundance," Kharon growled. "They've already taken her to Tartaros. You're too late."

It's not true, he willed.

Hermes wiped his brow with the back of his hand, leaving a streak of gunpowder. "Doesn't matter. That won't stop me."

"We needn't play this game," Kharon bargained. "We're practically brothers!"

"Am I the ugly one? I can't remember."

Just what Hermes needed: another fucking stalemate. He scanned for anything useful. A set of patio furniture. A side table with a silver tray. Not nothing, but not something either. He stuck out his foot and tipped the table. A bullet slapped the platter before it even hit the ground.

"Trying to make a run for it? I'll mow you down," Kharon hollered.

Hermes snatched the silver tray while Kharon was busy talking. A reflection of the room warbled over its filigree face. No sign of Kharon. Just Lily, whimpering in a puddle of blood and tears.

"What was the offer? The one that was better than mine?"

"Don't be sore!" Kharon shouted from behind his column. "You knew you couldn't trust me. I mean, look where I live. I'm just a soggy river rat that runs a tollbooth. They promised me money. And respect. Besides, you always hated the big-boy table."

"That I did," Hermes agreed.

"I thought you'd lose heart. Or interest."

Ouch. The adrenaline helped Hermes fight the last of Lily's toxins. And he needed all his wits. The longer he was held up here, the more time the Furies had to take Persephone to Tartaros—that most destitute of dungeons, where ages ago Zeus had banished the Titans. Tartaros sat at the bottom of an eternally dark pit at the center of the earth. An actual hellhole. Trapped with the Titans, Persephone would be subjected to the whims of the worst monsters for all eternity. If Hermes failed to reach her in time, he would grab his spelunking gear and descend the one-way trip. They would face the horrors together.

But what would happen to the earth? Hermes supposed it would freeze over. Life would wither and die.

And then what? What was the plan after?

The Furies were not creatures to have grand designs.

Hermes caught Lily trying to get his attention in the reflection of the silver tray. Her eyes indicated across the room—once, twice, thrice. When he didn't pick up the semaphore, she scowled and mouthed *you idiot.* Her eyes motioned left. *Over there! Over there!*

The syringe she used to poison him lay on the floor between Hermes and Kharon. It was still half full. *Oh.*

She huffed. He held up three fingers and counted down.

Three, two, one...

At the same moment she kicked the syringe, Hermes lunged. Kharon likewise made his move. Hermes fired his last round, hitting a bust of Hades just beside Kharon's head. Marble shards blinded the beast for a split second. A split of a second was all he needed. Hermes swiped the syringe and dove behind a closer column.

A chortle echoed. "You missed! I think you're out of bullets, if I counted correctly. And I'm good with math."

Hermes tucked the syringe up his sleeve. "You're right."

After counting to thirty, he tossed his gun across the floor and stepped out, hands raised.

Kharon's ugly green face peered around the column. "What are you doing?"

"What's it look like? I'm surrendering." Hermes stopped in the middle of the room. Lily intensely watched.

"Tartaros…" Hermes said. "There's no hope, then."

Hypervigilant, Kharon slowly emerged, revolver aimed for the heart. The gun looked like a toy in his giant paw. "You and me were BFFs. Pity that's over. Like everything else."

"You chose coin over bros."

Kharon shook his head in disappointment. His filthy hair flopped over his triangular ears, making him look like a disgruntled cocker spaniel. "If only you didn't get involved."

Using a sleight of hand, Hermes maneuvered the syringe between his middle and forefinger. Kharon cocked the hammer on his revolver, then hesitated, catching a glimmer. Light winked off a single drop perched on the invisible needle. Hermes launched, jamming the syringe into Kharon's left ear and plunging the fluid directly into his brain.

Kharon roared and reflexively crushed the revolver in his hand. Rounds popped off, shattering a mirror, slamming into walls—until Kharon abruptly stilled. His eyes glazed over. A vacant look erased his fury as the poison emptied his mind. Smoke trailed from the crushed pistol, which fell loose at his side. He slumped to the ground like a pile of dirty laundry.

Hermes patted him on the shoulder. "Sorry, old pal. But at least you'll forget this, too."

Lily chimed in, "You're welcome."

Typical Lily. One slightly unselfish act and she wanted a parade.

"Go to AA. You don't get my thanks."

"I don't want it." She crossed her arms in a huff, her nightgown now stained gold with her blood. "Besides, it doesn't matter. You likely won't survive what's coming."

CHAPTER TWENTY-SEVEN

THE LONGSWORD CLATTERED INTO the hull of the skiff as Hermes carelessly tossed it in. He braced against the bow to untie the mooring line. *Spoils of war*, he mused, stepping in next. The boat rocked, and he grabbed the dock to prevent his falling into the river of oblivion. Wouldn't want the Hermes myth to end with a slip and drown.

Two weather-beaten oars rested in fetid bilge water. He secured them to the rowlocks and pushed off into the mists of Lethe. Before the shore disappeared, a ghost rose atop the cliff.

Lily stood upon the ledge in her nightgown like a blood moon of ill omen. The distance between them stretched, heavy with sorrow and regret. The moment cast in bronze—eternal now—the last thing they would share. They would never set eyes on one another again.

The skiff slowly drifted into the current. Hermes only had to let the river carry him to the innermost circle of Hell, where Hades had constructed the gates of Tartaros. If Persephone were already imprisoned there, as Lily and Kharon testified, his quest had been over before it began.

Not tonight, Fate, my old nemesis.

He rowed harder on the left oar, turning the skiff against the current, then evened his strokes. His course was set for Elysium. The mist swallowed Lily's villa, then Lily, and finally the shore. Sounds began to trickle over the deceptively still water. An argument flared, quickly drowned by the clamor of a rowdy tavern. Grunts of lovemaking. The clang of swords in battle. Some faint. Some deafening. From every direction. The noises stacked upon one another, collided, suffocating the emptiness around his skiff. The farther he traveled, the more disorienting the river became. A cackle beside him. He spun to nothing. Then a cry of agony over his shoulder. Another shriek of laughter as if a woman leapt into his lap. Whether this was Lily's doing or some illusion, he could no longer tell. The air thickened, damp and cold, quivering with a death rattle. Visions of ancient lives played before the bow, to his port and starboard, as if projected onto the mist. Except this was no mist—it was the fog of memory, all the memories of those who crossed this river, the identities they sacrificed for paradise.

It was easy to get lost in the visions, as it was easy to get lost in the past. The only remedy was to focus on rowing, so Hermes redoubled his efforts. It was arduous work, his muscles still weak from Lily's toxic ploy. The oars cast whirlpools, brushing away each vision before another took its place. He lost all sense of direction, the exertion depleting his last reserves. His strokes grew ragged, lost their rhythm.

The skiff entered the doldrums—flat, endless, gray. Gray water. Gray mist. Gray boat. Even his skin looked gray. The boat creaked. Memories of ancient Greece floated listlessly by. Hermes lifted Lily's sword from the hull. Only a select few knew the way to Elysium. Hermes was one of them. It took inordinate effort to place the flat of the blade across the rail. The tip jutted over the water. He rolled up his right sleeve and leaned over the river. His reflection smiled back, though Hermes was not smiling.

Now came the hard part. He set his wrist at the edge of the blade and pressed with whatever might he had left, until the tip pierced his thick skin. The steel was made to cut down a god. Exactly what he needed tonight. A bead of ichor bloomed, and the blade beamed with the golden light of his sacred blood.

He took a deep breath, bit down on his shoulder, and ran his arm down the edge.

The pain felt terrible and wonderful. Feeling was important. His poisoned blood drained into his palm and dripped into the river, piercing his reflection. The poison yearned to return. The blood floated on the water like an oil spill, then began to expand—a blossoming rose that stretched and morphed into a water snake.

"That's the last time I bleed for you, Lily," Hermes said to his reflection, and collapsed back into the boat.

The oars were slick with his blood when he manned them once more. His shoulders rolled into the motion. The prow turned, and Hermes rowed after the golden snake. The snake led him farther onto the river, where the bottom became fathomless and the tide strengthened.

How did I learn the trick? Ask away. I can remember now.

It was the first summer after my banishment. Maps warned of dragons and sea creatures. The New World was not yet new to those who did not know it. Alexander was not yet Great.

Having conquered Persia, the young conqueror set his sights on the Achaemenid Empire. The invasion caused a rift between our Pantheon and the Sumerian gods—chiefly a very pissed-off Marduk from Babylon. Luckily, the Zoroastrians had recently established control over Persia, and their supreme Ahura Mazda was kind of an empty chariot…if you catch my drift.

Meanwhile, my banishment set off a furious negotiation between the Underworld and Olympus, given the rapid influx of dead Greek soldiers and converts in need of transport. The backlog had become a serious problem in my absence. It was a busy century. Thank you, Alex. It was agreed by Hades that I was allowed to travel only as far as Acheron before being rudely escorted back to Earth. On one condition, however: I was not allowed any contact with Persephone whatsoever—not on Earth, Heaven, nor Hell.

Like we listened. Every summer, Persephone and I met in secret in the dense, tiger-filled forests along the Narmada River in what is the heart of today's India, protected by the ever-accommodating Hindi Pantheon. But since Alex the Soon-to-be-Great's army was skirting the Hyphasis, the Greeks would soon be at war with the Hindus as well. Our typical refuge was no longer available. Vacation passes were canceled; the gods were recalled to Olympus to prepare for battle. All hell had broken loose—excuse the pun.

I was in the throne room on Mount Olympus, and it was the first time I'd been able to officially see Persephone in years. My seat on the council was temporarily revoked to placate a vengeful Hades, and I was only permitted entrance on official Messenger business. We were under the closest of scrutiny, thanks to Lily's persistent rumors and lies.

During a particularly fierce drunken brawl among the Olympians (one of many), Persephone stole away from her mother to pass me a note via a tiny fruit fly. I was to meet her behind the quarry, where the gods dumped their trash.

My head was on a swivel. If caught, we would only feed the lies. How Persephone could so easily brush it aside was a miracle. When I arrived, I found her buoyant, excitedly rocking on the balls of her feet. She had a plan.

"HELL?!" I shouted, flabbergasted. "Hell? You want us to meet in Hell?"

"Generally speaking," she whispered with an exuberant grin. "Right under their very noses. It would be perfect. They'd never expect us to go there."

"In summer?" I asked, wanting to make sure I heard her right. "You'd go back to prison for me?"

"Yes," she said without hesitation. "I have it all figured out."

She was beaming, enjoying that she had come up with a trick to rival the master of tricks. "We go separately—that's first and foremost. If we are caught, we can't be together."

"Clever," I said, with an eye roll that could move a mountain.

She huffed. "Don't do that. I'm not at the best part yet."

"Oh, there's a best part. I can't wait to hear it."

Her hands locked on her hips. "No sarcasm, please."

I sighed and nodded.

"Okay, so we go separately," she continued. "We use the same entrance you brought me through after the…incident. We use the mountain pass because no one ever uses it. It's too inconvenient and secluded. From there we go—"

"Hold the reins a second. What about your mother? Demeter will turn Earth to winter looking for you. Everyone will know you're missing as soon as you leave her side."

"Already handled. I've told Mother I need to be more independent and to know my role in a more intimate fashion. I insisted I'm spending my summers living among the mortals in disguise. I've thought of every detail."

I saw how much she needed this diversion. If I hadn't been so callous with Lily, we would never have been in this situation. This punishment on top of her suffering was my fault. I nodded, despite my doubts. Her confidence soared.

"Okay, now the best part…" She stretched the intrigue before throwing out her hands in a ta-da surprise. "Elysium!"

I couldn't believe what I was hearing. "Elysium? Not a chance."

"But it's perfect. Why would we ever go to Elysium? Lily's backyard. I'm giddy just thinking of it." A grin brightened her dimples. It was infectious.

"See," she declared. "You're smiling. You agree."

"I'm smiling because I can't help myself."

"We make a good team."

"Elysium's a fortress. And you, the most recognizable face in the Underworld—after mine, of course—want to slip past Lily, who started all of these rumors to begin with, and break into her paradise. Oh, and it'll be during summer!"

"I know it sounds risky, I know—"

"It's suicidal!"

She frowned. "Then the plan is perfect for you."

"Ha. Ha. Ha. So what? Are we sneaking in as servants? Am I hiding under your gown?"

"She didn't tell you then," Persephone smirked. "Guess you're not so clever in bed as I. After the thirteenth orgasm, a goddess will tell you just about anything. Including the secret entrance to her fortress. And I mean Elysium, not the one between her legs."

"That one's not so well guarded," I quipped.

Persephone shoved me. "Mean."

"I've given her far more than thirteen orgasms and she's told me no such secret."

She crossed her arms. "At the same time?"

Hermes smiled at the memory, then wiped it away from the mist where it had played out in front of his boat like a favorite television rerun.

A certain satisfaction came from remembering on the river of forget-fulness. Perhaps Hermes had conquered Lily's poison. Over the hump. Good immune system.

He sunk the oars into the river and rowed on, his vigor returning. The blood-sacrifice snake swam beyond the prow, leading him to paradise.

They'd never made it to Elysium that year. War broke out with the Hin-di Pantheon, and fearing a reprisal, Demeter clutched Persephone closer than ever, refusing to let her daughter out of her sight until she was de-livered back into the arms of her abusive husband. Hermes never had a chance to see if the trick actually worked. He was rowing blind, putting all his faith in thirteen orgasms from two thousand three hundred years ago.

The serpent accelerated, gliding over the glassy surface into the mist. Hermes lost sight of it.

"Damn." He released the oars.

Time to spill some more blood.

The second cut stung twice as badly. This time he was ready and grabbed the oars as soon as the serpent took off like a rock skipping the water. Sweat mixed with his golden blood and dripped into the hull.

Row. Row. Row. Row. Row.

Ahead, a pocket in the mist glowed with shifting neon—blue, red, green, orange. Hermes eased off the oars. The snake vanished again. He heard music and the blast of a foghorn telling anyone nearby to fuck off. Hermes allowed his skiff to silently drift. Sound carried over water, and he still felt too weak to fight if it was another trap.

A vessel approached. The chug of diesel mixed with the raucous energy of a big band jazz orchestra. Some Sinatra impersonator crooned "My Way" as the prow of a one-hundred-foot party yacht cleaved the mist like an axe. Beneath its largesse, Hermes may as well have been a rubber ducky in a bathtub. Several floors up, the deck was festooned with string lights and revelry. A champagne flute plopped into the water, followed by peals of drunken laughter.

"Oops, Roxana's lost her beverage!" a man cackled like a seagull. "Get Perseus to bring my beauty another!"

Hermes watched silhouettes appear on the deck. The man careened into his date Roxana, glittering in a silver gown, and gave her a sloppy kiss.

"Zeno, stop it!" Roxana pushed Zeno away. "You make mockery of me!"

"Don't cry over spilt champagne! Here, I commit mine to the river too!" Zeno's champagne flute soared over Hermes' head.

"Come on, everyone, champagne overboard! Let's christen our par-ty!" Zeno shouted to everyone's delight. The party guests tossed their bev-erages overboard. Several of the flutes crashed into Hermes' boat.

Roxana shushed the crowd. "Did you hear that? Something's down there!"

Without the strength to disguise himself, Hermes flattened into the rank water at the bottom of the hull. Guests converged at the railing above.

"Just a loose trawler," someone called out.

"Watch me piss on Lily's river," Zeno announced to fresh laughter. "Beware the hydra!"

The yacht churned past, saving Hermes the humiliation. The massive propellers jostled his skiff in its wake. He sat up, holding onto the sides as the current tugged his small boat like a sheet pulled off a bed.

Seagulls shrieked. The air warmed. And soon, the mist was pierced by spears of brilliant light, like a vanguard of soldiers waging war against the eternal night. Hermes crossed the battle lines into the embrace of Elysium. The fog behind him formed the fortress wall surrounding this most coveted of gated communities, guarding it from the rest of the Underworld.

Lily's trick had worked its magic, just as Persephone promised. Elysium, the White Island, in all its bleached glory, appeared floating on the horizon, wrapped in a serene Ionian day. Hermes shielded his maladjusted eyes as the most gorgeous rays nourished him. There wasn't an actual sun, of course—it was only an illusion, like a Disney resort on a Caribbean island, sheltered from the poverty.

Hermes rested.

There was no need to row anymore. Paradise beckoned.

***

Mere moments seemed to have passed when the screaming of a jet engine jolted Hermes awake. His boat listed, nearly tipping over, before slamming back with a splash. A red speedboat plowed by like a rocket-propelled lipstick, dragging two naked humans on water skis. Hermes caught their befuddled expressions before they were yanked away. It was easy to understand why. He looked like a walking mug shot. Dried blood, torn clothes, sopping wet—there were subway rats more camera-ready. He licked his palms and ran them through his hair. *That should do it.*

The majestic White Island greeted Hermes with all the swagger of a beauty pageant winner on a parade float. A sight to behold, and it wanted to be beheld. Hermes reached the base of its craggy cliffs, sunk in turquoise waters. Wildflowers and fruit trees ornamented with ripe citrus and pomegranates clung to the rocks as if to prove they could defy gravity. A family of golden ibex hopped along the ledges. Seagulls, herons, and all types of birds flittered among burrows. Trails connected whitewashed houses with blue-painted domes perched over the water like nesting egrets.

Around the island, rings of columns marked various temples dedicated to the gods. Hermes knew exactly which was built in his name. Unfortunately, the rituals did nothing for them. Gods couldn't benefit from devotion in the afterlife. Souls who continued to practice mostly did so out of habit, some out of gratitude, more often out of fear. Statistics showed temple attendance was higher in Elysium than anywhere else in the Underworld. Heaven was the land of goody two-shoes.

In hindsight, Hades should have instituted a more robust reincarnation policy and not presumed their religion would last forever. Only a trickle of the worthiest citizens admitted to Elysium were granted rebirth.

Hermes rowed on, searching for a beach to land.

A jangle of bells rang out from the island. A soul led four pack-laden donkeys along a narrow path, delivering loaves of bread, bottles of island wine, bricks of feta, and sacks of olives. Blue shutters flapped open on a house not far above the water. An elderly woman with a raisin face and auburn ringlet hair leaned out to beat dust from a rug. Elysium represented a glorified Greece wedded to the past, one that Hermes yearned for and missed. He waved, and the old woman and delivery boy returned his friendly greeting. For the first time since he had arrived in the Underworld, Hermes felt at home.

Rounding an outcropping, the port of Elysium came into view.

Hermes lurched to his feet, nearly capsizing the skiff. "No!"

Paradise was all terribly wrong. The bay, once an image of tranquility, now churned with a tangle of masts and rigging, clogged with yachts and pleasure barges flaunting vulgar names and political flags. The humble fishing boats that had lined the shore were nowhere in sight. Luxury hotels cascaded down from the Elysian Fields, swallowing the cliffs in marble and glass. Casinos and condominiums had squashed the quaint stone cottages, tavernas, temples, and markets. The beaches where Hermes once strolled in peace were swarmed with sunbathers, colonized by a forest of umbrellas like neon mushrooms.

Hermes would curse the Furies and their insatiable quest for profit, if he could. The change sickened his soul. He navigated the outer shoals, aiming for a small beach of polished dolomite where hotels cast shadows like piano keys over a tacky promenade.

The hull scraped the shallows. Hermes disembarked and waded ashore with Lily's sword at his side, the pistol clutched to his chest. Nude sunbathers basked in the everlasting sun like boiled lobsters. They glared up at the shipwrecked traveler blocking their light, eyes popping out of their burnt faces. The Fury sisters had opened the gates of paradise for any scum with enough coin to purchase a timeshare. Virtue be damned.

On the tacky boardwalk, Hermes dodged roller skaters, lizard walkers, and souvenir peddlers (refrigerator magnets and snow globes for everyone). There were at least a dozen Stardeer coffee shops started by a soul too lazy to properly rip off Starbucks. Still, every single location was mobbed with lines out the door. One of the cafés sacrilegiously operated out of a temple once dedicated to Athena, substituting piety for fair-trade macchiatos.

He forced himself to wear blinders and set his sights toward the crown jewel of Elysium.

The Tower of Kronos jutted up from the island's high interior plateau like a lonely participation trophy. A sphere of brilliant light served as the capstone, the torch that illuminated paradise. Its power derived from the steady reincarnation of souls occurring within—a certifiable green energy source, if there ever was one. The primordial white (more like apricot) light at the end of the tunnel was actually the miracle of rebirth. Every religion paid homage to the eternal battery in their own way. The Jews kept a flame burning above the ark. Christians placed a lamp before their tabernacles. The meaning changed over the centuries, but it started here.

Kronos had ruled during the Golden Age of the Titans after overthrowing his father, Ouranos, until he was later overthrown by his son Zeus. It was kind of a father-son bonding thing. The story went that generations after defeating Kronos in the Great War, Zeus took pity on his father, freed him from Tartaros, and granted him dominion over the Elysian Fields—which was kind of like giving Genghis Khan a seat on the local school board. The whole thing was a PR stunt masquerading as reconciliation.

Using the tower as a compass, Hermes entered the city. New Elysium assaulted the senses. Its maze of narrow alleys had been transformed into a façade for a shopping mall. The streets clattered with slot machines and the shouts of gamblers, which clashed with the wail of sirens forced to perform Jimmy Buffett songs at sidewalk bars for the eternal day drinkers. A noxious perfume of rose laced with gunpowder wafted from more knockoff shops with names like Guca and Prado. The latest earthly fashions in the window displays were about three decades late—tawdry and moth-eaten, more Goodwill than Rodeo Drive. But with everything old being new again, perhaps they were ahead of their time.

Hermes wove through the privileged souls decked in jewels and wreathed in garlands. They parted for him as if he were diseased, pinching their upturned noses. It was easy to read their minds. *Let them stare.*

He stepped into a plaza with a resplendent fountain. Riflescopes bristled along the rooftops. Hermes slipped under an awning outside yet another Stardeer. Keeping himself hidden, he moved umbrella to umbrella, weaving among packed tables with loitering writers clacking away on typewriters and gossiping brunchers festooned in ridiculous fur coats and feather hats. In between each lily pad of cover, he spied black eyes tracking his progress from above the street. The clopping of hooves under the foot traffic. A sinister presence lurked.

It was clear Hermes was walking into an ambush, but what other choice did he have? The demons held their fire, waiting for something. Or someone. He shoved through souls in line for a table, ignoring their protests, and veered off course from the tower into a labyrinth of white-washed alleys with bright blue doors and cascading purple bougainvillea, shooting glances back at the eerily picturesque lanes.

The roar of a sports car cut the calm like a suburban neighbor going to town with a chainsaw on a Sunday morning. A rust-stained white 1983 Lamborghini rolled across the alley's exit. Its engine idled, menacingly purring his name: HHHHHEERRRRRMMMMMMM, HHHHHEEEER-RRRMMMM. Then it revved: MMMMEEEESSS, MMMEEESSS, MMMEEEESSSS.

He scanned the rooftops. Hulking shadows crept along the ledges, dark as mine shafts. They tucked behind chimneys, draped rifle scopes over the tiles like a string of celebratory banners. Elysium tourists streamed obliviously past him. To his right, a café beckoned with an aperitif. To his left, a casino devoured pedestrians. The way back was choked by a gaggle of beautiful dames in evening attire.

The hooves shoved into stilettos were a dead giveaway: Empusai.

Hermes had walked right into a lobster cage. Incidentally, a lobster tank glowed in the café window, packed with the ill-fated crustaceans. Hermes could relate. Except he had no intention of going quietly into any pot of boiling water.

The Lamborghini door opened, ejecting an exuberant Tisiphone. The Fury's presence sent a primal fear rippling down the street. The writers stopped kvetching. The brunchers stopped gossiping. Tisiphone was the ultimate buzzkill. Souls flattened against the buildings, opening a clear line of sight between Hermes and Tisiphone like a Western duel. Inside the casino, a gambler hit the jackpot on a slot machine. The gleeful trill made an incongruous soundtrack to the doomed vibes.

"Well, well, well..." tsked Tisiphone.

"Well, well, well," Hermes returned with a courteous bow.

"You murdered my sister. What do you have to say?"

He considered every available response and went with: "Meh."

Directly above Hermes, a demon popped up like a carnival game, rifle shouldered. Hermes fanned his pistol and fired a single shot. The bullet hit the creature between the eyes. It tumbled over the ledge, landing on a pile of pancakes. The brunchers erupted in outrage as Tisiphone's army unleashed a hail of gunfire. Hermes dove into the casino. A bullet bit into his calf. Souls fled in terror. The fish tank exploded. Condemned lobsters scuttled to freedom.

Now injured, Hermes pinwheeled through squawking high rollers, a tornado of sequined dresses and tailcoats, until he collided with a poker table. Chips scattered everywhere, triggering a mad rush. His nose met a fist fortified with gaudy rings. Incensed gamblers glared through mascara and spray tans. Hermes had spoiled their fun.

A mob congealed, a hundred souls deep in every direction. There was nowhere to go.

"Where are all the virtuous? Huh?"

"Not here," answered a soul with a greasy combover and a popped collar.

The combover man attempted to shove Hermes, but for a mortal it was like trying to tip over a house. Hermes shoved him through a slot machine.

"We don't want your kind!" shouted another soul.

A shrieking woman hurtled at him, golf club arcing toward his head. Hermes caught the club mid-swing and ripped it from her.

"None of you care?" Hermes challenged. "Earth was your home!"

"Fuck Earth," shouted the woman who had thrown the golf club. She rushed him again. His timing was off. Somehow she managed to grab his gun. The weapon bucked. A round cracked. The woman collapsed screaming and clutching her stomach.

The circle widened as if hit by a shockwave. Hermes held out his hands. "Hold on. It was an accident…"

The dam burst. Snarling souls fell upon him like the jaws of a bear trap. They tore at his hair and clothes. Puny fists pounded his body. Hermes emptied his clip, but the souls were like ants, willing to sacrifice as many of their own to destroy the invader. For every soul that fell, another three replaced it. Hands encased his pistol. The weapon disappeared. So did Lily's sword. And his backpack. Hermes elbowed. Shoved. Punched. Tried to propel himself through the mob with his wings, but it was like pushing against a breaking wave.

The souls piled on. He couldn't breathe. Even his divine body had its limits…

Then the crushing weight abruptly lifted. The souls retreated. Hermes gasped for air. Ichor matted his hair over his eyes. He lay atop a pile of trampled souls and poker chips, feeling like an ashtray gang-raped by cigarettes. It took every ounce of energy to stand.

"Jackpot," said a familiar husky voice behind him.

Hermes turned around.

"Shit—" was all he managed. Tisiphone pistol-whipped him across the face.

He saw triple diamonds. Then nothing.

CHAPTER TWENTY-EIGHT

HERMES WOKE IN THE back of an SUV bouncing up a rough cobblestone road. The gas-guzzling ride felt almost therapeutically normal, except for his being pinned between two mouth-breathing demon henchmen. The stench of ripe cabbage cloistered the otherwise roomy interior, and no one bothered to roll down a window. Wart-like horns covered the demons like trunks of a Ceiba tree and poked into his sides. Their wide faces and fat necks resembled the Roman-descended mobsters they sought to emulate. Hermes tried to shift his hands, but they were bound in thick chains fastened to the floor. The metal was a special ore harvested in the Underworld and forged by the Uranian Cyclopes—the same blacksmiths who made Hades' helm and a variety of other godly knickknacks. The magic in the bands meant the cuffs were unbreakable. It must have cost the Fury girls their whole allowance. His efforts garnered a round of caustic stares.

"My nose is itchy," lied Hermes.

Tisiphone craned around from the front passenger seat with mom-ex-asperation. "No, it's not."

"That was some crack on the head."

"You deserve worse."

"So I've been told. Get in line."

"I don't believe in them."

They rounded a bend. Blinding light from Kronos' Tower poured through the windshield—a pleasant nuclear fallout glow. Hermes squinted while Tisiphone and her demons snapped on fancy shades.

"How much do I owe you for the ride?" Hermes said, his eyes watering.

"Oh, you'll pay, don't worry."

Tisiphone rotated back to send a text, probably to Alecto. Hermes started to hum a ditty, but a henchman elbowed him to shut up.

"How about a game?" Hermes asked cheerfully. "I spy with my little eye something that starts wiiitthhh…" He rolled his eyes around the car and stopped on Tisiphone. "The letter C."

No takers. Hermes turned to the demon on his right. "What about you, Sunshine? Any guesses?"

Sunshine bared his fangs. "Cat."

"Good guess, but no. I'll give you a hint. It rhymes with *runt*."

Sunshine thought about it some more. "Cat!"

Hermes sighed. "Sure. I'll give you that one."

Sunshine beamed triumphantly.

Tisiphone raised a middle finger over the center console.

Good. She's listening.

"Where's your sister? Not the one I killed—the other one."

"If you think you can trick me into sharing information, you're mistaken."

"Trick you?" Hermes lifted his cuffed hands and rattled the chains. "I wouldn't dare."

"You're irritating."

"Then you should have kidnapped someone else."

"I should stuff your godhood in your goddamn mouth and sew your lips shut."

Hermes forced a smile. It wasn't an empty threat. "Suicide bombers. Ever hear of them?"

"No. And I don't care to."

"That's a shame. I think you'd like them. They're humans who strap explosives to themselves and blow themselves up in places where they can kill other humans—as many as possible."

Her silence said she was clearly intrigued.

Hermes continued, "I've always been amazed how they convince themselves to do it."

"Enlighten me," she said.

"For starters, they're told they'll go straight to heaven. First-class ticket to Elysium."

"Makes sense."

"Good incentive. Doesn't stop there. They'll also get to spend an eternity with a bunch of virgins gone wild. Seriously, who came up with that idea?"

"Someone smart."

"No shit! Right?" Hermes played along. "It's a good deal. The humans are pretty clever—more than we give them credit for. It's usually some holy man—a priest, imam, whatever—who convinces some poor schmuck to blow himself or herself up. And by priest, I mean a self-interested twat. The recipe is quite simple. I'll share it with you if you like." He didn't wait for her to respond. "You drop some grievance, mix in a dash of dogma, a healthy pour of resentment and shame, some sexual repression—because why not?—add some more dogma, make it real fire and brimstone, and voilà! Easy-bake martyr. Best part: it's not like these suicide bombers can send a postcard from heaven to prove it was worth the effort. It's grade-A, top-notch bullshit. I've personally been to every heaven—never met a single terrorist being served an Arnold Palmer by a virgin."

"They wouldn't do it if it didn't work."

"That's what you'd say."

Tisiphone glanced at him in the rearview mirror. "Is this supposed to be a metaphor?"

"You're too smart for that."

"Don't start lecturing me on winter."

Hermes shrugged. "We're self-righteous. It comes with the territory."

Tisiphone gave a smile that landed like a sledgehammer. "Have you ever heard of a bird called a pelican?"

The question threw Hermes. "Yeah…seen one or two."

"Do you know how they die? It's wonderfully morbid and poetic. My favorite Earth story."

"I don't really go for nature documentaries…"

Tisiphone ignored him. "They starve to death because they go blind. And do you know how they go blind? The pelican searches for food flying above the water, and when it spies a school of fish—*WHAM!*—it dives, smashing through the water with enough force to snatch a fish before it darts away. Day after day. Slam. Slam. Slam. Now, every time it dives, it favors one side. After a while, after many dives slamming into the ocean, that eye dies. So what does the pelican do? These one-eyed pelicans? They still must eat. Must fish. They're not going to learn how to use a rod. No, they switch to the other side and dive and dive until their other eye no longer functions. They go blind. No more fishing. No more food. Do the other pelicans help feed their disabled brethren? No. Because it's nature. *You* designed it."

"Beautifully put," Hermes said. "And sadly, a myth. But let's not let facts get in the way of such a mediocre allegory. I assume I'm the pelican? Also, I didn't design anything. Ever heard of Charles Darwin? Evolution? None of us tossed the first pelican into the sky, nor did we hunch over a drafting table carving a lump of clay."

"That's exactly what Prometheus did!"

"With the humans. And that was probably a mistake."

The SUV went over a large pothole and bounced them up and down. Sunshine's bald spot thumped against the roof.

Tisiphone met Hermes' gaze in the rearview mirror. "The gods wrote the rules yet never lived by them."

"Hey, we're only gods—"

"Yet you made us color in the lines. Tell me how any of that was fair?"

"It wasn't. We broke our own rules quite often—me especially—but we never wrote the rules for the humans. They've always written the rules for themselves, for better or worse—usually worse. They just annoyingly attribute their laws to us. *We* never said a human couldn't covet their neighbor's wife or have sex with a sheep. *They* figured that out on their own."

"Not all of them…" Tisiphone said.

"Well, they're only human."

"The gods have rules. The humans have rules. But there aren't rules between religions," she said smugly.

Hermes hated the gotcha complex. "Right again. There are no rules governing the division of worship or to mediate a dispute, no league of pantheons. So technically, I guess freezing Earth is fair game. And you have your justification, as does every suicide bomber. And every pelican, if you're really committed to the metaphor."

She harumphed.

Hermes continued, "Let me drop some knowledge on you, though. And you're not going to find this on any fake Wikipedia page."

"Wikipedia?" she echoed, fumbling the pronunciation.

"Don't get distracted. What you need to hear is this: The universe is its own thing. It's bigger than the gods—new gods, old gods, extinct gods, gods yet to be born. Bigger than religion itself. As an unwritten rule, we don't fuck with it. Sure, we pluck the strings from time to time. We tinker, bend, smash atoms together. But we don't redefine what an atom is. The moment we start fucking with the fundamentals, we're just going to get—"

"Chaos," Tisiphone finished.

Ding. Ding. Ding. Ding. It always came down to that one word.

"That's the goal, sweetheart. That's the goal…"

She fixed her malevolent stare out the windshield, and they rode the rest of the way in silence.

***

They parked under a grand propylaion gate carved from the same marble that gave the White Island its name. Delicate archways latticed the exterior, climbing all the way up the Tower of Kronos, their patterns dissolving in the radiant solar flare.

After all the darkness and winter, the light practically seared his skin. Through the slits of his lashes, Hermes watched Sunshine rework the chains to keep them shackled together, which was nice because he hated goodbyes. A face mask was fitted over his head—the kind they give cannibalistic serial killers—and then attached to the cuffs on his wrists and ankles.

Hermes was yanked out of the SUV, stumbling from the force and into the radioactive glare. He immediately fixed his gaze on the ground, lest he go blind like one of Tisiphone's mythic pelicans. A battalion of demons in knee pads, shin guards, and salvaged armor converged around him like a roller derby bout. Sunshine jammed a pair of cardboard solar eclipse glasses onto Hermes' face. Finally able to look up, Hermes saw every demon wore those snazzy snowboarder shades. Not fair.

Almost immediately, Tisiphone ripped off his protection and stomped on the glasses. She furiously whirled to Sunshine and gestured the demon to her with a hooked finger.

"You. Come here."

Sunshine hesitantly obeyed, jerking Hermes forward in the process.

"What was that?" she quizzed him like a teacher catching a child misbehaving.

The demon dug the toe of his boot into the dirt and mumbled an apology.

Her lip curled, and she strafed her soldiers. "Compassion. That's what it was. Compassion!"

She unholstered a barbed scourge tucked into her belt and whipped Sunshine across the face, tearing a hole in his left cheek. Black blood splattered Hermes' sneakers. And here he had just cleaned them of Ker blood back at Lily's.

Sunshine wobbled, blood pouring down his chest and filling the pockets of his Dickies. But Tisiphone wasn't finished. She brought the scourge cracking against the poor henchdemon again and again, fueled by her preternatural thirst for suffering. She added a little hop and a twirl, and tossed the whip between hands like she was performing at some truly fucked-up talent show. The Miss Sadomasochist Pageant. Her face practically sparkled with glee. Few activities brought her as much joy. Sunshine crumpled to his knees, dragging Hermes to the ground, inches from the brutality, close enough to feel the whistle of the metal braids slicing the air. Each sickening smack was followed by tearing flesh as Tisiphone wrenched the barbs free. All because the offending demon dared to show kindness.

The rest of the malevolent army stood unmoved. Plenty of indifference to go around. Tisiphone lashed and lashed until Sunshine was nothing but mince. Finished, she whipped back her sweat-and-blood-soaked hair and tossed a set of keys to the next demon.

"Take his place."

The new supplicant removed the cuff from Sunshine's dead wrist and attached it to his own, hauling up a disturbed Hermes from a puddle of gore.

An exhilarated Tisiphone tucked the bloody scourge back into her belt, exhaling with satisfaction. "Better than sex."

Then she was on the move. Hermes was tugged up a squiggly pink walkway. The placenta led them into a grand hall that would put the LDS to shame. Like an otherworldly wishing well, everything was carved from a translucent Naxian marble that pulsed with a calming, hypnotic glow. Their footfalls echoed softly, creating a sound bath. The presence of Tisiphone and her heavily armed, flat-footed, flatulent demons in such a sacred space made his head throb from the dissonance. Or maybe it was the pistol-whipping. Either one.

Separating from the ethereal light, a dozen nymphs appeared. They flitted around to fit cotton booties over Hermes' sneakers and the demons' combat boots. Despite their maternal appearance, nymphs were fierce maidens with braided armpits and a distinct Woodstock vibe. When a nymph approached Tisiphone with a booty, the Fury smacked her with the back of her hand. The slap echoed through the chamber, and everything stopped. The nymphs deferentially folded their arms over their chests and bowed, but Hermes could tell they were seething.

"LEAVE!" shrieked Tisiphone.

The nymphs lifted their fallen sister and flitted into tiny chambers that honeycombed the tower.

Tisiphone marched on.

The hall split into two passages: one wound up the tower, the other spiraled down like a vein of water carving through limestone. Tisiphone chose down, of course.

The air warmed on their descent. The distant wail of a crying infant echoed up from the depths. Hermes couldn't help but act like a tourist—head spinning, eyes devouring. He'd never been granted access to the Tower of Kronos before, which was unusual, given that he had traveled most everywhere else. This was a truly holy place, so it made sense they had kept him out.

The demons jabbed him forward whenever he slowed, his shackles jangling with his shuffled gait. They passed a series of break rooms filled with brutal, hardened-looking souls—predators and gangbangers and warlords more suited to a supermax prison—smoking cigarettes around water coolers, reading porno rags, or brawling. Each chamber unveiled a fresh perversion. Every soul had a Roman numeral stamped on their forehead in scarlet dye. A peculiar detail. Goosebumps tingled over his own brow. Around and around, down, deeper, depraved. A pop-up brothel, serviced by exhausted nymphs. A poker game. An opium den. A familiar, repugnant face peered up from his pipe—a certain tyrant of Syracuse. A real bastard of a conqueror. Hermes paused, tasting the desecration as if he'd been forced to take a shot of sewage. These weren't just any old souls, but those beyond redemption.

The most wicked and vile. Evil.

This can't be right—

TUG! Hermes stumbled, wrists out in front. They were near the bottom. The ramp circled a pool of pink water flowing into a single drain like a puckered…

A bright green spark flashed above the hole. The infant cries grew louder. On the lower levels, the break rooms were replaced by a series of maternity wards, where a different breed of nymphs labored. Androgynous, elegant as orchids, their ivory hair floated over their simple white gowns, brushing the heels of their bare feet. There was no warmth, no love. That had been beaten out of them, clear from the scars and bruises.

The wailing reached its zenith as the fairy doulas glided among bassinets, checking forms on clipboards as they assessed which crying infant to cull for metempsychosis. It was as if these purest of souls expressed the despair their nymph caretakers could not.

Normally, this was a solemn, private rite. Not even the gods were allowed to witness a rebirth, but this sacred ritual had been corrupted too. The tower belched the evil souls back to Earth while spectators watched like it was a monster truck rally. Demons kept the beleaguered nymphs working at a breakneck pace, forced to reincarnate the wicked without pause. Though Lily had warned Hermes, it was still jarring to see firsthand.

They reached the holy of holies. The pool bathed them in a pink sweet-sixteen-party glow. Knee-deep in the baptismal waters was the head nymph. She turned at their disruption—they were a big tour group—her silver eyes afflicted with worry, sunken into her olive skin. Seeing Hermes, she seemed to lift ever so slightly with defiance—until a demon charged in and struck her with a baton, knocking her onto her knees.

Hermes growled, lurched to intervene, but his demon handlers yanked his choker, snapping his neck back. A heavy foot crashed into his spine, slamming him forward. The forced march pressed on around the perimeter. The head nymph pushed herself upright onto shaking legs, her gaze never leaving Hermes. Even through the slits in his mask, he could see the hope wither from her noble face.

If a god could be subdued, what chance was there for the rest of them?

A vile soul with Dahmer charisma waded into the pool, tossing his cigarette into the pure water. The man was naked. Battle scars covered his chest, and tattoos glorified his many rapes and kills. The head nymph numbly set her hands over his evil heart. A calm expression washed over him, and he began to regress in age, until a newborn floated at the nymph's feet. Her tears fell on the child, and she whispered a prayer into his ear.

The infant shrieked so forcefully he turned red. Perhaps he realized he would be forced to repeat all the mistakes of his past life. The nymph finished her benediction and released the child to float away.

The pool darkened to a burgundy swirl, poisoned by the wretched soul it was forced to ingest. The newborn traced the drain and then, sucked into the hole, ignited in a flash that momentarily blinded them all.

The soul ignited into a spark—the spark of life—and traveled up the tower to be reborn, unhurried and free, carried upon invisible wings of promise. For in this singular ascension lay the first, last, and only moment of perfection attainable to a human. Everyone—demon, god, and nymph—paused, transfixed, for even when defiled, it was beautiful.

"Cool, right?" Tisiphone said, smashing the transcendent mood.

"Cool," he said, muffled through his face mask.

The demon handlers shoved him onward. He caught one last look at the head nymph, aching and defeated, before he was yanked from the room of reincarnation.

They entered a dark passage, the air moist and the walls dripping with a slimy substance. The demons ahead and behind lit torches.

"This required a lot of planning," said Hermes to Tisiphone.

"No one's been paying attention for a very long time."

Hermes had a million questions but couldn't articulate any of them. Tisiphone indulged the quiet. Sometimes the best torture was being left alone with one's thoughts.

They brought Hermes to the closest approximation of a dungeon Paradise had to offer: the wine cellar. In Elysium, all roads eventually led to wine. Oil lamps dangled from the stone ceiling, illuminating six thousand years of vinification. It was Hades' pride and joy, a collection to give Dionysus a run for his money.

The demon handlers secured Hermes to the bedrock wall, arms and legs spread in an X. Tisiphone gestured to remove his face mask, and a small tasting table and chair were positioned in front of him.

She sat with her cheek resting in her palm, a dreamy expression that begged for a milkshake with two straws. A small wave of her other hand sent the demons away. The Fury girls preferred to torture in private.

"You killed my sister," she began.

"And to think I tried to keep a low profile," Hermes said.

She smirked. "I'm going to enjoy this."

"So am I." Hermes leaned forward tauntingly, cuffs digging into his ankles and wrists.

"Installing Odysseus as High Judge surprised me…I expected you to go the frat-boy route, one of your drinking buddies."

"I know. I surprise myself sometimes too. I do love Greek life, but I think warrior-king was the right move. Someone decisive, even-handed, sober."

"You gods love your nepotism. Did you think you injured us with your little revolt?" She made it sound as if Hermes had merely rearranged the furniture.

"I think your options have narrowed."

"They can have the Underworld. We're done with it. It's lost its luster anyway."

Done with the Underworld—and done with chitchat, apparently—as Tisiphone rose from the table. She stopped inches from his face.

"I want to remember you as you are now..."

Her skin crawled and bulged from the restless snakes squirming beneath. She lifted her forearm and, using her razor-sharp fingernail, made an incision between her elbow and wrist.

Hermes tsked. "You really shouldn't pick."

Unlike Megaera, Tisiphone was the Eryine of Retribution, immune to his provocations. She drew out a python, slick with her blood, and ran a finger down its spine. It hissed, cinching around her waist. No doubt it was highly poisonous. Her body writhed, the rest of the snakes surging toward the opening.

The python uncoiled, rising until the slits of its eyes looked into her beady eyes. Its tongue licked the air, tasting its victim.

Tisiphone addressed her snake. "Gods aren't any fun when it comes to torture. Their pain tolerance is so much greater than the mortals'. A shame, really. It dulls all sensation."

She released her pet onto Hermes. It wrapped around his neck like a choker. Hermes tried to nudge it off with his chin and blow air at it to no avail. The snake, now merely annoyed, turned its arrowhead back to its master for further instruction.

Tisiphone tipped her head. The snake whipped back and struck. Fangs pierced Hermes' jugular, injecting a sour venom. It struck again and again with lightning speed. Strike. Neck. Strike. Chin. Strike. Cheek. Strike. Shoulder. Strike. Chest. Poison seeped from the puncture marks, dripped down his face. Hermes thrashed against the restraints, but it only increased the snake's frenzy. On a pain scale of 1 to 10, it was holy fucking god.

The venom set his skin on fire. The agony like a power tool drilling into his brain.

"I've tortured so many gods. It takes so long for them to scream. It's more work than fun. Sometimes I think I've failed."

"You're doin' fine," Hermes panted, drenched in sweat, poison, and blood. Even the snake was exhausted.

"Thank you. I appreciate the encouragement. I've learned so much about us—our anatomy, our psychology. It's true we don't feel pain like the humans. But under our extraordinary armor, we're extraordinarily weak." She caressed his face, traced each of the bites, and shaved his evening shadow with nails as sharp as razor blades. "Our emotions are so raw, so pure. The smallest slight becomes the deepest insult. Heartbreak becomes murder. Laughter, an orgasm. Worship from a mortal…"

Her body pressed into his, humid as a summer night on a Louisiana swamp, her breath fetid and diseased. He looked into her hideous eyes and saw cockroaches and crocodiles. She dug a fingernail into his jugular, pushing it into him down to the cuticle, hooking him like bait.

"Every time they fall to their knees…ecstasy."

Hermes must have dissociated, because a single snowflake—so gentle and so pristine—suddenly floated down between him and Tisiphone. Its symmetry could only have been intelligently designed. It was sublime. Then he heard the distant pounding of drums. It sounded like the drums from the Blackfeet ceremony calling him into the sweat lodge. No sooner did he recognize the sound than the black portal appeared before his eyes, blocking Tisiphone's face. Hermes obeyed the call and crawled into the tortoise shelter.

Tisiphone withdrew her nail and snapped her fingers in front of his face. "Hello? Hell to Hermes? Where are you? Where did you go?"

Hermes wasn't home.

Her high interrupted, she snarled and slapped his face. "HERMES!"

But Hermes was in the spirit realm. Where she would never find him.

In the spirit realm, Hermes could sense multitudes, sense everything. He sensed impending danger—and, strangely, love. The blackness around him was a pool of primordial possibility. It was the essence from which visions were formed. Yet the vision his subconscious chose to escape into was one he did not expect.

Snow magically swirled around him. Towering mountains sealed off the horizons. He recognized the peaks. The Himalayan range. Hermes suddenly realized why this memory was so familiar. He had recently watched this tape. He turned around, and Persephone squeezed into his chest like puzzle pieces fitting together. Her cheek pressed into his shoulder, her tears soaking his shirt and instantly turning to ice.

"I'm sorry," escaped his lips, hovering in the frigid air along with his breath. "Maybe her leaving is a gift."

She detached from his embrace and flattened a snowman. The grief made her forget the cold, and her eyes slid over the snowy banks, unable to attach to anything in this foreign place called winter.

"A gift? My mother's vanishing?!"

It was the first time Persephone had seen snow—the day she told him her mother had vanished. Hermes had argued that Demeter's disappearance was not just a gift but the ultimate gift. He had been adamant; she had been apoplectic. The goddess of Spring was—and would forever be—perpetually in demand. The notion that she could represent both death and rebirth was a worship boon, a grade-A miracle. There were few things as impactful and present to all life on Earth as the turning of the seasons.

The seasons were woven into the fabric of existence: from the first tulips to the summer tan, from pumpkin spice lattes to snowball fights. The turning of Fall to Winter to Spring to Summer to Fall to Winter to Spring to Summer was endless, constantly restarting year after year. Persephone was the goddess of change and newness. As soon as you were tired of hot and sticky and barbecue, she gave you apple cider and Halloween. And when you got sick of foliage and sweater weather, you got to take out your skis, bask in commercialism, and listen to Christmas songs until you wanted to blow your brains out—and then, on cue, along came Persephone to melt the snow and give you newborn lambs and chocolate eggs. Hermes had wanted to shake her out of her silly funk and berate her to appreciate her good fortune.

When he was done with his rant, she had looked away to hide the tears spilling down her face. "I can't accept it…I don't want to."

"You have to," he had callously insisted. "You don't get how lucky you are. It's not fair, really, not to the rest of us. And then you reject it? Seriously? Persephone…like, seriously? What the fuck?"

She sank into the snow, and he sank next to her as the sun sank below the peaks. There was a lot of sinking going on. Shades of pink and purple danced across the mountains. The temperature plummeted, and when she stood, her body was rigid, a stiffness deeper than the cold. The snow crunched underfoot, a thin layer of ice newly formed over the surface.

"Okay. I hear you," she had said, turning to him with a smile confined to her lips. *Nailed it.*

Nailed it?! That's what he had thought in the moment? Her heart was an empty can, and he had stomped it flat to get a couple measly cents at the recycling yard. It wasn't agreement. It was appeasement. If only he hadn't been so thickheaded, so self-absorbed, he'd have seen how hurt she was—and how much of that hurt he had caused.

Minos was right, god help me!

He had accused her of being selfish when he had been selfish, rubbing her face in his bitterness and jealousy and then making her co-sign on the dotted line. Did he actually say she was blessed that her mother had vanished?! *Jesus Christ!* It didn't matter if Demeter had given Persephone purpose. It was not Persephone's purpose. Amid her profound grief, Hermes did what he always did: made it about himself. So she had boxed up her feelings and made peace, consigned herself to the worst type of loneliness: to be alone amongst those you love.

He had committed the sin of assholery. It was a mortal sin. Yet being immortal didn't let him off the hook. Could there be absolution? What if his amends was his purpose? Sometimes, purpose was not something ordained but chosen. That was clear now. So was his purpose.

But then, in accordance with the unwritten rules of the universe, his revelation was rudely interrupted. The real world came a-knocking in the form of a jab to his kidney.

The pain bored a tunnel through the Himalayas. A vision of Tisiphone appeared, distant and warped, as if he were looking through the wrong end of a telescope. He felt her fingers jamming into his side.

Oh right, I'm still chained to a wall in a wine cellar in Elysium.

The marble echoed with footsteps before she could harvest his organs. Intuition told him to return from the spirit world, and fast. Hermes thrust his consciousness back into his body to a scowling Tisiphone. She quickly stripped the snake from his neck, ripped it in two, and hid it behind her back just before Alecto entered the cellar. What a killjoy.

Tisiphone pasted on the innocent look of a child hiding a broken lamp. "I caught him! I caught him, no one else."

Alecto didn't acknowledge her sister. Hermes caught a wave of disappointment crest Tisiphone's face. The eldest Fury was draped in a resplendent ruby robe fit for a coronation—assuming it was by defenestration. Dainty bones decorated her hair, woven through her curls like a preteen's barrettes. The smallness of the phalanges could only be the remains of children.

He put up a fight, but I got him," Tisiphone tried again.

Alecto brushed her sister aside to face Hermes dead-on. "Martyrdom suits you."

"Yeah? I thought I'd try it on for a change..." Hermes squeezed out a smile, not easy with all the snake-venom swelling.

A loud metallic rattle whipped his attention to the stairwell. An ogre-sized demon lumbered into the cellar, its bald head brushing the high ceiling. Another unbreakable chain was strung over its shoulder like it was towing a ship. Hermes' heart pummeled his chest.

Alecto took the chain and gave it a violent tug. A pitiful pile of filthy rags crashed through a phalanx of demons and crumpled onto the floor. Inside the rags was a woman, he guessed.

The poor shivering thing was pale and emaciated. She stared at the floor so that Hermes could only see the top of her head, which was a cocoon of matted hair decorated with bits of straw and rat droppings. Steadying herself, she lifted a hand off the ground to shield her eyes from the light. A golden handprint was left on the ground.

A goddess beautiful as the first Spring tulip. *She's a goddess!*

"Persephone…" he croaked, unable to control his anguish.

"No more tricks," she groaned.

"It's not a trick. It's me," he pleaded, but she refused to look up.

Tisiphone laughed, but it was muffled and miles and galaxies away. Hermes felt like he was trapped in a shipwreck at the bottom of the ocean.

The ogre shoved in, heaving a sledgehammer over its lofty head before driving a spike through the chain into the stone. It was done to give Persephone so little slack her neck was forcibly bent into submission.

The spike may as well have gone through Hermes' heart. He had once promised Persephone his protection, swore she would never again be held captive. He had failed. Failed in the worst possible way. She was treated no better than a cow bound for the slaughterhouse. Worse still, Hermes had no authority. He possessed no scroll from Zeus. No pantheon stood at his back. He was a messenger without a message. A trickster with no tricks. A god without worship. A forgotten name. A relic. A nothing. No, less than nothing.

"It's me. It's Hermes." He willed her to see him, but it was clear she had been tortured—in both body and mind—unable to trust what was real. She shook her head and sealed her eyes shut.

"I'm sorry," he said. "Sorry for abandoning you, for being so selfish, for being jealous…"

"He's jealous too!" Tisiphone screamed in delight and clapped her hands excitedly like a superfan of *The Bachelorette*. "This is too rich, sister, so wonderfully rich."

Alecto allowed herself to smile—but only the slightest curl of her lip. "It's beautiful."

Hermes shoved them to the side of his consciousness. The world narrowed to just him and Persephone, supplicated on the floor. "I was always mad you had a role in this universe and I didn't. But you never had a choice, even in your mother's death. I was wrong. I always had a purpose too. I just couldn't see it…" A pause. "No, that's a lie. I knew it. I knew what I had to do, but I was selfish. I had a choice, and I chose to accept it.

My purpose should have been to help you carry yours. To not let you be so alone. I'm sorry."

He hung his head in shame. Shame. No more powerful emotion existed other than love. Then the softest voice—as if drifting across time and space—pierced his sorrow...

"Hermes? Is it really you?"

Every molecule in him snapped back to Persephone. Persephone. She was studying him as if he were a mirage. Hot tears washed away the venom on his face, burning as they crossed his many wounds. Hermes had never cried. Not once in his immortal existence. Here, in front of Persephone, before Alecto, Tisiphone, and an ogre of a demon absent-mindedly picking its nose—he sobbed. He wept freely and openly.

"It is," he blubbered.

"You big baby." Persephone smiled. She smiled spring showers and summer waterfalls, newborn foals and budding crocuses. Hermes laughed through his sobs, and Persephone joined. They were a slobbery, insufferable mess.

"This is disgusting now," Tisiphone was no longer excited. She covered her mouth with the back of her hand to hold in the vomit. "Sister? Can I put a stop to this?"

The scourge was halfway out of her belt when Alecto held up a hand. "Not yet. Let them have their hope, let them build their little sandcastle on the beach. Then it will be all the sweeter when we demolish it."

Tisiphone smiled. "Yes...yes! You're right."

"I'm always right."

Hermes blinked away the tears, as he couldn't wipe his face. He had heard the Fury sisters plot, but it didn't matter. All that mattered was connecting with Persephone. With bringing back...dare he say it...her humanity.

"I thought you might be another trick," Persephone struggled to speak louder than a whisper. "They made me think it was you so many times. But I think it is you this time."

"It is."

Doubt flashed across her features. "But Hermes doesn't apologize..."

"This Hermes does."

"How are you here?"

"I went looking for you, dummy."

"Now that sounds like my Hermes."

She sounded weak. Nearly broken—but not quite. Never. He wanted to hold her more than he wanted to do anything in his entire existence. He also wanted to crawl into a shell, curl into a ball, and weep forever. He wanted to break his chains.

Alecto suddenly gripped his chin. "There it is. Get mad."

Persephone was mere inches away. Hermes heaved against his restraints, lost himself to the rage. The Fury sisters practically vibrated with passion.

"YES!" Tisiphone shouted along with his screams—and strangely in harmony. "BREAK! BREEEAAAKKKKK!"

"AAAAAHHHHHH!!!" Hermes roared.

Tisiphone climaxed first, wings madly flapping, like a restless hawk on a falconer's arm, gripping the table until it splintered.

Hermes directed all his hate at the Furies. If a stare could burn, they would be scorched to ashes, and then those ashes would be pressed into diamonds. "I'll fucking strip your flesh! You'll wind up like your sister! I swear to myself! On my own oath!"

"Hermes! Stop!" Persephone pleaded. "You're giving them what they want!"

He couldn't hear her. Couldn't see her. All was fire. The three of them screamed.

"I swear on my own oath!" Hermes bellowed over their shrieks, his skin searing, delirious from the venom. "I don't need Zeus's permission to kill you."

In throes of pleasure, Alecto rushed her ogre and punched a hand into its chest, snapping ribs like dried twigs. The demon jolted—and then froze. She dug herself inside its cavity, found its heart, and popped it like a zit. The ogre toppled with a thud that rattled all six hundred thousand bottles of wine.

They went limp together. The room silenced. An exhausted Hermes wilted against his restraints. Persephone locked eyes with him.

"I'm sorry," he mouthed

"Me, too," she mouthed back.

Tisiphone wrapped a chain around Hermes' neck and directed his face to Alecto, who removed her arms from the ogre's chest, bloodied up to the elbows, raising them like a reveling surgeon. She sensually wiped the thick, greasy blood down her dress, then slipped a hand into a hidden pocket and withdrew a clenched fist. Slowly, with the flair of a musical theater major, she peeled back her fingers.

Persephone, who could not see what Alecto was doing behind her, watched the fear rise in Hermes' expression.

"What is it?" Persephone panicked—and she never panicked. She attempted to twist around.

"Don't look!" Hermes shouted, then begged Alecto. "Stop. You can't do this!"

The pomegranate in Alecto's outstretched palm was like a grenade without a pin. One side of the fruit bore a bite mark; the other was bruised from where it had fallen down the steps of hell. Hermes shook his head in grief. The puzzle solved itself. The pomegranate was still as fresh as that cursed night when Persephone ate three of its seeds. So fresh, the wound still leaked its crimson juice—high in antioxidants and the curse of eternal hell.

Alecto had somehow found the original offending pomegranate, the fruit that began it all: that began Persephone's misery and ended eternal summer, that cleaved the Earth in two. It was winter. She had been holding onto it for who knew how long—waiting, plotting. It was a testament to Alecto's hate, a symbol of Persephone's ruination.

All the air left Persephone. Hermes watched her mental state deteriorate, that crocus blossom trampled by an early autumn frost.

"Don't," Hermes begged her. "Don't give in to them!"

Persephone was finally surrendering to the Furies.

"The fruit carries the curse," Alecto said. "It will finish what Hades intended."

"NO!" Hermes shouted, until Tisiphone stepped behind him and tightened the choker, cutting off his ability to speak.

His eyes bulged. His mouth frothed. If only she would just look at him one more time, he could save her. But she was done. It was a terrible bit of magical thinking.

The Furies had proven themselves the stronger species. They had uprooted Persephone, the gravity of their hate sucking her into a grave. The wall behind him groaned. Several bottles flew from the rack and crashed at his feet.

Alecto savored his frustration, tasting it like a sommelier of woe. She pressed her thumb into the pomegranate's crown and split the fruit in two, juice bursting over her hands. Red capsules plumbed the inside like crystals on the wall of a cave.

Tisiphone released Hermes from his chokehold and moved to Persephone, jerking her head back by her hair.

"Don't let them do it. Don't eat! Please!" Hermes may as well have asked the sun not to set.

Alecto scraped a fistful of seeds and held the kernels above her head. Tisiphone forced the deposed queen to face her eldest stepdaughter.

Instead of a despairing goddess, Persephone suddenly became a portrait of defiance.

Alecto hesitated. Hermes saw the imperceptible shift from certainty to not. It was enough to steal what should have been the perfect orgasm.

"You're weak," Persephone said as a matter of fact, simply naming a thing as it was. A rock. A flower. A weak-ass Fury.

Alecto wavered. Juice trickled through her fingers.

"Alecto?" Tisiphone hissed. "What are you doing? Feed her!"

Alecto stared down Persephone. "I'm weak? You're the one on your knees, your brother chained to a wall, your husband usurped, your Earth dead."

"You're weak," Persephone repeated with Zen serenity. The response unsettled Alecto. Hermes was curious to see where she was going with this.

"This is our parting of the Red Sea," Alecto countered. "A great miracle to bring the humans back. On their knees, where they belong."

"It's an apocalypse—an end that will have no beginning. It's unsustainable."

"Many will die. Those that live will live according to our new faith. Without alternative. Without the other religions. As if they had any right to choose." Alecto stamped her words.

"They have free will—of which you've been deprived your whole existence. I'm sorry for that. You couldn't know…" Persephone paused. "Faith requires summer and winter."

"Wrong, stepmother. Summer is weakness. Laziness. Appeasement. Fear is the miracle. And what was promised requires their destruction. We will do our part."

Persephone looked upon Alecto with compassion. "Humans are immature. It comes with mortality. They should mourn every birth and celebrate every death. Only they can't. You want to drive them to darkness and despair? Their souls will freeze before they can muster a prayer. They won't have the heart for it."

"But they will pray. It'll be their last breath—and we shall answer! That was your mistake: you never answered their prayers! You had the power and never used it."

"Prayers are seldom answered because they need not be. Almost never, in truth. But worship can't exist without hope. Hope. It is a uniquely human trait. Alone among creation, they dedicate their short lives to it. They alone offer fealty to us—not of obligation, but by choice. Hope is their gift, their lesson. Their belief in our existence—us, immortal and beyond the borders of their understanding—that is the miracle. You will deny them hope. They won't survive. And neither will we."

"Despair I know. Darkness I know," Alecto's voice quivered. "In darkness, they crave fire. And a fire will be lit. This is only the first step. There are others. This is bigger than you will ever understand. By the time we're finished, you will be long lost—not even a memory."

"Do you know why we faded?" Persephone asked. "Our names and deeds studied instead of glorified? It's not for lack of miracles."

"That is exactly why! Our unwillingness to adapt, to convert," Alecto said furiously, now the one to lose control of her emotions.

Persephone looked like a saint, Hermes thought. She stared up at her stepdaughter and testified. "It's because we believe in resurrection. We faded because we were supposed to fade. In our time, the humans birthed democracy. Laid the foundation for reason. They honored our names and our stories—and they soared."

"THEY ABANDONED US! How can you forgive them?!"

Persephone didn't flinch. The cellar hummed with the energy of gospel. Hermes felt the power—felt it in his god bones—mesmerized as she preached.

"The humans found us in other ways. Other gods. And I am at peace. Because our stories guided them to better places, and better versions of themselves."

"And what of us? Are we better?" Alecto wiped black tears from her cheeks with the back of her sleeve.

Tisiphone stood frozen, mouth half open, unable to fathom her implacable sister so easily unraveled, so off her game.

"Tisiphone, it's time," Alecto snapped.

Hermes bucked against his restraints. "No—no, no, no! Alecto! Tisiphone! Don't do this." He turned to Persephone, feverish with desperation, heart crushed beneath the weight of failure. Here it was—the breaking point. "I'm sorry. I should have fought harder."

Persephone cradled him with her gaze, vast and infinite with love. "You did. You're here."

Tisiphone suddenly wrenched Persephone away, yanking her head back and prying open her mouth with her filthy fingers.

Alecto stuffed the seeds down her throat. Sour. Bitter with age. Loaded with vitamins and minerals (and fiber, but that was for later).

Tisiphone smashed Persephone's mouth shut and pinched her nose.

Hermes shouted, wailed, thrashed.

It took ages. A goddess could hold her breath a long time.

But then her throat spasmed, and she swallowed.

Alecto stepped back, breathing heavily, awed by her own victory. "Persephone is no longer mother of Earth. She is mother to death."

Hermes wept again.

Tisiphone finally released Persephone.

Persephone pitched forward, gasping, her mouth empty. She looked up to Hermes and whispered, "It's done."

"Don't say that," said Hermes. "Never ever say that."

Alecto lifted Persephone off the floor by her collar like she weighed nothing, and leered.

"I hear it takes a thousand years to adjust to Tartarus. The darkness is practically a living thing all the way down there. Perhaps it'll be better for her this time…not knowing who rapes her."

CHAPTER TWENTY-NINE

Victorious, Alecto emerged from the Tower of Kronos, dragging the Goddess of Spring behind her by the indestructible Uranian chain like an exotic pet. The light was too much for Persephone, a brutal shift from the endless black of her cell to a searing midday sun. It was for the best, perhaps, that she couldn't see the elite forces of the Furies gathered in the palace ward below. Demons and empusai, dressed in the old regalia, numbered in the tens of thousands. At the sight of Alecto, they banged their bronze shields and spears against their cuirassed chests. Their shrieks and grunts and jeers reverberated off the obelisk. To hell with dissociation. Persephone would stay in her body. She refused to feel shame. The worst was over. She accepted her fate.

The troops parted for a massive golden chariot pulled by centaurs, beaten into submission and yoked. The driver was an empusa with style. flaming hair blowing behind her like a flare stack. She forcefully choked the reins, stopping the centaurs at the base of the ramp. The chariot was instantly recognizable to Persephone, as it was to anyone who dwelled in the Underworld. It was the same chariot Hades rode into battle, that could cleave mountains in two and outrun a high-speed pursuit better than a white Bronco. It was the very same chariot from which he had kidnapped his bride and escaped back to Hell.

Alecto swept down the grand stairs, Persephone forcibly tugged along. A gleeful pandemonium swallowed them—a churning mass of armor and spears and hideous cries.

Alecto pitched her voice over the mayhem. "This was your queen! See her cast down. The old gods are RUINED!"

The mob stilled. Dumb faces trying to comprehend.

"Clap!" she thundered, and the demons erupted with applause.

Alecto wrenched the leash, tripping Persephone down the final steps. She fell into the mosh pit. The demons got handsy, pushing and shoving her into the chariot. Persephone towered over Alecto until a soldier forced her to her knees.

"Humans will sacrifice!" Alecto cried, exalted by conviction. "Wars will be waged in our names! It is our time to claim the sun!"

The ugly cheers reached an operatic crescendo. Alecto brayed a golden whip, cracking it against the miserable centaurs. They jolted into a trot, forcing a yawn in the battalion. Then they were descending the treacherous mountain pass high above a craggy landscape dotted by forest, before it flattened into the gold and emerald quilt of the Elysian Fields. The Mediterranean delights draped against the island's gleaming white cliffs, which spread to embrace the azure waters of Lethe. Tucked on the horizon was the town of Elysium, where even from a distance, the hotels and apartments seemed excessive, glittering under the eternal light of reincarnation.

After an age of stone walls and misery, Persephone's spirit soared.

They traveled in silence, save for the grinding chariot wheels and hooves clopping on the hard-packed trail. The brittle bones of children threaded through Alecto's hair rattled like wind chimes in the steady breeze of Paradise.

Alecto stole a glance at Persephone and saw not a trace of despair. Her jaw clenched like a fist. "Why do you care so much?"

Persephone sighed. So much for meditating. Couldn't she just enjoy the view in peace? Likely her last view of anything. *Nope. Fucking stepdaughters.*

"Care about...?" Persephone asked for clarification.

"Them."

"The humans?"

Alecto cocked her head. The skeletal fingers pinned in her hair tapped out a yes.

"You believe if they don't worship me, I shouldn't care?"

"That would make sense."

"That's your way."

"You forgive them?" Alecto scoffed, incredulous.

Persephone turned to her stepdaughter with pity. "There's nothing to forgive."

Alecto grimaced. Pity was its own weapon. "They're supposed to have evolved, but they've done the opposite—and dragged us down with them. They have lost the sublime."

"Ah," Persephone said, understanding now. "But maybe so have we."

Alecto charged into her rant. "They have no care for nature! They see only the world in terms of its usefulness—as if our creations are just for them to exploit. They obsess over tools, pay no attention to the wonders of the universe. They wish only for your power to be theirs. And as they have taken it from the gods, incrementally, piece by piece, what do they do? They use it for such silly, pointless things: anthrax and porn and Elon Musk and podcasts, Las Vegas and alcoholic slushies and Snuggies and... the list goes on and on."

Persephone shot her a sideways glance. "You sound jealous."

"That would be Megaera. She was the jealous one."

"I don't disagree with anything you've said."

"Then why do you care for them?! Why not join us?"

"No one asked."

Alecto raised an eyebrow. "You would? You would join us?"

"Fuck no."

"Then you don't care what happens to you?" Alecto simmered.

"Spring comes every year," said the Goddess of Spring.

"Not this year. No more."

"The humans will outlast winter...and you."

"You act as if you know it to be true," said a rattled Alecto, betraying her insecurity.

Let her see I'm no victim, Persephone thought.

"Individually, humans are burdensome and illogical. Collectively, they're an invasive, resourceful species capable of weathering any storm. They can live off leaves, drink urine, and turn to cannibalism...in the end, they survive. It's you that ought to be worried. You who won't outlast winter."

After a moment of heavy silence, Alecto whipped the centaurs into an unexpected gallop. Persephone gripped the brace woven into the chariot's shield.

Alecto cracked the whip again, harder, steering them dangerously close to the cliff.

"While the gods sat idle, we were forced to watch all we love leave us."

"I understand your pain," Persephone said. "But I'm not sorry for it."

Alecto took her eyes off the treacherous road to stare up toward Earth.

"Beloved stepmother, do you know the worst part of your arrogance? It's that you expected us to do nothing about it."

She tore a strip of silk off the chariot's lining and stuffed it into Persephone's hand. "Gag yourself...please."

She jolted the reins into a brutal turn. The chariot dangled over the abyss before crashing back onto the ledge and into an old wagon groove.

Persephone released the silk, and like a dove, it flew off the mountain and to freedom.

***

Tisiphone was having fun. Hermes, still chained to the wall, was not. "Boy, is this a marvelous day," she trilled. "And I intend to have many and more marvelous days in the days ahead. I'm so happy I could sing! Only...I don't know any songs. But I can dance!"

So instead, she danced—an old Greek folk dance, pirouetting in circles, accented by a quick hop and skip between toes. One arm wedged on her hip, the other held up like a kettle spout mimicking a flame in a breeze, then she'd switch arms and go again. The fly moves had been gifted to the Greeks by the Persians and Babylonians of Mesopotamia. Wine bottles crunched under her feet like cymbals clapping in time to her internal music. Giddy, she began to hum.

"Humming! Can you believe I'm humming?" she hollered, with a smile that would send schoolchildren crying for their mothers. "I've just won an empire, and I've never felt so free!"

The Fury eventually petered out, bending over with a finger held up. "I'm out of shape," she panted. "Hold on…"

What else can I fucking do?

"Wine," she finally managed between breaths. "Wine would be perfect. We need to rejoice. I've never rejoiced before."

Dizzy, she wobbled over to a rack and browsed the spears of wax-sealed corks.

She flashed him a smirk. "Nothing turns down here. Everything's aged to perfection. Quite marvelous."

"Yes," Hermes agreed. Other than his being tortured, this was now his most favorite room in the whole wide Underworld.

To the non-omniscient observer, Hermes appeared to have abandoned hope. It could not have been more the opposite. He was a tuning fork, aligning himself with a higher order of spiritual power. Meanwhile, Tisiphone searched for the perfect cabernet.

"Any preference?" she tossed the question over her shoulder like they were on a quick errand at the grocery store.

"Manischewitz," said Hermes.

She rolled her eyes. "Kill me now."

"With pleasure," he mumbled under his breath.

The Fury disappeared behind a rack of wine with a giggle. He heard a bottle slide from its perch, and she exclaimed, "Ah-ha!"

She reappeared with a stretched jug made of brown glass, caked in dust. It had two copper ring handles at the neck. "Roman vintage. From the private vineyards of Marcus Junius Brutus." She frowned at some memory. "A most disappointing protégé."

She wiped away the layers of time to examine the liquid. "Not a subtle wine. Heavy tones of rosehip and elderberry, with a finishing hint of amicide. Forty-four BC…to use the *Christian* nomenclature."

The cork popped with the sigh of a weary old man wishing someone would shoot him behind the barn. The fragrance required a quick whiff—

according to the sacred laws of consuming vino—before Tisiphone tipped it back and swigged like a sailor.

Feeling generous, she shoved the bottle into his lips and tipped it up. The thought of drinking from the same surface as her was as appealing as French-kissing a bulldog after it drank from the toilet. Yet he was parched and jonesing for booze. No sooner did he taste wine than she opened her hand and let the bottle drop. The rare vintage exploded onto his feet.

"Oops. What a mess." Tisiphone covered a giggle, behaving like a child showing off the marker drawings she made on the walls. "I better clean that up."

She crouched out of his eyeline, and he could hear her sift through the shards. The top of her matted head contained several nests of baby vipers that hissed menacingly. "Who needs fancy instruments when one can improvise with what's right in front of you..."

She lifted a large shard into his view to consider it in the light. It was obviously suitable for the task—whatever that task would be.

Her eyes traversed his chest, torso, and legs, down to his bare winged feet. She wet her lips. "Mmmmm," she murmured.

He felt her caress his right foot with her calloused fingers, as if he were being massaged with a chunk of jagged shale. Then he felt her rip off his dirty mud and blood splattered sneakers, exposing his winged feet.

"Be careful with those." Hermes thrust his chin at the Converse. "They're one of a kind."

She tossed the sneakers over her shoulder. "I prefer Nikes."

Of course she does...

The broken glass teased down his leg, like a barber with a straight edge, starting at his knee, down, and down, until she wedged the shard into the joint where his trademark wing met his non-trademark ankle.

"Oops," she presaged.

In a swift, hard thrust, she dug the glass into his flesh. Snip.

Waves of hot agony rushed through his body, unlike anything he'd experienced in eternity. He leaned into the chains. "Take 'em all."

"With pleasure." She seized his left foot and sawed.

Two wings down, two to go.

Hermes blacked out.

When he came to, Tisiphone was sitting cross-legged in a pool of his golden blood, clapping in delight. His severed wings twitched on the floor like dying fish in a puddle.

She took the amputated wings and flew them through the air like toy planes, making engine noises as she soared them past his face.

She waited for Hermes to scream. Howl. Curse. Thrash against the chains. Anything.

Yet he gave nothing.

He watched himself from a thousand leagues away, from the spirit realm, where he was connected to all things—all the pain in the universe, and all the happiness. It was all just energy.

Energy was neither good nor bad. It just was.

He felt Tisiphone's energy curdle, from merriment to seething fury, unaware that his emptiness was anything but empty.

The opportunity to torture a god came once in an eternal lifetime, and he could sense from his spiritual perch that, to prepare, she had denied herself victims for months to heighten the arousal.

Defiance was expected. Explosive and emotional she could work with. Not this. Not nothing. He was cockblocking her sadomasochistic orgasm.

He turned away to journey further beyond the borders of himself. There was strength in the earth yet, hibernating deep within its veins. The universal energy of the spirits was raw and pure. When channeled, it was a fuel more powerful than any worship. For this energy came from within, not from without.

Self-reliance was not a requirement. Not every journey must be traveled alone.

It was time Hermes called forth the spirits of Spring to save their goddess.

To do so, he needed to send a message. Not an email. *Fuck email.*

But the spirits only listened to those worthy of being heard. They would require a sacrifice to show he was serious.

A serious god.

When was Hermes a serious god?

He knew what he had to do. Just a small thing. So simple.

Floating in the primordial darkness between the couch cushions, Hermes imagined a lighter.

Boop. A small plastic Bic appeared. Simple as that. Snap of a finger. Answered prayer.

Honestly, it was rather disappointing. As a god, he would have preferred something silver or gold, flashy yet tasteful—not something you could buy at a gas station for ninety-nine cents. But, hey, this was about relinquishing the ego, so it made sense in an ironic, cosmic way.

Hermes lifted the hot pink Bic (Jesus, it was hot pink) and, with his calloused thumb, sparked its flame.

All that was left was to do the self-immolation bit.

Hermes touched the flame to his heart. It was a dry husk these days. Easy kindling.

His ego instantly caught fire. It was time to let go.

He sent his burning ego dashing through the realm between realms, a message from the Messenger. His spirit, now free of himself, moved faster than a comet. In defiance of the divine laws of his pantheon, he threw open all the doors and windows to his body, presenting himself as passage into the Underworld.

Calling all spirits! Any who wished to join his crusade was welcome. Hermes the doormat.

He did not have to wait long for an answer.

He felt the first passing spirit like a bolt of lightning from Zeus's arsenal.

It erased the barrier between mind and matter and married its existence with his. Another joined. Restless and eager. Then another.

Until Hermes was at once the Sun and the Moon, empty and full, all things and nothing.

Hermes was the Infinite.

The shackles went taut. The cellar groaned, warping where his unbreakable chains were fastened to the stone.

Tisiphone was too busy playing airplane on the floor to notice the impending danger above.

The wall bulged.

At once, everything shattered—an explosion that shook the entire realm.

His fists collided. Ten thousand bottles crashed as Hermes took down the cellar in an avalanche of marble, granite, and wine.

He fell upon an unsuspecting Tisiphone with the force of a volcanic eruption. She furiously scratched at the Uranian cuffs digging into her neck. The terror on her face was justice for her reign of terror.

He found a snake coiled just below her throat and dug it from her flesh. Tisiphone gasped and gargled.

He fastened the python into a noose and strung her up.

Her skin writhed, the snakes under her skin in a frenzy to abandon their mistress. They sought out every orifice to escape, and if they could not find one, they ripped her open from the inside.

Tighter, he pulled. Tighter.

Her windpipe cracked. Venom leaked from the corners of her mouth.

Tisiphone fell limp and was no more.

CHAPTER THIRTY

HERMES CHARGED UP THE phallus of reincarnation, his denuded feet bleeding out the gills of his sneakers from Tisiphone's masochistic orgy, golden treads marking the white marble—a bad habit now trailing him from the Vatican vaults to Lily's villa and the halls of Paradise.

The reincarnation of wicked souls continued, if not accelerated, and though Hermes wished to intervene, there was no time. None of it would matter if he didn't reach Persephone before Alecto brought her to the Gates of Tartaros.

He raced around the seashell chamber, a blur between the ribbed columns, his last two wings fluttering—fast, but not the electric current speed he could produce before with all four.

They'll grow back...in time, in time.

He burst into the great foyer, startling a horde of demons and Keres. They leapt up, determined to stop him, but Hermes was unstoppable. Spirit energy surged inside him. He cleaved through the creatures like a ship breaking waves. Armor splintered. Columns toppled. The tower shook under his withering assault, and a portion of the ceiling caved in, exposing a honeycomb of antechambers. Frightened nymphs peered down at the fury of a supercharged god. He retrieved a broadsword buried beneath the rubble and hacked down the great doors in one strike.

On the steps outside, an empusa spun around with a half-eaten tuna sandwich in hand and a Seinfeld lunch pail at its feet. In the courtyard below, Alecto's elite battalion stared up at Hermes in shock. Break time was over.

Hermes seized the empusa by her flaming hair, used her as a shield, and charged the army. The beast became a pincushion as thousands of arrows, bullets, and spears whizzed past. The two sides collided halfway down the ramp. The empusa's hooves became a perfect battering ram, flattening rows upon impact, hurling soldiers over the cliff. A shudder of dread rippled through Hell. His steroidal might was greater than their collective strength.

Advancing into the courtyard, he brought a Spirit World–sized reckoning. A tornado of flashing steel. Faces swarmed and broke before him. The yard became a swamp of trampled bodies. The smart demons dropped their weapons and fled, some leaping to their doom rather than face a god's wrath.

Until there was only one. One lonely shadow demon, trembling, a wet stain spreading down its khakis. It brandished a sorry dagger with little enthusiasm. Hermes, still riding the spiritual gravy train, merely flicked his hand. The demon's head twisted off its neck like a bottle cap with a final sickening crunch.

The courtyard fell silent.

Chest heaving, skin burning, Hermes released the spirits, lest they consume him entirely. He closed his eyes and thanked them, feeling the energy slip away. Opening his eyes again, his tunnel vision widened, and his muscles loosened. He felt like a rubber band stretched—perhaps permanently—beyond its form.

Sometimes it's good to get it out of your system.

He waded across the scarred plaza to a battlement, finishing off any demon still moving with a quick spear thrust to the skull. From the ledge, he surveyed the White Island, sighted the port town of Elysium and the flotilla docked along the river. A large red sail unfurled above a Greek warship—the largest vessel by far. That would be Alecto.

His ruined feet would be unable to cross the distance. He needed speed. About a dozen war chariots were parked out front of the tower, but more conveniently, so was Tisiphone's Lamborghini with half a demon stuck through the windshield.

After scraping the carcass off the hood, Hermes located the keys in the ignition. Seat belt? Check. Mirrors? Check. He shifted into drive and slammed his mangled foot on the accelerator. The tires skidded over the blood, and he fishtailed down the mountain faster than a nonna headed to Sunday mass.

Low to the ground, he lost sight of Alecto's warship as it readied to sail, but the race car glided like water through a pipe. It was the next best thing to flying.

On the plains of Elysian, Hermes blew through a checkpoint. The demons assumed he was Tisiphone and let him pass. Rose petals swirled past his tinted windows as he steered into the old city. The cobblestones wreaked havoc on the low clearance. A tire burst, and the shredded rubber made the sound of a wet cloth slapping against the ground—but who hadn't played a little fast and loose with a rental car?

In a last hurrah, Hermes gunned his princess mobile through a final barricade of chariots guarding the harbor. The car accordioned, and Hermes found himself settled next to the engine.

The hot mess lurched to a stop on the docks. He kicked open the door to Alecto's trireme towering over the river, bristling with two stacked rows of oars manned by several hundred slaves. Its twin red sails billowed, making for the deeper, faster current of the River of Oblivion, where it quickly sank into the fog.

Hermes needed something small and fast and ready to sail. Most importantly, he needed to find something now.

At the end of the dock, a paltry, single-mast pleasure barge with a small square sail was tying onto the mooring. A silk canopy enshrouded the deck, filled with pillows for its owner and guests. The boxy shape made it unsuitable for a chase but fine for a lazy cruise around the island. The thirty slaves shackled to the oars would, however, be useful.

Alarm bells suddenly resounded throughout Elysium. The rest of Alecto's demons had learned of his escape and were regrouping along the harbor behind him.

Abandoned by their Fury, they were afraid to confront him directly, so instead began firing from afar. Gunfire crackled, splintering bits of dock while arrows and spears landed around him.

He ducked behind the Lamborghini, where a dead cacodemon lay jammed under the wheel. He plucked a Winchester revolver embedded in the creature's skull and sprinted for the pleasure barge.

The barge heaved sideways as he leapt aboard, upending canapés and crudités and jugs of wine. Demons surged onto the dock after him.

Hermes took stock of his commandeered craft. A plump nobleman was cursing him out from the comfort of his daybed, cheeks purple with rage and dress soiled with deviled egg. His young harem retreated into a frightened pile.

Not one to ask permission, Hermes simply chucked the pedophile overboard. The harem jumped into the river after their master, then swam for shore, abandoning him to the weight of his jewels.

Hermes ripped the mooring line from the piling and whirled to the slaves, who represented the diversity of lands the Greeks had once conquered. Under a steady barrage of gunfire, they huddled with their heads tucked between their knees, hands clamped over their skulls.

"ROW!" Hermes roared. "RRROOOWWW!!!"

Muscle memory kicked in. The slaves grabbed their paddles and heaved. Hermes assumed the rudder, and they cleared the dock seconds before the demons could board.

The barge scraped the anchored yachts until they cleared the harbor. The demons kept firing, but the missiles splashed harmlessly in the water.

On the river, Hermes steered toward the swirl of fog that separated eternal day from eternal night, where Alecto's warship had vanished. A shadow of the prow appeared like a ghost ship dead ahead.

"THERE! We've got them!" he shouted excitedly. The slaves couldn't care less. They were ordered to row, so they rowed.

Alecto's ship was larger and faster. His pleasure barge was infuriatingly sluggish. The trireme easily slipped away, enveloped by the mist. There was no chance of catching her outright—and once in the fog, he could only steer by intuition.

He gripped the rail, strained his godly eyes. The memories of Lethe were too thick.

At least he knew where they were going. And there was only one way to get there.

"Faster," he commanded his slaves in vain. Indeed, they were his slaves now. He felt the current grip the bottom of the vessel, pulling them faster.

The sky darkened as they passed back into eternal night. Soon, he knew, the river would take a turn for the treacherous.

"Ease the right side. Half strength," he ordered. The right rowers slackened, and the barge veered left into the current. The haze beyond the bow took on the burnt-orange glow of a distant forest fire. A hiss rose. The acrid smell of smoke filled their nostrils.

"Make ready!" Hermes strode the deck with manic energy, shouting encouragement. "Do not be afraid! Row, and I'll get you back to paradise! With overtime bonuses for everyone!"

The golden hue deepened across the river like a malevolent smile. They were not headed for the great tanning bed of Elysium. One after another, the slaves released their oars and trembled—clearly not getting the memo about overtime.

That hiss swelled into a piercing scream. A gust of scorching air blasted over the barge.

Hermes seized the rudder tight as he could and bellowed, "GET DOWWNNNN!"

They reached the turbulent conflagration of the Underworld's two great dichotic rivers, where the Oblivion violently met the Phlegethon. Water smashed into lava, exploding in napalm-like spouts. The mist flashed into scalding steam. The slaves dove for cover. Those too slow shrieked as their skin cooked and bubbled with blisters. An Ottoman slave screamed as his eyes melted.

The barge drifted sideways, dragged toward a whirlpool off their starboard.

"To the oars!" Hermes pulled his slaves out from beneath the benches and thrust them back to their posts. "If you don't row, we all burn!"

Boiling water spun the barge. They spiraled around a vortex stretching open beneath them like the jaws of a fire-breathing dragon. A torrent of white-hot steam belched upward, threatening to air-fry them in an instant.

Hermes charged the gangway. "You want to burn for all eternity? THEN ROW!"

The slaves took heart, inspired by the god who stood against the heat. They took up their oars, faces flushed, and heroically bent their backs as scorching water sprayed.

"Dig deep!" Hermes kept up his cheerleading.

A slave lost his face to a steam bath, his agony joining the chaos. His absence created a dangerous drag. Hermes sprang into the vacant post, seized the scull. Forward. Back. Forward. Back.

"Through the fire! Forward. Heave! Heave!"

His efforts picked up the slack of thirty men, and the crew gained new vigor. Together, their oars fought back, digging out of the whirlpool.

The current picked up speed, hurtling them toward the River of Fire. Their clunky pleasure barge was all wrong to navigate these waters. Hermes needed something nimble and light as an arrow. They were on a floating pizza box.

He breathed deep and prayed to Persephone. *Guide me through this, sister.* For good measure, he prayed to the spirits that had bailed him out of the Tower of Kronos, too. He had burned his ego back in the wine cellar and now had no problem praying to whoever—or whatever—would help him through this gauntlet.

The steam thinned, leaving the air oven-hot. Ahead, a wall of flames stretched across the river. They were closing in on the Phlegethon. A red wave crested ominously above the bow. The rhythm of the oars faltered. The slaves wavered, their tears lost in sweat.

"There's nowhere left to go but into the fire," he shouted over the volcanic rumble.

The rows of terrified visages latched onto his words. Hermes was too cynical for inspirational speeches, but the moment demanded a cliché. Humans loved their clichés. And in this existential crisis, the impending doom stirred his inner high school coach. A time for platitudes and soapboxes.

Though they were damned, dammit if he was going to let his one chance go to waste.

"There are few moments in our lives—or afterlives—that require us to give everything we have within us," he began, embracing his halftime locker room moment. "To tap those last reserves. Since returning to the Underworld, I've accepted anonymity, swallowed insults, humbled myself before my enemies, self-reflected, torched my ego, and eaten more spoonsful of shit than an assistant in Hollywood. Have I deserved it? Hell yes. I've been a selfish, vain god for more centuries than I can count—obsessed with worship, then raging at its absence. Filling the void with tricks and mindless distractions that caused harm to everyone else, including those I supposedly loved..."

"GET TO THE FUCKING POINT?!" a slave piped up.

Hermes frowned. So much for the pep rally. Still, the speech was good for something, as he managed to rally himself.

"ROW! That's the fucking point! Row on, and I promise you rebirth. Row hard. Row fast. ROOOWWWWWW!"

Inspired—or simply scared shitless—the slaves snatched up their oars. Their efforts tripled. Hermes slammed his full godly force into the rudder and braced for impact with the cresting orange tsunami.

All right, purity of fire, bring it on.

The prow plowed up the wave of lava in a violent crash of sparks and pumice. The Phlegethon grabbed the barge and propelled them toward the depths of the Underworld. From the rudder, Hermes witnessed the oars catch fire. The sail and linen canopies burst into flames. Flames licked their aft and starboard and crawled up the mast. Everything was being consumed.

The slaves again abandoned their posts, huddling at the center of the barge. The deck pulsed with embers. Hermes stayed the course, scouring the choking smoke against the stinging in his eyes.

Downstream, a lambda flashed in the firestorm like a red-hot cattle brand pulled from a pile of coals. The Spartan war symbol was painted on the bow of Alecto's warship. It might as well have been a beacon.

Despite the ray of hope, the whole of the pleasure barge was now engulfed. And they were sailing into a crematorium. There would be no phoenix-like rebirth if sunk. A spiritual rebirth, maybe—but it's hard to live a higher calling while trying to match dental records.

Hermes reached for the rudder and burned his hand. It had become too hot to steer, leaving them at the river's mercy, careening them into a narrow canyon of blackened stone and toward a series of drops.

He tore strips from the nobleman's bedding and wrapped his palms like a boxer preparing for a fight. The silk curled as he reclaimed the smoldering rudder and centered them in the current.

They shot over the first lavafall.

The prow slammed into the bottom like a hand slapping a bug. Then the pleasure barge jolted back upright, rocking violently side to side as they fought to stay balanced. Somehow, they were still buoyant. Downstream, the back of the trireme materialized in the smoke. His vessel finally showed its advantage. Far lighter than Alecto's warship, they had begun to gain on her. The Viking ship broke through the lava with its anvil prow, doing all the work for Hermes. He only had to keep his barge in their wake.

Framed by the raging firestorm like Lucifer himself, Hermes seized the moment. "Do not despair! We've almost made it to the Island of the Damned!"

Bad choice of words.

The riverbanks were lined with blazing mangroves, their trunks crackling and splitting. Crucified to each tree was a soul begging for mercy. This was the valley of the irredeemable. It was practically Christian in its fire and brimstone. Except none of the tortured souls had been condemned to this fate. They had willingly bound themselves to these burning posts, seeking the inferno to burn away whatever plagued their souls—however long it took—until cleansed or consumed.

Hermes affixed his gaze to the warship. To Persephone. To hope.

They were close enough that several demons fired arrows at them. The shafts burst into flame before they could even land. Alecto appeared along the stern with a loathing that scorched just as hot.

A sudden cry from his oarsmen spun Hermes to his ship. A crack had split the center of the deck. The planks bowed upward. Blue flames pried their way into the barge like the tentacles of a sea creature. More flames climbed over the gunwales. They were beginning to sink.

The slaves cried out to their god.

"What do we do?"

"Help!"

Prayer was their only chance at deliverance now.

The river widened before them, which meant it was also shallow. They had reached the shoals, a perilous maze of superheated coals that stuck up like broken, necrotic teeth. The barge began to turn broadside and drifted toward a glowing boulder.

Hermes darted back to the rudder—but there was nothing left of it but a band of copper.

"Crash positions!"

They hit along their starboard side. The barge buckled, throwing them off their feet. Cinders and flames exploded. Four slaves were pinned between the ship and a massive molten stone. Their screams were wrenching. He scrambled to save his brave crew, but the magma piled up beneath them, slamming the barge up the side of the glowing boulder.

They were about to capsize. It was a wretched choice: save the four souls or save the rest and his ship.

Hermes ripped the broken mast from the deck, wedged it between the barge and superheated rock, and shoved all his weight. The hull scraped along until it dropped back into the river. The pinned slaves were promptly sucked under the ship and burned to ash.

It was the last burning straw. Hermes collapsed, knees scorched, and wept in front of the mortals who had never witnessed a god cry. But he no longer cared. Hermes could be vulnerable in front of humans. His emotions moved his slaves to tears, and soon they were all bawling. A great, big, blubbering mess.

The catharsis quickly ran its course like a bout of IBS. Stripped to the studs, Hermes felt a strange, unexpected calm. He wiped his cheeks, leaving streaks of soot and forced himself upright, onto his weary feet. He turned back to the ship, nearly broken in two.

The River of Fire had settled into a black marshland where the lava had cooled. Pillars of steam rose from the moonscape. Their crippled barge lurched to an anticlimactic stop, embedded in bubbling quicksand. Despite their severe burns, his heroic crew extinguished the last of the flames with blankets, doused them with buckets of sand and wine, and even used their own urine.

They had survived. Just barely.

Hermes manned the shattered, charred bow and sighted the Island of the Damned. Alecto's trireme had survived too and had anchored close to the shore.

A gangway from her ship slapped the ground and her crew of demons raced to disembark.

Hermes smiled. *There's still time.*

He was the god of luck, after all.

"Make ready to land."

CHAPTER THIRTY-ONE

"MAKE READY TO LAND!" Hermes bellowed to the confusion of his slaves. It was something he had always wanted to say, though it was more a figure of speech here. There wasn't really any land for which to make ready. He hadn't spent much time sailing.

Their barge had come to a complete and permanent stop, nestling into a concrete-like mixture that would make it a permanent fixture. The slaves made a clumsy, half-hearted effort at lowering a gangway assembled from burnt scraps. Since it couldn't support his weight, Hermes vaulted over the rail.

He hit the hot, oatmeal quicksand with a wet punch. To a mortal, it would be instant death; to a god, it was more pedicure spa treatment. He sighed audibly as his injured feet sank into the warm, soothing mineral bath. The balm sealed and cauterized the wounds and would help them heal.

He glanced back at his crew on the smoldering deck, milling about in shock. At some point they would have to find their way back, unfathomable as it seemed.

In the distance, Alecto and her escort had made slow progress, as she required her demons to lay planks on which they could travel over the boiling mud. Some had even offered their bodes as stepping-stones.

Hermes had his chance. With a wrench that engaged his entire core, he tugged his right foot free. Hot air tickled his toes and he suddenly realized—His was sneaker gone?

He whirled back to the hole where his foot had been, but the ooze had already devoured his precious Converse. The same happened to his left foot, the suction tearing off his sneaker like a carjacker.

The beloved Fastbreak Mids, those mighty steeds which had loyally served him through the whole of Hell—and which had been worn by *the actual fucking* Michael Jordan at the 1984 Olympics—were now consigned to a concrete grave.

Oh well, he thought, refreshingly detached. *Sacrifices must be made.*

He resumed, barefoot now, one sucking step at a time. The effort was monumental.

Alecto had reached terra firma when she realized Hermes had not only somehow survived the Phlegethon but was now devouring the distance behind her. She lashed out at her entourage, and they broke into a sprint, their boots thudding on the hard earth.

Hermes plowed through the thick sludge, finally reaching the planks that Alecto's demons had so helpfully laid.

A rearguard train had assembled on the planks, two abreast, to stop his progress. He easily bowled through the soldiers, hurling them into the quagmire where they became entombed, leaving a lone claw here and there to stick up from the quicksand, forever frozen mid-wave. *Goodbye to you, too.*

He was on a roll, his journey almost at its nadir.

Don't stop believin'!

Solid ground was a puzzle of cracked clay, like the bottom of a dry lakebed. Hermes had made it to the Island of the Damned.

Almost instantaneously, the black horizon hurtled away like an ocean ripped into a tsunami. The swelling darkness swallowed Alecto and her army. He became disoriented, like a bird colliding with a window. This was the end of the world—and it was endless. Dispiriting by design, no soul could survive here for long. Fitting that Zeus had chosen this site to hold the Titans. His father had a good eye for real estate.

He did a three-sixty as if lost on a street corner, picked a direction, and ran. Finding no sign of Persephone, he turned and ran the opposite way. He did this pointless suicide sprint several times. The flats were simply too flat—stretching vast distances, wreaking havoc on one's sense of scale. And it wasn't like Alecto was waving around a glow stick. That would have been helpful.

Thwarted, he finally stopped. Terror scaled his lungs, clung to his throat. It was a cruel bait and switch. His victory had been swapped out for defeat. He wanted to rip open his chest and tear out his heart. *How could he give up now? How could he allow Alecto to win?* He spun again, trapped in a shattering silence.

And then a familiar voice—capital V—piped up from the quiet:

I am a god. And there are no gods. All humans are gods. All gods are human.

Hello, Voice, Hermes replied, frustrated. *Thanks, but no thanks.*

The Voice didn't appreciate his sarcasm.

I am a god. And there are no gods. All humans are gods. All gods are human.

The Voice was fucking with him—had to be. It seemed like an age ago that Hermes had stood atop Mount Olympus and sworn an oath to himself, to the masters of Fate, that Hermes, Messenger of the Gods, Trickster, dashing, handsome bad-boy hero, would journey to the deepest depths of hell—to the end of the end of all ends—and bring Persephone home.

Well, here he was. And the Voice had come to hold him to his word.

I am a god. And there are no gods. All humans are gods. All gods are human.

"Thank you. Just great. Real helpful!" he shouted acidly at the void.

I am a god. And there are no gods. All humans are gods. All gods are human.

"I get this is rock bottom…but fucking come on! COME ON!"

I am a god. And there are no gods. All humans are gods. All gods are human.

"I am a god! Okay? You happy now?! I'm a god. What good has that ever done me?"

I am a god. And there are no gods. All humans are gods. All gods are human.

"YES. YES! I am a god!"

His breath hitched. An electric jolt. Something severed inside of him.

I am a god. And there are no gods. All humans are gods. All gods are human.

It was doubt. Doubt and shame. Doubt and shame fell away. Past cleaved from present. His spine straightened. Moved by some holy spirit. Filled with that divine mojo. Caressed by the hand of Fate. Not in a creepy, rapey way—but consensual.

"I am a god!"

I am a god. And there are no gods. All humans are gods. All gods are human.

"I AM A GOD! Now give me a goddamn sign!"

Ask and ye shall receive.

Flames gushed into the air along the horizon with the gusto of pyrotechnics at a pop concert. The outline of a soaring keep materialized. Salvation!

Hermes staggered forward, unable to believe his eyes. Call it Fate, Deus Ex Machina, the omniscient will of the third act—his prayer had been answered.

He almost shouted "hallelujah!" but figured that would be a bridge too far.

Flaming geysers fanned across the battlements of a fortress carved from obsidian blocks, each the size of a double-decker bus. There was no ornamentation or embellishment, just sheer sheerness. Two bronze doors stood at the center, tall enough for the Empire State Building to comfortably stroll through, and it wouldn't even have to duck. All who stood before the Gates of Tartaros were humbled.

Sprinting toward the gates was Alecto's army, a porcupine of armor, spears, and rifles. Persephone, he surmised, was cocooned at the center.

Get down! shouted Fate.

Hermes flattened out of sight before he was spotted by Alecto or her demons. Ear to the ground, he felt a distant vibration tremble through the dirt. Moments later, the entire island violently shook.

Alecto signaled her war party to halt. The demons cinched tighter, facing outward with their weapons. They were armed to the claws and teeth. A swarm of Keres took flight from the ranks, circling like gnats above them.

The rumble took on a syncopation. A pattern of doom emerged.

Doommmmm. Doommmmm. Doommmmm. Doommmmm.

Footsteps. Not one, but two. The footfalls came from opposing directions, their shock waves briefly overlapping under Hermes like two passing waves.

Alecto had rung the wrong doorbell.

How to free Persephone before the beasts arrived?

Hermes wracked his trickster brain. The landscape presented an impossible challenge. There was no cover. If he tried to rescue Persephone now, he would be charging directly into gunfire and arrows. Alecto would mow him down as easy as a target on a firing range.

He crawled forward, staying just outside the pyrotechnic glow, stopping close enough to see the snorts of steam rising from the legions. The minor earthquakes steadily rose in magnitude, nearly bouncing him off the ground with each footfall.

At last, the giants lumbered out of the darkness on either side of the gates. These weren't just normal giants. They were G.I.A.N.T. giants. They were the Hecatoncheires, the "hundred-handed ones." Ten stories tall and gifted with one hundred arms (hence the nickname). Each hand wielded a crude weapon: mace, sword, club, crossbow, slingshot.

Their patrol circled the island, but the signal fires had called them back. They blasted grumpy huffs, clearly unhappy to deal with visitors. There weren't many conjugal visits for the Titans.

As the histories told it, Zeus had freed the Hecatoncheires from the pit they now guarded in exchange for switching sides. They had helped turn the tide in the war against the Titans. There were five Hecatoncheires known to legend, but thankfully only two had shown up now. Their names were probably Huey and Dewey. Huey and Dewey were twin brothers, as ugly and dim-witted as they were lethal, with permanent bedhead. Their eyes were large and set too far apart, and about ninety percent of their minimal mental faculties went into coordinating the logistics of one hundred arms. Spiked bands decked their wrists. A loincloth the size of a sail covered their unimaginable bits. No neck, all muscle—they only needed a beer cozy and a wife-beater to complete the look.

The twins met in front of the gate and greeted each other as they did in their culture, with a series of grunts and farts. Then they rotated to search for who dared visit the Gates of Tartar Sauce.

Hermes cursed their arrival. The Hecatoncheires were seven hundred tons of complication.

Stall any longer, and he could lose his chance to save Persephone. Rescues hinged on preparation, observation, and—most importantly—timing. It took everything in his power not to act. Sometimes the best course was to do nothing. A plan would come. *It had to.*

The cocoon parted, and Alecto stepped forward to address the giants, the Uranian leash clutched in her hand.

Hermes' heart skipped a beat.

There she was. Wrenched into his sight. Persephone.

Alecto turned back to speak, lips twisted in malice. Hermes couldn't hear what was said, but Persephone obediently lowered to her knees. Further debased. He nearly leapt to his feet but forced restraint. The urge to act burned behind his eyes. He wanted to break out of his own skin.

But one misstep would lead to her ruin—Earth's ruin.

He had to play this smart.

Persephone remained unreadable. Whether her stoicism was strength or despair, it was impossible to tell. They had reached the Gates of Steak Tartare upon the Island of the Damned, where no Spring could germinate.

You're not alone, Persephone. I'm here.

Against the obsidian world, Alecto stood out like a bride at a funeral. "Hecatoncheires!"

The cretins stirred, searching over her head.

"I am Alecto, daughter of Hades!"

At the mention of their king, the giants lowered their gazes. Alecto barely crested the bunions on their toes.

"I come to you as Regent of the Underworld. Minister of Moral Crimes."

She stepped forward, undaunted.

Ballsy.

"I command allegiance! Do I have it?"

Hermes held his breath. *Please don't bow. Please don't bow.*

The two giants slowly bowed.

He should have gone with impulsive. Thanks to his dawdling, Alecto had the allegiance of the universe's biggest, baddest, dumbest WMDs.

Hermes sensed her triumph like he was downwind from a garbage truck. He punched the ground in frustration. A puff of ash flew into his eyes.

"Damnit," he cursed, temporarily blind. There wasn't anything but his dirty cuffs to rub off the grit, and that only made it worse. He paused.

A smile graced his dimples. Nothing like a sharp poke in the eye to get the trickster juices flowing.

Blinking furiously to restore his vision, he zoned in on Alecto.

She thrust out her finger. "Open the gates!"

Huey and Dewey rumbled their consent like a whale song echoing over the flat expanse. Hermes removed the Winchester revolver from his jacket—taken from the demon in Elysium—and fished out a single .357 Magnum bullet. The round slotted into the cylinder with a satisfying click. One bullet.

The Hecatoncheires splintered off to either side of the bronze gate, arms swinging like tentacles. They each clutched a lever thick as a sequoia's trunk. It took twenty hands apiece. In unison they tugged. Behind the fortress, a series of gears groaned to life. A crack resounded like someone throwing down a tectonic plate at a Greek wedding. The gates split down the center and slowly spread. And Hermes got his first glimpse of Tartaros.

The island drained into a monstrous pit which was…well, a hole. But not just any hole. It was a really, really, really big hole. Like, a really, really big one. The sinkhole was more of a black hole—a black hole that had sucked in another black hole. The rim of the cavity was surrounded by elaborate statues of the twelve vanquished Titans, commemorating his parents' victory in the cosmic war. Total Olympian move. Super tactful.

The pit had a gravity of its own, vacuuming up hope. This was the last crossroad. Hermes could feel the presence of Eshu, the God of Crossroads, at his back. No more waiting. No more thinking. His mind was empty. Free of doubt, Hermes had faith.

On his mark for a last sprint, he bent his knees, muscles poised like a coiled spring.

Inhale.

One. Two. Three.

Exhale.

GO!

He was a missile. He was a brother. He was a god. Entering the shadow of the colossal Hecatoncheires, he was a reckoning.

A cacodemon spotted him first, a stain on the horizon, and cried out in alarm. Alecto spun from the gates, and Persephone lifted her gaze from the ground. He caught the surprise on her face, which quickly reconstituted—her eyes begging him to save himself.

Sorry, sis. There's no turning back now. Fate led me here. I am a god.

Alecto shouted something, but Hermes couldn't hear her over the rumble of the gates and the flatulent exertions of the Hecatoncheires. The demons formed a shield wall around Persephone, and the hovering Keres notched their bows.

His heart was his compass. His mind a supercomputer calculating distance and velocity. He would stay the course no matter what. Momentum and surprise were on his side.

Two hundred yards...

Alecto had become distracted by Hermes. The Hecatoncheires abandoned the levers to watch too, expressions befuddled and eyes wide. Perfect.

Hermes closed his eyes. There was no need to aim. Fate held the gun. The bullet would find its mark. He had faith. The trigger pinched his finger.

The moment stretched an eternity, held in suspense—then time snapped back with a shriek louder than a train whistle. Hermes had hit his mark.

Alecto and the demons spun to Huey, bellowing in agony, ten of his hands slapping over his right eye, which resembled a popped zit thanks to the .357 Magnum round embedded in it. Having released the lever, Huey's half of the gate slammed shut with enough force to crumble the attached battlement. An alarmed Dewey tied off his chain and rushed his injured twin. Huey thrashed and threw his brother back. Not knowing what to do, Dewey whined and stamped his feet like he had to go potty. The Underworld trembled. It was a bizarrely tender moment, in a playground owie sort of way. It also meant the gate was open and unguarded.

Huey wailed and bashed one of his clubs against the obsidian wall. His remaining eye locked on Alecto and her demons.

Alecto's swagger departed faster than a 2 a.m. burrito. She reeled in Persephone and backed into her troops, discreetly ordering them to retreat.

The circling Keres didn't get the memo. Belligerent, thick-headed buzzards that they were, the Keres brandished their spears and bows at the giants.

Big mistake. No...giant mistake.

The Hecatoncheires raised two hundred pointy, spiky, blunt objects.

Hermes grinned. *This just needs a little nudge in the wrong direction.*

"Stop him!" Alecto shouted as Hermes rushed the nearest demon.

He elbowed an ogre in the face, snatched its musket, and slid under a row of spears like a runner stealing a base. Easy aim now. The iron shot burrowed into Dewey's ear.

Alecto whirled back to the giants. "Oh no."

Two epic war cries answered the provocation, like a trumpet heralding the end of days. The demons shit their britches.

"HOLD THE LINE!" Alecto screamed futilely.

In an instant it was every-demon-for-itself. Armor-plated terror jostled past Hermes, nearly knocking him down. He sprinted in the direction he last saw Persephone. Clubs smashed like falling meteors, cleaving craters out of the flats. Some demons valiantly fought the giants, but they might as well have been armed with toothpicks.

Three Keres locked on Hermes as they wove through a tangle of giant weapons. Hermes scanned his options and ran headfirst toward Dewey and one of his beefy arms swinging a scythe the size of a windmill's sail. The Keres formed into a strafe maneuver and dove. Claws out. At the last second, he threw himself into a crater. The blade whistled overhead and cleaved the three Keres into six.

He was running on an overdose of adrenaline, mouth dry, body tingling. His heart pounded out an action movie soundtrack—lots of hard-charging Taiko drums and macho power chords. Crawling to the rim, he got a worm's-eye view of the mayhem.

A buzzing between his ears wouldn't quit. It was Morse code for *keep moving.*

Hermes jumped back into action, frantically searching for Alecto and Persephone. Oversized projectiles hurtled past. It was like navigating a carnival game called the Blitz. Demons were stomped and squished and blown to bits. Keres exploded like kamikaze mosquitoes hitting a bug zapper. And the hands. So many hands. Big hands. They pounded, snatched, smashed, bashed, and poked. Hermes had never seen a Titan in action before. Now he understood why Zeus had both feared and used them.

To his left, a path to the gate opened, and he took his chance.

A cacodemon was suddenly madly sprinting alongside him, its mouth frothing. They ran neck and neck like it was a high school track meet. A shadow crested above. Hermes stuck out his foot and the cacodemon face-planted.

SMASH!

A club the size of a semi-truck drove his competition into the dirt, the force of the impact blowing Hermes off his feet. He tumbled head over heels, coming to rest on his stomach, staring down the sight of a slingshot with a boulder yanked back in the pouch.

The massive projectile launched. Hermes rolled out of the way. The boulder skipped past, carving a path of destruction—

There! Hermes spotted Alecto in the boulder's wake. The Fury towed Persephone by the leash. They slipped through Huey's legs unnoticed, headed for the open, unguarded gate.

Hermes ran into the danger zone. His only thought was Persephone. A mace bulldozed the way, whipping a mountain of dirt into the air. He climbed the avalanche, surfed down the other side, where a dozen demons hacked at one of Dewey's thumbs. Dewey ground the pests like a child crushing ants. Above, Huey loaded a bolt into one of his many crossbows, gears cranking, his remaining eye tracking Hermes.

Persephone. Persephone.

An arrow the size of a tree thwacked out of the crossbow and nearly skewered him. Hermes zigzagged toward the gate as missiles fell from the sky. Each shaft struck and knocked him off his feet. Each time, he picked himself up and ran harder. A bolt with a Ker speared on its tip burrowed into the ground directly in front of him. He wove through the newly planted forest and caught a final glimpse of Persephone as Alecto tugged her past the gate.

Persephone! Persephone! PERSEPHONE!

A broadsword cut off his route. Hermes chased his reflection down the blade toward a mace embedded in the splintered ground. The weapon wrenched free. Hermes mustered all his adrenaline and leapt, seizing one of the spikes as Dewey pried the weapon free.

The battlefield whizzed away, rapidly shrinking as Hermes hung on for dear life. The mace halted mid-swing, leaving him clutching the spike beside Dewey's ear—a grotto with stalactites of foul-smelling wax. Drool streamed from the giant's sloppy grin as he cheerfully stomped and crushed. Mayhem was his happy place. Dewey targeted a group of demons racing back to Alecto's warship, but it had been commandeered by Hermes' slave and was now casting off.

Hermes pumped his fists. "Way to go, guys!"

The shout was directly in Dewey's ear. Dewey grunted and spun in confusion.

Hermes found himself face-to-eye with Dewey.

"Hi."

Dewey's head cocked to one side. "Hi."

"Good chat. Think you can give me a lift?" Hermes jerked a thumb backward toward the gate.

The giant snarled, revealing a row of yellow teeth like school buses stuck upright. That would be a no. Then he violently shook the mace. Hermes wrapped his arms and legs around the spike, riding it like a bull at a rodeo.

Dewey bellowed in frustration and launched the mace back for another pitch. This was it. Hermes braced. The mace whipped over Dewey's head.

At its zenith, he let go.

Momentum flung him as if from a catapult. He soared over the fortress, toward the black hole of Tartarus, graceful as a flying pig. Directly below, Alecto dragged Persephone to the rim of the pit.

Now for the easy part. Nose down, Hermes clamped his hands to his sides and took aim. At just that exact moment, Persephone happened to turn and look up to the strangest sight she would ever behold. Hermes winked, just to put an exclamation point on the spiritual moment.

Alecto caught the slightest curl of a smile grace Persephone's lips, the aberrant sparkle of amusement in her eye. She whirled around. Her wings reflexively snapped out like airbags, knocking Persephone into a statue of Hyperion.

Alecto launched into the air. Fury and god collided. They smashed into the ground beside Persephone, who teetered on the edge of Tartarus. Her shackled wrists reached toward him, but Alecto bucked her feet into Persephone's stomach at the same time she tackled Hermes. Her wings pinned his shoulders and legs with their steel barbs, the leathery surface bristling with thousands of microblades that would shave him to death if he so much as twitched.

"Hermes!" Persephone cried out. Then she vanished over the edge.

"NO! Persephone!" An atomic blast detonated in his brain. His thoughts vaporized.

She was there. Now she wasn't.

The chain shackled to Persephone slithered over the rim, racing after her into the abyss. It wrapped around the statue of Hyperion, sawing through a stone arm.

There was a chance to save her. Hermes hurled himself toward Tartarus, but Alecto's talons dug through his collarbone, nailing him to the ground. She couldn't stop laughing, the sound of it like a chainsaw attacking a fence. Her face bulged and roiled like wet clay as the nest of snakes beneath her skin writhed, stretching her wicked smile wider and wider and wider.

She threw her head back and shrieked. "I win! I win! I win—"

Hermes head-butted Alecto. Her nose flattened into her face with a wet crunch. Stunned, she dropped backward onto her ass.

Persephone. Save Persephone.

He scrambled to the ledge, prepared to jump. No light penetrated the black hole. There was nothing. Nothing there. Nothing.

A flash of gold erupted directly below him like a streak of lightning across the night sky. Persephone peered up at him, a gash illuminating her brow. The divine blood washed over her face, revealing her in the darkness.

Hermes traced the chain that shackled Persephone back to the rim. By some miracle, it had snagged the bust of Hyperion, who had been sculpted shielding his eyes from the glare of defeat. The chain had caught on Hyperion's outstretched blade, the very same sword he had surrendered in defeat. The irony of it briefly flitted through his mind. Saved by Hyperion, the Titan of Light, who had participated in the castration of his father Ouranos to usurp his own father's reign. First Ouranos, now Hades. The cyclical power of transgenerational trauma was a bitch.

The sound of drums suddenly pounded up from the pit below Persephone. The Titans stirred. Hermes imagined the monsters eager to catch the fall of an Olympian.

"Just hold on!" he called down to Persephone.

"Not like I have a choice!" she called back.

He grinned and began reeling her in. In two great heaves she rose halfway up. Her eyes suddenly widened in terror. "WATCH OUT!"

A set of fangs ripped open the side of his neck.

Alecto attached to his back. The chain slipped from his grasp, burning through his hands. Persephone plummeted into the blackness. The rungs counted down the seconds to her doom.

Snakes lashed at Hermes from Alecto's hair. He grabbed her by the vipers and wrenched. She bit down on his chin and a chunk of flesh ripped away. He roared, not in pain but for Persephone. He was losing her all over again. He couldn't lose her. He couldn't.

Golden ichor rained onto Tartarus and fed the starving pit. Alecto seized Hermes by his ankle and spread her wings. Swept off his feet, the back of his head smacked the ground. Stars erupted across his vision.

"Don't," he begged. Gods weren't supposed to beg. But by god, Hermes would beg if he had to. "Please. Please, Alecto. Don't."

Alecto hovered in place, treading air, her wings whipping up a storm. A god dangling helplessly in her talons, pleading for mercy—this truly was the pinnacle of her dominion. She was the apex. And apex Furies didn't grant mercy.

Poor Hermes.

Hermes stared at the right-side-up Alecto from his upside-down view. The blood rushed to his head. He wanted her to taste this victory. To savor it for as long as she could.

Alecto took the bait. Rising higher.

Climbing and climbing. She wanted to make this orgasm last forever.

"Hey! Fluffernutter the Destroyer!" Hermes rudely interrupted. Alecto looked down. Her triumphant smile collapsed. Directly below Hermes was Persephone, standing on the ledge.

"How?" Alecto stammered.

Hermes flashed an ebullient grin, which from her perspective looked like a frown. Attached to his finger was a ring. Actually, it was a rung. A rung from Persephone's chain. Alecto had inadvertently rescued Persephone, drawing her up from the pit.

She had been tricked by Hermes.

Persephone slammed her cuffs against Hyperion's blade and split them in two. Free at last.

An eternal lifetime of terror cosmically rebounded on Alecto. She ditched Hermes and attempted to flee the scene. He landed on his back next to Persephone, still wearing his smile as he watched his sister whip her former chains like a rodeo star.

"Go get 'em, partner!"

Persephone released the chain. The metal cracked against Alecto, coiling around her leg. A savage tug brought the last Fury down with a satisfying thud. This was no longer a fight, but Hermes saw no reason to intervene. Let Persephone have her fun. If anyone deserved to indulge in a little vengeance, surely it was his sister.

Alecto clawed toward the gates, nails carving trenches in the dirt as her mangled wings flailed uselessly. Even if she could cry for help, who would answer? Beyond the fortress, the Hecatoncheires continued to make mincemeat of her army.

Alecto looked back and beheld Persephone, Goddess of Spring, Mother of Earth, framed against the edge of the world. It was futile to try and escape.

Persephone dug her heel into the Fury's back. This time Alecto begged and pleaded. It would have been easier to convince the world not to spin. Persephone ripped the pinions from Alecto's spine like a fly pinched between her fingers.

Hermes flinched and had to look away. When he turned back, Alecto was twitching and flopping and screaming. Persephone casually brushed the feathers from her dress. There would be no mercy. It was time for the unceasing one to meet her ironic end. Persephone seized Alecto by the scruff like a wrestler going for the showstopper knockout and dragged her past Hermes to the edge of Tartarus.

Alecto flailed. "Help me! Mercy! Don't let her do this!"

Hermes waved goodbye.

No hesitation. Persephone hurled the last Fury over the void like she was tossing a sack of garbage. "FUCKING STEPCHILDREN!"

Halfway over the pit, Alecto flapped her arms since she no longer had any wings. There was nothing to stop her from falling. And fall she did.

Hermes leaned over the abyss. Alecto plummeted until she blinked out of existence. It would probably take weeks before she hit the bottom. "Well…that was overkill."

Persephone stumbled away from the ledge and unleashed a primal roar four thousand years of frustration in the making. A full, cathartic, fist-shaking shebang. And then all at once she fell silent. Her gaze stalled over the pit, unfocused, as if she'd spilled too much of herself.

Unsure the outburst was over, Hermes gave her a tentative pat on the shoulder.

She blinked and turned to him. "Now what?"

"I think we go home," he said.

Home. The word turned on the waterworks. Without warning she pitched sideways. Hermes just managed to catch her, keeping her upright, forehead to forehead. Their tears flowed together, tributaries of pain and loss merging. Hermes had long imagined this moment, their grand reunion, yet there was nothing grand about it.

He parted her hair. The face behind the bangs was not one he recognized. A shadow self-cast that he feared would resist the light. Her eyes searched his and found them unfamiliar too. They harbored separate traumas neither could yet put to words. It was too much after so much. They turned away and stared into the void like strangers.

Hermes spoke first. "I went to Olympus."

"Oh yeah?" Her voice was hoarse and soft.

"I saw our father…"

"Wasn't what you expected."

He nodded.

"And you asked if he would give you a message to deliver," she continued.

Another nod. The totality of all the moments that led to this moment seemed impossible to process. A lesser sister might step on his silence. Prod and probe. Instead, she let him be.

"This journey to you…" He paused. The right words were so hard to find.

She found a smile enough to pass for encouragement, though it weighed more than she could carry. "Worthy of Homer? Worthy of poems and legends? Worthy of eternal relevance, passed down through the ages into movies and ancillary IP?"

"Not exactly," he said.

"Well, Homer still wanders somewhere. I can put in a good word. Though he's a bit possessive—'my ideas,' as it were."

He exhaled, hand over his chest. "I need a minute to think."

She stared into the pit with an ache just as fathomless. "A minute…I have more than a minute. I have an eternity."

It was the pomegranate. She had eaten the cursed fruit that bound her to hell. Hermes had lost even when he had won. "No! Fuck the rules! Fuck the system. We'll figure this out."

She tilted her head back, eyes closed in resignation. "You can't change this any more than I can. It is the way it is."

The injustice of it thrust him to his feet. "Persephone—"

She didn't want to hurt him. But reality was reality. "It's over—"

"NO," he said more forcefully.

"What do you mean no? It's not up to you."

He searched the hellscape. Another idea slowly dawned. It couldn't work. *Could* it work? The madness of it gleamed in the wild eyes that he returned to Persephone. "I'm really, really, really sorry about this."

Her cute little brow furrowed in confusion. "What are you—"

She never finished the question. In one swift move, Hermes wedged his fingers into her mouth like a dentist examining a cavity and stuffed them down her throat.

He jumped out of the way as Persephone pitched forward and vomited the contents of her stomach into the pit. It was his worst nightmare. Projectile vomit. A stream of purple pomegranate juice gushed from her lips. Then, oddly, it was followed by a puff of yellow petals. They looked like the train of a flower girl at a wedding.

Hermes grimaced and looked away, fingers plugging his ears. "Thatta girl. Get it all up."

After a brief pause, he took a chance and squinted, fighting back his own sympathy vomit. She heaved again, heaved until there was nothing left. When it was finally, mercifully over, he gently massaged her back.

"All done…all done…there you go. Don't you feel better now?"

She didn't answer, slumping into his shoulder.

He pulled her close and decided to never let her go.

The rain of vomit vanished into the darkness of Tartarus. Hopefully Alecto remembered to pack an umbrella.

CHAPTER THIRTY-TWO

Persephone lost consciousness as soon as the last seeds were expelled. Would forcing her to vomit up the cursed pomegranate do anything? He hadn't a clue. It was a last-ditch Hail Mary. Hermes couldn't rest until he returned her to Earth. But would Spring return with her? If he was wrong, and she was indeed bound to the Underworld, then returning her to Earth would be the end of her. And what then? Would it also be the end of life itself?

The God of Luck and Trickery and Celestial Messages, Ferrier of Souls to the Underworld, swore to himself that if Persephone met the worst of Fate, he would join her on the other side. Perhaps there was no afterlife for a god. Perhaps this was all there was. Hermes was prepared to accept the great unknown beyond the known.

This must be hope. This must be faith.

Look, Ma, I have faith!

He scooped her up and whispered a prayer of gratitude, and one for the strength to begin the journey home. The attendants of the Underworld appeared to have faith too. Passing through the Gates of Tartarus, Persephone cradled across his arms, the Hecatoncheires ceased their tantrum, allowing Hermes to walk unmolested across the field of carnage. Hermes stopped before the ancient warriors and mumbled an apology. Huey and Dewey considered it, accepted it, and then tussled for a few tense moments over who would be most gracious to their queen. Since Dewey still had two eyes, the argument tipped in his favor.

Dewey extended one of his hundred hands for Hermes to climb aboard and proceeded to carry them across the Underworld, first following the Phlegethon, and then each successive river—Lethe, Acheron, Cocytus, and Styx.

Persephone slept through the whole ride. It was almost annoying, like looking across the aisle on a red-eye flight to see a fellow passenger snoring away peacefully, just begging to be "accidentally" elbowed on the way to the bathroom. Occasionally, Persephone stirred and moaned, but she hadn't spoken nor opened her eyes over the unbearably long trek back across the Underworld.

Hermes was astonished to find that even in the short time since he had arrived in Elysium, the realm appeared to have recovered from the Furies. Supreme Judge Odysseus and Commander Aegos were driving the demons back into the crevices of Hell in a series of fierce urban combat operations. The battles were briefly suspended as both demon and human souls stared in wonder at the immortal giants lumbering past, doltishly waving down like they were a royal at a jubilee.

Once the Hecatoncheires passed, it was *game on!*—and back to the slaughter.

Hermes stayed out of sight, ensconced within the calloused terrain of Dewey's palm, focused only on Persephone as the giant made great strides across the realm. Dewey deposited them at the base of the back stairs to Earth. At a loss for words, Hermes merely nodded his thanks. Dewey understood and needed nothing else.

Hermes lifted Persephone and began the long ascent.

Time became obsolete, his progress marked only by the fading scent of death. He carried the still-unconscious Persephone up the endless steps, through soil, dirt, rock, and stone. With each step he prayed. *Hold on. Hold on. Hold on.* Until, quite suddenly, a blue dawn cleaved the darkness. The light shimmered like an aquarium. The cave was entombed in frost and sealed by a frozen waterfall.

He looked down at Persephone. A thin wisp of steam escaped her purple lips, bringing a sense of relief only in that it proved she was still alive. Barely.

Earth was just beyond the wall of icicles. He kicked his bare heel into the stalactites and shattered the last frozen barrier.

His heart sank. No trees, no cabins, river, lake, animals. Only snow. The great backbone mountains were invisible against a white sky. All of it buried and bleached like a carcass. Earth was gone. Winter had triumphed.

Hermes trudged endlessly onward, no destination but hope, cheeks cracked but too cold to bleed, Persephone swaddled against him, his only purpose now to keep moving, to keep her warm and her heart beating. They reached what was once her valley, and he sank into the drifts. There was nowhere else to go—no spring or summer, not on Earth nor in Heaven. Her heartbeat weakened against his own, faint as snow against the sky.

If all that ever was and is and would be were in this moment, then the end wouldn't be so bad, he thought.

A white flash suddenly ripped apart the sky. Hermes tracked the streak of light as it fell from the heavens. The star crashed beyond the white horizon, sending up a plume of snow like a faraway smoke signal.

Minutes later, a figure approached, a mirage treading atop the powder like Jesus on the Galilee. The angel wore a simple black cloak and an elegant, checkered wool scarf. Snowflakes collected in his hair, ears red and nose kissed by frost.

"You came back," said Gabriel, slightly in disbelief.

Hermes dug himself out of the prodigious snowpack and lifted Persephone.

"Do something!" The command was practically frozen on his lips.

She was draped across his arms as he thrust them out to Gabriel, offering her like an anguished parent handing their child to a pilot on a war-torn tarmac. "I'll pray to your God. Whatever he can do, just ask him to do it. Please."

A Greek god begging a Christian archangel...once there was a time Hermes would have been mortified by the thought. Not anymore. This was desperation beyond desperate-times-call-for-desperate-measures. A humbled Hermes stood before Gabriel, not as a god, but as a brother trying to save his sister, a man seeking salvation.

Gabriel stood over the prostrate, humbled Hermes, his trademark judgment absent.

"Don't you do that!" Hermes croaked. "Don't you shake your head."

Too late. Gabriel shook his head. "An angel of the Lord can do nothing for a Greek god. All we can do is...have faith."

Shame threatened to crush Hermes like a submarine sinking to the bottom of the ocean. "I tried to save her...I tried. It wasn't enough."

A spasm from Persephone sent him into a new level of panic. He laid her down as she grabbed at her throat, gasping, unable to breathe. Her thrashing carved jagged wounds in the fresh powder—no delicate snow angel, but some ruined, tormented shape.

Hermes rocked helplessly back and forth, arms squeezed over his chest. "What do I do? What do I do? What do I do?!" The question was like a chant. Maybe if he clapped his hands and said he believed in magic, she could be brought back to life.

The angel elbowed Hermes out of the way. "Move!"

Rolling Persephone onto her side, Gabriel pried open her mouth and tipped her head to clear her airway. Red sprayed the white.

Gods don't bleed red.

The thought somehow registered within Hermes' terror.

"What are you doing?"

"Shush."

Gabriel proceeded with the Heimlich maneuver. Persephone was limp as a rag doll. Each thrust sank them deeper in the snow. Hermes couldn't just watch from the sidelines. He needed to do something, but Gabriel thrust out his wing to block him. "Stay back!"

The Heimlich didn't seem to be working. Gabriel lifted Persephone and folded her forward. With the heel of his palm, he delivered a final, forceful smack to her back. Her body shuddered. A single pomegranate seed shot out of her mouth. Then she went limp.

Dead.

Hermes buckled. His world snapped in two.

She's dead. This wasn't how it was supposed to be.

The archangel laid Persephone within the icy crater as if it were a casket and then backed away. His wings folded in defeat, and he clasped his hands to bow in prayer.

Hermes rushed in and planted a tender kiss on her forehead. "Don't go. I'm not ready."

Tears froze on his cheeks. If only he could shrink himself out of existence. That was what he wanted right now. Instead, he could only hug his knees to his chest, chin burrowed. This is how they would be for the rest of eternity. He would stay like this, watching over her, and never move again.

Beside him, an unnatural warmth emanated from the single ruby pomegranate seed.

Gabriel felt it too. They both turned curiously to the kernel as it melted the surrounding snow like a hot ember. Then it vanished, boring a hole through the ice.

Far below them, the seed struck the soil with the force of a thunderbolt, sending a current straight into Earth's heart more effective than a defibrillator. The shock wave pulsed outward from beneath Persephone, rippling in all directions across the tundra. The mountains trembled, triggering distant avalanches. Another shock wave detonated, stronger than the first. A stunned Gabriel looked to Hermes. This was way beyond his pay grade.

Hermes scrambled to place a finger to Persephone's neck. They waited and waited...

"There's a pulse!" The beat of her heart produced another shock wave, then another, each one building upon the last.

"It's Earth...Earth is waking up..."

The blizzard broke suddenly like a fever. The clouds shredded above them, separating into floating icebergs cracked with sunlight, igniting the snow into a field of diamonds. Hermes squinted and raised a hand to shield his eyes. Gabriel slowly spun in a circle, eyes filled with wonder, as if waking to the first light of creation. For all their rules against magic, and hatred of the old gods and their meddling, his people did love a good miracle. He extended a hand, catching the last snowflake of a long, long, too-long winter.

Spring had arrived.

Gabriel watched the snowflake melt in his palm, a flicker of jealousy, and then turned back to Hermes. "You didn't think to try that the first time?"

Hermes shrugged. "No one asked."

Gabriel rolled his eyes. "Old habits—"

"Die hard."

"I'm guessing this will create quite the hiccup."

Gabriel sighed. "Yes. Monotheism can be a bitch sometimes... humans are so literal."

"So are gods. Sometimes."

Gabriel brushed the snow off his travel cloak. "Miracles aside, we have a few concerns outstanding."

"Wow. That was fast. She's not even regained consciousness." Hermes frowned and deliberately placed his attention on Persephone. He tucked his jacket under her head.

"Afraid so," Gabriel said.

"Look, if it's about confidentiality, you don't have to worry."

"There is that…yes…"

"No tell-all books, no late-night appearances for me…I'm done. I don't even have my fingers crossed behind my back—look, see." Hermes wiggled his uncrossed fingers.

Technically, crossed fingers did not have any magical nullifying power over spiritual agreements—or any other agreements, for that matter. However, Hermes didn't want any more trouble with the Catholics. He was quite done with trouble. For a while, at least.

"Fair enough. But you'll want to hear this." Gabriel's words were like storm clouds on the horizon. He dramatically peeled off his gloves to show he meant business. "It's come to our attention that the blame for this…freak weather anomaly…well, it doesn't rest solely upon Greek shoulders."

"Freak weather anomaly? Is that gonna go in the official press release? Or am I just supposed to take you at your word?"

Gabriel's eyes narrowed and his expression hardened, giving Hermes hot flashbacks of their first meeting in the Vatican courtyard.

"My word actually means something."

"Oh. Perfect. So I'm not going to be the fall guy?"

"It would be easier for all of us if we could just blame you."

Hermes scoffed. "That's a relief."

"The Furies didn't act alone. Coordination was required."

"No shit."

"We've gathered intelligence—"

"That's a first. But why are you telling me?"

Annoyed, Gabriel looked away and dug his loafer into the powder. "We need help."

"Thank you," Hermes said. "I know that was difficult for you to say."

Gabriel swung around with a scowl that could blot out the sun. "We need the help of someone with access to all realms. A god inside."

Hermes heaved a great big sigh and readied to depart, lifting Persephone in his arms. "Whelp…I'm sorry, I'm not a messenger anymore."

Hermes started to walk away.

"No, you're not."

The angel's words stopped Hermes cold. "Do I have a convert?"

"An admirer, but don't take that to the bank."

Gabriel unbuttoned his coat and reached inside. Hermes instinctively braced. The sunlight glinted off an evidence bag as Gabriel held it aloft. A bright, neon feather that could have come from a peacock or a toucan was sealed inside. The feather had circular patterns in shades of red, blue, and green.

"Do you recognize this?"

Hermes made a show of squinting. "Nope. Don't recognize it."

Of course he recognized the Baach feather he'd stolen from the Vatican vault a lifetime ago. While the new Hermes—the one that had this second lease on eternal life—had sworn to be honest and pious, he didn't agree to be a chump. Nowhere in the Holy Scriptures did it say he had to incriminate himself.

"The one in our vault had a pair," Gabriel continued. "Would it help if I reminded you of your immunity with the Holy See? Our deal for...well, the deal was for you to deliver a message, and only deliver a message."

Hermes lifted his eyebrows. "About that deal..."

Gabriel grumbled. "Yes. You upheld your end of the bargain, we uphold ours."

Hermes adjusted his hold on Persephone and walked back toward Gabriel and the feather. "Yeah, well, now that you mention it, it does look familiar."

"It would also look familiar to Lilith, the Jewish demoness and once the guardian of a certain classified prison that never existed."

"Uh-huh." Hermes nodded. Gold stars for denial. Looks like they had something in common after all.

"You've been through Hell, so I need to catch you up on some other news—a series of catastrophic earthquakes in Central and South America. Entire countries devastated...millions lost. Obviously, the state of Latin America concerns us greatly. I believe there are larger forces at work. Do you understand the purpose of the feather you stole?"

"Makes a great duster—high shelves, ceiling fans—"

"No. It contained an antidote. This one here contains the poison it counteracts."

Hermes suddenly wanted to get as far away from this conversation as possible. "Okay. Good to know."

"You're not protecting anyone. We know you gave the other feather to Lilith, in payment for her information—information that allowed you to access our vault."

"Did I now?"

"Immunity," Gabriel reminded.

"Right. Yeah. Maybe I *did* give it to her."

Just when he thought he could ride off into the sunset…

But Gabriel didn't pursue the grievance.

"Do you have any clue why she wanted it? Out of all the things she could have asked for and received? Why that feather?"

"I don't know," admitted Hermes. It was the honest-to-God truth. Gabriel could see it. "I was curious. But Lilith does love her kinks. So, yeah, it was strange—but on brand."

"Yet you didn't bother to ask…" Gabriel slipped the poison feather back into his coat for safekeeping. "Lilith didn't just sell you information. She sold you out. I believe she was a part of the plot to kidnap Persephone."

The realization was beyond devastating. He had been a pawn. Both brother and sister had been pawns. Ichor pounded in his godly ears. Suddenly, Hermes couldn't bear to look at Gabriel. His thoughts skidded over the snow like a runaway toboggan.

"Where's Lilith now?"

"I was hoping you could tell me," Gabriel said.

"Who set me up?" Hermes demanded.

"That's the million-dollar question."

Hermes stared past Gabriel, a glacial stillness, a force that could carve mountains. Lilith was no mastermind. There were others. More than one, as the spirits had prophesied. He thought he heard the distant rumble of Chaos, that most destructive power.

Rather abruptly, Hermes made up his mind. "Beer. For or against?"

Gabriel puffed out his chest and stuck his chin into the air. "I like beer."

"Good. So do I."

Was the angel's posture arrogance? Or was he just a regal son of a bitch? The answer suddenly didn't matter. Hermes found himself admiring this honorable, loyal servant of his god.

Yes, that beer sounded nice.

"Feel free to call," Hermes said.

Gabriel nodded. "We will."

EPILOGUE

Persephone woke groggy, as if from an afternoon nap, stretching under her sheets, sunlight dappling her cheek, the edge of a migraine playing the tambura beneath her brow. She opened her eyes to her old bedroom, just as she'd left it. A warm breeze, pollenated with the scent of summer, billowed her blue curtains, pawing against her arm like a Labrador eager to be at her side.

Around the room was evidence of a vigil. An open copy of *The Divine Comedy* rested on a wicker chair; bouquets of sunflowers, daisies, bluebells, and lilacs exploded on the dresser; a bowl of vegetable broth had cooled on her nightstand. Peering past her pillow, she noticed empty mugs on the floor, along with every dish, cup, plate, and bit of cutlery she owned. Evidently, her caretaker did not know how to use a dishwasher. But that didn't bother her. A wind chime sang outside, along with several varieties of birds that trilled and chirped happily.

At the back of her mind were memories—dark ones—but she did not want to reach for them. Not yet.

My caretaker. Someone had bathed, combed, and washed her hair, dressed her in a clean nightgown. The house, she discerned, had been diligently repaired from the battle that had raged that fated day.

It wasn't just the furniture that had been repaired. The whole of Earth had been repaired…

A persistent *thud—thud—thud*—echoed from somewhere, the sound of metal cleaving the ground. Clods of dirt tossed in the air outside her window. *Thud, thud, thud.*

She sat up, wiggled her toes at the edge of the bed. Her legs felt weak from lack of use, but she was whole too, and, as she noticed in a mirror, a tad pale. Too much time in the Underworld killed your tan.

She followed the sound of digging through her home, which was in the process of a serious remodel. Someone had been working to put everything right—exactly the way it was—down to the cedar plank floors. Hand-shaved shingles were piled in the living room, ostensibly to fill the gaping hole in the roof. She was grateful and touched, yet oddly, she wasn't sure she wanted everything back the way it was. It felt like a time for new beginnings.

Persephone slipped onto her porch, gently brushing her new porch swing, wet with a coat of Carolina blue paint. The sun danced on the emerald prairie after a recent July storm. A thin herd of half-starved buffalo grazed on a carpet of seedlings sprouting across the rolling valley. Cumulus clouds galloped toward the north.

Not everything was perfect, however. The land bore scars of the terrible winter that had only just receded—trees splintered under the heavy snow, swollen rivers carving wide, muddy banks—but Earth was a determined spirit, eager to recover. Every branch bristled with buds, and wildflowers were exploding with vibrant colors like the crescendo of a fireworks show. This part of the world had seemingly unfurled from the pages of a fairytale.

A black sparrow settled on the banister in front of her, claws tucked under its breast, yellow eyes calmly observing.

Beyond the porch, her vegetable garden had been replanted. Rows of tomatoes—all shapes, sizes, and colors—climbed their trellises. There was turquoise bushy kale, heads of broccoli, reams of spinach, and purple eggplants. Her fruit trees, berry bushes, and grapevines had been equally tended to and brimmed with life. Her heart soared.

Thud. Thud. Thud.

The curious digging resumed, coming from the back of her cabin. She followed the wraparound porch to the east, where she found Hermes in her yard, flannel shirt open to catch the breeze, clunky yet functional work boots half sunk in the dirt, hoe in hand.

Manual labor did not come naturally to the Fabio of gods. He clumsily whacked the soil and sent another clod flying into the air. Progress, be it mortal or divine, came slowly. Baby steps.

She leaned against a post, wistful, content to watch Hermes work. *This is my paradise.* A leaf brushed her hand—seven green fingers waving up at her. Ubiquitous as they were. She rubbed the fuzzy buds between her thumb and forefinger and shook her head. Hermes had cultivated his own paradise—the ganja kind. She didn't know whether to laugh or cry. So she did both.

Hearing Persephone, Hermes abruptly stopped his assault on the earth. Her laughter was sweet as summer rain on parched soil.

He wiped the sweat off his brow like a true farmer and said, "Hey."

"Hi," she returned. "Whatcha doin'?"

"Growing shit. What does it look like?"

She burst into a fresh round of laughter, laughing until her sides hurt.

He wedged his hands on his hips and frowned. "What's so funny?"

"Nothing," she said, beaming.

"Welcome home."

He smiled back, and joy overflowed her soul. Persephone was indeed home.

***

Golden clouds haloed the Backbone Range as a late summer sun set behind the prairie. It was nature's most sublime and longest-running show: 4.543 billion seasons and counting. Hermes and Persephone sat in the tall grass, arms interlocked as if they intended to chain themselves together for the rest of eternity. The cabin sat way off behind them, content to wait for their return. Neither was in a hurry for this time together to end. They could easily stay all night under the stars and watch the sunrise. And do it again tomorrow. And the tomorrow after tomorrow. And so on, and so on.

Hermes turned to his sister, her gaze lost beyond the western sky. Oh, how he could relate. Often, in solitude, he would come back to awareness with a jolt, realizing that for some unknowable amount of time, his own stare had slipped beyond the sighted, falling off the page of a book or the screen of his phone.

Was her stare the stare of someone lost or someone found?

Since her return, Persephone suffered from recurring nightmares. She always woke to him keeping guard at her bedside. He said it was to prevent another abduction, but what he didn't say was that he had nightmares of his own and only felt at peace seated in the corner of her room.

They both hurt. They had both gone through separate horrors and been recast, though into what, neither could yet say. Hermes chose to say nothing of his journey, determined not to add any further burden upon his sister's conscience. The added lines on his brow and the tinge of gray that streaked his golden locks said enough anyway.

He wanted to ask her to share, but knew the story would be the same. This wasn't something they could force. Not now. All they knew for certain was that they were not who they once were.

Her nightmares would pass in time, sure. Persephone would heal as Earth was healing, the two being connected. Understanding that made it somewhat easier. Yet there was nothing easy about his own process. That he would have to figure out on his own.

Later. Later, and not now.

Now was perfect.

"Sometimes you're an enigma to me," he heard her say, and slowly came back from his thoughts.

"It's not intentional," he said.

"I should hope not. You know, I'm lucky to know the god of luck."

Her profile was cast in golden light. She was beautiful and gentle. She was a wonder.

"You once asked what the messenger of the gods is supposed to do when there are no more messages."

That piqued her interest. "And? Is he to screw around for all eternity? Do tell. Inquiring minds want to know."

"He grows up."

Without warning, tears gathered in the cradles of her eyes.

He sat up, worried. "What's wrong?"

"Nothing. It's just…" She struggled and then turned to him, his little sister, looking up to her big brother.

"Just don't outgrow me."

The trillion-pound weight of her abduction momentarily lifted off his heart. His soul—if a god indeed had one—soared into the grace note of the sunset.

He opened his mouth to respond, but Persephone tensed, startled in the way she did so easily these days. He followed her intense stare across the valley, aimed at three strange bedfellows striding out of the west. Two of the three cut enormous silhouettes.

"It's okay," he said. "I've been expecting them."

It took a heartbeat for her to register the shadow of sadness in his voice. A shudder of apprehension stole her breath. Their fragile summer of healing had come to an end.

Resolute, they rose to meet the three travelers. Persephone recognized Gabriel, whom she knew only through professional circles—various conferences, interfaith mixers. The other two stood back, rather standoffish, one significantly larger than the other.

Gabriel and Persephone exchanged pleasantries and comments on the weather, strained by subtext. Hermes called Gabriel his "Catholic compadre," much to the archangel's annoyance, and then boasted of his new maturity and the way he could always make friends of his enemies.

"Not true," Persephone and Gabriel replied in unison.

Gabriel gave Hermes a less-than-gracious once-over. "You seem different."

"I'm evolving," Hermes said, and went for a fist bump.

Gabriel just stared coldly until Persephone interrupted. "What is this about? You're both supposed to hate each other. My brother stole countless treasures from the Vatican…"

That caught Gabriel off guard. He struggled for an answer.

"Way to put the kibosh on the feel-good vibes, Sis."

Persephone was undeterred. Her skepticism ran deep. "How do you go from hunting my brother so ferociously to embracing him?"

Gabriel and Hermes shared a conspiratorial look.

Her gaze shuttled between them, missing nothing. "I see…"

Hermes abruptly changed the subject. "So, altar boy, how's the new pope workin' out?"

Gabriel stared at him blankly and chose not to engage. "Managing."

"Come on, I hear the guy's a rock star."

Hermes waited for a thank-you. Gabriel gave him the middle finger instead.

"Boys!" Hermes called to the two travel companions looming behind the archangel. "Get your clay keisters over here."

The copper-tanned giants shuffled forward through the prairie, massive hands wringing, clearly starstruck. Hermes introduced the two golems. "The small one goes by Chaim, and this big fella is Moishe."

Chaim leaned toward Moishe and loudly whispered, "He wasn't kidding—she's a real shiksa goddess."

Moishe also seemed to lack for social cues, staring intently at Persephone.

She mumbled to Hermes, "What's a shiksa?"

"I think it means pretty...Wait until they meet Aphrodite."

Moishe perked up. "Audrey? Did he say we get to meet Audrey Hepburn?"

Chaim slapped his brother in the chest. "No, you fool! Trim the hair out of your ears. He said we get to meet Aretha! Aretha Franklin."

Hermes dug his palm into his forehead while Gabriel and Persephone tried to follow the golems' back-and-forth.

"Aretha, the Queen of Soul! Why would we meet Audrey Hepburn?" Chaim continued. "Think. Use the keppeleh. Sometimes you're so thick, God help me—" He turned to the actual gods. "Not you two. Ours—" Back to Moishe. "What would you do without me, huh?"

"Aretha Franklin's dead," Gabriel interjected. "And so is Audrey Hepburn."

Chaim looked crestfallen and whipped off his cap. "Oh...may their memory be a blessing."

Moishe followed, sweeping off his crinkled fedora. "May their memory be a blessing." Then he turned back to Persephone. "I love Bette Midler. Do you love Bette Midler?"

Persephone blinked, overwhelmed and slightly alarmed. "Yes...?"

"Is she dead too?" Moishe asked.

Hermes jumped in. "They're your new bodyguards. Chaim and Moishe spent a hundred years guarding the gates of Prague."

"And remind me, how'd that turn out for the Jews?"

"Ouch," Gabriel muttered.

Chaim and Moishe grimaced and grumbled, obviously insulted.

"I don't need protection," Persephone insisted.

"I disagree," Hermes insisted back.

"So do I," Gabriel insisted on top of the insistence.

Persephone threw him daggers too.

The archangel held out his palms to soothe any hurt feelings. "I'm afraid the times demand it. And these...golems, despite their...

quirks…are effective. I can vouch for that personally." He shot Hermes a loaded glance.

"The goddess will listen to the goyim. Watch," Chaim said behind his hand to Moishe, yet loud enough for everyone to hear.

It was two against one. Her arms slowly uncrossed. Persephone finally relented.

"Persephone. That's my name. Just Persephone."

"We's gonna join, make sure nobody tries nothin' inappropriate." Chaim squeezed her cheek to seal the deal. "Then we go with you to Hell. Much fun. Big thumbs-up."

Four massive clay thumbs rose into the sky.

Persephone sighed, taking measure of the two massive golems. "Where will they sleep? I don't have…room."

"We don't sleep, Miss," Chaim answered.

She forced a strained smile. "Oh…great…"

Moishe bobbed his head enthusiastically as if he were selling an extra feature on a car she didn't want to purchase. "And we're handy around the house."

"Maybe keep them away from any do-it-yourself projects," Hermes suggested.

Moishe grunted. "Jesus was a carpenter."

Chaim piped in, "The Jews made us to do the hammering." He tapped the side of his head again. "Smart."

Hermes stepped in front of Persephone to cut off the impending explosion. "They're here to stay. Now say thank you."

For a harrowing moment, it wasn't clear which way she would go, but then, resigned, Persephone turned to her new security detail. "You are noble protectors of your people, and I am honored to welcome you into my home. Thank you."

Their copper cheeks flushed. She extended her hand, and Chaim pumped it up and down, gentler than expected.

Gabriel rested a hand on Hermes' shoulder. "It's time."

His stomach plummeted back to the Underworld. How could he leave her so soon? A serious case of codependency had flourished, and now he was set to abandon her again. Another broken promise. Persephone seemed to read his mind and squeezed his hand. Every parting was difficult, but this one felt like death.

Gabriel signaled the golems to give the brother and sister some space and the three of them walked toward her cabin.

"You'll be safe here with them," Hermes said once they were alone, unsure if he was trying to convince her or himself.

"Once I recover, I intend to join your crusade."

"You can't say *crusade* anymore. Not politically correct."

She sighed. "I have a right to find who did this to me, did this to Earth."

"I know. I know..."

They hugged, holding on as deeply as any two beings who love possibly could.

He took a deep breath, inhaling this into his memory. "I know what I'm supposed to do now." His voice was muffled against her heart.

"Good," she said. And that was all he needed to hear.

Hermes looked past Persephone to Gabriel, waiting for him on the porch swing, slowly rocking back and forth. There was a certainty Hermes hadn't felt in ages. He had to go. He had to leave her. His next mission would be just as consequential. The fate of the universe depended on him. It had been ordained. Yada, yada, yada.

He looked to the golems next. They had already assumed their new roles. The ancient protectors stood sentinel upon opposite hilltops, officiously scanning the horizon for any threat to the shiksa goddess. He would be leaving Persephone in good hands—solid, clay hands.

Persephone also watched her solemn protectors and let out a sigh. Maybe she wanted to further protest the arrangement. His sister did prefer her solitude. How could he blame her? She had a lot of responsibility on her plate. She deserved a refuge, she deserved peace. But that argument would be for another day. This day was ending.

There was another possibility. Maybe she possessed the same calm, the same sense of purpose.

Yes. That felt right.

The last peel of sunlight disappeared behind the mountains like the last grain of sand slipping from an hourglass.

"See you tomorrow," she whispered to the sun.

"See you tomorrow," he echoed, saying goodbye to a most precious day.

They stood side by side, unrushed by time, by the seasons, and the laws that made them, as the world faded to night.

Hermes turned to his sister, not knowing if or when he would see her again.

"Thank you for waiting."

Acknowledgements

THANK YOU IS A small phrase to stack against the massive influence and profound support that made this dream a reality. I'm endlessly grateful to my family, especially my parents, Leslie and Lou Rubin, for their inexhaustible support; to my brother, Matt Rubin, and the game of Mad Libs on Moonlight Beach that sparked this whole thing; and to my sister-in-law, Steph Rubin, and the latest addition, Maddox. I secretly look forward to reading him this book. And of course, to the best dog in the world: Rosie.

A mountain of gratitude goes to the incomparable, unsinkable Marianne Moloney, who has stood by my side, had my back, and blazed many paths ahead of me since the very beginning, and always with unflinching Brooklyn ferocity. To my editor, Guy Intocci, thank you for demystifying the wonderful process of book editing and making it so fun.

A special thank you to Mark Byrne and the way of CEPA. More than just a teacher, he is forever a mentor and friend. I'm also grateful to Meg Peckham. I'm so sad she didn't get to see this book in print, but her red pen will forever blaze across my pages.

Thank you to Erica, Bob, and Cheryl Rhode, who imprinted my childhood with a love of literature during our impromptu *Harry Potter* book club meetings.

I also appreciate all the writers in my corner. Thank you to the longest-running writers' group, the Oxnardians: Matt Witten, Bonnie MacBird, Harley Jane Kozak, Patricia Smiley, Jonathan Beggs (in memoriam), Craig Faustus Buck, Linda Burrows, Jamie Diamond, and Bob Shayne. And to the former 18th Street Coffee crew—now the nomadic coffee crew—thank you for providing the best reason to procrastinate: Byron Willinger, Phil De Blasi, Steve Waverly, and Daniel Greenspan.

Finally, thank you to everyone I've left out, and my (sincere) apologies to every mythology scholar who is sure to tear their hair out at the liberties I've taken in this story. I most assuredly did not set out to be the next Edith Hamilton or D'Aulaire.